BLACK LEGION

More Chaos Space Marines from Black Library

• BLACK LEGION •
by Aaron Dembski-Bowden

BOOK 1 – THE TALON OF HORUS
BOOK 2 – BLACK LEGION

• FABIUS BILE •
by Josh Reynolds

BOOK 1 – FABIUS BILE: PRIMOGENITOR
BOOK 2 – FABIUS BILE: CLONELORD

• AHRIMAN •
by John French

BOOK 1 – AHRIMAN: EXILE
BOOK 2 – AHRIMAN: SORCERER
BOOK 3 – AHRIMAN: UNCHANGED

NIGHT LORDS: THE OMNIBUS
by Aaron Dembski-Bowden
(Contains the novels *Soul Hunter*, *Blood Reaver*
and *Void Stalker*)

KHÂRN: THE RED PATH
by Chris Dows

SONS OF THE HYDRA
by Rob Sanders

WORD BEARERS: THE OMNIBUS
by Anthony Reynolds
(Contains the novels *Dark Apostle*, *Dark Disciple*
and *Dark Creed*)

STORM OF IRON
An Iron Warriors novel by Graham McNeill

THE SIEGE OF CASTELLAX
An Iron Warriors novel by C L Werner

AARON DEMBSKI-BOWDEN

BLACK LEGION

BOOK 2 OF THE BLACK LEGION SERIES

Black Library

A BLACK LIBRARY PUBLICATION

First published in 2017.
This edition published in Great Britain in 2018 by
Black Library,
Games Workshop Ltd.,
Willow Road,
Nottingham, NG7 2WS, UK.

10 9 8 7 6 5 4 3 2 1

Produced by Games Workshop in Nottingham.
Cover illustration by Raymond Swanland.

Black Legion © Copyright Games Workshop Limited 2018. Black Legion, GW, Games Workshop, Black Library, The Horus Heresy, The Horus Heresy Eye logo, Space Marine, 40K, Warhammer, Warhammer 40,000, the 'Aquila' Double-headed Eagle logo, and all associated logos, illustrations, images, names, creatures, races, vehicles, locations, weapons, characters, and the distinctive likenesses thereof, are either ® or TM, and/or © Games Workshop Limited, variably registered around the world.
All Rights Reserved.

A CIP record for this book is available from the British Library.

ISBN 13: 978 1 78496 753 6

No part of this publication may be reproduced, stored in a retrieval system, or transmitted in any form or by any means, electronic, mechanical, photocopying, recording or otherwise, without the prior permission of the publishers.

This is a work of fiction. All the characters and events portrayed in this book are fictional, and any resemblance to real people or incidents is purely coincidental.

See Black Library on the internet at

blacklibrary.com

Find out more about Games Workshop
and the world of Warhammer 40,000 at

games-workshop.com

Printed and bound by CPI Group (UK) Ltd, Croydon, CR0 4YY

It is the 41st millennium. For more than a hundred centuries the Emperor has sat immobile on the Golden Throne of Earth. He is the Master of Mankind by the will of the gods, and master of a million worlds by the might of His inexhaustible armies. He is a rotting carcass writhing invisibly with power from the Dark Age of Technology. He is the Carrion Lord of the Imperium for whom a thousand souls are sacrificed every day, so that He may never truly die.

Yet even in His deathless state, the Emperor continues His eternal vigilance. Mighty battlefleets cross the daemon-infested miasma of the warp, the only route between distant stars, their way lit by the Astronomican, the psychic manifestation of the Emperor's will. Vast armies give battle in His name on uncounted worlds. Greatest amongst His soldiers are the Adeptus Astartes, the Space Marines, bioengineered super-warriors. Their comrades in arms are legion: the Astra Militarum and countless planetary defence forces, the ever-vigilant Inquisition and the tech-priests of the Adeptus Mechanicus to name only a few. But for all their multitudes, they are barely enough to hold off the ever-present threat from aliens, heretics, mutants — and worse.

To be a man in such times is to be one amongst untold billions. It is to live in the cruellest and most bloody regime imaginable. These are the tales of those times. Forget the power of technology and science, for so much has been forgotten, never to be re-learned. Forget the promise of progress and understanding, for in the grim dark future there is only war. There is no peace amongst the stars, only an eternity of carnage and slaughter, and the laughter of thirsting gods.

Peter Jackson once said: 'We all felt like Luke, but we all wanted to be Han.' This one's for Gav Thorpe and Andy Chambers. We all felt like Gav, but we all wanted to be Andy.

DRAMATIS PERSONAE

In alphabetical order

AMURAEL ENKA

    Black Legion warrior, born of Cthonia. Master of the Flesh Harvest. Former Medicae Quintus of the Sons of Horus. Tenth of the Ezekarion.

ASHUR-KAI QEZRAMAH

    Black Legion warrior, born of Terra. Sorcerer and voidseer of the warship *Vengeful Spirit*. Sixth of the Ezekarion.

CERAXIA

    Mistress of the Arsenal, born of Sacred Mars. Former Mechanicum governess of the Niobia Halo outpost at Gallium. Seventh of the Ezekarion.

DELVARUS, 'LORD OF MONGRELS'

    Black Legion warrior, born of Novus Principa. Warchief of the Riven.

EZEKYLE ABADDON

    Black Legion warrior, born of Cthonia. Master of the Black Legion. Commander of the warship *Vengeful Spirit*.

FALKUS KIBRE

    Black Legion warrior, born of Cthonia. Commander of the Aphotic Blade. First of the Ezekarion.

ILYASTER FAYLECH

    Death Guard warrior, born of Barbarus. Apothecary of the Death Guard of the Kryptarus warband.

ISKANDAR KHAYON

    Black Legion warrior, born of Prospero. Lord of the Ashen Dead, and Blade of Abaddon. Third of the Ezekarion.

LHEORVINE UKRIS, 'FIREFIST'

    Black Legion warrior, born of Nuvir's Landing. Commander of the War God's Maw. Fifth of the Ezekarion.

MORIANA, 'THE WEEPING MAIDEN'

    Human prophetess, born of Jaragh. Twelfth of the Ezekarion.

NAGUAL

    Daemon, born from the Sea of Souls. Bound to Iskandar Khayon.

NEFERTARI

    Eldar huntress, Trueborn of Commorragh. Bloodward to Iskandar Khayon.

SARGON EREGESH

    Black Legion warrior, born of Colchis. Prelate of the Long War. Second of the Ezekarion.

SARONOS

    Warp Ghosts warrior of unknown origins. Captain of the warship *Tartaran Wraith*.

TELEMACHON LYRAS, 'THE MASQUED PRINCE'

    Black Legion warrior, born of Chemos. Lord of the Shrieking Masquerade and Champion of the Black Legion. Fourth of the Ezekarion.

THAGUS DARAVEK, 'THE LORD OF HOSTS'

    Death Guard warrior, born of Barbarus. Warlord of the Kryptarus warband.

TOKUGRA
> Daemon, born from the Sea of Souls. Bound to Ashur-Kai Qezramah.

TZAH'Q
> Mutant beastman (*Homo sapiens variatus*), born of Sortiarius. Strategium overseer aboard the *Vengeful Spirit*.

ULRECH ANSONTYN
> Iron Warrior, born of Olympia. Champion of Thagus Daravek.

ULTIO, 'THE ANAMNESIS'
> Advanced machine-spirit reigning over the warship *Vengeful Spirit,* born of Forge Ceres on Sacred Mars.

VALICAR HYNE
> Black Legion warrior, born of Terra. Master of the Fleet and commander of the warship *Thane*. Eighth of the Ezekarion.

VORTIGERN
> Black Legion warrior, born of Caliban. Lord of the Black Lions and commander of the warship *With Blade Drawn*. Ninth of the Ezekarion.

ZAIDU VOROLAS
> Black Legion warrior, born of Nostramo. Subcommander of the Shrieking Masquerade.

TERRA

The Gods hate us. I truly believe this.

They need us. We are their fuel. Our thoughts and deeds are what give them life. They *are* us, in the most literal sense. Every nightmare, every wound, every death – it all feeds them, it all fuels them, forms them. And no, they are not individual, reasoning entities as a sentient soul could ever comprehend. They are unreasoning forces, emotion and action given etheric shape, burning forever behind the curtain of corporeality.

But they hate us. I am convinced of it.

My brothers do not agree with me in this matter. Lheor believed they were mindless and without intent, that they could not hate us because they could not hate, nor love, anything. Ilyaster believes they are generous – even kind – but one must know one's own desires when dealing with them, and see the strength in even the most cursed gifts that they give. Telemachon sees them as distant, fascinating creatures, preferring his own intimate and secret forms of faith. Sargon believed, with all the fanaticism of any fervent worshipper, that the Gods grant us what we deserve, not what we desire. He used to insist that it is the purpose of our existence to live up to what the Gods wish us to become. That our blood and sweat must ever be spent in reaching the potential that the Pantheon sees within us.

Even my dear, misguided brother Ahzek believes that they are presences – rational, irrational or otherwise – that can be outfought and out-thought. Ahriman's belief could charitably be called optimism, or harshly considered to be ignorance. I suspect it is that terrible and compelling blend of both: naïvety.

But I am convinced that they hate us. They laugh at our dreams. They mock our ambitions. They fight us to enslave us, knowing they need us. They crave champions for their causes, elevating us, offering more – always more – to achieve our goals, only to abandon us and destroy us when we act against their whims. This is more than simple malice. Malice is crude and practically instinctive, a thing even beasts can comprehend. No, this is spite, and spite requires consciousness, emotion, the capacity for bitterness and wrath.

But they reserve their fiercest hatred for Abaddon. Oh, how they despise him. They hunger for him, fighting each other for the honour of attracting his ironclad soul into their clutches. The Pantheon hates him the way parasites or addicts resent that which sustains them. Without Abaddon, they have no hope of victory. If he would only choose one of them, if he would only commit his destiny to one of the Gods, it would bring the Great Game of Chaos to its final moves.

But then Abaddon would lose. He fights not for the

Pantheon, those creatures that hate how they need him, nor does he care about their Great Game. He fights for himself, for his own ambitions, and for the brothers at his side. He fights for the Legions cast aside by the Emperor. He cares about the Imperium we built with our blood, sweat, bolters and blades – and he wants it back. He cares about returning to the godling that gave us life and seeing the Emperor bleed for all His failures. He cares about brotherhood, the unity of the damned, the wrongs that were done to all of us.

And therein lies the root of the Gods' spite. They beseech him. They beg him. They betray him in spite and then crawl back in the hope that he will bow to them.

But the power is ultimately Abaddon's, and that is what the Gods can never forgive.

His greatest strength is also his deepest flaw. Because he will not bow to the Pantheon, they will forever betray him and work against his ultimate triumph. It is said that Abaddon's destiny is an ouroboros, the serpent devouring its own tail, as the Pantheon chases a submission he will never give, and he chases a triumph that may never come.

And so I tell you this, as true as I have ever been in my entire life: Abaddon's entire existence is devoted to breaking the cycle. We, his brothers, are his instruments in forcing fate onto a new path.

And thus, I am here. Captured, if you believe my gaolers, though I came to their door and surrendered my weapons of my own will.

I am still blind.

Strange, the things you can become used to. The darkness that stole my sight weaves treacherously around my other senses, tainting them, leaving them unreliable. Even time is a traitor. It no longer plays faithfully through my mind.

Eyeless and chained in place, the only way to measure the passing of time is by the beat of my twin hearts. Yet that rhythm becomes deceptive when silence is one's only companion; minutes can malform into hours, yet hours may pass as wayward moments.

How long have I been here on Terra? How long have I called this cell home? How long has my only company been the archival servitor that shares this space?

Why do you not speak, Thoth? Because you will not, or because you cannot? I hear the soft rhythm of your breath, so I know you are not fully automated. Yet your quill scratches on and on, committing these words to parchment. You are mind-reaved to a state of simplicity, perhaps, mono-tasked to avoid the moral threat I represent. Is that it?

I am wasting my breath with these questions.

I know what your masters want. They wish for more, always more, more recollections and reflections of an era that was myth to their society thousands of years before any of them were born.

I am not without pride. I am not immune to the temptation to lie, to reweave past failures and injustices as victories for the sake of my own esteem, to say that the Black Legion's rise was so inevitable, so born in righteousness, that we ascended with nothing but the acclaim and awe of our brothers and cousins. Yet for all my faults, I am not a petty soul, and there is no gain in spinning lies for Imperial ears.

This, then, is the truth. The Black Legion's history is drowned with blood, much of it our own. If it was easy to despise the dying Sons of Horus for their treachery and weakness, it was easier by far to loathe their reincarnation for its strength and defiance. Put simply, we refused to die. And oh, how our brothers and cousins hated us for it. How they tore across the Eye, hunting us for the twin sins of drawing breath and seeking to fight fate.

Sometimes we fought them. Often, we fled. Those were not days of pride, but nor were they days of outright defeat, for even as we fled from the vengeance and jealousies of our kindred, there were those that sought us out with a mind to fight alongside us.

Our ranks swelled, timeless night by timeless night. At first almost every recruit was another exile, another wanderer, another disgraced or disgusted soul that came to us in search of a new beginning. Some wished to cleanse themselves of the past and stand beneath a new banner. Some wished to taste once more the purpose of brotherhood after the endless battles within the Eye had broken their old bonds. Some sought to deceive us. They were purged, fed to the creatures that writhed in the dark of the *Vengeful Spirit*'s deepest decks.

Soon we recruited not lone warriors or squads, but warbands and warships. Time and again, Abaddon scattered us across the Eye in divided forces, bringing word of his return to his beleaguered Legion, offering amnesty and alliance to any that wished to join with us. Most of our new loyal brethren were the survivors of the shattered Sons of Horus. They came for one reason above all: survival. A dying Legion on the edge of extinction was suddenly presented with three of the most iconic symbols of its former strength. The Legion Wars raged on, yet here was Ezekyle Abaddon, here was Falkus Kibre and here was the *Vengeful Spirit*. Such an echo of their bright past was surely their greatest chance of survival in a realm that still hungered for their blood.

Exiles and idealists from every Legion joined us. Vortigern brought his solemn and wayward Lost Lion warband into our ranks. Amurael Enka came next – a brother who has had every chance to betray me across an eternity and yet never once wavered in his loyalty. Then Chariz Terenoch, the Wonderworker, who forged the blade I carried after the destruction of my axe Saern. He was the first of my former brothers among the Thousand Sons to surrender his Rubricae to my mastery.

Then came Zaidu and his vile cannibals, who inevitably fell into Telemachon's favour, followed by Delvarus and his brutal Secondborn, once Legion brothers to Lheor and formerly the guardians of the great warship *Conqueror*, flagship of the World Eaters.

None of our foes could overwhelm the *Vengeful Spirit* head on. Nor was Ezekyle content to exist for survival's sake and let only stragglers and exiles swear oaths of fealty. He wanted more. He wanted a Legion. Not one of the eighteen Legions of the Great Crusade; his vision was set higher, founded in the principles of rebirth. He wanted the first and only Legion of the Long War.

As tribal conquerors have done since the ages of antiquity, we offered our foes a choice: serve us or be destroyed. Those that chose to swear allegiance to Abaddon were permitted to join our fleet or garrison our strongholds, with some of those humbled warlords even joining Ezekyle's inner circle. Few chose destruction, though true to our word, we let none survive once they had chosen defiance.

Through blood and fire we raised ourselves to a place of, if not pride, then at least less dire shame. We commanded a fleet. We were the lords of thousands of warriors, each one sharing our ambitions to be more than we had been.

Though we were still hunted by our rivals – and none pursued us more bitterly than the last living Sons of Horus who spat at us for corrupting their legacy – we no longer lived with the blade of extinction against our throats.

Abaddon's aggression bordered upon obsession, almost into the realm of madness. He committed us to battle after battle, not only to crush those that offered defiance but also to come to the aid of beleaguered warbands that had sworn oaths of alliance. The Sons of Horus suffered worst of all, still plagued as they were by the shame of their defeat at Terra. Many were the times we tore through the formations of predator fleets hunting Sons of Horus warbands, fighting them back long enough for their prey to either flee or to stand with us against their attackers.

There was precious little luck to this. Abaddon courted the services and loyalty of sorcerers and seers above almost any other recruits. Ashur-Kai, called for so long the White Seer and now navigator of the *Vengeful Spirit,* found himself in a position of incomparable value. Nor was he alone – a coven of prophets and oracles formed, and when Abaddon's seers whispered, he took heed of every word.

And it worked. Ezekyle Abaddon, who had been First Captain of the XVI Legion and a renowned hero of the Imperium, became a champion to the Sons of Horus. Unprecedented numbers of them abandoned the green ceramite of their old Legion and adopted the colourless distinction of our nameless warband, fighting again beneath his banner. First for survival, and then, as we all believed, for something more.

That most potent and pure of motivations.

Revenge. Vengeance bought at any price.

I, too, had changed. I no longer suffered the nightmares

of wolves. The somnolent reflections of my burning world had receded, and with them faded the helpless hatred that had tasted a little too much like fear. Memories of grey warriors no longer howled through my mind, just as Gyre no longer walked by my side or guarded my slumbering form. Gone was the Fenrisian axe I carried into battle. Gone too was my armour of cobalt and polished bronze. The ceramite I wore was colourless, edged in dull metal.

I was remade. No longer a soldier of the Great Crusade or a heretic of a failed rebellion, I was a warrior of the Long War – as I have been every day since, as I will be until my final breath. Perhaps that last gasp of life will be within this very cell and it shall taste of this stagnant air. I don't know.

This is what I do know.

I am he who tells of the rage of angels. I am the emissary that speaks the blasphemies of a false god's exiled sons.

I am Iskandar Khayon, called Khayon the Black, Breaker of the Crimson King, Raider of Graves, Lord of the Ashen Dead, Third of the Ezekarion, Lord Vigilator of the Black Legion. I am the judge of my brothers' sins and the taker of traitors' heads. I am what my brother needed me to become – now, as ever, I am his blade at the throats of his foes. I am a blinded, tortured prisoner in Inquisitorial shackles. I am the Herald of the Crimson Path.

The seeds of our conquest were born in the fallow ground of Abaddon's own ambition, but we cannot ignore the whips that cracked against his back. Let us speak, then, of Moriana and Thagus Daravek.

Daravek, the battle-king and Lord of Hosts, remains my greatest failure. Few others have come as close to killing our dreams of vengeance as Thagus of the Death Guard, at the head of his armada.

And as for Moriana... Look for that name in your own ancient records, inquisitors. You will find her there, secreted within the deepest shadows. Doubtless her presence spread the same poison among your roots that it spread among ours.

Let this archive chronicle the beginning of what the Imperium now calls the First Black Crusade. I will tell you of the roots of the war and the first bloody battle when at last we broke free of our warp-wrought prison, when an ancient knight-king fell into darkness and when my brother sought to claim the sword fated to end an empire.

I swear to you on whatever tattered scraps remain of my soul, every word on these pages is true.

From shame and shadow recast.
In black and gold reborn.

PART ONE
MY BROTHER'S BLADE

'...Daravek Thagus Daravek he bled us he butchered us even Ezekyle didn't know the threat we couldn't have known it is Khayon's fault Khayon is to blame my brother Khayon he could not do it he could not do as he was ordered Khayon was blind he could not see the traceries of fate and he would not believe...'

> – from 'The Infinity Canticle', sequestered by the holy order of His Imperial Majesty's Inquisition as an *Ultima*-grade moral threat. Purported to be the unedited, raving confession of Sargon Eregesh, Lord-Prelate of the Black Legion.

I

WEAPONS

'Khayon, I know you're here. I can smell your mongrel stink.'

Daravek's voice was a rusted hacksaw, a thing of flaky corrosion and rotting edges. 'Show yourself. Let us finish this.'

He was talking a great deal, almost always a sign of desperation in a warrior. I dared to think that control of the situation was slipping through his fingers, and challenging me like this was the only way he could try to reassert his dominance.

Around us, above us, sirens were crying out their warnings. They had been doing so for several minutes. In Daravek's defence, he had done very well to last this long.

But I had him. At last, I had him. Tonight I would bring his bones to my lord Abaddon.

Thagus Daravek was an immense, bloated monster, swollen by the favour of his patron Gods. Wet filth crusted the overlapping plates of his battle armour, sealing the seams with undefined biomechanical vileness. The ceramite around his torso and one of his legs was warped with diseased swelling and fusion of the flesh within, and horns of bronze thrust through punctures in the mangled armour. The bronze spines were veined, somehow alive, and bleeding vascular promethium. The vulture's wings that rose in ragged majesty from his shoulder blades were spindly, trembling things despite their size, the feathers and tattered bones burning in heatless waves of warpfire. Ghosts, or things that looked like ghosts, reached out from those flames.

'He is here,' Daravek said, deep and low, as he paced. His jaundiced eyes drifted from warrior to warrior among his elite guard. Blood decorated his face from the slaughter so far. It bubbled, slowly dissolving on the active blade of his axe. 'I know he is here, riding within your bones. Which one of you was weak enough to fall to the mongrel magician?'

Even as I clenched my consciousness away from the risk of discovery, even as I dissolved my essence thinner than mist and threaded it through the blood of my host body, I felt a stab of irritation at the word 'magician', uttered in Gothic heavily accented by life in the highlands of Barbarus.

But now was not the time to amend the warlord's ignorance.

'Was it you, Symeos?' he asked one of his warriors. The metal chamber shook around us. Statues to incarnations of the Undying God and the Shifting Many trembled, given shivering life by the assault on the fortress. Symeos tilted his helmed head, bearing his throat before his master's blade.

'Never in life, Lord Daravek.'

Daravek levelled his axe at another of his closest brethren. Some of them shared the same traits as their liege lord – the warped bloating of preternatural disease, the encrusted corruption of once pristine battleplate. This one did not; he was cadaverous in a drier, more ghoulish sense. There was something parched about him, something that spoke of undesecrated tombs beneath the earth, decorated with the untouched dust of centuries.

'Ilyaster?' Daravek asked. 'Was it you, brother?'

'No, my lord,' Ilyaster said with the ugly rasp that served as his voice. He was unhelmed, and the words were a carrion-scented breath through blackened teeth.

Daravek swayed to the next warrior. To me. His eyes met mine, his toxic respiration caressing my face. 'Tychondrian,' he said. 'You, brother?'

I was also unhelmed. I snarled through jaws that could barely close due to the length of my uneven fangs.

'No, lord.'

The fortress gave another titanic shudder around us. Daravek turned away, laughing, truly laughing. 'You could all be lying, you worthless wretches. Nevertheless, the day is far from done. We must get into orbit. We will go where Abaddon's mongrel cannot pursue.'

I was instrumental in the birth of the Black Legion, yet the truth is that I was absent for many of the battles that formed its genesis. While my brothers waged war and fought to survive, I worked in an isolation that bordered upon exile. I cannot say that I never resented Abaddon for this, but I have always understood it. We each play the part to which we are best suited, and he did not need another general, or yet another warrior. He needed an assassin.

This is not a rare role for souls of great psychic strength among the Nine Legions. We possess talents and masteries that make murder something of a specialty. In a realm where deception and assassination are plagued by a million unnatural considerations – where stealth and a sniper rifle are next to useless; where physical laws scarcely apply; where every single foe is preternaturally resistant to venom and poison – those with the power to remake reality make the finest murderers.

Use of the Art, manipulating the matter of souls, allows one to bypass such limitations. A warrior who may never best his brothers with a blade can bind daemons to his will. The same warrior, who may be mediocre with a boltgun and bear no awards for either valour or mastery, can rewrite the minds of his foes to his own wishes. A marksman that has learned every scrap of intelligence about his target may try to predict his foe's actions, but a sorcerer that has seen into his enemy's soul knows every iota of lore without needing to resort to crude guesswork. And if you give credence to such things, the sorcerer may have walked the paths of fate and seen a host of possible, probable futures, and can manipulate events to bring about the most desired ends.

Yet if I am making this sound easy, I am doing a disservice to the slayer's craft. Most of these undertakings are monumental. Many are impossible without a coven of allies and apprentices, both of which I have used in abundance across the millennia. Sometimes, however, I work alone, and those sorcerers capable of such feats must be psykers of immense strength. I do not say this lightly. My reputation among the Nine Legions has been hard earned, and there are precious few sorcerers able to match me in might. Most of those that can tend to waste their talents in the unreliable impracticalities of precognition and prophecy. A tragic waste. Some say the best blades are those that are never drawn, and there is wisdom in such a philosophy. But power must be wielded, tested and trained, lest it wither on the vine.

You have heard me speak of Ahriman before. I know you know his name, from his many predations upon the Imperium. My brother, my naïve but most admirably honest brother, Ahzek Ahriman once told me that he alone among the Nine Legions stood above me in talent with the Art. It was typical of his habit for blending humility with arrogance, to say nothing of manipulation.

I cannot speak for the veracity of his words. In the long years of my life, while almost all of my sorcerous rivals lie dead, a few of them came close to killing me. There are others whom I would never wish to face, and still others that carry reputations equal to, or greater than, mine.

In our Legion's early years, I played my part as expected. My new duties for Abaddon required a breathtaking amount of preparation, and I adhered to these requirements with unfailing focus.

I was never swift in my work. I was, however, very thorough. When Abaddon needed haste, he sent warriors or warships to do his will. When he needed precision, when he wanted a point made or a lesson learned, he sent me.

When Abaddon first told me he required Daravek dead, I knew not to expect any deep conversational insight as to how he wished me to achieve his goal. It was always my place to study the target, to ascertain the consequences of various methods of death and to bring about a result most favourable to our emerging armies and the warrior-monarch that led us.

Abaddon expects results. Any one of the Ezekarion requiring the painstaking force-feeding of information, unable or unwilling to compose battle plans in his own right, would be discarded or destroyed as useless. The same stands for the chieftains, subcommanders and champions that fill the officer ranks beneath us.

This serves a twofold purpose. First, although he leads the Black Legion's greatest battles and oversees our function, in this manner Abaddon forces his ranking officers and elite bodyguards to constantly adapt and act on their own initiative.

The second purpose, no less vital, is one of trust. By this delegation his closest brothers know they carry his trust. The rest of the Legion, and the entirety of the Eye itself, knows this as well. The Ezekarion speaks with Abaddon's voice. Each one of us wields his authority. You cannot overstate the exultant effect this has on morale.

It was my duty as Abaddon's silent blade that brought me to the fortress of Thagus Daravek, Warlord of This, Master of That, Butcher of Them and a dozen other titles that I refuse to consign to parchment even all these millennia later. One of them mattered more than the others, and that is the one I shall use: the self-styled Lord of Hosts.

He challenged us at every turn, a warlord who wanted to rival Abaddon, and thus he was sentenced to death. Our emissaries to other warlords would arrive only to find that oaths had already been sworn to Daravek. Our fleets would translate into a system only to sail into one of Daravek's many ambushes.

We of the Ezekarion, and the armies we commanded, had been bleeding the Legions for some time, carving them apart as we fought for our right to exist. None retaliated with the same ferocity as the Death Guard, and no warlord was as wilful, or as dangerous, as Daravek, the so-called

Lord of Hosts. The title fit. On more than one occasion he had gathered fleets comprised of warbands from several Legions, tasked with the purpose of resisting our rise. Yet always he avoided direct conflict with Abaddon. Always he remained one step ahead of us, refusing to come within range of the *Vengeful Spirit*'s guns.

For every victory we earned through the running blood of his warriors, he stole one back in kind. He had to die.

I was Abaddon's instrument. It took months of watching, waiting, hiding and scrying to locate his sanctuary world, and I was blessed with fortune as well. Traitors within his ranks stood ready to work with me. I could not fail. I *would* not fail. Not this time.

Daravek and his warband laid claim to a world of calcified pain. Despite the madness of those words, they are neither weak poetry nor a strained metaphor. The planet's crust was formed of tortured breaths, fearful dreams and the echoes of human and eldar agonies throughout eternity, all of it bleeding from the warp and rendered into a cold landscape of knuckly, misshapen bone.

This would have left me enraptured during my first years inside the Eye. When I walked the world's surface, however, I was neither breathless nor awed. My mind was elsewhere, tangled in other difficulties. This was my fifth attempt on Daravek's life. As useful as I was to Abaddon, his patience was not without limit.

'Kulrei'arah,' Nefertari had informed me before I left to undertake the duty. That was the name this globe had once carried as part of the eldar empire.

We had no name for it. It didn't deserve one.

If you touched the osseous ground with bare skin, you could feel the senseless, red reflections of the dreamers and sufferers whose torment formed this place. Even without touching the bony earth you could hear the murmurs rising from its cracked, marrow-stinking surface.

What wracked imagination had conjured such a planet into being? Was this Daravek's psyche at insidious work, shaping it to his desires? Or was it merely the Eye's etheric discharge taking form – the warp's excremental run-off changing a world without any guiding will?

And yet, as daemon-haunted worlds are weighed, the climate and landscape of this nameless sphere were practically tame. On Sortiarius, the home world of my former Legion, it rains the boiling blood of every liar ever to draw breath. In the season of storms, this sanguine tempest is often acidic enough to dissolve ceramite. Some say this is Magnus the Red's rebellious subconscious at play, scourging himself for his past treacheries. I cannot speak to the truth of the matter, but it sounds appropriate for my father, as conflicted as he is.

Patches of this nameless world's surface had, through preternatural corrosion or unrest, been reduced to deserts of bone dust. It was within one of these oceans of skeletal powder that Daravek's fortress lay, half-buried in the dust of eroded nightmares. Its crooked spires reached skywards, surrounded in a fog of toxichemical mist. Monstrous industrial mouth-vents along the sides of each tower breathed the poison gas across the surrounding desert, offering yet another line of defence. Despite this, the bastion was still a place of pilgrimage to the beastmen and mutants that populated the world – their bodies, given over to varying degrees of rot, lay across the desert in their scattered thousands. This latter element fascinated me. What would bring these creatures on such a pilgrimage, into the face of an almost certain death? What did they believe awaited them within the fortress' walls, those few that were strong enough to walk through the poison mist to reach it?

I recovered several of the corpses for educational purposes. Speaking with the shards of their souls, I ascertained from their pious wailing that they left their subterranean tribes and marched upon Daravek's castle of corroded iron in the hopes of elevation into his ranks. He would hardly be the first to try and pervert the gene-seed implantation process to function on mutants, adult or otherwise, but tales of success in altering the Emperor's original ritualised process were – and still are – as rare as you might imagine.

After each summoning I would sheathe my *jamdhara* knife, hurl the shrieking ghosts back into the warp's winds and incinerate the remains to erase any evidence of my investigations. Avoiding detection was paramount. Slowly, invisibly, I began my infiltration.

It took almost a year of psychic permeation before I was ready to kill Daravek. Everything had to be precise. It had to be perfect. I could take no risks this time.

I still wonder if I acted too swiftly.

The creature's name was a gathering of syllables that I would struggle to pronounce aloud, despite speaking several hundred linguistic variants of humanity's proto-Gothic root tongue. This creature, whose thoughts were a turmoil of bestial instinct and slavering loyalty to its armoured masters, toiled its life away in the fortress' dark depths. Here the only sounds in existence were the brays and yells of the menials raising their voices above the ceaseless crash of coal-fire machinery. This was the creature's life, from birth to death.

In this dark realm, the creature moved among its kindred, clutching a rusted and broken machine strut, almost two metres in length. It thrust this primitive spear through the back of a second creature's neck, ripped it free, then wielded it as a club to shatter the face of a third slave. This third unfortunate fell to the ground, raising its arms futilely as it was impaled through the chest.

The spear was now bent, rendering it useless. The creature left it in its kinsman's chest and turned to the others drawing closer in the stinking, crashing darkness. It could kill one of them, perhaps two, but dozens of red eyes gleamed back in the gloom. Jagged war-shrieks and more human-sounding cries of anger and fear sounded out through the dark.

The creature did not fight its kinsmen. It turned from them, took three running steps and hurled itself into the pounding, rattling mechanics of the closest machine station. The pistons slammed. The gears ground. The creature's final thought, not surprisingly, was washed red with panic and pain. The machine slowed momentarily, then chewed through the obstruction.

This happened again and again. One of the creatures would erupt into sudden violence, killing without warning, striking down those at its side. Several simply threw themselves into the jaws of struggling mechanical engines.

Within the space of a single minute, eleven of the machines had stalled, jammed by dense clogs of flesh and bone.

In one of the spires, a legionary overseeing the work of high-level functionary slaves stared unblinking at a console that started to flash with red warning signs. He was already dying when the console's alert runes began flashing, suffering catastrophic ischemic shock as a carnival of messy embolisms savaged his brain.

The Space Marine – a warrior named Elath Dastarenn – remained standing. He stood slack-mouthed, dead-eyed, and keyed in several codes to deactivate the console's warning sigils, silencing the terminal from reporting its findings elsewhere.

I believe he said something mumbled and meaningless as his synapses flared those final times. Whatever the wordless murmur was supposed to mean, I cannot speculate. Bodies, and the brains that drive them, do strange things as they die.

The legionary holding the rank of Armsmaster ceased speaking halfway through addressing his squad. He drew his sidearm in a slow snarl of arm servos, placed the bolt pistol's mouth against his left eye and discharged a bolt directly into the front of his skull.

Atop one of the gunship platforms, a crew of mutant thralls braved the toxic gases with rheumy eyes and blood-pocked rebreathers, working to refuel a Thunderhawk. One of them unlimbered a crude flamer from beneath her cloak, a weapon she did not have the clearance to possess. She had spent several days building it piece by piece, despite lacking the intelligence to do so, and now brought it forth to bathe her companions in a roar of semi-liquid fire.

She ignored her flailing, dying herdmates, even when one of them crashed into her and ignited her gas-soaked clothing. Aflame now, she pushed the nozzle of the jury-rigged short-burst flamer against the refuelling port of the grounded gunship, but nothing emerged when she pulled the trigger. Her last act was to thrust her burning arm directly into the hole that opened into the promethium tank.

I saw the explosion just under a minute later from where I watched, several kilometres away on a low ridge.

On several other towers, anti-aircraft cannons rotated and lowered, no longer scanning the low atmosphere for threats, instead tracking the flight paths of the fighter wing patrolling above the ramparts. The servitor-brains inside these turrets would later be found boiled alive in their suspension-fluid cradles. Long before that, however, they spat volley after volley of cannon fire into the sky, bringing down most of their own aerial defences.

The primary cannon – an anti-orbital annihilator fusillade – detonated in the middle of this treacherous display due to its fifty-strong crew of mono-tasked servitors acting without orders, overriding all fail-safes and overloading the poorly maintained power cells set in the weapon's foundations. The three tech-priests tasked with overseeing the primary cannon's function had slaughtered one another without warning or reason, acting in cold and calculating silence, effectively abandoning their servitor wards.

I saw this explosion as well. It was considerably brighter than the first.

Power began to fail across the fortress. Partly this was because of slave crews turning on one another. Partly it was due to the sabotage of several power generators. And partly it was because one of Daravek's own elite warriors, the legionary's armour heaving to contain the disease-bloated flesh within, had fused several melta charges to his own body and detonated them at the tri-cortex plasma locomotor that controlled coolant for the fortress' entire reactor district beneath the planet's surface.

An uprising began in the fortress' depths when a legionary powered down and deactivated the prisoner cells, flooding the lower levels of the castle with warp spawn, devolved mutants and mortal captives who were being kept as food. The legionary cut his own throat with his chainsword before he witnessed the fruits of this labour, and the vox speakers in his gorget that demanded reports heard nothing but his last breaths gurgling through his destroyed vocal cords.

Several legionaries rampaged through the warband's barracks and armouries, butchering their unprepared brethren and slaughtering arming slaves. Each of these wayward warriors was inevitably killed in turn by his brothers, but not before each had done what damage he could. Within each victorious squad, another warrior would then turn on his brethren without warning, unloading a boltgun at point-blank range into the backs and heads of his brothers, or carving limbs from bodies with a power sword before being finished by the survivors.

Dying daemons clawed their way from several of these corpses, their soulless lives extinguished on the floor by the bodies of those they had possessed. Others I simply abandoned where they fell, moving my senses and consciousness to the next warriors whose souls I had spent months studying in preparation for this night.

One by one, death by death.

* * *

I remember every man, woman and child whose mind I touched, whose body I puppeteered, whose flesh I gouged out hollow as a haven for a daemonic parasite, purely because of what I am. A legionary's brain is sculpted to retain everything from the moment of his awakening as a Space Marine to the second of his demise.

Far from the fortress, I was sweating in my armour and chanting, endlessly chanting, hunched in the confines of a crawl hole I had dug with my bare hands. Even with my consciousness free of my body, I felt my physical form reacting to the pressures I was placing upon it with such a protracted psychic sending: the ache of my over-bent spine; the tickle of saliva running from my moving mouth; the painful spasms of my twitching fingers.

Months and months of preparation had led to this moment. Soul by soul, being by being, I moved through the fortress, touching some minds as a mere caress, amplifying their basest instincts and spurring them to bloodshed. Others, those I had silently and unknowingly prepared over the many months, I plunged myself into, knife-like and savage, tearing their consciousnesses into mist, overriding the function of their muscles and bones with my will.

Even among those I had been spying upon for months, hollowing out for this specific purpose, resistance was tenacious. I was weary and their souls were strong, and rather than waste time seeking to overcome them I would move onto others. I was too focused on my work to keep track of every failed attempt, but in more than one district of the fortress my attempts to rally the slaves against their masters failed, as did my attempts to force the Death Guard to butcher their slaves.

It was working, though.

Bulkheads that led to avenues of escape were sealed and overridden with their mechanical processes shot. Corridors were collapsed with explosives. Gunships that managed to lift off were brought down by fire from the battlements. Section by section, district by district, the fortress was cast into darkness and pitched into disorder. A year's work, all culminating in a single evening. The jaws of the trap slowly closed.

It was not perfect, but by the lies of the Shifting Many, it was close. So damn close.

Soon it was time to hunt Daravek. I sank my unseen claws into one last prepared and vulnerable mind, tearing his shrieking, violated thoughts free and binding my own in place. I settled into this new host, gathered my strength and waited.

Daravek was by no means easy prey, and he was anything but a fool. He had reacted with precision and competence, moving through the fortress himself, quelling the uprisings through the brutality of his axe and by ordering entire sections of the fortress sealed, flooding them with alchemical toxins to extinguish any living resistance. It might have worked had the sections actually been sealed, but many of his unit leaders and subcommanders were mind-eaten wrecks that failed to comply with his orders, or were murdered by their subordinates before they could act. In many cases, they were dead before they could even receive his orders.

But despite all my preparation, I was building an uncontrollable fire in haste and with imperfect tools. Daravek felt my nearness. He knew what was happening, knew this was the payment for resisting Abaddon's past approach and offer of alliance. He had seen this before. Not on this scale, not to this degree of precision, but he knew the hand that held this blade.

'Khayon is here,' he had said.

He halted his massacring advance in one of his ritual chambers, demanding answers from the remaining bodyguards at his side. They endured this with stoic, regal loyalty.

When his eyes locked to mine, I felt the toxicity of his breath against my mutated face. 'Tychondrian,' he said to me. 'You, brother?'

I snarled a denial through a fanged mouth that the warp had mangled and reshaped into something of absolute lethality.

'No, lord.'

He laughed. By the Pantheon, he was enjoying this. 'You could all be lying, you worthless wretches. Nevertheless, the day is far from done. We must get into orbit. We will go where Abaddon's mongrel cannot pursue.'

The chamber shook once more with the discord I had orchestrated across the fortress. Daravek turned away from me, levelling his gaze upon the next warrior of his inner circle. All I had to do was shift my stance, lengthening my shadow beneath the flickering glare of the overhead lights so that it touched Daravek's in lightless union.

I forced my psychic command into that patch of conjoined darkness.

Now.

Prosperine lynxes, extinct with the annihilation of my home world, were ill-named for comparative purposes. Before their destruction, they had resembled the equally extinct

Ancient Terran *tigrus*-cat or the sabre-toothed *smyladon* rather than any other feline: hugely muscled, bulky with strength and speckle-striped in natural warning to ward off other predators. However, they eclipsed even those prehistoric beasts in size. A Prosperine lynx's great head, with an arsenal of spear-tip teeth, would reach the height of a Legiones Astartes warrior's breastplate.

That is what leapt from Thagus Daravek's shadow. Claws first, the beast melted out of the darkness and launched, roaring, onto the warlord's back in a move of impossible agility.

In shape it was a Prosperine lynx, but in form it was purely daemonic. This creature possessed neither flesh nor blood, and its fur – black and striped with lighter grey – was closer to smoke than hair. Its claws were the length of gladii and formed from volcanic glass. Its eyes were the kind of white that burns.

I was moving the moment it struck. I spun to the warrior next to me, igniting the lightning claws I wore as gauntlets. I could – *should* – have slaughtered two of the other bodyguards before they could react, but I was slowed by the unfamiliar might of the Terminator war-plate around me. Nor were cumbersome lightning claws my weapon of preference. I carved through the closest Death Guard only for the blades to lodge within the corpse for precious seconds. When I dragged them free, my chance to slaughter Daravek was lost – though he still thrashed beneath the daemon-cat's weight and fury, his other bodyguards now moved between us.

Reality bleached down to flashes of instinct and insight, cutting, weaving aside, swinging left and right with the cumbersome claws. Despite my gouging Tychondrian's consciousness free of his flesh, his body still resisted my control. He had been stronger than I expected. That made me slow.

Tychondrian's body was a limping, bleeding ruin by the time I reached Daravek. Scarce seconds had passed, but it was an assassin's eternity, where every heartbeat counted. The taste of failure was already running its bitter way over my tongue. I knew, facing the embattled Daravek as he wrestled with the thrashing, snarling lynx, that I lacked the strength to finish him from within Tychondrian's shredded form.

Nagual, I sent. Even my silent voice was ravaged. Tychondrian was dying, the distraction of weakness rather than pain flooding through his fading muscles and slowing his internal organs. I was down on one knee, unable to force myself back up as the body died around me. *Nagual... Finish him...*

Master, the lynx sent back in acknowledgement.

Not a word in truth, just a ripple of awareness, yet the lynx was struggling alone. Daravek gushed a flood of alchemical flame from his wrist projectors, bathing the creature that thrashed upon his back and shoulders like a living cloak. Nagual's smoky corpus caught fire, and the beast vanished.

Suddenly unbalanced without the daemon's weight, Daravek took a moment to turn and stabilise himself. In the same second, the daemonic feline roared from my shadow, leaping out to crash into the Death Guard warlord once more.

Cannot kill alone, sent Nagual as his fangs scraped sparks across the ceramite of Daravek's shoulder guards. His claws found better purchase, tearing mangled shreds of armour plating free and ripping through the meat beneath, yet each savage wound sealed almost as soon as it was carved. *Prey is blessed. Gifts from the Undying God. Gifts from the Shifting Many. Cannot kill alone.*

I couldn't rise. I couldn't shoot. The arm I raised did not end in a double-barrelled bolter clutched in an armoured fist; it ended raggedly at the elbow, severed moments before by one of the other bodyguards' blades.

'Khayon.' Daravek spat my name from his bleeding mouth, advancing on me, step by slow step. 'I. See. You.'

The daemon's snarls turned frantically feline as Daravek gripped Nagual's biting face over his shoulder and began to sink his fingers into his skull.

Master!

I tore myself free of the useless husk that had been Tychondrian, suffering the disembodied vulnerability of an unseen etheric form. My body, my true body, was kilometres from here – hunched and chanting and utterly useless. In the air around me, I felt the shivery threat of shapeless daemons drawn to my unbound spirit, hungering for the taste of a human soul. No time for caution.

I closed myself around Daravek, seeping through the cracks in his armour, sinking into the pores of his skin, driving into the meat of his mind. Possession is among the most desperate and difficult ways to attack a soul. It rarely works without intensive preparation, and he sensed me at once, as surely as if I held a blade to his throat. Immersion within a soul comes with a horrific sharing of overlapping senses as the brain plays host to two souls, awakening the mind with painful hisses of meshed memories and sending burning stabs of sensory input along overburdened optic nerves.

Not this time. Daravek's spirit was iron. Trying to puppet

his flesh was to shout into a storm; I was hopelessly overwhelmed against his strength. He repelled me from his flesh through force of will, and hurled the daemon-cat away through force of muscle.

He was bloodied and battered, cut off from the survivors of his warband, his fortress falling around him – yet he still lived. He turned, paying no heed to the blood he vomited down his chest-plate, disgorging internal filth through the grate of his teeth and seeking me, wild-eyed and raving.

No. Not seeking me. Seeking my ally, the traitor now revealed in his midst.

'Ilyaster.'

One of his inner circle still lived. Ilyaster, that patient and parched creature serving as Daravek's herald, standing as ever with his liege lord's scythe of office in his hands. He too was wounded from the fray, his Cataphractii plate mauled and spitting sparks from its back-mounted power generator. I had not touched him, nor had my daemon familiar.

Ilyaster pulled the ceremonial weapon from the corpse of the brother warrior he had just beheaded, and raised it to ward off his own lord.

'You.' Daravek's mouth ran with black blood as he regurgitated the accusation. 'You betrayed me. You summoned Abaddon's mongrel. *You!*'

The shadow-lynx advanced from one side, Ilyaster from the other, wounded but determined.

Now. It had to be now. Daravek could destroy all three of us if he was allowed to retake control of the battle.

But I had nothing left. I hurled myself into him once more. He repelled me without effort, as defiantly as though his soul were warded by steel.

Weakening by the moment, I drove back into his mind,

thinning myself into near-nothingness, offering no solid presence for him to repel a third time. I did not need to master his flesh, merely steal a moment of opportunity.

No assault this time. This was attunement, a harmonising with his body's mortal processes. I flowed through his physical form, riding his blood, feeling the singing sting of adrenaline and electrical impulses from his nervous system.

Pain.

I willed pulses of flame to dance along the cobweb of his nerves, forcing his muscles to contract, to clench, to spasm.

It was enough. Enough to loosen his grip on the axe, enough to paralyse Daravek the span of a single breath.

The daemon-beast was a hammer weight of taloned shadow against my face and chest. The ceremonial scythe was a lance blow cracking into my side. I felt myself falling to the ground, weighed down by the body I had suffused with suffering.

Feed! The daemon's snarls came with each jarring, reaving blow of his clawed paws. *Feed! Blood! Meat! Life!*

I was Daravek in that moment. Every word was a thunder crack against my shattering skull. The daemon, the minion of Abaddon's mongrel assassin, was taking me to pieces. I could not move. My armour was shattered by my own ceremonial scythe in Ilyaster's hands.

And yet, I was laughing. Daravek was laughing. I had no power to compel him to such a reaction.

Khayon. I spoke my own name, forcing my spirit into cohesion, keeping myself together. *I am Khayon. I am Khayon.*

Memories flashed, acid-vile in their intensity, of warriors I had never met and wars I had never fought. Strangely it was this, of all things, that Daravek hated me for most. This voyeuristic sharing of his thoughts; this defiling insult of living inside his skull. And yet, even then, his snide laughter echoed all around me.

He backhanded Ilyaster hard enough to shatter the other warrior's breastplate and moved for the immense doors leading to the fortress' teleportation chamber. I had to stop him. I had to kill him.

But I could not. I could not hold myself inside his form. He would not let me. He hurled me from his flesh with the ease of a man waving aside an insect. My shock only made it easier for him to shed my consciousness from his own, and he did so with silent psychic laughter.

Almost, Iskandar! Almost, this time.

He repelled me with such brutality that all sense and sensation fled from me. I saw nothing, sensed nothing, and merely plunged through blackness. At the end of my strength, only oblivion awaited.

For a time, I did not exist. For a time, I was past consciousness. In that deep and timeless black, I remember only one thing: when it began to end. There came the sensation of fangs, jaws that closed together in the nothingness. Weapon-teeth sank into whatever was left of Iskandar Khayon, biting down into the matter of his lost soul.

Jaws that arrested my endless fall, that held me in a bladed, impaling embrace... and that brought me back.

I woke with the arrhythmic drumming of my twin hearts straining inside my chest, and a gasp of bitter air spearing its way into my lungs. My vision returned, but slowly, victim to smears and hallucinatory blurs.

When my muscles ceased spasming, I managed to rise on unsteady feet, appalled at the weakness of my limbs. Sweat greased my flesh in a disgusting coat. Blood had trickled from my eyes, my ears, my nose, my gums. The pressure in my skull began to ease as I sucked in great heaves of air, fuelling my locked lungs and overworked hearts.

Nagual emerged from the shadow cast by my crouching form, licking blood from his obsidian teeth.

Master? the daemon lynx asked, as if I were not standing right before him.

Is it done? I was so drained, I could not be certain I was even reaching outside my own head, let alone to my distant daemon. *Is he dead?*

The great cat turned back towards the burning fortress, kilometres away and far below us in the desert bowl.

The prey fled. Could not kill alone. Had to save you, master. Your soul was lost.

Breathless, exhausted, I exhaled into the nameless world's reeking wind and looked up at the stars, where Thagus Daravek and his surviving brethren were surely safe aboard one of their warships, no doubt already sailing to yet another hidden sanctuary that would take me years to find.

Defeated, a failure for the fifth time, I looked down at the lynx. I would go to the fortress and claim it for Abaddon. I would find out if Ilyaster still lived. And then, after this latest loss, I would go home.

II

AMONG THE OCCLUDED STARS

Abaddon was alone when I returned. He watched the smoke-wreathed stars as I approached him, looking out at the escort ships holding a perimeter around the flagship.

We were hiding. The fleet – what little of it that I could see – lay at anchor in the very deepest nothingness, shrouded in a region of the Eye's densest mists. The *Vengeful Spirit* was vulnerable, protected only by a clutch of destroyers, frigates and light cruisers.

We were more fortunate than many other warbands. Abaddon has always seen value in sorcerers and recruited them to our cause by any means necessary. In a realm where Navigators are hopelessly lost to madness and so many warships sail only by hurling themselves into the tormented oceans and trusting the whims of the Pantheon to bring them into new hunting grounds, our vessels were guided by those gifted in the Art. Though far from a fail-safe method, use of sorcerous void-guides was the best – and indeed the only – way to keep our fleets in cohesion.

My brother and I stood in one of the spinal observational spires overlooking the dark vista of the *Vengeful Spirit*'s backbone battlements. Outside of battle, he was often to be found here. As time had passed, as our armies had grown, as the assaults to steal the *Vengeful Spirit* had increased in number and intensity, Abaddon became evermore a warlord of the Eye rather than the simple, blunt instrument he had been as First Captain of the Sons of Horus.

And yet.

And yet Ezekyle himself diminished in ways few eyes outside the Ezekarion seemed to see. The malady that struck him burned slow in his blood, eating at him month after month. He grew distracted, insular, listless. The life in his golden eyes never faded; rather it seethed and turned sour. He had begun to grow apart from those of us he had brought together.

He led us, still. His lapses and distractions had not yet threatened to compromise his leadership, but the more feverish and gaunter he grew, the more uneasy some of us in the Ezekarion became.

Soon enough, he stopped sleeping. Sleep is rarely a concern for the warriors of the Legiones Astartes. We are able to subsist on mere hours of such healing rest each week, and we are capable of long periods without it entirely, albeit with a strain upon our physiologies. Yet Ezekyle claimed he no longer sought the respite of slumber at all. Instead he was almost always here between battles, staring out into the teeming half-dark between the Eye's occluded stars.

Sometimes I could almost sense what tore at his thoughts. Something? Someone? A presence, voiceless but far from silent, existed somewhere out there in the deeper dark. It called to him. Or threatened him. Or cursed at him. I could not tell.

I could not tell if it was even real or simply some echo of his own aura, refracting across the infinite. To look into Ezekyle's soul was always a matter of discomfort. He was but one man, alone and unbreakable, but his soul swirled with thousands of other voices forever pressing against his being. Was one of them stronger than the others? Was that what I was hearing?

He had always refused to enlighten me, and nothing I could do ever pierced his aura. I wondered if he even heard the presences on a conscious level. He did not seem to. I confess that his distracted stoicism has always chilled me – the warp itself, the galaxy's own reflection, cries for his attention and yet he resolutely ignores it.

The pressures of such an existence must be beyond reason.

The night I returned, he looked ravaged. We were alone but for my great lynx of shadow and obsidian, which prowled around the chamber, the fluxed heavens reflecting on the surface of his pearlescent eyes. I had not yet seen any of my brothers except Abaddon – most were away with the other fleets, fighting – and Ezekyle's summons had come the moment my boots struck the *Vengeful Spirit*'s landing deck.

Abaddon wore his battleplate – once the dark wargear of the Justaerin, though in the unreliable timelessness since the destruction of Horus Reborn he had already made several modifications. Another aspect that set Abaddon apart from many of our brothers was his refusal to rely on armourcraft slaves. Abaddon refused to let anyone tend to the maintenance and modification of his black war-plate. The trophies that hung from his armour were all those he had hammered into place himself. The trinkets and charms were those he had carved or fashioned. The repaired patches and sections of reinforcement were each done by his own hand. A legionary has no choice but to let machines and thralls aid in his armouring, when the ceramite plates must be mounted and driven and drilled into place, but that was the limit of Abaddon's tolerance.

He turned to me. Life seemed to pour back into his features.

'Iskandar,' he said. He was bathed in the light of the poisoned yet purified stars. Despite his throaty Cthonian drawl, he spoke my name with the Tizcan pronunciation. I have always appreciated the gesture. 'Back at long last.'

'Where is the fleet?' I asked. 'Blood of the Gods, Ezekyle, we are practically alone in the void.'

'Engaged elsewhere. Engaged several elsewheres, in fact.' He related the whys and wheres of our forces. We were scattered to the warp's winds, engaged in a dozen theatres of war at once. Falkus and his warband – the Aphotic Blade – were bringing destruction to Denarcus. Lheor and Zaidu were reinforcing Ceraxia at the Thylakus Expanse. Vortigern, Telemachon and Valicar were also prosecuting conflicts elsewhere. Our forces were divided as part of Abaddon's endless ambitions, raiding some foes, negotiating with others – the endless and fragile cobweb of warfare and diplomacy was being woven even here in our warp-shaped prison, and the swiftest, hungriest of its weaving spiders was my golden-eyed lord.

As he spoke, the Prosperine lynx padded to his side the way a tamed hab-feline would trail after its owner. Abaddon ran his unclawed fingers through the daemon's spectral fur.

'Nagual,' he said in greeting.

Nagual's rumbling purr sent shivers through the deck. 'I like this one far more,' Abaddon continued. 'It's much more honest than your wolf ever was.' I was not sure what he meant, and rather than let me reply, he gestured with the Talon to bid me begin my report.

'My brother,' I said, 'Ilyaster Faylech and his brethren await your welcome.'

'Good.' Abaddon nodded, his bulky figure framed by the hazy void outside the observation deck's blast windows. 'And?'

I went to one knee, a knight of yore before his liege lord. 'And I failed you.'

His breathing became a rumble, the promise of thunder to come. 'Thagus Daravek still lives.'

I did not think Ezekyle would kill me. I did not, however, expect to leave this encounter unscathed or unscarred. 'He lives, lord.'

'Is there some aspect of my leadership thus far, Khayon, that leads you to believe I look kindly upon failure?'

'No, lord.'

'And failure of this magnitude?' he said slowly, opening and closing his clawed hand. 'You are my blade, Khayon. What use is an assassin that cannot kill?'

I almost shamed myself by arguing, insisting that Daravek represented my lone failure. While this was true, pleading the case would have been unforgivably pathetic.

Abaddon rested a single claw point against my forehead. It would take a mere twist of his wrist to flay my face from my skull. I had seen him do it to others in the past. He wore the Talon almost all the time now. Rare were the encounters when one could address our overlord without the light of a distant sun or a chamber's lumoglobes reflecting off the wicked scythes lengthening from his fingers. They scraped together with dry rasps when deactivated. They spat the unstable sparks of an ancient, arcane power field when alive. Horus had considered the Talon a symbol of his office as much as a tool of war. Abaddon considered it simply a weapon to be wielded, but he was not blind to the symbolism of wearing a trophy of that particular patricide.

'Report,' he said. 'Tell me everything. And get up, fool. You are no knight, and I am no king. We are brothers here.'

I rose as he lifted the Talon away, biting back my surprise. I could sense the anger burning off him the way a sun bleeds heat, but he seemed too weary to care.

I looked at him closely for the first time since arriving. A subtle strain tautened his features. He looked more than unhealthy – he looked plagued. His deterioration during my absence was undeniable. I had to say something.

'Ezekyle–' I began, only for him to wave my concern away. 'Report first.'

I did as he commanded. I told him of my mission and of the preparations I had taken. I told him of the final night of battle and of the Death Guard defectors that Ilyaster – our wounded ally in Daravek's ranks – had brought with him. I told him of the assets won and the number of foes destroyed. I told him of the desecrated bodies impaled upon the battlements that I had left in my wake: a lesson to warbands of the Nine Legions that our offers of alliance were to be taken as seriously as our threats of vengeance. And, last of all, I told him of the failed trap through which Thagus Daravek had fled.

At the conclusion, Abaddon said nothing. He looked down at his Talon, the great claw closing and opening once more. Outside the observation deck's blast windows, I could see the murky forms of several craft, a few of our own gravely depleted fleet at anchor within the malleable void of Eyespace. I couldn't make out any details at this distance but I knew that – like the *Vengeful Spirit* and like our own ceramite – their hulls were black, darkened through psychic fire, atmospheric descent and the charring of battle damage. Black not simply to replace the colours that we had once worn, but to eclipse them. Black to acknowledge our shame. Black to symbolise freedom from the past, to declare our loyalty to none but ourselves.

'I cannot do it,' I finally said, breaking the uneasy silence.

He chuckled as if I spoke in jest. 'Is that so?'

'I cannot kill him, Ezekyle. I have tried with every iota of my strength. I cannot do it.'

Abaddon levelled his gaze to mine. 'He is stronger than you?'

'No.' There was no need to lie. 'No, he is not. I would feel that, and I would admit it, were it true.' I trailed off, unable to explain it to either of our satisfaction.

'You have returned to me in failure from a mission that you assured me, most zealously, was destined to succeed. I suggest you do better than stuttering half-answers through clenched teeth, Khayon.'

'I cannot kill him,' I said again. 'When I try, he brushes me aside. It is like fighting the tide with nothing but shouted words. No matter how I hide myself, he senses my presence. No matter how I strike at him – subtle, slow, swift, vicious – he banishes my efforts.'

'So he *is* stronger than you.' Abaddon shook his head. 'You Tizcans. When will you learn that there is no shame in admitting that others may know more than you, or possess greater strength?'

I dared to step forwards, feeling my temper flare. 'It is *not* a matter of strength. If it were, then he and I would fight, Ezekyle. We would be locked in a contest, one seeking to overpower the other. This is more than that. He laughs at my efforts. He throws me aside the way you would cast off a cloak. I have no answers, brother. I have never felt anything like it before.'

I watched as he turned and walked away from me with a slow orchestra of grinding servo-joints. Once, this chamber had been an observatory. A place with no purpose in war, if such a thing can be countenanced on a Legiones Astartes flagship. A hololithic table stood in the centre of the room, damaged from previous battles but still functional. Abaddon used his free hand to trigger a prepared sequence of images. He called up hololiths of each of the vessels sworn to our cause; not merely the subfleet around the *Vengeful Spirit*, but the entirety of that to which Abaddon could lay claim.

I stared at the visual litany spread before me in a vista of flickering light. This was more than a fleet. This was a Legion's armada. We had come so far, yet we had so far still to travel. I suspect that looking at such signs of progress gave Abaddon comfort. I was content to see him distracted by anything that turned his anger from me, even this anaemic, hollow irritation that was far from the disappointed rage I had expected.

'You must try again. No other warlord has as much of our blood on his hands as that Barbaran dog. Daravek must die.'

'As you command, lord.'

He laughed at my neutral reaction, and I was gratified to see even a flicker of his former charisma resurfacing. Yet he either sensed my thoughts or had grown adept at guessing them, for the smile swiftly passed.

'You are watching me as if I may shatter into pieces. Enough of your useless worrying, Khayon.'

Finally, he spoke of it. I would not let this chance pass. 'You look weary past all endurance. Why do you not let me help you?'

'Help me?' The mirth in his eyes soured further. 'I send you where you are needed, to do what must be done. You are my blade, brother, not my nursemaid.'

'All of the Ezekarion can see that something is wrong within you, but I am the one that sees how deeply it has taken root. You are plagued by something, something I can almost see and hear myself, even as it hides in the warp's winds. It grows stronger, its burden upon you heavier.'

He realised then that I was not going to let this lie, as I had on all previous occasions. Perhaps I would have been content to trust him and refrain from pressing the matter had he not appeared so eroded and gaunt upon my most recent return.

'This presence,' he said slowly, and suddenly he looked hungry. Starved, even. 'This voice that you sense – have you pursued it to its source?'

'I have tried,' I admitted. 'A thousand times and more. There is nothing there. No source.'

'Khayon.' His voice was a growl, a low breath, a purred threat. It was a sound more suited to the jaws of a beast than to the mouth of a man. 'You are overstepping your authority.'

Ezekyle Abaddon is the consummate soldier, and he embodies everything that a warleader must be to thrive within the Empire of the Eye, but he is not without his flaws. One must always be careful when dealing with him. The wrath that makes him a warrior without peer boils beneath the surface of his skin at all times, ever ready to erupt. And his patience with me was scarce enough that night already.

'I overstep nothing,' I replied. 'Speaking the truth to you is my duty, Ezekyle. Just as the Mournival once counselled Horus Lupercal.'

He sneered at the mention of his primarch father's informal and grotesquely insufficient guiding council. 'The Mournival failed. I know that better than anyone, for I was part of it.'

'It did,' I agreed. 'And you were. But I do not intend to let the same mistakes occur a second time. You were ignorant then, Ezekyle, and your place was to give counsel to a deluded fool. We are all far more than we were in that age of moronic optimism. What haunts you, brother? What is it that eats away at your psyche and soul?'

I thought I had him. He had warned me against pursuing the matter, but I trusted that the wisdom and sincerity of my words would finally penetrate the armour of his secrecy.

'You aren't an insolent soul, Khayon. It isn't in your nature. Insubordination is something you must be driven to, not something in your blood. Why, then, do you persist with this?'

'I know what I sense.'

I saw another flicker of temper at the edges of his eyes. 'Your nebulous concerns are born of the very fact you have no idea what you are sensing. If you knew, you wouldn't keep asking.'

'Then tell me, Ezekyle. Tell me what lies in the warp's cry. The Eye itself is shrieking your name. Unborn daemons drift around you in a halo of torment. What is out there? What calls to you?'

I knew, the moment his eyes met mine, that I had overstepped. His mouth hardened into a thin line. He idly stroked two of the Talon's blades together with a whetstone rasp.

Nagual growled, sensing my unease across the symbiotic bond. *You have angered him,* the beast sent to me, forever simplistic in his emotions. *His soul boils.*

Abaddon's cold gaze drifted to the daemon. Because of the growl? Because he could sense what the creature was saying? An interesting possibility – unwelcome, but interesting.

Silence, Nagual.

'That is your father speaking, sorcerer,' said Abaddon. 'You speak with the vanity that Magnus the Red bred into your bones – that sense of knowing more than anyone else, of knowing best. The arrogance of believing that you alone know what to do with wisdom. You see something you don't understand and it blisters your mind because, in your arrogance, you are so certain that you alone can deal with it.'

'It is *not* that,' I vowed. 'I wish only for you to trust me, to trust all of us among the Ezekarion. We are your counsel and your bloodwards. We are the voices sworn to always speak the truth before you.'

He rounded upon me, looking down with cold anger barely held back. 'You are the only one that accuses me like this, Khayon. You are the only one that whispers your doubts and pours them into my ears. You are the only one that scratches at the walls of my mind and demands entrance, desperate to witness my every thought. The others trust me, but you alone do not. Not the proud and wise Iskandar Khayon. Why is that?'

He didn't let me answer. He silenced me with a gesture and continued, 'You stare at me with suspicion. And I will tell you why, sorcerer. It's because you are afraid. Afraid that I will fail you as our fathers failed us. Afraid that after rediscovering brotherhood I will be deceived into abandoning it once more. Afraid that the madness that claimed Horus will seep into my skull and leave me the same preening, deluded husk he was towards the end of his rebellion.'

I said nothing. There was nothing to say. To deny even one of his words would be to insult both of us. He had spoken my thoughts as if he had read them from a parchment page.

'If you wish to speak to me, Khayon, speak from wisdom, temperance and trust. Speak from ignorance if you must. That, at least, is palatable. But do not speak from fear.' He shook his head in something approaching disgust. That simple gesture shamed me far more than his accusations. 'Sometimes, brother, I swear that you have forgotten how to hate. All that remains is suspicion and fear. I will have no cowards at my side.'

I took a step closer, feeling my teeth clench, feeling my hands closing into fists.

I am no coward. I knifed the words into his mind, not by intention but by sheer force of belief. He tensed at their impact, and after a moment he smiled.

'Perhaps you aren't.' The ragged harshness left his voice. 'You truly believe I need your aid, brother? That I am so fragile I will fall victim to the same delusions that ruined our fathers?'

I dared a smile, though there was precious little joy in it. 'It is more that I have a healthy loathing of the creatures that call themselves gods. The warp is alive around you, Ezekyle. I sense that, without a doubt.'

He fell silent after that. I can recall it with crystalline clarity even all these millennia later, the way he weighed the decision before speaking. To trust me or to chastise me? To believe that I was sincere in my concerns, or to believe that I was foolish and fearful?

'Very well, Khayon. I will give you the answers you seek. We will speak of this when you return from Maeleum.'

I stared at him, seeking to keep pace with this sudden shift in his thoughts. Maeleum? What madness was this?

'Why send me there?'

'Why do I send you anywhere?' he countered.

'But there is no one to kill on Maeleum. There is nothing there at all.'

'You think so?' His tone was neutral enough that I couldn't tell if he was baiting me or honestly asking.

I was surely correct, after the casualties sustained in the rebellion against the Emperor, and the losses suffered in the massacres that took place within the Legion Wars. The Sons of Horus had bled and bled and bled, most often at the hands of their former allies who punished them for their desertion at Terra. And as for the survivors, most of our warriors and officers alike were drawn from the Sons of Horus, who had followed Abaddon and Falkus back to their crusading home aboard the *Vengeful Spirit*. How many could truly remain on their adopted, desecrated home world? Maeleum was lifeless now, the tomb of a dead Legion.

But Abaddon has ever known more than he reveals. Even then he had eyes and ears everywhere across the Eye, sequestered in places and delivering messages unknown to even the Ezekarion.

'I am taking the *Vengeful Spirit* to lift the siege at the Anvidius Conjunction,' he said, painfully calm, painfully reasonable. 'And thus, I need you to go to Maeleum in my stead.'

Not a mission of murder, then. Something worse, something to which I was far less suited.

For a number of reasons, I was rarely our Legion's chosen emissary. That dubious honour was most often reserved for

Telemachon, and in those early days he was both warlord and herald. It was an honour that I was glad to concede to him, for the role of diplomat was one I despised, though I did once ask Ezekyle why he so rarely selected me.

'There is more to forging alliances than intimidation and threat. You're too cold. Too detached, too guided by reason. Too...' and here he paused. 'Too Tizcan.'

'Those are surely virtues, not flaws.'

Abaddon looked at me as if I had proven his point.

And so others were far more commonly chosen. Ezekyle would send them ahead of our main fleet, bringing terms to rival warband leaders, requesting their alliance or their surrender. As one might imagine, these consular missions met with varying receptions.

In the very beginning, Telemachon's arrival was often a source of amusement. Abaddon was believed dead and the *Vengeful Spirit* had sailed away into that tremulous space between history and mythology; thus Telemachon was seen as a mad soul, a warrior trapped in the past, bringing words of impossible doom to uncaring warlords. Those that remained unconvinced were soon illuminated by the presence of what they had previously believed impossible: the *Vengeful Spirit* tearing through their fleets or razing their cities with blissful ease.

Most recently, with so many warbands gathering beneath Daravek's merciless gaze in opposition to our rise, the receptions our emissaries received were ever more hostile.

My previous ambassadorial effort had ended in abject failure. Ezekyle had ordered me to make overtures to the warband of Korosan Myrlath, one of the few remaining Sons of Horus, Abaddon's own former Legion.

'I will see your will done,' I promised.

'No, Khayon.' Abaddon was quite serious. 'I don't want him dead. You are to go as an emissary.'

I remember saying nothing for several seconds. I needed time to process this. 'Is this an example of dry Cthonian wit?' I asked.

'No, brother. Not this time.'

And so, emboldened by my lord's trust, I swallowed my reluctance and made the journey.

It went poorly. They captured me despite my peaceable intentions and hauled me before their overlord's throne. There I was paraded and mocked before Korosan's court.

I felt the kiss of a blade against the back of my neck. Its thrumming power field spat sparks of searing energy against my cold armour plating.

'We meet at last, assassin,' Korosan Myrlath greeted me.

I looked up as far as my executioners allowed. They kept me held low, forcing me to remain on my knees before their lord's throne. I managed to lift my gaze to Korosan's amused stare. Time had changed him as it had changed all of us, and he too wore his sins on his skin. He had fused to his armour, becoming a thing of biomechanical arrogance, his ceramite weeping stinking, bubbling blood from between its plates.

'Today I am merely an emissary,' I replied.

This delighted him, despite being the truth. 'Of course you are, Khayon. Of course you are. Do you have anything of worth to say before we see your sentence carried out?' He did not rise from the throne of rusting, twisted iron. I was not certain he could rise from it. He seemed bound to the throne where his armour had bonded to the corroded metal.

'I was not aware that I was on trial.'

'No? But Thagus Daravek will pay richly in plunder for your head.'

'So you have already bent the knee to the tyrant,' I replied, forcing into my voice a mirth I did not feel.

This earned a chorus of fresh laughter from the gathered warriors. Sensing their masters' amusement, the beastmen and mutants around the throne room erupted into an orchestra of bestial noise. I waited until the howls and roars faded. I could do nothing else.

'Abaddon's pet assassin,' Korosan grinned as he spoke the words, 'accusing others of tyranny. What grotesque irony is this? Speak your master's message, slave, and then we shall be done with this farce.'

'Abaddon's message remains unchanged,' I replied. 'Daravek seeks servants. Abaddon seeks brothers in arms. Forswear your oaths to the tyrant. Sail with us and take revenge upon the Imperium. Join us, or die.'

Korosan smiled, showing two layers of teeth. His armour, once cast in the green of the Sons of Horus, was lost to a stain of verdigris and crusted over with colonies of barnacles. A sword was driven point-deep into the deck before the throne. Its hilt was of human ivory, its blade some kind of sharpened, shifting stone. He kept one hand on the weapon's pommel at all times. I could hear the faint scraping sound as he ran his armoured thumb up and down the grip.

'You're quite serious,' the warlord said, 'aren't you?'

I resisted the urge to fight against the two warriors holding me on my knees. 'Wholly serious. My lord has no wish to destroy you.'

More laughter. I ignored it. This time, so did Korosan. 'No wish to destroy me? No, perhaps not. He wishes only for me to bow to him, as Horus' heir.'

That was the moment I realised I was dealing with a fool.

I felt suddenly blessed that I would not be calling this blind, proud creature 'brother'. He was unworthy of fighting at our side.

'I am no slave. Every warrior in history has fought under a warchief's orders. Every soldier born has followed an officer's commands. Even generals obey kings. I will not listen to your childish mind fumble and misunderstand the benefits of unity and brotherhood. This is your last chance. My lord would have you as an ally.'

'He would have me spurn my oaths to the true Lord of the Eye,' Korosan said with a sneer. 'And I will shed no tears of regret over disappointing your weakling master with his stolen Talon. We will return your dismembered corpse to your precious lord. That shall serve as my answer to his generous offer.'

He gestured to one of the warriors behind me, the one holding his blade against the back of my neck. 'Ectaras. Do it.'

I said nothing as the blade rose. The crowd roared their acclaim.

I heard the whining protest of the descending blade. I saw the filthy, gore-mattered deck beneath me. There was no poetic thunderclap of the sword's impact, no revelatory flash of my life awakened from memory to play out as theatre before my eyes.

The sword fell.

I died.

After I died, I opened my eyes. The command deck of the *Vengeful Spirit* was just as I had left it, with my brothers and sisters of the Ezekarion and our gathered slaves, awaiting my return. I mourned the loss of the Rubricae whose armoured husk I had stolen and possessed for my journey.

Poor Zaelor now lay headless in the midst of Korosan's court. Surely they would defile his remains once they realised the empty shell wasn't my corpse.

'Well?' Telemachon asked me. I ignored him, turning to Abaddon.

'Negotiations,' I admitted, 'went poorly.'

Abaddon seemed unsurprised. I suspected then, as I have suspected ever since, that he did not wish Korosan to stand with us at all, but appearances of fairness had to be maintained. He had sent me knowing Korosan would refuse me.

His response was typically focused. 'Kill them.'

And so we did. We committed our burgeoning fleet to the skies above Korosan's world, to rain fire upon nineteen thousand warriors, thralls, slaves and minions. Korosan himself was taken alive at the battle's end. Abaddon gave him to the Aphotic Blade, who impaled and crucified him upon their battle standard. Servitors intravenously fed him the bodily waste of our Legion's slaves to keep him alive. He survived for five miserable months.

Such is the price of defiance.

In the observation spire on the night of my return from Daravek's nameless world, Ezekyle's assured gaze finally made me abandon all attempts to argue. As far as he was concerned it was already settled: I was bound for Maeleum.

'Your return is timely,' he added. 'The *Viridian Sky* is refuelling and rearming to prepare for passage to Maeleum. Transfer aboard once you leave here.'

The *Viridian Sky* was Amurael's ship, and one of the fastest in our fleet. Amurael Enka had been a Son of Horus, even down to sharing many genetic facial markers with the fallen primarch, much like Abaddon. That had once been seen as an omen of great fortune in the XVI Legion. Less so, now.

Amurael was also the newest of the Ezekarion. My voice had been one of the firmest in favour of his inclusion.

'Amurael is a far finer ambassador than I, especially if you wish someone to carry word to any Sons of Horus remaining on that pathetic crypt of a world.'

'You always assume the worst,' he chided me. 'This is no mere emissary expedition. Far-point telemetry probes have warned of a vessel making planetfall on Maelum.'

I breathed in through my teeth. Telemetry within the Eye was disgustingly unreliable. Some of our probes – deployed in abundance across our expanding territories – functioned via cores of surgically implanted astropathic minds, others operated through pulses of echolocation in a planet's atmosphere. In truth, telemetry was of hardly any use in the true void either, but it was prone to giving readings of raw madness in this realm where the warp and reality blended together.

'Telemetry,' I ventured carefully, 'tells a great many tales.' It was not the first time I had said this. It was not even close to the first time.

Abaddon's smile was slow and severe, the jaws of a trap squeezing closed. 'In this instance it tells a tale that aligns with Ashur-Kai's vision dreams, and I refuse to ignore providence on that scale.'

I did not share the value Abaddon placed on prophecy either. Not then. Not now. I didn't ask what my former mentor had seen in his visions. It didn't matter; whatever it had been would have been couched in metaphor and exaggerated significance, no doubt.

'I will go,' I said, surrendering to the inevitable.

Abaddon watched me with a nameless expression that betrayed none of his thoughts. 'We will speak of your concerns over my soul when you return. You have my word, brother.'

It was enough for now. I nodded my compliance.

'And try not to die on Maeleum, Khayon. I need you alive.'

The Cthonian sense of humour is born from lives spent in near-feral gangs inhabiting the lawless tunnel-communes of profitless, used-up mine networks. It is best summed up by a theme of blunt, dry grimness. It is not quite sarcasm; rather it is closer to a deliberate tempting of fate.

I have never found it particularly amusing.

Something flashed behind his stare. I felt it in the same moment – some pull on the threads of the void outside the ship, a caress of a new presence within the nebula – the same way mortals would sense the opening of a door in their chambers.

We both turned to the vast window, looking out at the gas-wreathed stars. Abaddon's teeth showed as a row of ivory knives. In the same moment, a female voice sounded from the mouths of the black iron gargoyles fashioned into crenellations along the chamber's walls.

'Ezekyle,' said the *Vengeful Spirit* to her master. 'Eight ships have translated in-system. The *Exaltation* is hailing me.'

'Tell Telemachon that he is just in time.' Abaddon looked at me as he spoke. 'And inform him that he is going on a journey with Amurael and Iskandar.'

I resisted the urge to sigh. As I said, I have never found Cthonian humour particularly amusing.

III

A LEGION'S GRAVEYARD

Maeleum.

The flames of atmospheric entry cleared away from the cockpit windows to reveal a realm of corroded metal as far as the eye could see. Dead ships hung in the sky, belly-ripped and hull-torn, lingering like swollen clouds ready to shed rusted-iron rain. No engines kept them afloat, nor did any auspex sweeps sing back with any signs of life. They drifted in the unhealthy sky, immune to gravity, pulled from orbit yet unwanted by the ground below.

I confess, the sight stole my breath. This had been the vanguard of the fleet that had laid siege to Terra. Now our gunship veered around these monuments to lost wars, these carcass embodiments of how far the mighty had fallen.

The planet was deep within the territory claimed by our confederation of warbands, though we had little cause to defend it and even less cause to return there. In keeping with Abaddon's wish that we look to the future rather than mourn the past, he treated Maeleum with both contempt and indifference, depending on his mood.

The landscape was a stain of industrial cancer. I had been expecting a ruined city. What I saw was a wasteland: a continent of rusting wreckage spread below us across the bombardment-wrecked geoscape, with grounded warships that had once served as hives and habitation spires.

So many daemon worlds within the Eye seethe physically, even tectonically, with their masters' whims and under the pressures of the wars that rage across their surface. But Maeleum, blighted haven of the Sons of Horus, was a place of memoriam and decay. All weapons, all places, all living beings have a reflection in the warp, no matter how fragile or faint. Maeleum emanated an aura of funereal rot.

This was where a Legion had come to die.

'God of War.' In my shock, I breathed Lheorvine's favourite curse.

Telemachon stood by my side. The turbines upon his back had long since fused to the rest of his armour, and the silver faceplate that hid his ravaged features was now bound to the skin and skull beneath. His metallic face showed neither emotion nor expression, resembling the pristine and perfect features of a young king's burial mask. A fair reflection of what his face had once been.

Years before, Abaddon had given the first of his loyal brothers a gift – shards of silver from the broken blade that had once belonged to Sanguinius, the fallen primarch of the Blood Angels Legion. The shards were beyond price; flooded with agonisingly potent psychic resonance, fuelled by the wounds the blade had inflicted over the many decades and thrumming with the death-scream echo of the primarch who had been holding it when he was cut down and slaughtered.

I used my shards in the forging of Sacramentum, the sword born to replace my lost Fenrisian axe, Saern. Lheor had arranged for his shards to be fashioned into the razored teeth of a new chainaxe, a weapon he had then lost within a span of mere months. For all I know it may still lie submerged in the choking swamps of the moon Narix, where we locked blades yet again with the Word Bearers.

And with his shards, Telemachon had fashioned a new face. The faceplate of his helmet was blue-veined silver with eye-lenses of opal, lit crimson from within. When I looked at him, I saw the wasteland of Maeleum reflecting filthy and orange across his argent features.

'The years have not been kind to this world,' he said in his honeyed voice, unflawed by processing through his helm's vocaliser. 'Nor have the guns of the Legions.'

I wondered: had he been here those years ago when the Emperor's Children raided Maeleum for plunder, to pluck the corpse of the First and False Warmaster from where it lay in state? Sometimes Telemachon had alluded to his presence in that battle. Other times he denied it.

As we made our approach, I could tell he was at least partially moved by the sight, his aura muted, his gaze sweeping silently over the revealed vista.

I did not despise him then, at least not to the depths that would follow. This was before the years where the two of us sought in futility to end the other's life, before we divided the Black Legion with our bitterness, bringing our brothers to civil war. Soon the decline would begin. Soon the mistrust between us would start to fester. But that day, as we made planetfall, the old grudges from his treachery at the Siege of Terra and my subsequent manipulation of his mind were fading wounds, allowing us the luxury of indifference to one another.

Strangely, of the three of us, it was Amurael who was the least affected by the sight of Maeleum's landscape. To him this was a homecoming, a return to the world he had fought for and defended against the other Legions while he still wore the green of the Sons of Horus. Yet as the gunship descended over his adopted home world, he merely showed his jagged teeth in a smile. Our surprise amused him.

'Maeleum was never a place of beauty,' he said. 'Little changed with its abandonment.'

The gunship streaked over the rust wastes, bearing down on the coordinates given up by our telemetry beacons. Amurael was at the controls, seeking one particular downed ship among the fallen horde.

'There,' Amurael said, sighting it first.

A strike cruiser. A Legiones Astartes strike cruiser, no less.

The ship lay within the grave it had dug for itself, half-buried and forlorn yet not entirely stripped of its majesty. The warship's final moments were illustrated in the rotten earth of the wasteland, where it had left a chasm carved by its ploughing crash. It had impacted like a gouging spear, not a falling needle, and had ripped open a wound in Maeleum's junkyard flesh as testament.

It wasn't one of ours. I knew that much the moment I saw its corpse.

What little remained of the vessel's superstructure was naked of allegiance. Its wrecked hull showed no sign of markings – at least none that had survived the crash, the fiery atmospheric entry or the abrading winds of the Eye's warp-stung void. Thus it belonged to no warband I could name.

That was perhaps less noteworthy than it seems to

Imperial minds. The warbands of the Legions, and those that declared independence from the Legions that had sired them, were forever bedecking themselves in new icons and sigils, marking new leadership, new ways of waging war, new victories. The life-reviling Purge were drawn from extremists among the Death Guard. The Steel Brethren were wayward brothers of the Iron Warriors. The Sanctified were blood-maddened sons of Lorgar. And on and on it went.

Yet this ship was more than unmarked, it was practically unchanged. The Eye hadn't managed to twist its hull to reflect the sins of the warriors within.

The three of us shared a glance. No one had any answers.

'Come in low,' Telemachon advised, 'and land in the shadow of that cruiser. If there are survivors, I'd rather take them by surprise.'

'That will make for a long walk to the crash site,' Amurael remarked.

'I have no other pressing engagements,' said Telemachon.

As we made a landing approach, it was a matter of finding somewhere stable amidst the dead-hulk rust yards. Retros fired, slowing our descent; we looked out of the cockpit windows upon a wasteland that showed no sign of society. Instead it echoed with the cries and gunfire of battles lost long ago. Our vox-network was worthless, crackling with the babble of ghosts and Neverborn, no words of which we could be sure were sentient at all, let alone directed at us.

The gunship's landing claws crunched into the rotten earth. We made ready to disembark. Amurael checked his bolter, slamming the magazine back into place. I could sense the thoughts unfolding behind his eyes. It reminded me of Abaddon, who held a similar expression whenever he oversaw a battle plan, giving orders that adapted and reacted to the movements of the enemy forces.

I led the way down the assault ramp. The gunship's crew were Rubricae bound to my will, performing the duties of gunners with the voiceless, patient serenity that my automatons devoted to every command I gave them.

Defend. I sent the order into the hollow helms that served as their minds. The animated suits of ceramite armour readied bolters and blades, ready to stand eternal vigil if it came to such a fate. They made for perfect guardians, providing no sorcerer was strong enough to wrest them from my will. I doubted there were any warbands left on this world to threaten them.

I took only four of them with me, beckoning them with a wordless telepathic pulse. Amurael's warriors walked with them, a small squad of his chosen men. They kept their distance from me. I had always kept company more with my own ashen dead than the living warriors, but it was strange to me, how the rank and file of the Black Legion perceived me. I was evermore removed from them in my duties as Abaddon's blade.

'Lord Khayon,' they greeted me with various murmurs. I returned the greetings with a curt nod.

Nefertari also deigned to accompany us, emerging from the gunship's interior. She wore her crimson suit of overlapping battleplate, spined and spiked and cast from the alien resin-bonded materials her species favoured. I had done precious little research into the origins of her armour – nor was she eager to enlighten me whenever I asked – so the two of us were left caring only for its effectiveness. It was constructed with pockets of buoyant gases within its resinous layers to make it preternaturally lightweight, a design philosophy born of her kind's inhuman inventiveness.

She touched a silver medallion piece in the hollow of her throat, activating the jewelled micro-force field generators embedded in the scarlet suit's overlayer. Kinetic barriers of Imperial make will groan with machine thrums or insectile buzzing. In contrast, Nefertari's armour produced a whispery sibilance, near silent.

'I told you not to bring that thing,' Amurael said to me.

'She is useful,' I replied.

'It will attract the Neverborn.'

'She can handle the Neverborn.' I turned to Nefertari. 'Scout ahead. Return with word of what you find.'

She favoured Amurael with a cruel, disgusted smile, and spread her wings to stretch them. A moment later she pulled them in close to her back, broke into a run and kicked off from the ground on the third step. She leapt skywards. Her wings cracked open. As simply as that, she was gone.

Telemachon watched her ascent, his eye-lenses tracking the beat of her wings. Amurael scarcely glanced her way.

'Allying with that creature is the most disgusting perversion,' he said. 'It amazes me that you tolerate it.'

This was not an uncommon refrain among my brothers. It didn't matter that I was hardly the first among the Nine Legions' warband leaders to ally with aliens inside the Eye, or even to possess one as my champion. Mutants, chem-born, daemons... A warband drew its champions from wherever it discovered efficient and willing murderers. But it was Nefertari's breed that revolted my brethren. She was the daughter of a species that had, in its arrogance and ignorance, given birth to the Eye. Lingering remnants of the eldar race were considered favoured prey for many Legion warbands.

'She is useful,' I repeated. 'And she has won every duel she ever fought for me.'

'She would last all of three seconds on a battlefield,' he pointed out.

'That could be said of many warband champions. And I would never commit her to a battlefield. She is a killer, not a warrior.'

Telemachon finally turned away from her receding shape in the sky. 'Let's go.'

We walked, following the tiny silhouette of my sky-borne bloodward.

Seeing the ship closer brought no answers, only more questions. We watched its corpse from the lip of the canyon it had gouged.

It still looked Imperial. Its time in the Eye had evidently been impossibly brief. While the crenellated, cathedral-like wreckage little resembled the glass spires of my home – Tizca, the now-dead City of Light on long-lost Prospero – I still found that the Imperium's stark Gothic architecture held its own bleak majesty.

Nefertari did not. When she returned to us after her scouting flight, my bloodward offered her perspective on the merits of the Gothic aesthetic.

'Even your voidcraft are repulsive.' She spoke her own tongue in a sibilant murmur. 'Can your species shape nothing of beauty?'

I let that pass. She was always difficult when she hungered, and I'd not let her feed in some time.

'What did you see?'

Her wings rippled, sinews crackling, then folded close to her back. 'We have been beaten here. Your kind are already present in the ravine.'

'My kind?'

'*Elayath ahir vey,*' she said in her mellifluous tongue. I knew the expression; its literal meaning was 'deformed barbarians'.

'Legionaries,' I clarified for Amurael's benefit.

Nefertari spat venom-darkened saliva onto the ivory ground. Her pierced lips mangled into a sneer. I found her revoltingly inhuman at the best of times, but when her gaunt features twisted into those subtly alien expressions, echoes of the ancient xenos-hate stirred in my heart.

'Your former Legion-kin, no less,' she said.

The Thousand Sons. Here.

Prey. By my side, the beast that wasn't a beast gave a low, throaty growl. Nagual's sending was a wordless thought, a concept rather than language. The lynx turned that pale gaze down to the distant wreckage and licked his sabre-fangs. He moved like a gliding lie, the way a shadow ghosts across a surface, not like a natural-born beast at all. *Prey,* he sent again.

Perhaps. Be calm, Nagual.

'How many warriors did you see?'

'I saw only a single gunship. Small. Smaller than ours.'

A Thunderhawk, then. 'It seems this wreck is attracting a great deal of interest.'

Nefertari smiled, entirely unlovely, showing too many teeth. As we drew away from the others, she spoke in low tones. 'You are gilding your exile in grandeur it does not deserve. Your precious Ezekyle is no longer even subtle in his commands, is he? "Go here, Iskandar. Go there. Go wherever I wish, kill whomever I demand, so long as you remain out of my sight and cease staring into my soul."'

'You know nothing,' I said. Abaddon had promised me answers upon my return. I would hold him to that.

'I know I care little for what pathetic mysteries lie within this fat and ruptured carcass of cold metal,' she replied. Her voice was as dry as the warship's desert grave.

I was in no mood for her mockery, nor would I let her irritation stain my fascination.

'Khayon.' Amurael called to me, summoning me back. I moved to where he stood with his warriors, watching the wreck through magnoculars. His colourless armour was dusted grey by the desert's gritty breath. Flecks of the black beneath showed in patches where the dust had not yet taken hold.

His warriors moved away from me, believing they were being subtle about it. My four Rubricae remained motionless.

'Movement?' I asked Amurael.

'Movement,' he confirmed. His skin was almost as dark as Lheor's, with bony protrusions at his cheekbones and brow ridges. Whatever handsomeness he'd possessed as a human was destroyed not only by his ascension to the Legiones Astartes, but by the osseous alterations to his skull since coming to the Great Eye. The small spines pushing through his face cast him in the image of something mythical and daemonic. I wondered what sins were in his heart to shape him so.

Amurael locked his helmet back into place with a snake hiss of air pressure. His faceplate was a snarling visage of bone and ceramite, bestially crowned by dark biomechanical horns curling back from his temples. We have an expression for such warp-wrought changes on our flesh and armour: 'The Gods know his name'. We use it for those that have attracted the Pantheon's attention and favour. It is not always a compliment.

'Well,' he said, 'let's go introduce ourselves.'

Few worlds within the Eye are as serene as Maeleum, since so few are as dead as Maeleum. In a realm where ceaseless tides of psychic energy manifest as avatars of warring gods alongside their embattled mortal followers, Maeleum was a place of haunted peace. It was a world destroyed, its fortresses broken open and empty, its people slaughtered or simply gone. The philosopher in me found it an effective if crude symbol for the Sons of Horus themselves, who had danced on the knife blade of extinction for so very long.

I have heard tales that insist Abaddon returned here after slaying Horus Reborn, and there he competed against rival captains in pit fights and honour duels, eventually emerging victorious and leading the fallen officers' men away with him, proud to march under his orders.

Perhaps there is the taste of truth in that, though I never saw such a thing. I may have been elsewhere, in the exile of my work as Ezekyle's unseen blade. I have learned not to rule out any story, no matter how unlikely it sounds.

But what I witnessed was altogether more proud, more defiant, but somehow more sorrowful.

I have spoken of the warbands that we crushed in battle, and of those that surrendered when they witnessed the *Vengeful Spirit*'s guns ripping through their fleets. I have told of those warbands whose fortresses we defended ourselves, coming to their aid in the knowledge that we were gaining appreciative allies or new, grateful recruits.

The Black Legion's rise is filled with more of those tales than even I can relate. Tales of those willingly bending the knee, and opposite stories of those submitting with supreme reluctance before coming to realise that there was strength in this new unity.

These tales are exactly what one might expect in such an ascension. This chronicle will gain nothing for relating them in yet more detail.

But there were others. Other exiles from this very planet, weary of eking out an existence in the rust and ash that remained. They were the warriors that had held on to the bitter end, unto the very edge of extinction, calling themselves Sons of Horus no matter that their foes murdered them for it.

We encountered them aboard vessels lost or crippled in the Eye, all personnel dead or in Legiones Astartes hibernation through activation of their sus-an membranes. We met them on beleaguered, war-riven warships limping towards us, seeking sanctuary in the *Vengeful Spirit*'s great shadow. The exiles, the wanderers, the unlucky – all of whom drifted away from Maeleum, little by little, in a slow, desperate diaspora. The last inhabitants of a dying world, they finally sought something more than survival. That brought them in search of Abaddon.

It is no exaggeration to say that these Sons of Horus were among our most fervently loyal recruits. When I say that we are the Legion of the Long War, I speak of our rebirth and of our lord's belief that blood and gene-line are irrelevant. What matters is the hate in a warrior's heart and the skill with which he wields a blade. But I am also speaking of those last, lost souls. They were the ones who endured the final days of the XVI Legion, and they know, better than any other, what it is to cling too long to the echoes of the past.

Amurael was one of these final exiles. When he had approached us years before aboard his ship, the *Viridian Sky,* a swift dagger of a frigate, he sailed towards us with weapon decks cold and void shields lowered. At the time, seeing this approach from where I stood on the *Vengeful Spirit*'s command deck, I had laughed at the boldness of the manoeuvre. Abaddon had not.

'That's Medicae Quintus Enka's ship,' my brother had said, as surprised as he was pleased. To gain an Apothecary of Amurael's rank would be a savage coup for our warband. It is true to say the Nine Legions, locked in the Eye, have far greater trouble recruiting and sustaining their numbers than we ever had while reinforced by the flesh harvests of the Great Crusade.

Amurael had come aboard with over four hundred warriors and thrice the number of tech-priests, Legion servants, skilled serfs and Cybernetica war machines. At the head of this ragged host, Amurael had approached Abaddon and the Ezekarion on the landing deck and cast his bolter to the floor by Ezekyle's boots.

I wasn't alone in considering this a sign of submission. We all believed it a symbolic gesture of surrender – Abaddon was already welcoming his former Legion brother into the fleet – until Amurael drew the power sword sheathed at his hip and thumbed the activation rune. Ezekyle, less plagued by his unspoken burden then, had bared his rune-scratched teeth in a grin.

'An interesting way to greet an old commander,' Abaddon said.

Amurael carved the air, loosening his wrist. He looked battered, wounded and weak. No doubt he'd had to fight his way from Maeleum to reach us, bleeding every step of the way. Yet still he stood defiant.

'If you can best me with a blade, Captain Abaddon, you will have my loyalty and the loyalty of my followers.'

One could not help but admire his tenacity.

After the duel, as the *Viridian Sky* was being hauled in by tugs and overseen for repair, Abaddon summoned Amurael to a gathering of the Ezekarion, those souls trusted most by our lord, whose voices he promises to always hear, and who are permitted to call him by his informal first name. Amurael was sworn in as our tenth member, though our warband already numbered in the tens of thousands.

'I sailed from Maeleum,' he confessed at that conclave, held in Lupercal's Court beneath the faded and dusty banners of the Great Crusade. This was the chamber in which the First and False Warmaster had conducted his councils. Abaddon had sealed it off from the rest of the ship, allowing its use only for the Ezekarion. I believe he enjoyed the gesture's ironic symmetry.

'What remains on Maeleum?' asked Falkus, who had abandoned the world himself years before in his quest to find Lheor and me, bringing us to Abaddon's side.

'Almost nothing,' Amurael had replied. 'Only our shame.'

We walked the war-salted earth of that junkyard world, ankle-deep in scrap metal, every step a grinding clatter. Nagual stalked at my side, bleeding into shadows and emerging elsewhere, choosing his own path through the rubble. Even with the daemon's feline grace, metal shifted and strained beneath his weight.

When you stand upon a world within the Eye, everything feels alive. The air itself is blended with the warp's etheric elements, rendering psychic senses lamentably unreliable. I felt the presence of living beings nearby only in the vaguest, most sourceless way, as useless as hearing voices in the mist without sensing anything of direction.

Amurael led the way, the searchlight on his backpack cutting across the ruinscape, illuminating the detritus. He soon gave up scanning our surroundings with his auspex, wholly unsurprised at the flawed readings he was getting. He remained entirely unfazed, walking confidently around and through the corpses of slain warships.

Bunkers and silos amidst the wreck-waste offered glimpses of sanctuaries, though even these were damaged, scorched by incendiaries or bleached and mangled by far deadlier, toxic weaponry.

When we reached the enemy gunship, sheltered in the overhanging shadows of the wrecked vessel, I took the lead.

'Do not fire,' I voxed to the others, 'unless fired upon.'

What did the Thousand Sons see as we approached? A small coterie of warriors emerging from the ruined, rusted earth, with no sign of how they had arrived. Each of us wore battle-riven armour with trappings of corroded gold. Our battleplate was black, banishing old colours and old allegiances with the totality of an eclipse. We did not call ourselves the Black Legion. That name came from those we faced across the fields of battle. It was a curse more than a rallying cry in those distant days. 'Black Legion!' they would howl in mockery, with all the disgust of calling us orphans, traitors, scum.

The grounded Thunderhawk trained its guns upon us, cannons whirring as they rotated. I advanced on the first of the Thousand Sons, a warrior in flowing robes and carrying a staff crested with crystals, showing him my open palms.

'I am Iskandar Khayon,' I told the leader of this modest blue host.

His brethren drew closer. Every one of them was a Rubricae, silent in their obedient vigil, boltguns clutched to their breathless chests.

'Iskandar Khayon died at Drol Kheir,' their master replied. How many times had I heard those words now? Even Lheor and Falkus had heard it and believed it, before we went searching for Abaddon.

Wearying. So very wearying.

'I am Iskandar Khayon,' I repeated, as I always repeat after the accusation.

'No, you are the thing that wears his face.'

I removed my helmet then, hoping it would promote trust rather than convince him to abandon his misguided belief. Barefaced in the dusty wind, I looked between the lone living sorcerer and his ashen dead sentinels. He seemed to be alone but for his slave-warriors. Even the footsteps in the worthless earth told of his recent arrival and lacked the turmoil that many warriors would have made with their tread.

My own Rubricae marched to my side. I had brought only four with me, each one a moving statue of scorched black and charred gold, their cobalt paint long burned away and their Kheltaran helmets casting long shadows under the weak light of this world's two pallid suns. Behind them, Telemachon, Amurael and Amurael's squad of warriors kept their bolters low, awaiting the results of my attempted diplomacy. Nefertari said nothing and did nothing, except silently hunger.

'I see Khayon's alien at your side,' the Thousand Sons legionary said, 'but where is Khayon's axe? Where is Gyre, his tutelary?'

'Your doubts are irrelevant,' I said with a smile. 'I am Iskandar Khayon.'

The sorcerer inclined his T-visored helm. 'You may think you are. I will leave you to your delusion. What do you want here, Black Legionnaires? Salvage?'

'No.' I gestured to the ruined hulk. 'Answers.'

'Then we seek the same thing.'

'Perhaps so,' I agreed, 'but this is our domain. And you, my countryman, stand within my Legion's territory.'

'A nameless, mongrel Legion,' the sorcerer said. That accusation, so very common, had long since lost its bite. A few of Amurael's warriors shared grinding chuckles across the vox.

'Indeed,' I agreed once more. 'And if you leave now, we mongrels will let you live.'

The sorcerer said nothing. Perhaps he knew I was lying.

'Are you here alone?' I asked.

'I owe you no truth, traitor.'

'What of your vessel in orbit?' I pressed. 'We saw nothing in the system.'

'As I said, I owe you no truth.'

I felt myself smiling again, this time with markedly less warmth. 'You are coming across as quite hostile, friend.'

'Your name is spoken often among our Legion – Khayon, the Raider of Graves. Am I to believe you will let me leave here with my Rubricae? That you do not intend to steal them like the harvests of ceramite and ash you have already reaped from so many of my brothers?'

'You have a mere fourteen warriors. I am not so starved for power that I'd kill you for these scraps.'

His laugh was a bitter thing. 'How merciful of you.'

'I don't recognise you,' I said, referring to the Eye-born changes of his armour. 'By what name do you go now?'

'I am Aklahyr.' I sensed the ripples of his aura shift,

emanating a grim amusement. 'If you were truly Khayon, then you would know me.'

Now that he had revealed his name, I did know him. Like so many Thousand Sons officers, myself included, he had been a scholar as much as a warrior.

'Aklahyr the Erudite,' I said. 'Banner-bearer for Bejarah's Company. I read your treatise on the significance of iambic pentameter in Kantori summoning verse.'

'Those days are behind me. Behind us all. I serve Thagus Daravek now.' His helm dipped slightly. In shame, that he served the Lord of Hosts? In judgement, that I did not?

'I know the name,' I admitted.

He gave a grunted exhalation through his vocaliser. 'Indeed you do.'

'Why are you here?' I asked, one last time. 'This is our dominion, Aklahyr.'

He was helmed and his expressions were hidden, but I could feel derision radiating from him, flavouring his unseen aura with disgust and doubt. I could feel how this was fated to end. He didn't believe that I intended him no harm. More than that, he hated me. He ached to swing his staff.

'You should guard your emotions better,' I chided him. 'They betray your violent intent.'

Trinkets and talismans rattled against his robed armour plating as he shifted his stance, levelling his staff towards us. His voice was a resigned murmur.

'Let us get this over with.'

'Very well.'

The Prosperine lynx snarled by my side. I gestured for him to hold back. Nefertari likewise stepped forwards, but I shook my head. Warband leaders often allowed champions to duel before a battle – for amusement, for morale, for the chance of attracting the eyes of the Gods – but Aklahyr was alone, and I had no wish for Nefertari to fight in my place.

I drew my sword in place of the axe I had lost years before, that Fenrisian blade long ago broken by the cloned son of a false god. Sacramentum gleamed in the day's sick light.

What followed was brief and, with due respect to the dead, rather uninspired.

Once it was done, I scoured his Rubricae. Bathing them in psychic flame, I burned the blue from their armour plating and withered their tabards and loincloths to charred remnants, repainting all fourteen ceramite husks through sacred incineration. Once stripped of their former colours, the pack of voiceless, mindless warriors fell into dignified lockstep with the four Rubricae already attending me.

I am Khayon, I told them. *I am your lord now.*

All is dust, they chorused back in telepathic whispers as dry as the rust around us.

Nefertari crouched over Aklahyr, running her fingertips across the rents in his armour. She breathed slowly, slanted eyes half-lidded, her inhumanly white flesh darkening with a hue of ruddy health. I knew her revitalisation wouldn't last long, not with the suffering of only a single dying soul. I would need to let her gorge herself soon, else the soul-thirst might leave her weakened and less useful to me.

One by one she sniffed her stained fingertips, taking the scent of Aklahyr's blood. She refused to taste it, fearing corruption, and yet she gouged her fingers back into the torn-open armour, rooting around, firing his dying nerves and amplifying his final spasms.

'Nefertari. Enough.'

She hesitated at my order, on the edge of defiance, before

reluctantly finishing off poor, stubborn Aklahyr with a swipe of her flensing knife across his throat. The sorcerer's spasms finally ceased. If it matters for the purposes of this archive, his final thoughts were to curse me.

Amurael, who had been watching with bored regard, keyed a code into his narthecium gauntlet, deploying a bonesaw and several carving knives.

'Out of the way, alien.'

She rose, stretching her wings again. 'I am not going inside that mausoleum of cold metal,' she said, gesturing to the ship. 'It has been too long since I tasted the freedom of the sky.'

Such a futilely poetic sentiment. She wanted to hunt, to see if there remained anything worth bleeding on this husk of a world. I waved a hand, granting her permission. She launched upwards, taking to the air in a gust of swirling grit.

Amurael had crouched in her place by the dead Thousand Sons legionary, preparing to harvest Aklahyr's progenoid glands. His bonesaw gave a high whine.

'This won't take long,' he assured me. 'One less sorcerer at the Lord of Hosts' side, at least.'

I looked over at him. 'Daravek haunts us even here.'

'True.' Amurael began carving. Blood arced. 'You really should have killed him when you had the chance.'

The ship was dead within as well as without. We walked its powerless halls, witnessed its annihilated statuary, held uncaring vigil over its slain crew. My hopes sank the deeper we travelled, for the devastation was almost total. If we had come here for salvage, we would have been destined to leave disappointed. The fact the strike cruiser would never sail again was beyond contestation, but scarcely a metre of its hull was left unscarred.

Yet salvage was not our concern. As I had told Aklahyr, we wanted answers.

Even a dead ship isn't silent. Buckled metal whines under pressure. Leaking fuel and coolant will hiss and fizz and trickle and drip. Footsteps reverberate for a kilometre or more, echoing back along avenues of mangled metal, their rhythms distorted, until the senses are half-convinced whole armies march up ahead in the shadows.

The cruiser's layout was perfectly familiar to us, a mirror of so many Legion warships constructed from the same Standard Template Construct. Yet my unease grew, chamber by chamber. Have you ever returned to a familiar place, an old haven perhaps, or a place that burns strong in youthful memory, only to find its soul has changed with the passing of time?

We passed through a grand monastic chamber with gaping holes that had been backlit windows of stained glass. Whatever scenes they had depicted would remain a mystery, now shattered into millions of coloured diamonds that crunched underfoot. A row of golden statues had become a toppled, defeated phalanx amidst the detritus. A great aquila of pale stone, once mounted upon the wall with great wings outstretched, was rubble at our feet.

And everywhere were bodies clad in cream robes ripped by claws and turned black with blood. The corpses were far from pristine. Each one was someway fused into the decks or the walls, partway through the process of being absorbed into the world that was now their tomb.

I knelt by one of the human corpses, taking a fistful of its lacerated robe. The sigil on the cloth was a crudely sewn cross, all four tips flared.

'The Brethren of the Temple of Oaths?' I spoke of the VII

Legion's elite, those rare guardians that stood as sentinels over Rogal Dorn's own flagship, the *Phalanx*.

Amurael used his boot to roll one of the other bodies. The same symbol showed on her hooded robe. 'Legion thralls,' he agreed in word though not in tone. 'And that's the Brethren's cross,' he added with reluctance. It still felt wrong.

These were Legion-serfs, yet the symbol on their breasts was one we had never seen in such widespread context. These were the halls of a Legiones Astartes warship, yet they were bedecked by parchments listing battles and benedictions I had never heard of, against alien foes I had never seen. In stockpiled armouries we found Legion weaponry that similarly eluded easy recognition. The Phobos boltguns and patterns of pistols that my brothers and I still wielded were treated here with the reverence of museum relics, cradled in stasis fields, some of which had survived the crash. Other, sleeker designs of weaponry were racked in place or scattered across the chambers alongside shattered suits of that rarest of wartime treasures: Legiones Astartes Mark VII battleplate.

This last aspect twisted my innards most of all. The wargear had all the hallmarks of mass-production, down to the armourers' marks engraved upon the ceramite. Yet even in the time of shame when the Throne-loyal Legions scoured my brothers and me from the Imperium, chasing us into the etheric prison of the Eye, this pattern of armour had been scarce in the extreme.

And it was black. All of it, black. Not the conflicting yellow and black of the Brethren of the Temple of Oaths, studded with Imperial victory wreaths and the fist symbol of their Legion. This was all straight black, draped in knightly tabards, adorned by chains.

It was Amurael who gave voice to the question pressing against the confines of my skull.

'Khayon,' he said, turning a broken, unfamiliar bolter in his hands. 'How long have we been gone from the Imperium?'

Sometimes my Inquisitorial hosts ask me to explain the unexplainable. Over the course of my captivity I have related the form and function of many aspects that define life in the Empire of the Eye. Within that realm where physical and corporeal laws go to die, temporal stability is another maddening casualty. Time exists only as a fractured idea, different for every one of us.

I have fought beside warriors of the Legions for whom the Imperium itself is a distant memory, even to eidetic recollections. It doesn't matter to them why the Long War began, nor even how it will end. They have been fighting it for an eternity. It is all they know.

On the opposite side of the same coin, I have known warriors for whom Terra is scarcely a memory at all – the same adrenal rage that flowed in their veins during the Siege still beats through their bodies now. For some of them, chronologically speaking, it has been mere months or a handful of years since their exile began.

As for myself, I have undertaken missions on my Legion's behalf that took days to succeed, only to return to Abaddon and the *Vengeful Spirit* to learn that years had passed aboard our flagship. The reverse is also true. More than once I have waged war in the Black Legion's name for years, even decades, only to find that practically no time has passed at all.

But even this is seeking to define the undefinable. We are speaking of a concept that cannot be tamed with words.

The truth is both simple and devastatingly complex. The truth is that most of us no longer care about time. It means nothing to us anymore. Marking the passage of days and months and years is almost impossible. We fight when we must fight. We kill when we must kill. We eat and drink to sustain ourselves. We sleep when our bodies force somnolence upon us. There is no routine, no harmonious schedule of order. We breathe and bleed and breathe and bleed. There is only existence, moment by moment. You are alive or you are dead.

And that is the truth our Imperial counterparts most struggle to understand. When we lock blades with the Space Marines of loyal Chapters, and they pour scorn upon us for a bitterness that has lasted ten thousand years. When we have little idea which thin-blooded newborn conclave of hypno-indoctrinated soldiers is hurling itself against us with oaths the Emperor Himself would have found insane. The truth is that it is no ancient grudge rolling on through the cobwebs of old, old minds. Our hatred is still hot. Our wounds are still fresh. It has always been this way, and it shall always remain so. Time cannot dilute the venom that flows through our hearts, for time no longer exists.

I could not tell you how many years have passed for me since I first set foot on a warp-touched world within the Eye. Sometimes it feels as though I was breathing Terran air only weeks ago. Sometimes I feel incalculably old, weighed down by the pressure of conflicting memories; things that feel as though they happened to other souls, in other lives.

Time is a mortal conceit, a product of the material universe, and we are bound by no such laws.

***

We found the first warrior's body. He had died in battle, not killed in the crash. Whatever daemonic forces had swept through this ship like an ill wind, this black-armoured warrior had claimed several of them with bolter and blade. Ichorous residue marked the deck and walls nearby, where daemons had dissolved after the destruction of their physical forms. The same blood marked the teeth of his chainsword.

The dead warrior wore a cross-marked tabard over his armour plating, the sigil matching that of the slaves we had seen earlier. A length of chain bound the sword to his wrist, either simple good sense to keep hold of a weapon in the chaos of melee or a nod to the gladiatorial pit-games fought on the most primal and bloodthirsty worlds.

Or by the most bloodthirsty Legions. This was a common enough custom among the World Eaters. Even former XII Legion warriors among our number still held to the tradition.

'Who goes first?' asked Amurael. A few of his warriors stood nearby, red eye-lenses tracking the shadows, the thrum of their active battleplate a subcurrent of growling sound.

'I will do it,' I said.

I crouched by the body and drew my ritual jamdhara dagger. The helmet came free easily. I began to carve, scalping the corpse as though I were some tribal primitive claiming a battle trophy. My brother Falkus and his Aphotic Blade are keen collectors of the skulls of fallen champions. I suppose the principle is much the same, but I had no taste for such grisly plunder.

I broke open the skull for the cold feast within.

Once life has left a body, decay sets in at once. A corpse's internal cohesion breaks down, the binding particulates and processes no longer holding together. Despite no visible sign of rot, I could taste the onset of entropy when I chewed that first mouthful of brain.

I swallowed and proceeded to force my way through the rest of the bitter meal. Then I closed my eyes.

I waited.

Not long after, I had the answers I sought.

IV

WHERE PAST AND PRESENT MEET

They called themselves the Black Templars.

I learned this, and so much more, with that first taste of brainflesh.

How much ink has been committed to parchment in detailing the myriad warlike uses of Legiones Astartes enhancements? So much is made of our capacity for perfect recall, of saliva glands that produce hydraklorik acid, the imperviousness of our reinforced bones and the might of our layered muscle and sinew. Far less is spoken of the biological gift that turns cannibalism from heathen ritual into revelation.

The gene-seed organ responsible for this gift is the omophagea – called, in the oldest scrolls, the Eighth Step of Supremacy, or 'the Remembrancer'. It takes root within our bodies, attaching to the brain and nervous system through fusion to the spinal column and digestive tract. Though we are gene-forged to steal sustenance from almost any organic matter, even the flesh of our fallen enemies, it's through the omophagea that we also devour our foe's memories. Nerve clusters in our stomachs carry pulses from the digesting meat to our minds, which the post-human brain interprets as instinct and insight.

A beast's flesh transfers its awareness of its existence, of its surroundings, its struggles, its hungers and its dangers. You sense the nearness of its predators and the taste of its prey. A human's eyes show a blighted palette of a thousand images over the course of the person's life, including that soul's very last sight.

The brain makes for the finest meal. It offers unparalleled insight from a gallery of stolen emotion and memory. You see another being's memories as if they were your own: unreliable, often hazy, occasionally excruciatingly vivid. Their instincts overlay yours, your emotion and reason entwines with those of a life you never led.

It takes discipline to suppress the narcotic qualities of this merging. The sensation can become an addiction all too easily, for it offers pleasure as well as power. In the Thousand Sons we had couched the act in ritual and solemnity – praising the warrior-scholar virtue of 'knowing your enemy', and quelling any guilty pleasure in the cannibalistic act.

Of course, such feasts of flesh are hardly uncommon when any warband emerges victorious over another – look even to the Imperium's own record of supposedly loyal Chapters, especially those of the Blood Angels Legion's genetic descent. Flesh Eaters. Blood Drinkers. How do bands of warriors earn such names, I wonder?

But I am getting ahead of myself. Those were names still many years in the future from the night aboard the shattered warship.

That night, my senses swam with the reflected shards of another life.

I run through a forest, cooled by the dapples of shade beneath a high sun. The rock in my fist is reddened with the dark blood that bleeds from a broken skull.

I stare up at the stars from where I lie in the long grass, and I wonder: where is Terra? Which star warms the Emperor's Throneworld?

I stand before a warrior taller than any other I have ever seen. He tells me that I am chosen, that I am to come with him. The blade of my bronze knife breaks against his armour plating. I scrape my fingernails bloody as I fight. He tells me this is good. He tells me that he chose right.

I sit within a stone chamber, where the walls and floor and even the air is as cold as ice. I speak words of mumbled reverence as I brush sacred oils upon the teeth of an unpowered chainsword. I perform this rite with my bare fingertips, adding the blood from my cuts to the unguents.

I rise from my restraint throne as light blasts into the drop pod. My bolter kicks in my hands, roaring at the inhuman creatures that throw themselves against us. Their chitinous hides burst apart beneath each impacting shell. Impure gore streaks me, streaks all of us, painting our armour with foul flesh, staining our tabards. I am shouting as I kill, and the words are like sunlight and life and the adrenal thunder of blood running hot in battle. The words embody me, my brothers and the heroes we strive to emulate. The words are everything.

No pity.
No remorse.
No fear.

I kneel before my marshal, lowering my head to the hilt of my downturned sword. I breathe in the dusky scent of myrrh from the smoking incense braziers, and I speak my vows of loyalty, of virtue, of courage, of zeal. The Chaplain walks before us, leading the chanted chorus. I feel his eyes upon me, watchful for flaws in my demeanour, listening for any whisper of insincerity.

He will find no flaws and hear no lies. I am worthy of this honour. I will not fail my brothers. I will not fail my Lord Dorn. I will not fail High Marshal Sigismund. I will not fail the Immortal Emperor.

I stand before my arming thralls within my private sanctum. Armour drills whine and lock tight inside the sockets already surgically gouged into my flesh. I am dressed in ceramite. Weighted by it, rendered complete by its sacred burden.

My sword is pressed into my left hand and chained in place, inviolately bound to my forearm. Around me, the serfs chant my name in monastic baritone.

I stand on the bridge, arrayed with my brethren before Marshal Avathus' throne. We stare into the tainted void ahead, where reality puckers and ruptures in the grip of unreal forces. This is the prison into which our ancestors cast our traitorous forebears. We stand before the very mouth of hell.

I fight in the collapsing corridors of a dying ship. My weapons are sundered, my armour is broken, my body reduced to red ruin. Creatures – daemons, they are daemons, they can only be daemons – claw at me, bearing me down, pulling me apart while I still draw blood-tasting breath.

No pity.

Teeth fasten to the flesh of my face, biting in, grinding down, straining, scraping, cracking.

No remorse.

I push the cleaved remnants of my sword up into quivering, fatty flesh.

No f–

I was myself once more, metabolising the stolen memories. Telemachon and Amurael indulged their curiosities as well; I could see them working through the ingested lives, trawling through the recollections for slivers of deeper insight. Telemachon was helmed, of course, but I could see Amurael's features ticking with involuntary muscle responses to the emotions and traumas of the dead Black Templar's long life.

'Angevin,' he said. 'The warrior's name was Angevin.'

I had felt the same sense of identity when I first tasted the memories.

'They came into the Eye willingly,' he added. 'Scouting and exploring.'

'Hunting,' Telemachon amended. 'Hunting *us*.'

'We have to warn Ezekyle.' I had not intended to speak those words, but now they were spoken, the truth of them bit deep. 'If these Templars stand vigil outside the Eye, it may change everything.'

Telemachon shook his head. 'No matter how many of them are waiting for us, no matter if they meet us with every warship in the Imperial Fists fleet, they won't have enough iron in the void to stop us breaking free.'

'Perhaps not,' I conceded. 'But they would have enough to leave us deeply scarred. Do you believe Abaddon wishes to lose hundreds, even thousands, of the warriors we have so painstakingly recruited?'

'To say nothing of the casualties we'll sustain when

Ashur-Kai guides us out of the Eye,' Amurael warned. This, too, was true. No few warbands had lost vessels in the desperate storms that raged at the Eye's edge. Our prison was viciously adept at keeping us caged. 'If we emerge piecemeal in the face of an enemy fleet...' Amurael let the words hang.

'Guesswork,' Telemachon replied smoothly.

'Preparation and consideration,' I replied.

Khayon, a voice breathed, and my spine tightened.

Amurael spoke up, supporting my words. I was not entirely certain of the specifics of what he said. Telemachon replied. I do not know what he said, either. The voice I was hearing belonged to neither of them.

Khayon.

Nagual padded closer, claws scratching the deck. He bared his fangs in a slow growl.

Who calls, master?

I do not know.

Telemachon and Amurael were still conversing, the former doing so while he took blood and flesh samples from the fallen Templar, the latter speaking while examining a compact but blocky pattern of bolt pistol I had not seen before.

Khayon.

I rose slowly, looking towards the archway mouth of the western corridor. The crash had broken this portion of the ship, leaving the deck sloped, leading down into yet more powerless dark.

Khayon.

I heard Telemachon's armour purr as he turned to me. 'What ails you, assassin?'

I did not turn to look at him. 'Someone is here.'

I heard the echolocation clicks as Amurael reactivated his auspex. I felt Telemachon staring at me, though he remained silent.

'Nothing,' Amurael confirmed.

Khayon.

'I sense a presence,' I said. 'Nearby. Within the city, or whatever the closest settlement is called. It knows my name.'

'Male? Female?' Amurael asked. 'Is it even human?'

'I cannot tell. It is less than a whisper.' And this was so. If you can imagine the impression of lips moving, mouthing your name, without breath to give sound to a voice.

'Your miserable alien?' Amurael snorted the question.

'She has no psychic capability,' Telemachon answered before I could, and his rich voice carried a seedy reverence that made my skin crawl. 'Her soul is far too delicate.'

'It is not Nefertari,' I said. 'Whoever it is, I am not even certain they are alive. This is a world of mournful echoes and unquiet ghosts.'

'Then ignore it,' was the swordsman's suggestion.

Khayon. Khayon. Khayon.

I could not ignore this. For someone or something to gain access to my mind, even to brush my surface thoughts like this, spoke of a being with considerable power and significant intent. Trap or not, I was going to find the answer to this mystery. I reached after it, finding nothing but mist, mist, mist.

'It is coming from deeper in the ship. Or... no. From beneath the ship.' I looked to Amurael. 'Are there any subterranean fortresses nearby?'

The former Sons of Horus legionary took a moment to answer, and his aura flared with uneasy light. Something in my words had discomfited him.

'Several.' Amurael's eyes met mine. He wiped the smeared evidence of his investigative cannibalism from his mouth.

One of his legionaries clarified. 'Lord Khayon,' the warrior said, 'the Monumentum Primus is only thirty kilometres from here.'

I hesitated. That possibility had simply not occurred to me. 'We are near the Tomb of Horus?'

'Yes, Lord Khayon.'

Khayon. The presence was a needling caress inside my skull. *Khayon. Khayon. Khayon.* I clenched my teeth against its unwelcomely tantalising touch.

I rose to my feet. 'Show me the way.'

The ship had fused with the earth, amalgamating with the fortress complexes beneath the surface. Here was another world entirely, a realm of fallout bunkers, interconnected trench mazes and subterranean chambers. The Black Templars strike cruiser had speared into the ground and swiftly found its wreckage bound in the mutated grip of the realm below.

Everywhere I looked corrosion was rife, the decay of the world above creeping down here in infections of rot and rust. Power lapses plunged whole portions of the complexes into darkness, and what light remained was strained and weak, flickering on the edge of failure. The truth of Maeleum was just as ugly as the lie, for soon enough we were walking through chambers and corridors littered with industrial detritus and the half-eaten bodies of slain humans, beastmen and legionaries alike.

Most of the dead Legion warriors wore the armour of the Sons of Horus, left to rot where they lay. The purple and puce of the Emperor's Children was also in evidence, along with shades marking resting places of fighters drawn from the other Legions. Most of these bodies had been gouged open by fleshsmiths and Apothecaries, their progenoids harvested in the heat of battles fought long ago.

The charnel-house smell penetrated my armour and sank into my senses. I could feel it in my pores. I could taste it, that sour meat stink, on the back of my teeth.

Amurael's warrior, Dejak, led us deeper. My retinal display tracked the depth, and it wasn't long before my fragile telepathic thread to the Rubricae aboard our gunship thinned and severed, leaving them unbound. They would fulfil their last orders, but I couldn't reach them to see through their eyes or issue them new commands. Nor was I about to stop and achieve the necessary meditative focus to re-commune with them.

Dejak stopped at a junction, his helm panning across a long, arcing bloodstain along a bolt-punctured wall. Nothing about it seemed any different to the rest of the biological mess we'd seen in the complex so far.

Telemachon and I glanced at one another. 'This smear of sanguine filth is notable in some way?' I asked Dejak. I suspected that Lheor would have made some irritable remark about fine Cthonian art. As much as I wished for his presence here rather than Telemachon's, I did not miss what passed for his wit.

'It's a sigil, lords.' Dejak walked down the left-hand corridor without bothering to illuminate us as to what exactly about the blood smear informed this decision. He was with Amurael at the head of the squad, deferring to his lord.

We followed once more. Telemachon's clawed boots clicked and scraped with the percussion of each of his footfalls.

'A gang sign, I suspect.' His mellifluous voice murmured over the vox, to me alone. 'A marking of territory. An echo of what once was, on now-dead Cthonia.'

'Most likely.' I was not certain where this conversational gambit was going, but I knew Telemachon, and I knew it was leading somewhere.

'Lekzahndru,' he purred my name with the Gothic twist of his former home world. 'Tell me,' he added, beneficent and smooth, 'of Drol Kheir.'

Bolters crashing in arrhythmic percussion. Energised blades thunder-clapping against burning war-plate. Blood running hot, steaming in the cold, marshy air. Life becoming vapour, red smoke curling from riven ceramite.

'There is little to say.'

'And yet,' said Telemachon, 'so many of our cousins among the Legions do have something to say, and they all say the same thing.'

Iskandar Khayon died at Drol Kheir.

'It was a battle,' I replied. 'A vast one, but not a glorious one.'

'How so?'

'Why does this matter?' His fascination was unjustified. Several warbands from various Legions had banded together against several others and waged war across the ever-shifting ground of a daemon world, warring for territory. What else was there to say? Battles of that kind took place every hour of every day somewhere within Eyespace. Drol Kheir was unremarkable beyond the immense casualties sustained, when the Death Guard had rained alchemical toxins upon their allies and enemies alike.

'But,' Telemachon pressed, 'whose side were you on?'

I was scarcely listening to his irrelevant purring. Something on his armour drew my eye.

'Hold,' I commanded. He turned back to me, his impassive, beautiful silver faceplate meeting my gaze and targeting locks.

I tore Telemachon's sidearm free of its leather holster, pulling it into my hand with a drag of telekinesis. I turned the ornate bolt pistol in my fist, looking at the curious decoration hanging from the polished gold grip. Tokens and charms were common on our weapons and armour, but I'd never seen him with this keepsake before.

A feather. A single black feather. I tore it from the fine golden chain that bound it to the pistol grip and crushed it in my hand.

'Is this from her wings?' I demanded.

'But of course.'

'You diseased creature. Stalking her. Watching her.'

'And more.' The onyx of his eyes flashed with reflected light. Telemachon was smiling. His facemask didn't change, but I sensed whatever was left of his face behind the silver twisting in mirth.

I ground the remnants of the feather beneath my boot. In the same moment, Nagual ghosted silently from the shadows behind Telemachon, his muscles bunching with the urge to leap.

No, I sent to my lynx.

I will end him. My mind inferred the *tigrus*-lynx's violent eagerness as words, though as ever no words were spoken. His jaws parted slowly, readying volcanic-glass sabre-teeth the length of swords.

No, Nagual.

His thoughts curdled, becoming a fusion of expectant sensation: the rending of ceramite beneath unbreakable claws, the hot rush of human blood upon the tongue...

Nagual. I sent the command as a blade to break through the beast's closing mind. *Obey.*

He heeded me, but only just. Only because he had to, lest he risk my displeasure.

I missed my wolf, lost to Horus Reborn all those years before. Where Nagual had hunger, Gyre had possessed intelligence; where Gyre was a gifted huntress, Nagual was a ravening destroyer. He had his uses, but I was increasingly certain that I would banish him soon, just as I'd banished every other failed successor to the wolf I still mourned.

All of this transpired in the merest of moments. I looked from my lynx to Telemachon, and the words I spoke were not the ones I had intended to speak.

'Do you value your life so little?' I asked him, surprising myself with my own honesty. 'This hunger for her will be the death of you.'

The swordsman tilted his head, regarding me through his backlit eye-lenses. 'Is that concern I hear in your voice, Lekzahndru? Can it be that you fear for my well-being?'

Loyalty to Ezekyle's vision had so far prevented our mutual distrust from becoming disgust. We had sworn to be brothers and never to harm one another, an oath taken at Abaddon's behest when we first carved the Legion symbols from our armour. Telemachon had stolen several artificer slaves to artfully paint his armour black. I had simply charred the paint from my own and blackened it with conjured wisps of warpfire.

We were far from our lord now, but my adherence to his vision was inviolate. I believed in Abaddon's ambitions; I would not break with his trust. I tossed the pistol back to Telemachon.

'The same rules that govern you and me do not apply to

Nefertari,' I pointed out. 'If you continue to antagonise her, she will kill you regardless of our oath.'

'And you fear bearing the blame for her actions?' Damn him, I could hear the smile in his voice. 'Ah, no, it isn't that. What you fear is far more territorial. It makes your skin crawl, doesn't it? The chance she may come to treasure my attentions. You fear that the Youngest God looks through my eyes, seeking to swallow her soul.'

I stared at him, at the argent and flawless face he presented to brother and foe alike. Words eluded me for several seconds. How was one supposed to react to such baiting?

'Spare me the deluded twists of your broken mind,' I said. 'I do not interfere with the preening, wailing things you call minions. Do not meddle with my coterie, either.'

'As you wish, Lekzahndru,' he replied smoothly. He reached to run his fingers through Nagual's striped greyblack fur, but the daemon gave a throaty warning snarl. Telemachon pulled his hand back. 'I see,' the swordsman said, perfectly calm. I could feel him smiling again.

Amurael was watching us, as were his warriors. The servos in Amurael's neck snarled as he shook his head.

'If you're finished, brothers?'

Chastened, I fell in behind him once more. Greasy amusement still radiated from Telemachon's aura. I felt it as an itch against my skin, impossible to ignore.

Part of my irritation was that he'd spoken the plain truth. If he baited Nefertari into crossing blades with him, the blame would fall on my shoulders for not controlling her. Abaddon tolerated her only because I had made it clear I wouldn't cast her aside. She was too useful to me.

I wouldn't let myself consider Telemachon's other insinuations. His sick craving for her was born of his hunger for sensation, any sensation at all, and the god that flowed in his bloodstream cried out to devour Nefertari's eldar soul. Being near to her caused him pain. Even the slow creep of agony she caused him electrified his nerves with pleasure.

Wretched parasite, I thought.

Master? My simple-minded familiar's senses met mine.

Not you, Nagual.

The Faceless Man?

How many times had I imprinted Telemachon's name upon what passed for Nagual's mind? Each attempt was an exercise in futility.

Yes. The Faceless Man.

The Faceless Man. How apt. To his own men, the warriors of the Shrieking Masquerade, Telemachon was most often called the Masqued Prince. I preferred Nagual's title.

I will end him, the great cat promised me. Flicker-flash sensations hissed through my thoughts – the salty heat of running blood, the useless thrashing of prey with my jaws locked around its throat...

No, Nagual.

Breathe the command and it will be done.

As tempting as it was, I did nothing of the kind.

The first chamber of worth we reached was among the more tragic sights I have ever witnessed. Deep within the complex, Amurael led us into an apothecarion that far exceeded any military medicae centre in both grandeur and purpose. Colossal vault-tanks rose like fortress walls, all instrumentation and console circuitry pulled apart and riven by chainblades. The archive banks, where priceless genetic material had been held in stasis-locked storage, were looted and destroyed in deliberate spite rather than by the incidental damage of war. Every container that had once held vital chemical cocktails of preservative fluids was smashed and dry, now home to hives of insect vermin making their lairs in machines that had once granted transhuman life.

A gene-seed repository. I recognised the place's purpose as soon as I saw it. The importance of these hallowed halls is burned into the very marrow of every Legion warrior.

Telemachon similarly needed no elucidation. He laughed softly upon entering, the sound slow and wet and entirely sincere at the devastation of this priceless place.

Amurael had been Medicae Quintus within the Sons of Horus – a ranking officer by any judgement. He walked through the chamber as if in the grip of a dream, no doubt seeing the shades of what had once been overlaying the truth of what was. He examined shattered machinery and useless tools, saying nothing as he explored.

'Was this your laboratory?' I asked him.

'No. Mine was always aboard the *Viridian Sky*. The warriors of my company never risked storing our gene-seed reserves on Maeleum, even before the Emperor's Children came for the Warmaster's corpse.'

Something occurred to me then that hadn't before. When the Children of the Emperor raided this world and defiled Horus' corpse for use in their bastardised cloning foundries, they surely wouldn't have resisted plundering the XVI Legion's gene-seed depositories.

Twice the insult. Twice the desecration.

'There's nothing here,' Amurael declared. 'Let's go.'

Nagual was busy, breathing corrosive smoke into a colony of slug-like creatures that crackled and popped as they dissolved. He licked the resulting sludge up with one swipe of his tongue, swallowing noisily.

To me, I sent.

The lynx obeyed, his eyes glowing with the absorption of more daemonic matter. We walked on though the rusted dark. And to think I had been concerned about playing ambassador on Maeleum. We were not emissaries. We were practically thieves.

Thieves in a realm where everything of worth had already been stolen.

A journey that should have taken us no time at all instead took over a week, in the time-lost way one judges such things in the Eye. So many of the tunnels had mutated closed or fallen into ruin, we found ourselves constantly doubling back and seeking alternate routes. Added to that, the labyrinthine complexes beneath the earth shifted when you dared take your eyes from the passage ahead, leading in conflicting directions again and again. Truly the warp had riddled its way through the stone of this world's core and twisted the planet to its indiscernible whims.

And all the while, *Khayon, Khayon* echoed in my skull. Never louder, never quieter, never weaker, never stronger. Just... there.

Our armour sustained us, feeding nutrients back into our systems and infusing us with synthesised chemical feeds to maintain alertness and health over protracted deployment. The leathery flesh of the dead – even their bones – would offer us sustenance if we chose to indulge, but we were a far cry from starvation. Telemachon sampled those cold delicacies purely out of choice. I made no comment each time I saw him removing the lower half of his faceplate to do so; eating the unburied dead was something most of us had done in times of desperation, and there was no denying that necessity had become preference among many warbands banished to the Eye. By Imperial standards, such feasts are the least of our sins.

I learned that the entirety of Maeleum was connected beneath the surface, with freeholds and subterranean fortresses linked by tunnels and trenches. The deeper we moved, the more evidence pointed to abandonment rather than annihilation. Signs of conflict lessened, replaced by signs of desolation. The bodies we found had expired from hunger or thirst as often as those torn open by raiders' weapons. The Emperor's Children hadn't penetrated to the deepest levels in huge numbers. When they had passed this far, it was as slavers and plunderers, eager to get their spoils back to the surface. Thus, they had sacrificed an invader's thoroughness for a pirate's prudence. Even some of the armouries weren't looted fully, though the weapons we found there were in various states of dysfunction.

One of the wonders we discovered in the depths was a great transit route – powered down and empty now – with an underground conveyor rail tunnel between one fortress and another. The mutants that thrived down there in the lightless deeps prayed to the powerless rail-engines as iron gods, beseeching them to awaken from their slumber. I could not guess how many generations of Legion slaves and serfs had interbred under the Eye's influence to produce these sorry creatures.

I pitied them, though more for their uselessness and ignorance than from any sympathy. Amurael and the others ignored them. Telemachon found them delightful, hunting them the way a beast would hunt herds of weaker prey. He laughed joyously as he raced away into the darkness, returning later with blood spatters drying across his armour.

Nagual ached to give chase to them as well. I allowed it each time, if only to distract my lynx from pulsing his hungry insistence that he would kill Telemachon if I but asked. I wondered if Nefertari, alone on the surface all this time, had found similar prey.

Amurael focused only on the gene-seed depositories. He didn't hold much hope of locating actual genetic material, knowing that all of it would have been destroyed or long since rotted within failed preservative machinery. Instead, he sought to rekindle what systems he could bring back to a semblance of life, seeking data above all. He worked with his customary focus, draining wounded data-archives of any lore they could be coaxed into surrendering.

I was tempted to ask if he was delaying our journey, taking these alternate routes to rifle through old apothecarions.

Khayon, the voice caressed the inside of my skull, a constant whisper against the back of my eyes. *Khayon. Khayon. Khayon.*

'What are you doing?' I snapped at Amurael at one point.

'Compiling a monograph,' he said, as he watched an information feed inloading into his narthecium's storage coils. 'A treatise on every aspect of the Legion's gene-seed. This is a rare opportunity. I want every word ever written about the process, from basic schema and flawed experimentation all the way through to stable modification.'

'We can already maintain what we have,' said Telemachon.

'Barely,' Amurael replied without looking up from his vambrace console.

'Our numbers won't fall if we're diligent.'

Amurael still didn't look up. 'They will over time whether we're diligent or not. But this isn't only about the gene-seed supplies we already have.'

'Names,' I said, interrupting their burgeoning disagreement. 'Ezekyle is not only gathering gene-seed data, he is gathering names. The name of every Son of Horus entered into the Legion's archives as confirmed dead.'

This was typical of Abaddon's precision. He was compiling an archive of who still lived, tallying the fallen and survivors alike. It was the best way of knowing what percentage of the remaining Legion was already sworn to us, sailing as part of our fleet. The rest would be hunted down, and recruited or killed.

Amurael's nod told me that I had assumed correctly.

'I was made for greater deeds than administrative archiving,' said Telemachon. 'Be swift. This place bores me.'

It took another two days to reach the Tomb of Horus.

The sarcophagus was empty. Where once Horus had lain in state – arms crossed over his chest, hands gripping the hilt of Worldbreaker – there now stood a great coffin of empty cracked marble. Its proportions were appropriately massive, only making its emptiness more pitiable. The gold leaf inscriptions were gone, broken by boots and hammers. Towering windows of stained glass, once backlit in this subterranean sanctuary, were holes in the high walls, while the scenes of glory and rebellion they had once depicted were reduced to diamond rubble that crunched beneath our boots. Skulls that had once been the trophies of innumerable conquests were particulate bone dust, swirling slowly in the stagnant air.

Amurael's men were commanded to wait. We went in alone.

Khayon, the whisper brushed against me once more. Still sourceless, still directionless.

Once this fortress had been called the Monumentum Primus. Now it was a ruined castle deep within Maeleum's crust, shaped from slave-hewn rock and the eroding bones of monstrous warp serpents.

I have been in places that stank of tawdry, useless prayer, and I have walked worlds where I was the only living being, yet no fane or cathedral ever felt so crass as that crypt, and no prison or place of lonely pilgrimage ever felt as desolate.

I was not sure whom I despised more – those that had prayed here as fools kneel before an altar, or those that had defiled this tomb out of blasphemous ambition.

The crypt was lifeless but far from empty. Wraiths gathered here in worship, ethereal and near silent. Here were the shades of kneeling beastmen, their avian crying and bestial braying stolen by time, rendered down to breathy impressions of the sounds once made by living throats. Here were warriors in the viridian battleplate of the Sons of Horus, standing in austere reflection or duelling over their father's bones. Here were invading Emperor's Children, laughing, killing, executing.

Hordes of fighting warriors. Hosts of worshippers. Moments in time overlapping, conjured by the spiritual significance of this hallowed ground.

'Iskandar,' Amurael said, low and solemn. 'If you would.'

I nodded. With a gesture of my hand I banished the unquiet dead, pushing the manifest energy from this vast chamber. It was like scattering a handful of sand to the wind. Devoid of those echoes, the chamber grew truly silent. Alone now, we approached the sarcophagus.

The body this coffin had cradled was years gone, first hauled away like a hunter's kill to be dissected on the unclean slabs of III Legion butcher-surgeons, then recovered by Abaddon and the very first of his Ezekarion after the destruction of Horus Reborn. What remained of the Warmaster's corpse – the genetic plunder that was all Fabius Bile had left intact from the looted cadaver – was housed safely within the Apothecarion Apex aboard the *Vengeful Spirit,* stasis-sealed and guarded by a hundred of our Syntagma war robots, linked to the Anamnesis' conscious control.

You might think, ignorantly but not unfairly, that Horus' genetic samples alone would be enough for us to engineer an endless supply of the nineteen biosynthetic organs necessary for implantation to create Space Marines from human boy-children. This is not so, no matter any individual Apothecary's genius. The Emperor himself envisioned the process, which speaks to the intellect required to first bring it into being, and put it into effect with the immense technological impetus of the Throneworld and its unprecedented access to relics of the Dark Age.

Even now in the Imperium, an Adeptus Astartes Chapter can be rendered slowly extinct by the theft of its gene-seed, despite its medicae-warriors possessing all the information and support necessary to re-engineer new progenoid glands and create new Space Marines. Indeed, such defilement is one of the Nine Legions' preferred punishments; nothing drives a Chapter to such desperation, nor tars them with such shame, as the theft of their future.

And as for the Legions themselves? Would we raid our thin-blooded cousins and descendants in the Imperium if we could render new gene-seed organs with ease? Would we slaughter each other over fragments of lore or tithe fortunes in service and materiel to the Mechanicum's daemon-forges if we could simply engineer miracles without their priceless expertise? We bind daemons into our war machines to keep them functioning. We forge new amalgamated horrors of daemonic flesh and cold metal to replace technology we can no longer maintain.

Remember this, for context is precious in the comprehension of this tale. For all that we mock the Imperium in the way you make a virtue of small-minded ignorance, we too have lost so very much. Perhaps even more. Your masters have sealed knowledge away from you, incinerated it, or it has been lost through the natural passage of time. We, on the other hand, have watched it slip through our fingers even when we tried to keep it close.

Nowhere exemplified this better than the shameful crypt on Maeleum.

One of the ghosts refused to disperse. It watched the three of us approaching, turning old, old eyes to each of us in turn. I felt the fall of its judging gaze upon me like a threat, a blade stroking against my armour. How long had it been here? Had it always been here, even when this sepulchre had been inhabited by the Warmaster's deluded sons, only taking shape in the vacuum left by their absence?

The spirit was human, though its soul was boiling with the memories and emotions of accumulated centuries. Whoever it had been in life, it had witnessed sights and lived an existence far in excess of those allotted to a typical mortal span. Its form, that which we call a *corpus* when speaking of warp-born entities, was stable and unchanging. Its long hair was dark and ragged. Its skin, much like mine, was the dusky melange common among civilisations that rise in the equatorial regions of worlds like Terra. It wore a traveller's cloak of faded black, and simple, travel-worn clothing. Tears stained its cheeks, tears of white ink; those four trails of sorrow were tattoos of tiny scripture from the corners of its eyes.

It was – or had been in life – an unmutated human female.

I reached for the warp ghost a dozen metres away, fingers curled as if to crush its throat with telekinesis. The air whirled with an unseen breeze in answer to the energy I summoned. The spirit's hair trailed in the breeze.

Telemachon hesitated in his approach. I heard the fibre-bundle cords in his armoured collar purr as he tilted his head. Amurael halted a half-step after, looking between the apparition and the scanner display on his narthecium gauntlet. At my side, Nagual watched the spectre with glowing eyes, his jaws parted. Venom dripped from his sabre-teeth.

Khayon, came the whisper one last time, and the ghost smiled.

'Iskandar Khayon,' said the wraith, its voice completely human. 'Telemachon Lyras. And Amurael Enka.'

I lowered my hand. The rising wind died. The three of us said nothing, confronted suddenly by a human woman where no living being had any right to be.

'You will take me to Ezekyle Abaddon.' She said it not as a command, but as if she were speaking of a memory. A memory that hadn't yet happened.

'And why would we do that?' I asked.

'Because I bring him a warning,' she replied, perfectly calm, 'and I will deliver him a future.'

Amurael and Telemachon merely stared at her. I was the one to ask the question on our tongues.

'Who are you?'

She told us. She gave us a single name, though others would grant her many more titles across the years to come. And that was how I met Moriana, the Weeping Maiden, Oracle of the Despoiler, Prophetess of the Black Legion.

V

VENGEFUL SPIRIT

We brought Moriana before Abaddon – not as the messenger she claimed to be, but as the prisoner she truly was. She walked between two of my Rubricae, and no matter how prepared she was, she still flinched at the wall of sound that met us when we walked onto the bridge.

The fleet was at muster by the time we boarded the *Vengeful Spirit*. Even as we translated in-system, other vessels were breaking into the sanctuary of our nebula, engines running hot, seeking to fall into anchor formation around the flagship.

I heard Ashur-Kai's voice long before I set foot on the *Spirit*.

I sense great unrest around you. His psychic tone was usually touched by his former role as my master, yet now it was discoloured by urgency and concern. *Explain yourself, Sekhandur,* he sent, using the variant of my name from its classical Gothic roots. *Why are the tides of fate crashing against your soul?*

As dramatic as ever. I should have realised he would sense Moriana's presence the moment we translated in-system. *We bring a captive from Maeleum.*

That would explain the warp's turmoil around your vessel.

We had been slowed on our return, true. I was not even close to being as gifted at navigating through the tumbling tides of Eyespace as Ashur-Kai was, though I had returned as swiftly as I was able.

You sound uneasy, my brother.

All is not well, Sekhandur. Lheorvine and Zaidu are about to kill one another, apportioning blame for their losses at Thylakus. Valicar, Ceraxia and Vortigern have returned bloodied by fleets sworn to Daravek. We encountered our own difficulties with his minions, as well. Can you not see the ship?

I could. On the oculus, the *Vengeful Spirit* was clawed prow to stern with superficial damage, the extent of which did not worry me; the simple presence of it did. It had been duelling vessels that were strong enough to break through its shields.

Tell me everything, I sent.

Just get to the command deck. I heard the age-old commanding tone of my former mentor in that order. *You will see for yourself.*

And so I did. A wall of sound, the uproar of rage and recrimination, washed over us as we entered the bridge. The bridge after a battle was usually a place of celebration and, not uncommonly, drunken or ecstatic torture of enemy warlords. Their corpses – or soon-to-be corpses – were hauled into place among the war banners hanging from the strategium's roof, and warriors engaged in raucous contests of strength, vows of brotherhood or violent displays of adrenal joy to celebrate the victories that brought these new trophies.

I have been told that Imperial Space Marines sombrely reflect after their triumphs, kneeling in monastic reverence before statues of their idols and worshipping representations of their heroes – a somewhat different aesthetic to the pit fights, the howls and the cheers that follow our victories, where bragging is an art and a warrior's reputation is all. Yet the sensation I walked into on the bridge that day was thicker, somehow fouler than usual. The frustration of hundreds of beaten warriors, their emotions meshing, created a psychic echo of their defeat that settled upon me like a funeral shroud.

Tokugra was the first to greet me. Ashur-Kai's daemon-crow fluttered to alight upon my shoulder, regarding me with eyes that had seen stars born and die, and had shined with amusement all the while.

Boy, it greeted me.

I had not been 'Boy' to Ashur-Kai for centuries – the days of my adolescent apprenticeship were long past – but Tokugra referred to me by nothing else.

Nagual snarled at the crow. The two daemon familiars glared at one another in bestial dislike before, as ever, the crow took wing and put distance between itself and its warp-kin.

The command deck was alive with heaving bodies and shouting voices. Most of the activity centred around the raised dais where Abaddon's throne sat unused. Warriors were yelling accusations and refutations, demanding answers from each other, and demanding that others heed their words.

'Stay close to me,' I told Moriana, and threaded the same

command through the minds of the Rubricae that guarded her.

We passed beneath Ultio, the Anamnesis, in the chamber's very heart. She turned gracefully in the pale azure fluid of her suspension tank. She was the calm heart of the storm, serene in her amniotic haven amidst the shouting masses. The cognition cables tendrilling from her head to the machinery atop her life-support prison swayed gently in the artificial womb-fluid, forming a serpentine crest where each industrial snake carried her thoughts throughout the ship's receptive systems. The fluid was clean, constantly filtered and infused with nutrients by the humming machines set in the tall glass tank's foundations.

She stared forwards, scarcely seeing with her eyes at all. Her vision was spread across the many thousands of gun-imagifiers and hull-scryers set along the *Vengeful Spirit*'s battlements. When she spoke, her mouth moved but produced no bubbles in the artificial womb-fluid. Her words intoned across the bridge with a voice not wholly unlike the way she had spoken before her immersion.

Sister, I sent to her.

'Ezekyle,' she said, the black stone vox-gargoyles in the chamber's rafters calling out above the multitude. 'Iskandar, Telemachon and Amurael have returned.'

In life, she had been Itzara, a young woman of Tizca. In death, she had first become the Anamnesis – machine-spirit at the heart of the warship *Tlaloc* – and then, gaining strength and identity upon fusion with a new vessel, she had become Ultio, the heart of the *Vengeful Spirit*. She was the ship itself, and its hull was an extension of her body, its armour plating her skin, its plasma reactors her organs.

She swirled a hand through the fluid of her tomb-cradle,

not quite a wave of greeting. Her thoughts were a ceaseless process of trajectories, damage calculations and a deeply resonant awareness of the souls aboard the ship she commanded. It was painful to touch a mind like that for too long. Too inhuman.

Abaddon watched from the raised dais where his throne was set, though he considered the command throne to be little more than pageantry, sitting on it only when receiving emissaries or supplicants from other warbands.

Sargon intercepted me before I could reach the throne. He wore the blackened ceramite we all wore, though his was bedecked in tattered scrolls I had no intention of reading. The monkish surplice he wore over the battered power armour was pockmarked and war-torn, its painstakingly inked scripture ruined by scorch holes.

He looked young, barely more than a Legion initiate, his smooth skin the typical duskiness of those born and raised in the City of Grey Flowers on the long-lost desert world of Colchis. He had lacked vocal cords since long before I had met him, purportedly losing them to a cut throat in the Siege of the Imperial Palace. For several years he had relied exclusively on the hand gestures of Legiones Astartes battle-sign and using his simplistic psychic efforts to speak through the mouths of any nearby corpses.

Time had changed the method, if not the need. His shoulder guards were warp-fashioned things, horned daemonic faces of bio-ceramite leering from the armour plating, slavering bloody spittle, occasionally lashing their too-long tongues at the air. It was through these faces that he spoke, both voices in guttural harmony.

'Iskandar,' the two faces spoke. Neither of them looked at me – for reasons beyond me, both were always blindfolded with layers of chains. They licked their fanged teeth, chittering to themselves between words.

'Sargon,' I greeted him. 'What is all this?'

'Revenge,' he said, leading me onwards. 'The Gods have a sense of humour if this madness is anything to judge by. Half of our fleets limped back to the muster. Every captain and warlord brings the same tale – Legion resistance. *Organised* Legion resistance. Thagus Daravek took your latest attempt on his life personally.'

I said nothing, not wishing to speak yet again of my failure.

'You should have killed him, Khayon.' Sargon's youthful features remained gentle as he gripped a howling female beastman by the back of the neck and hurled her out of the way. Her herd-kin scattered before our advance. 'Worse,' Sargon continued, 'he savaged the War God's Maw and the Shrieking Masquerade. Lheorvine blames Zaidu. Zaidu blames Lheorvine.'

I had no chance to answer. He blindly backhanded another crew member aside; the servitor toppled into those nearby, and we pushed through the crowd together, where most of the Ezekarion had gathered around Abaddon's dais surrounded by dozens of their warriors. Here, the feeling of frustrated defeat blanketing the chamber reached its apex.

Zaidu was facing Lheor, ahead of baying packs of their men. Zaidu, bedecked in skulls on chains, his armour scraped bare of colour, was a clawed and avian malformation of a man. Taloned feet scratched the plasteel decking beneath him. The turbines on his back whined, powering up with his acidic thoughts. Every movement he made was a sudden jerk or a twitch, adding to the aura of ravenous energy he exuded.

The laughter through his sleek helm was a staccato croaking. 'Your words, Firefist, they are a child's puling wails.'

'Don't call me Firefist.' Lheor's dark, patchwork face showed rows of glinting metal teeth. Shivers ran through him, not a sign of fear but of physiological desecration and simple blood-need. The Nails were biting into his brain – he was struggling to keep control of himself.

Zaidu managed to cackle and growl at the same time, evidence of the mutation within his throat. 'Your words,' he said again, 'they are the bleating of a weakling.'

Lheor roared, spit flying from his metal teeth. 'I lost men because of this creature's cowardice.' He levelled his chainaxe at Zaidu, but his words were aimed at Abaddon. 'We lost the battle because of this harpy. Let me kill him, Ezekyle.'

Abaddon stood halfway up the stairs leading to his throne. He looked gaunter than even when I had last seen him, his jaundiced features speckled with blood from who knew how many hours, days or weeks before.

'Calm yourself,' our overlord commanded with a tired sneer. Never had I seen him look so exhausted. 'You're frothing at the mouth, Lheorvine.'

'I want his head!'

Zaidu's reply was a laughing screech that had all the charm and humanity of talons raking over sheet metal. 'The Masquerade did all that was asked of us, Lord Abaddon. Firefist's warriors failed to hold their lines. The War God's Maw, they are weak. Daravek's men killed them before we could reach them.'

Lheor drew his hand back, ready to slam his axe blade into the deck.

No! I sent in an urgent blade of psychic warning. To drive a weapon into the ground before a brother was to initiate a blood challenge – a Cthonian gang ritual that Abaddon had allowed, even encouraged, to spread through our warbands.

Lheor's face twitched as his cranial implants reacted with boiling heat to the unwanted pressure of my silent voice in his mind, but it was enough to force a moment's hesitation. He lowered the blade. The watching crowd bayed their disappointment.

Telemachon shoved past me, moving to Zaidu's side, and the jeers turned at once to cheers. The crowd scented blood now.

'Say nothing more, brother,' Telemachon ordered his lieutenant. 'Let's cut to the truth, shall we?'

Zaidu immediately nodded in wordless compliance, remaining at his lord's side. Lheor looked between the two of them, still straining to hold himself back with the leash of Abaddon's wishes.

'Lyras.' Lheor made the name an accusing growl. 'Your dog cost us the battle at the Thylakus Expanse.'

Zaidu indeed said nothing, at least not aloud. I could hear the faint click of vox-relays from his helm, as well as Telemachon's.

'In my absence, Subcommander Vorolas is invested with my full authority,' Telemachon said calmly. His aura rippled with the first stirrings of excitement, of anticipation finally ripening.

Lheor kept his eyes on Telemachon. 'We have pict-feeds, gun imagifiers, vox archives and sworn oaths that stand testament to your bastard subcommander failing to reinforce us and leaving my vanguard to die.'

Ah, how familiar, I thought, though my blood was running cold. I did not like the prickling amusement radiating from Zaidu. It was a piss-stain of smug satisfaction souring his aura. This unfortunate scene had the ripe stink of premeditation.

'I understand your displeasure,' Telemachon replied, as reasonably as I had ever heard him sound. 'And I trust Subcommander Vorolas' account differs from yours?'

Zaidu twitched one shoulder, followed by a tic-jerk of his head. 'We fought to get to them, Lord Lyras. How we fought! But the War God's Maw, they know nothing of tactics. They cannot hold to a battle plan. They advanced too far, too fast. Firefist's men, they were already taking savage losses by the time we reached them.'

Lheor's response to this was, by his standards, rather calm. He spat onto the deck before Zaidu's boots, the acid eating through the metal floor.

'You're a liar, Zaidu.' Lheor followed the disrespectful gobbet with more accusations. 'A liar, a coward and your word isn't worth a damn here. I am Lheor of the Ezekarion, and I say you lie.'

He looked to Abaddon for support, but none came. I stared at Abaddon's passivity – and in that moment, the die was cast. Lheor threw his axe. It hammered into the deck before Zaidu's boots. The Raptor cackled his nasty excuse for laughter.

Telemachon's aura flared with the caress of rich, snide delight. He was the one that stepped forwards, his hands on his sheathed swords.

'I hear your words, my dear brother, and like you, I am of the Ezekarion. As Subcommander Vorolas' commanding officer, I accept the challenge in his place.'

Lheor spat again. He wiped his mouth with the back of his gauntlet. 'I challenged your pet, Lyras, not you.'

'Indeed?' Telemachon turned fractionally to Zaidu, and their two helms bent together in melodramatic affirmation. 'Do you see the axe on the deck, Subcommander Vorolas?'

Zaidu's reply came as a reassuring hiss. 'I do, Lord Lyras.' The theatrical innocence in his vile voice was beyond grating.

'Then I accept the challenge on Subcommander Vorolas' behalf,' Telemachon restated. 'Such is my right, as his lord.'

To his credit – or rather, in an unsurprising sign of his own zealotry – Lheor did not hesitate. He drew the saw-toothed flensing knife at his hip and stepped forwards, facing our warband's finest warrior with a naked grin.

'Is that what you want? I care not whose blood runs for this, Lyras. Yours or that screaming dog's – it's all the same to me.'

In the years to come, I would often think back to this moment. The sight of Lheor advancing on Telemachon, our warband's finest bladesman, carrying nothing but a skinning knife in his hand. Lheor is long dead now, fallen on Mackan, as I have said before. But this is the man I remember, the grinning and confident warrior that faced the perfect swordsman, carrying only a dagger.

Ezekyle? I sent to my lord. *Do something before this madness gets further out of hand.*

Abaddon watched and said nothing. He looked weary beyond reckoning, but his eyes met mine and he nodded, finally giving me the signal I needed. I drew Sacramentum, and she flashed sacred silver in the strategium's sick light.

'*Enough.*' My command was both spoken and driven into the minds of everyone present. The beastmen whined and lowered their heads in submission. The warriors regarded me with a mixture of reluctant obedience and resentment that I had stepped forwards to break the promise of bloodsport.

Telemachon did not look at me. 'You have no right interfering, Lekzahndru.'

Lheor shared the sentiment. 'You can have his pretty burial mask, Khayon, once I've carved it from his skull.'

I cut the air between them with Sacramentum's shining length. 'You,' I addressed Telemachon, 'are duelling no one on anyone's behalf. You think me blind to this transparent ploy? And you,' I aimed my blade at Zaidu, 'may expect my summons later. If you refuse to speak the truth in this matter, Zaidu Vorolas, I will tear it from your mind.'

I looked between Zaidu and Lheor. 'Now both of you, *back down.*'

Zaidu obeyed at once, moving away with Telemachon, but Lheor did not. Spittle gleamed on his chin, and he watched their retreating forms with bloodshot eyes, still gunning his chainaxe.

'Coward.' He drooled the word with a stalactite of saliva, then shouted it louder, setting off another chorus of cheers. I pulled Lheor aside, dragging him by the pauldron.

You foolish bastard.

He winced at the silent knife of my voice, cursing me and snapping back, 'Get out of my head.'

'You foolish bastard,' I said aloud the second time.

Above us, Ultio drifted in her tank, her nude form a silhouette in the amniotic fluid of her artificial womb. Several of the Syntagma stood nearby – the war robots and cognitively enslaved cyborgs she commanded were bristling with weaponry. The human and mutant crew knew to stay clear of her mechanical enforcers. To the beastmen clans that served us, the Syntagma were machine angels that obeyed the ship's soul.

Lheor bared his iron teeth, his features twitching. A

particularly painful spasm forced one of his eyes to screw closed and his mouth to pull to the side for two heartbeats.

'You're lecturing me, you uptight cur? The Shrieking Masquerade caused more casualties among my warriors than that Gods-cursed Daravek you failed to kill. Zaidu is lucky I brought my grievance before Abaddon instead of killing him back on the Thylakus battlefield.'

Luck had nothing to do with it. One of the ways Abaddon promoted unity was by overseeing disputes and duels between chieftains and warlords himself, rather than letting them slaughter each other out of his sight, according to their own whims. A subtle touch, but one of the many ways in which he sought to impose laws over our chaotic way of life. If nothing else, I admired his monarchical intentions.

'Zaidu is baiting you,' I said to Lheor. 'I cannot imagine that you do not see that.'

'I see it.' Lheor sucked his saliva back through his teeth. 'I'm not blind. That Nostraman wretch, I'll pull his hearts from his chest and–'

'And if that challenge had been allowed?' I interrupted. 'Telemachon will fight in Zaidu's place. If Ezekyle had not ordered me to act, brother, you would be locking blades with the Masqued Prince this very moment instead of receiving a lecture from me.'

'I'd rather have the duel.' Lheor's left eye screwed shut as his cheek gave another wrenching spasm. Anger still rippled from him in an unpleasant breath against my sixth sense, but it was lessening now, a tide on its way out. 'The Masqued Prince,' Lheor said in a growl. 'Ha! I'd cut him to pieces.'

I stared at him for several seconds, amazed, truly amazed, that he honestly believed what he was saying.

Deluded or not – and he most certainly was if he thought he could outfight Telemachon – Lheor was calming down. That was good. That was all I needed for now. I turned back to seek Moriana, only to see her slipping free of my Rubricae, moving forwards, a dark serenity spreading through the crowd around her.

This lone, unaugmented human strode towards Abaddon, strode past mutants and monsters and warriors, and we watched her as if enspelled. Surprise was writ plain across many of my brothers' faces. Even the mutants and braying beastmen, who had been so eagerly praying for bloodshed to erupt between their masters – for there was no finer entertainment than seeing their betters bleed – fell silent.

Moriana walked to the base of Abaddon's dais, and there she stood as tall and regal as a human could amidst a horde of monsters and mutants and gene-forged warriors, the least of which still towered above her.

'Ezekyle Abaddon,' she said, her gaze lifted to his. 'May we speak?'

He stared at her, and I will never forget how he showed no surprise at her manifestation. I do not know if he knew her from before our exile to the Eye, nor if he had been expecting her, but I do know that there was no surprise in his eyes when she stood before him. Perhaps he was merely too drained to react, but I do not believe so. There was something else at work that day, perhaps the fate that our seers and prophets prattle of at such length.

'Speak,' Abaddon bade her with a ripple of the Talon.

Moriana spoke. She told my gathered brothers and sisters what she had already told me, Amurael and Telemachon on the graveyard world of the XVI Legion.

* * *

Back on Maeleum, she had claimed to be a seer. More than that, she swore she had foreseen our arrival within Horus' tomb.

Moriana had been on Maeleum for some time, drawn by its spiritual resonance and its place at the crossroads of fate. She claimed to know nothing of the downed Black Templars vessel, and her aura flickered with truth when she made that claim. She likewise knew little of those black-clad warriors herself, deflecting our irritation by insisting she had far worthier tales to tell.

We let her speak. As she did so, she led us from the crypt, back to the wreckage-strewn surface and onwards into the wilderness of the eternal rust yards. All the while she spoke of how her dreams had driven her into the Eye itself and then to Maeleum.

'I bring a warning to Abaddon of a rival to his throne by the name of Thagus Daravek. More than that, I bring word of the Imperium as it is, not the empire that you once knew.'

The possibility of deceit was foremost in our minds, yet how could we resist such lore? She answered our questions, some clearly, some with evasions.

The Imperium she spoke of was a realm unreal to us. In the centuries since we brought fire to the sky above the Imperial Palace, our names and deeds were not just consigned ever deeper into history, they were increasingly woven into mythology.

Knowledge of the rebellion – a conflict she called 'the Horus Heresy', the first time I ever heard those words spoken – was ever more guarded and sequestered. Imperial authorities twisted what had happened in the war when they acknowledged it at all, and it was far more common to suppress any facts through sanction and even execution.

Worlds deemed too tainted by the truth were declared forbidden ground, blockaded from trade and transit, struck from astrocartographic charts and severed from astropathic communion until generations had passed. Some were even cleansed of life and resettled by harvests of colonists and itinerant pilgrim populations.

Hope and ambition were no longer the currencies of mankind. In an age of spreading peace, the truth was becoming myth. The people of humanity's empire turned their devotion to soulful adherence in prayer and duty, while the Imperium's armies forgot how they had once warred upon each other and instead turned their weapons outwards, to the xenos races that had retaken their territories after the failed Great Crusade had dissolved in civil war.

I listened in absolute awe. Nothing in the mists of her aura suggested any deception. If anything, she seemed to be taking care with her words, for fear of overwhelming us or provoking incredulity. I wished for nothing more than to tear her mind apart, ransacking her memories for all she had seen and all she had felt within this new Imperium. The only thing that stopped me was simple caution – she was adamant that she must meet with Abaddon, and I knew my lord would need to meet this outlander for himself.

Moriana spoke on. Whole worlds had been reshaped, their continents given over to graveyards and necropolises, mourning not the slain on either side of our nearly forgotten war but the more recent dead of the last several hundred years: the innocent martyrs of the God-Emperor's faithful flock.

The God-Emperor.

The God-Emperor.

Language cannot convey the effect those words had

on me. I will do all I can to explain it, knowing that every explanation is wrong, for no wordcraft can truly shape an impression of what I felt the first time I heard that title.

'The God-Emperor,' Moriana said again, when Amurael asked her to repeat herself. He had stopped as if struck, his thoughts running so acidly rancid that I felt them pressing against my senses.

Telemachon had been exultant, roaring his laughter to the sky, so gripped by euphoric revelation that I thought his twin hearts might seize. If you have ever walked an asylum's halls, you know that laughter. It is something beyond mirth, beyond elation. It is a release, a dam that breaks in the back of the mind to let madness pour forth, preventing the brain from drowning in poison.

The God-Emperor. I tried to repeat Moriana's words but my mouth refused to give them shape. I was laughing myself.

Telemachon could barely breathe. The laughter sawed in and out of his faceplate's vocaliser, wheezing and wet, hacking as if he'd ruptured something in his throat. Amurael stood dumb, trying to process what he had heard. Trying and failing.

Yet Moriana was far from finished. She spoke on, telling us of the Cult of the Emperor Saviour emerging from the disorder of the rebellion's aftermath. Uprisings of this cult were commonplace on countless worlds, subsuming whole systems in this tide of new belief. The Emperor, revered as the source of the Astronomican, allowed travel between humanity's scattered worlds. The Emperor, Master of Mankind, Bane of Aliens, the one true deity.

A god.

They believed the Emperor was a god.

I knew how and why this had happened, even before she said another word. It happened as it always happens, as any scholar of their own species' history can tell you: it happened because the helpless masses were fearful, and because the powerful wanted unchallenged control. Every religion rises for the same reasons – the lower tiers of a society crave answers and comfort, needing rewards in an afterlife to justify the harshness and grimness of their lives. And to prevent uprisings in search of better existences, their rulers institute a creed that keeps the masses obedient and compliant.

Meekness, obedience, submission... These become virtues that the oppressed must embody in pursuit of a greater good or a later reward.

To stand against the prevailing belief becomes not just philosophy but heresy. Heresy worthy of execution. And so control is maintained by the strong over the weak.

'The God-Emperor,' I finally managed to say. There have been many times in my life since then that I have cursed that title or cringed at hearing it cried by His deluded followers. But that day, damn me for my naïvety, I was laughing with Telemachon. A cruel, spurned mirth, not the amusement of the victor but the bleak joy of the beaten. That laughter was a purging, like shedding an uncomfortable sheath of skin.

'Much of the Imperium already adheres to the word of the sect as gospel,' Moriana continued. 'The Temple of the Emperor Saviour has a far wider reach and deeper roots than the petty cults that flowered during your rebellion. The *Lectitio Divinitatus* was a child's bedtime candle compared to the sunlight of the beliefs now gripping the Imperium.'

All these thousands of years later, deep in what scholars

name the Dark Millennium, the Ecclesiarchy grips the whole Imperium in an inviolate hold. Moriana spoke of its rise as an inexorable ascension, only a handful of centuries before its formal, final adoption as the Imperial Creed, backbone of the Adeptus Ministorum, state religion of the Imperium of Man.

And all of it, *all of it,* founded from the very beliefs that the Emperor had sought to destroy.

Just as the Emperor had been betrayed by His sons, so too had the fool been betrayed by His own empire. Blind and rudderless without its monarch to guide it, the Imperium was devolving into superstitions and half-truths. No wonder we were already close to being myths.

'The Word Bearers won.' Telemachon was on his hands and knees in the dust, blood trickling from his unmoving silver mouth. He laughed and heaved and vomited and laughed, speaking between dragged breaths and violent convulsions. 'The Word Bearers won. They eat dirt and drink shame. They chant prayers to the unwanted truth through bloodied lips. They lost everything. And yet they still won.'

'I did not fight for the Word Bearers' vision,' Amurael snapped. 'None of us did. Our ideals were higher and worthier than the pedantics of divinity.'

He looked at me as if expecting my support. I could not give it. What ideals could I claim, truly? I had fought in the rebellion because there was no choice. The Wolves razed Prospero and stole the choice from us. I waged war upon Terra because my side was chosen for me.

'What of you?' I asked Moriana. 'You are older than your physical form. Your soul is far older than your flesh. You have lived for centuries within this new Imperium, have you not? What, then, of your beliefs?'

She stared at me, measuring me by some silent criteria. I

could tell from the flaring corona of her aura that my words had surprised her. I felt her thoughts shifting, following this new path.

'I believed the same,' she admitted. 'For many years I believed Him to be a god. I was instrumental in spreading the belief myself.'

Images, memories, swirled slowly behind her eyes. Before they could resolve, she somehow felt me looking within her skull. A wall of mist swarmed across my sixth sense. I had met no other mortal who could defend themselves with such swiftness and ease, but I'd seen enough to confirm my suspicions.

'You still believe it.'

'I know what I know,' she said. Her voice turned melancholy but ironclad in the same moment, all doubt gone. 'A god or not, His power renders Him indistinguishable from divinity.'

'This is not the kind of theosophic discussion our liege lord enjoys,' I warned her.

'No? And yet you'll take me to Abaddon whether you wish it or not, because you know he would never forgive you for leaving me here. There is more that I cannot say now. So much of what I know is only for Abaddon to hear.'

'For his ears alone?'

'For his ears first.'

'You expect us to allow that?'

She endured my doubt with a priestess' patience. 'You'll have to accept it, Khayon. Not only here and now, but in the many years to come.'

There was no unkindness in those words, yet they made my skin crawl. Telemachon was still coughing and chuckling. 'Perfect,' he was saying. 'Perfection itself.'

I had to help him to his feet. 'Medic,' he called out mockingly to Amurael as I lifted him to stand.

'I fail to see what's so amusing in all this,' said Amurael.

'The perfect jest,' Telemachon replied, a grin in his honeyed voice. 'Don't you see? We are all part of the perfect jest.'

All of this, she told Abaddon and those of us gathered on the command deck. Telemachon was speaking softly among a group of his Shrieking Masquerade warriors. Lheor was calm, stunned to silence. Amurael looked disgusted. None of us moved, none but Ultio, who turned in her amniotic sanctuary, looking down across the crowd at one warrior in particular.

'Ezekyle?' she asked. Her voice was a murmur from the mouths of a hundred brass gargoyles in the rafters. The *Vengeful Spirit* itself, prow to stern, shuddered in sympathy with her concern. She was a weapon, a beast of war, and she feared for the soul of her master.

Abaddon watched Moriana, his eyes glassy, mouth parted to show a glint of his filed, rune-etched teeth. He inclined his head, a reassurance for the ship's machine-spirit and a bid for Moriana to continue.

The prophetess spoke on. I will not relay everything she said; much of it you already know from Imperial annals, and a great deal more holds no relevance all these thousands of years later. To us, it was madness strung together in sentences. To you, it would simply be history.

Even as I relate the details now, my recitation conveys none of her moments of indecision or the halts within her speech. Moriana has never been a natural speaker. A listener, perhaps – it has been my experience that she hears everything spoken and uses it to her advantage when the time is right. But she lacks a demagogue's easy charisma or a preacher's fervent conviction, and yet we all stood rapt as she ministered to us with the unwelcome truth. The imperfections in her delivery that day only added to her sincerity. The hesitations in her cadence as she sought the right words only reinforced the importance of what she had to convey. And so we listened, drawn into the spell she wove.

One of her most compelling habits was to speak without meeting her listeners' eyes, her head tilted just so, her gaze unfocused, as though she was used to relying on senses beyond sight.

'I feel your anger,' Moriana called out to us as she neared the end. Her voice was cracked and dry. 'I see your broken battleplate and the dried blood of your wounds, and I am here to share a warning beyond the words I have already spoken. I have walked the many webs of fate. The greatest threat to your ascension rises with you now. He hears the same call to unity that you all hear. He follows the same goals, along far different paths. You know him as Thagus Daravek, the Lord of Hosts.'

It would be an exaggeration to say that every eye turned to me in that moment, but many did. The Ezekarion, privy to Abaddon's plans, along with their closest warriors – they all glanced towards me. At my side, Lheor gave a dirty, grunting chuckle at the sudden shift in attention, while I heard Telemachon's mellifluous laughter from across the chamber.

'Thagus Daravek,' Moriana repeated. 'In every future where he lives, Ezekyle Abaddon does not. In every future where he unites the Legions, the *Vengeful Spirit* burns in the void. If he leaves the Eye and steals your fate from you, then your newborn Legion dies.'

The bridge dissolved into immediate uproar. Moriana raised her hands to bid the crowd be silent, though her efforts were useless. The roars went on, adding to the percussive thunder of weapons beating against armour in militant rhythm.

I heard and felt no paucity of rage in that bellowing cry. It unnerved me in a way little else could, for it laid bare the arrogance with which we draped ourselves. We had grown so strong, so used to our own victories, that the idea of defeat had become anathema. Perhaps, just perhaps, it also resonated a little too much like fear.

I looked back to Moriana. Abaddon had descended to her side, and he lifted the Talon high, lightning snapping between its bladed claws, bringing the gathering to a swift silence. He did not need to say a word; the gesture itself was enough.

Moriana thanked him with a nod. 'Kill Thagus Daravek,' she said to him. 'Kill him and take your place beneath the gaze of the Pantheon. This is your destiny.'

That word again. How it plagues this tale.

Destiny, I sent to Amurael in irritated disgust, but Ashur-Kai overheard my psychic derision. He pulsed his disapproval to me from his raised platform above the bridge, where – as the warship's voidseer – he guided the *Vengeful Spirit* through the tortured heavens.

Do not lecture me, I sent back before he could do so. His attempts to convince me of the merits of prophecy had already failed over several centuries, and his reprimand was easy to ignore now. Prophecy. Destiny. Fate. Ah, the infinite power of hindsight. Prophets or prophetesses may speak whatever they wish, and apply it like a soothing salve over the wounds of any event – once the moment has already passed. Prophecy is unreliable at best and the embarrassing artistry of charlatans at worst.

Abaddon, silent all this time, finally spoke. He said that which I had hoped to hear, the only words that mattered.

'You speak of the Pantheon's gaze, but I will never bow to the forces that deceived Horus Lupercal.'

Moriana looked up at our lord, ferocity in her dark eyes. 'But Thagus Daravek will. And he will take your place on the paths of fate.'

I felt like spitting. Surely my brother could not be dragged in by superstition and naked manipulation.

'Ezekyle,' I said, 'must we listen to this?'

Sargon looked aghast at my interruption, as did Ashur-Kai. Both were clinging to Moriana's every word. Abaddon gestured for me to hold my tongue, though there was no anger there.

'Let her finish, Iskandar. Let's see where this leads. Thagus Daravek has been a thorn in our side for decades, prophetess, but why do you so fiercely demand his death? What does he intend to do?'

'He intends what you intend, Ezekyle Abaddon. That which calls to you also calls to him, and already he makes ready to claim it before you can. Despite all of your ambitions, you are left with a simple choice – wield the sword that you see in your dreams, or be killed by it.'

VI

EZEKARION

I know the cadence of that beating heart. I know the smell of that skin, the tang of those bionics, the scent of those consecrated weapon oils...

Inquisitor Siroca. We meet again. Welcome, dutiful agent of the Throne. Welcome to my parlour. Please forgive me for not offering you refreshment; the warded chains that steal my sixth sense and bind me to this pillar have savaged my ability to play the kindly host.

I feel your gaze upon my eyeless face as keenly as these hexagrammic restraints that sear my flesh. You have come for answers, no doubt, but to which questions?

No. Say nothing. Let there be no pretence between us. I know where you have been and what brings you back before me now. Your scrabbling, delving efforts into your order's deepest archives have dredged up mention of Moriana, just as I warned you they would.

You are beginning to believe me, are you not? You are beginning to believe the words of an arch-heretic.

Moriana is one of those names that slither through the veins of history. Is it the same woman? Can it be true? Can it be that one of the founders of your sacred Inquisition is the very creature that whispered prophetic poison into my brother's ear? Can it be that the inceptor of your precious ideals chose later in her unnaturally long life to abandon them? Was she a warrior-handmaiden of the Emperor who saw the light, or an archaeoscientific vizier in one of His laboratories who looked too long into the dark? Both? Neither?

Someone before you has been seeking truth in the shadows. Where did you find this lore, Inquisitor Siroca? In whose archives were these words hidden? Your master's perhaps. The man or woman that taught you and trained you, the merciless predecessor that fashioned you into the weapon of Imperial law I sense before me now.

Very well. Keep your silence. I will speak on.

We made ready for war in the wake of the prophetess' words. The fleet mustered. We left garrisons at our grandest fortresses and arranged the barest-bones patrols on the edges of our domain, but the heart of our sanctuary nebula played home to almost every able vessel in our armada, from the vastest battleship to the sleekest frigate to the bulkiest troop-conveyor.

The Ezekarion oversaw this great gathering, while Abaddon – in a move that shocked all of us – sealed himself away in seclusion with Moriana.

The officers' perspectives on this were divided. Ashur-Kai was captivated by the new seer, aching to speak with her, his scarlet albino gaze shining with a hunger no different to that of a starving man suddenly presented with a feast. He craved her insight and wanted nothing more than to follow the paths of fate at her side, learning all that she knew, seeing all that she had seen.

'Ezekyle has sealed himself away from his sworn inner circle,' I argued with Ashur-Kai at one point, as we stood upon the *Vengeful Spirit*'s bridge atop his navigation platform above the rest of the command deck. 'How does that not trouble you?'

'He has questions,' my former master replied. 'She brings answers.'

'He has never exiled himself away from us before.'

'This is beginning to sound like the tantrum of an ignored child,' Ashur-Kai replied, his tone mild. But I would not be dissuaded by mockery, no matter how gentle or well intentioned.

'Think of his degeneration these last years. Think of the voices in the warp that sing his name, practically praying to him. And now this? Do not mistake my caution for cowardice.'

He turned his white features to me, and I knew from the starved look in his retinal-red eyes that I was arguing in futility.

'She has brought the answers our lord sought. The only good is knowledge, Sekhandur. The only evil is ignorance.'

'That is a saying uttered by as many fools as visionaries,' I pointed out, 'and an attitude that has led to damnation more than once. The last man to speak those words in my presence doomed our Legion.'

Boy, Tokugra psychically cawed at me from its master's shoulder. *Boy is frightened.*

Hush, crow, lest I feed you to my lynx. Nagual would enjoy that.

'You should not be afraid,' Ashur-Kai continued as if his

familiar had spoken true. 'See her arrival for what it is – an opportunity like no other.'

'I do not trust her,' I said, which were words I would say innumerable times across the centuries to come.

'Then don't trust her,' Ashur-Kai said as he turned back to the oculus, his long white hair falling to half mask his features. 'But don't waste the chance to learn from her.'

He had every reason to be ill-tempered and distracted given his role in the war to come. He was the armada's most gifted voidseer, tasked with coordinating and aligning the efforts of every sorcerer in the fleet for the attempt to break out of the Eye's pull. To even brush against his mind was to feel a dense web of overlapping murmurs that threatened to drag me inside, adding my presence to the processes of what must be calculated and the variables that must be considered. We were asking our voidseers to sail near blind and deaf through a realm where physical law had no grip, and to maintain the fleet's formation while doing so. In all the years of the Nine Legions' exile, nothing on this scale had yet been attempted. We were certain to lose several ships, and braced to lose most of them.

'Ezekyle will summon us when he wishes us to attend him,' Ashur-Kai insisted. He met my eyes with his watery albino gaze. Fascination for all that Moriana represented still burned there, no matter how distracted he was by the coming trial.

I touched my fingertips to my heart in that old Cthonian gesture that had crept its way through the Legion – the gesture of one speaking the truth. 'Sometimes I wish I had your faith, master.' The old honorific, just this once. It made him smile before he turned away and resumed his work.

Among my other contemporaries, between their faith,

patience or indifference, none of the Ezekarion shared my preference for caution. Telemachon reacted to Moriana's favour with Abaddon much as I had suspected he would. His behaviour was nothing but parasitically loyal, to the point that he even stationed several of his Raptors outside Abaddon's palatial quarters, ostensibly standing guard with Falkus' Aphotic Blade. It was a gesture rather than a necessity, but – as ever – it was a cunning and valuable one. Moriana took note of it on her emergence, just as she noted those among the Ezekarion that showed less in the way of trust.

We risked much as the fleet mustered. We lost territory that was left inadequately defended, surrendering it to the other Legions rather than put up doomed resistance. The heartlands of our dominion remained as heavily patrolled as we could manage, but we paid in lost worlds at the frontiers. To our rivals and indeed many of our allies, we practically vanished from the Eye, concerned only with amassing our strength in secret.

Around the *Vengeful Spirit*, a fleet gathered of such size that even jaded veterans often stopped to stare at the host of warships at anchor in the murky void. Valicar, once guardian of Niobia Halo and now master of the fleet, was in constant contact from aboard his battleship, the *Thane*. His trust in Abaddon was absolute; he exloaded a stream of updates to the flagship with calculated efficiency, oversaw the muster in Abaddon's absence and never once demanded to speak with our liege lord.

We made ready for the war we had wanted to wage for centuries, yet I could not overcome my hesitation over the true reasons we would be fighting it. 'The sword,' Moriana had said, with such perfect assurance. 'You have a choice,

Ezekyle Abaddon. Wield the sword that you see in your dreams, or be killed by it.'

None of us knew, not then, what the sword was. Abaddon had told us nothing before retreating into seclusion, except that we were to make the final preparations to leave the Eye. Moriana's words were all the more unsettling for the way she knew that which we did not.

That sword. By the Shifting Many, how much of what we have done has its roots in the wielding of Abaddon's sword? Oceans of Imperial blood have run beneath that blade's edge. Rivers of our own have flowed because of it. We fought a crusade to claim it. We have spent an eternity slaughtering those that would take it for themselves.

In Cthonian, the blade is called *Usargh,* or 'Oblivion'. In Nagrakali, the blunt mongrel tongue of Lheor's former Legion, it is *Skaravaur,* or 'Crownrender'. In Tizcan Prosperine, the language of the city of my birth, it is *Mal-Atar-Sei,* 'the Shard of Madness'. To Nefertari's people it is *Sorathair,* 'the Thorn in Reality', a name spoken only as the blackest curse. These are all imperfect translations of the weapon's true name, for the blade was forged in no mortal realm, nor was it fashioned by mortal hands.

In the wordless, soul-borne language of the warp's winds, within the eternal howling of the daemonic choirs, echoes the name *Drach'nyen.* This is no word as the human mind would understand it, for it is not an utterance but a concept. Within the eternal song of howling, weeping madness is the fate-spun promise of the Emperor's death, of His Imperium carved clean of ignorance and false faith.

That chorus, that concept roared into daemonic essence, is Drach'nyen. This is what our languages try and fail to distil into spoken words. Usargh, Skaravaur, Mal-Atar-Sei...

They are all aspects of the same thing: Drach'nyen, the End of Empires, a creature with its genesis in the warp-threaded conviction that it exists only to kill humanity's king.

That which you call Chaos, or the Ruinous Powers; that which we call the Pantheon – this essence, this energy, does not obey us. It is not an entity unilaterally supporting us, or a reliable weapon that serves our needs. It uses us. It elevates us, for the purposes of its own whims. It is a force of honesty, true, making us wear our sins on our armoured skin, but it is also the essence of absolute deception, shifting and warping whatever it wishes to pursue its own conflicting ends. It is the crashing, clashing energies of every memory, emotion and agony felt by every human since the dawn of time, with the same suffering of countless alien species flavouring the resultant matter.

It can be used, but only if you are willing to be used in turn. It can be worshipped and begged, but only if you are willing to risk damnation along with ascension. It is a force flowing through the veins of reality, one that chooses us and marks us as its puppets as well as its champions. That cannot be stated enough.

It is not *on our side*. Many of us spend our lives fighting it and resisting it far more often than beseeching it.

Abaddon's blade is one such aspect. As I hang here, chained and bound in the tender care of your Inquisition, though I crave to be back with my brothers and doing the Warmaster's work, there is one comfort in my captivity: it is a blessed relief to be this far from Drach'nyen.

I can still hear it whisper at the edge of my mind even with my powers stripped from me. But I can no longer hear it laughing. No longer does it seep into the core of my being, a distraction and an infection, a daemon only content when it is rending reality apart and leaving formless Chaos in its wake.

It is said that the weapon is only a sword at all because Ezekyle wills it to take that shape. I can tell you this is true. It is not a sword. It is scarcely even a daemon. It is said among the Legions that this was the Gods' first gift to win Abaddon to their cause. If so, it was by no means their last.

But I do not believe it was the first. No, that dubious honour belongs to another. Drach'nyen was the second of the Pantheon's treacherous bribes. I have no doubt that the first was far more insidious, no less bloodthirsty and calls herself Moriana.

Abaddon maintained his self-exile for weeks, taking counsel alone with his new prophetess. When at last he emerged, he summoned us to Lupercal's Court. Every one of the Ezekarion answered this call, even Ashur-Kai and Valicar, who were both reluctant to leave their duties in the hands of their lieutenants for any time at all.

I answered that summons with a sense of purpose I had not felt in some time. Ezekyle had promised me answers upon my return from Maeleum, and one way or another, I would have them. That included enlightenment regarding this sword that Moriana insisted Abaddon was fated to claim. No more whispers of what may or may not be. It was time for answers. I would tolerate no refusal.

The Ezekarion assembled in Lupercal's Court. Here, where the failed Warmaster of the Imperium had gathered his lackeys and minions, Abaddon instead gathered his brothers and sisters. We stood beneath banners of Imperial conquest long since rendered meaningless by our betrayals, and in this great chamber where galactic civil war was first planned, we took a quieter counsel amongst the cobwebs. Horus had listened to cheers in here, with half of the Imperium chanting his name. We listened to the squealing of rats and the wet feasting sounds of things that had mutated far from their verminous origins. Whatever they were, they and the rats they had evolved from kept to the shadows.

Sanguinius was there. Noble Sanguinius, Primarch of the Blood Angels Legion, was there in all his glory, and I saw Sargon hesitate upon entering. He considered the primarch's manifestation an omen, and likely a bad one.

Sanguinius was formed of psychically resonant crystal, as were all of the echoes of those slain aboard the *Vengeful Spirit* throughout its long history. Corridors and hallways across the ship were rimed with these outgrowths, and they formed most frequently after battle or tumultuous journeys through the Eye. I had become accustomed to them – they had been the very first things we had seen when we initially came aboard the *Vengeful Spirit* in our hunt for Abaddon. They were mindless statues of hazy crystal, easy to dismiss unless one were foolish enough to touch them. They 'sang' when touched, psychically offering numbed images and sensations of their deaths in last, useless gasps of a soul's energy. The phenomenon had briefly fascinated me, but I soon relegated it as beneath notice.

Sanguinius had died aboard the *Vengeful Spirit,* and here his ghost remained, as the warp-saturated steel of the ship's hull resurrected the primarch along with the other fallen. This was not the first time I had seen Sanguinius' crystalline shade. I had shattered it once, intrigued by the potency of the crystal shards, and one of them served now as the smooth pommel jewel of my force sword, Sacramentum.

The crystal primarch always regrew, sometimes here, sometimes elsewhere, just as the other crystal corpses across the ship always regenerated after shattering.

Ashur-Kai bowed his head as he passed the kneeling angel, paying respect to the agony etched upon that perfect face of stained diamond. Most of the others ignored it, save for Lheor who gave a pained grin at the sight. He idly swung his chainaxe as he passed, the weapon's teeth briefly roaring, biting and breaking one of the immense wings from the body.

I felt a twinge of psychic expression from the crystal ghost, a stab of false pain from the psy-crystals.

'Another glorious victory,' I chided my brother. He turned the grin on me, moving to my side. There was no real amusement in his eyes.

The first surprise was that Ilyaster joined the gathering, his desiccated visage and patchy remnants of hair rendering him skullish and without humour. His sunken gaze drifted across those of us that had already gathered, and he nodded with a formality he would soon learn was unnecessary in this company.

'I am Ezekarion,' he said in his desert-tomb voice.

None of us argued. He was welcomed with nods and a few fists banging against breastplates. He too halted at the sight of the now one-winged crystal incarnation of a dead primarch, kneeling in torment beneath the banners of old wars. He processed what he was seeing, but rather than mutilate the thing he simply walked around it, just as absorbed in the history hanging from the gothic rafters.

These meetings of the Legion's commanders were the most visible efforts to bring order from disorder. We would speak of supply lines, resources, materiel, formations, crew numbers, targets, duties... In short, we would behave as if we were an organised fighting force, not a disparate conclave of warband leaders bound together in a realm that defied physics and military logistics. Every warrior would speak their piece, citing their relevant contributions. Abaddon, in turn, would hold court in relative silence. He knew the value of letting his subcommanders exercise their authority and – as with any army – feed on their various rivalries. Officers were driven not just to excel before Abaddon and earn his sparse praise, but to exceed the deeds and usefulness of their kindred's warbands, impressing the Ezekarion and putting themselves in the running to serve the Legion's highest commanders.

Abaddon was cautious with his compliments, but one truth was always in evidence: those who quelled internal rivalry within their warbands, either by charisma, murder, or ritual challenges – those who could be *trusted* to fight reliably and not abandon battle plans at the whim of their own blood-greed or to heed the calls of the Gods – these were, without fail, the warriors who were most often rewarded. To them fell the positions of honour and glory within every assault, and the Ezekarion leaned most heavily upon them to secure victory. They became the backbone of the Black Legion.

War-frothing raiders and treacherous mercenaries have their uses in any conflict, do not doubt, but Abaddon has always willed the Black Legion to be more than another gathering of howling slavers and psalm-chanting reavers. As common as those aspects are within our ranks, we do not let ourselves be defined by them. No true organisation would be possible if we did.

None of us were surprised when Moriana entered. The

only unexpected element in her appearance was that she wasn't at Abaddon's side. She didn't make anything of her entrance, merely walking through the great double doors and taking her place near to Telemachon, who stood with calculated insouciance. She greeted him with a hand briefly on his vambrace, the gesture somehow sisterly. Their heads bowed together in murmured conversation. She smiled as she spoke, and his aura flared in response, a greasy brightening of bitter amusement.

We stood in a loose circle, gathered but separate, as was our informal custom. Falkus, the First. Sargon, the Second. I, the Third. Telemachon, the Fourth. Lheor, the Fifth. Ashur-Kai, the Sixth. Ceraxia, the Seventh. Valicar, the Eighth. Vortigern, the Ninth. Amurael, the Tenth. Ilyaster, the Eleventh. And Moriana, though she had said nothing of it, evidently the Twelfth.

Ezekyle was last of all, stalking with slow, grinding growls of his Terminator battleplate. At gatherings of our warbands, he would always take the focal point of attention, drawing all eyes towards him and calling out across the gathered masses. Here, among his trusted kin, he merely joined the circle we had formed.

Once more I was struck by how unconscionably weary he was. If we had expected his time alone with Moriana and her serpent-tongued prophecies to illuminate and revitalise him, we were both right and wrong. Ferocity blazed in his eyes, the ferocity of reborn purpose, but it was the effort of a man on the very brink of ruin. Whatever had rejuvenated him, be it knowledge or something more sinister, it was also eating him alive.

'The fleet will sail for the Eye's edge,' he ordered. 'We will declare war on the Imperium and the corpse that occupies its throne. If Sigismund's Black Templars stand in our way, we will break them. If Thagus Daravek opposes us, we will destroy him. If any of you have questions, now is the time.'

So casually did he state his galaxy-changing intent that several of us smiled, myself included. But as expected, all eyes turned to me, so certain that I would be the first to speak. This time, however, it was Ashur-Kai.

'We are prepared, Ezekyle. Every void-guide and sorcerer aboard every vessel in the armada is ready to weather the storm.'

I could see the weight he bore on his shoulders, and for a moment I felt a stab of sympathy. He fought a war I could not help with, one far harder than the games we assassins played. He had to lead the Legion from unreality into reality, breaking us free of a prison the Gods themselves kept closed.

'You have my trust and faith,' Abaddon replied solemnly.

'My thanks, brother,' Ashur-Kai said, inclining his head.

Abaddon looked around the circle. 'Who else?'

They all looked to me again, but I did not speak second, either. That fell to Amurael.

'We sail for the Imperium,' he said. 'An event we have all fought and bled to bring about is finally here, and every warrior in the fleet stands ready. Outside this ship, a Legion's worth of warships await our signal to sail. But I'm asking you, brother to brother, why are we declaring war on the Imperium now?'

Ezekyle looked across the circle at him, golden eyes locked. 'This is what we have hungered for,' he replied. 'This is what we have worked towards. You ask why we will declare the war now? Because we can, brother. Because, finally, we can.'

'That isn't what I'm asking. Do we wage this war by your command?' Amurael indicated Moriana with a cursory wave of one hand. 'Or on her whim?'

'This war is a matter of *vindicta*,' Abaddon replied, using the High Gothic word for vengeance, knowing its resonance among our kind. 'It has always been about revenge, Amurael. *Our* revenge. Moriana's appearance is merely a fortunate twist of fate. We would sail with or without her. You know this, brother.'

Amurael nodded, though not at once. The hesitation was telling even if I had been unable to read the surface thoughts drifting through his aura – he trusted Abaddon, but Moriana was an outside agent, and she stank of manipulation more than measured guidance.

Moriana, for her part, said nothing. That was wise, for Amurael's sentiments were shared by most of us there that day. We accepted her, or at least tolerated her, but we did not know her.

'Does it matter?' asked Vortigern. His face was severe, his expressions forever cold. In all my life, I have met no soul as serious as Vortigern of Caliban. 'I will fight by your side either way,' he said to Abaddon, hand resting on the hilt of his sheathed sword. 'Whatever this human's motivations may be, they are irrelevant to us. Our plans remain unchanged, do they not?'

Lheor nodded, the movement a brief jerk of the head. Even back then, he was beginning to lose control of his body, his nervous system at the mercy of the adrenal pain-engine in his skull. 'Matters to me,' he grunted. 'Tell us what the witch said, Ezekyle. No secrets here, eh?'

Abaddon nodded. 'No secrets here,' he agreed. 'And answers will come. Armsmistress, you have remained silent thus far. I would hear your thoughts if you would share them.'

Ceraxia towered above us, looking down from within the shadows of her hooded robe. I could just make out the softly rotating eye-lenses in that shrouded gloom, and the dark metal polish of her resculpted form. Her segmented, scorpion-like legs hissed and clicked with adjustments of minute pistons. Each of her lower limbs ended in a great blade that left scratching dents in the deck. This four-armed, spider-legged machine-goddess drew forth from her robe the Black Templar's helm that I had recovered from Maeleum, and though it would have undoubtedly made a more emphatic point if she dropped it onto the deck, such was her reverence for its manufacture that she kept it clutched in two of her hands, close to her red-robed form. Not a trophy to her, but a holy icon.

'I care naught for the poems of seers,' she said, emitting her words from a vocaliser formed by her fused, clenched golden teeth. A pale light flickered through this metallic fusion with every syllable. 'Or warriors' reasoning for revenge. The fleet is ready, so the fleet shall sail. We have evidence of further wonders developed by the Martian Mechanicum in our absence from the Principal Materium. Examples of such treasures must be brought into our possession, unmade, remade and knowledge of their form and function secured for our own use.'

I cut through this with a chop of my hand. 'With respect, Ceraxia... Ezekyle, tell us what we came to learn. Tell us what devours you, and what this seer means when she speaks of fate riding upon the blade of an unclaimed sword.'

'It's always you, Khayon,' he said with a weary smile. 'My assassin, and my accuser.'

'I am what you need me to be, brother.'

He met my eyes, nodded once in acknowledgement, and then, at last, he told us.

VII

VINDICTA

I will not relate every word that passed between the Ezekarion in that meeting. So much of it you already know, and the rest you have surely inferred.

Suffice to say that we spoke of the warp's whispers and their weight against his mind, and we spoke of the creature that cried out within those etheric tides, the creature that called itself Drach'nyen. That monstrous and deceitful entity's existence has its place in the tale to come, but it was not, in truth, the focus of our gathering.

Primarily, we spoke of the coming war and the reasons it would be waged. It has ever been thus, even in the Ancient World, when mankind was bound to the surface of Terra and battles were fought with spears and shields and riding beasts and warships of wood. Warlords have always considered the notion of a *casus belli,* the reason for committing to war. This was no mere raid we planned to harass the Imperium's frontiers. This was to be a clarion call, summoning allies and warning foes.

This was to be the declaration of the Long War.

And here, my Inquisitorial gaolers, we must speak of scale.

There are those among the Legions, and scribes of what few Imperial texts are permitted to exist, that suggest the entire crusade was fought purely so Abaddon could claim his blade. This is brazen falsehood. Hundreds of thousands of legionaries would spill from the opening Eye, with millions of mutants, humans and daemons in a tidal horde behind them. Most of them knew nothing of Drach'nyen then, and most know nothing of it now. They have their own lives to live, as pathetic and stunted as those existences may be.

That false coin comes with another side, of course. There are those that believe we wished to surge forth and take Terra in the first breath of the war. Ignorance of this staggering scale is the rawest, rankest madness.

The road to Terra is the most fortified, impossible series of battles imaginable. Wars are not fought in one engagement, but piecemeal: campaign after campaign, city by city, fleet by fleet, world by world. Even if we could bring our wrath to Terra in a single strike, what use would it be? The rest of the Imperium would remain unconquered, and would descend on Terra to cut our throats while we celebrated our temporary triumph.

Horus Lupercal had half of the Imperium's forces, and he still failed to take the Throneworld, deluded creature that he was. We have a fraction of a fraction of those galaxy-spanning warhosts. Horus began with – and lost with – more than we could ever muster. As the Imperium reeled in the wake of the rebellion, so did we. As it has struggled to recover all these millennia later, so have we.

For all of the ways in which the Legions are stronger than we once were – with our daemon-engines and Neverborn allies and the myriad gifts of our spiteful Gods – there are twice as many ways in which we are weaker. Supply lines no longer exist, leaving our guns starved of shells and our warships hoarding diminished supplies of energy and resources. Few warbands can lay claim to the materiel of a Mechanicum cruiser or a forge world within the Eye, and those that can must fight endlessly to protect it from rivals. Slaves die or lose their minds to the warp as easily as they breathe. Whole fleets scatter to the warp's winds, for Eye-space is far less stable than the material realm. Battleships die of thirst, fuel-dry and crippled in the dark void, to be forgotten or swallowed as part of a macro-agglomeration space hulk.

Warbands fight amongst themselves over ammunition, territory, plunder, even clean water. Champions that aspire to replace their warlord masters fight duels or sink to betrayal in order to rise above their former stations. There is no true agriculture in the Eye, no harvest worlds supplying sustenance necessities; whole worlds and fleets survive on the flesh and bones of the unburied dead, or the warp-stained roots of alien plants, or the corpulent bodies of mutant livestock. Commanders and warband leaders, even of the same Legions, wage war against one another over matters of pride or power, or to win the all-too-brief favour and dangerous blessings of the erratic Gods.

Worst of all, recruitment for the Nine Legions is a matter of hellish difficulty. We lack anything like the reliable resources we once had to sustain ourselves and maintain our genetic lines. I could not even begin to estimate the number of 'bastard' legionaries born after the Heresy, forged with gene-seed raided from Space Marine Chapters loyal to the Golden Throne.

And all of this is before the long and difficult journey to actually escape the clutches of the Eye, which is, as I have stressed, our prison and our punishment for failure as much as our haven. The Eye's edges are where the storm rages hardest. Ships seeking to leave are torn apart in those reaping tides. Do you not think we tried? There is no swifter way to lose warships than by hurling them towards the Great Eye's edge.

Perhaps I paint an ugly picture with all these truths. We are so much stronger than we were, yet so much weaker. We have such zealous purity of purpose, weighed down by impoverishment, treachery and desperation.

I will not lie, not even here, for deceit would be useless. The Black Legion's history carries its share of shame and bitterness as well as the glories we clutch with such pride. Some Imperial scholars cannot imagine why we have not yet won. Others cannot see anything but defeat in our future. There is no clear truth. It is all smoke and mirrors, all illusion and confusion.

Of that fateful night when Abaddon revealed the source of the dreams that dragged at his consciousness, it is not the gathering of the Ezekarion that stands out to me. It is what came after, when our nameless Legion's warlords returned to their warships, and I alone remained at Abaddon's side. Even Moriana was dismissed. After their shared seclusion, Abaddon seemed to have no further use for her. At least, not for a time.

'Khayon,' he said, as the others left, 'when was the last time we sparred?'

It had been a great while. Years, in truth. My place was

often away from the Ezekarion, and away from the ashen dead I ostensibly commanded. My place was wherever Ezekyle pointed on a hazy, shifting star map and said he required someone dead.

We duelled, our swords live, power fields crashing and spitting each time the blades met. Lupercal's Court was our arena, and we fought for hours beneath the dusty weight of Horus' failed rebellion.

Ezekyle is a barbarian. A slayer. In battle he is a warrior without peer, but his strength is in the force of his presence, the relentless viciousness of his assault. To meet him on the battlefield is to know, without doubt, that your life will end if you stand and face him. He does not fight, he merely kills. That is not to say he is unskilled. His talents are supreme, his focus inhuman, his speed supernatural. He is a force of murderous nature, his weapons never still, his eyes ever aware, alert to every shift and tension of muscle in his foe.

In ages past he would have been called a battle-king, one of those ancient Bronze Epoch monarchs that fought in the front lines and inspired his men in the chaos of the shield wall, rather than a ruler directing a war from afar, or only fighting in tediously honourable single combat.

Outside of battle's heat, no matter how he trains, he lacks the depths of brutality and viciousness that make him so formidable in true war. He is perfectly capable of duelling with a sword in training bouts, but it has never been his gift. Any one of the Ezekarion could, at their best, match him blade on blade. Telemachon and Vortigern could defeat him with relative ease.

We fought alone, our armour illuminated in the flicker-flashes of aggravated power fields. The banners above us flashed as if in a lightning storm, the breaths of displaced air from our colliding blades setting them gently waving in the false breeze.

It is strange to think back to how he was then, before the Pantheon showered him with blessing after blessing. When he was just Ezekyle, my brother and my sworn lord, not Warmaster Abaddon, Chosen of the Gods. In time, I would scarcely be able to stand near him, forever bathed as he was in a rippling, replenishing saturation of soul-matter, with the warp itself forming a choir heralding his every move. He could not growl without even his closest warriors edging away, nor nod without thousands of daemons shrieking in acclamation.

But not yet. I could see the silhouettes of unborn daemons seeking birth through his aura, feeding on his hatreds, and I could see the way the warp focused upon him as though he were a nexus, but such things happen to many souls of significance inside the Eye. I did not know then that I was witnessing a mere fraction of his future majesty.

As we duelled, two other presences joined us. The first was Nefertari, whom I sensed watching us from where she sat among the arching rafters. She should not have been here, but beyond a curl of Abaddon's lip as he too sensed the alien, he gave no further reaction. The second was Nagual, who melted out of the shadows and watched the fight with burning white eyes.

Master, he greeted me. I could do little more than pulse back brief acknowledgement. Sweat rimed my face. My vision danced with smears of afterlight, blurring with the lightning cracks of the two meeting blades.

'Nagual,' Abaddon greeted my lynx, his breathing ragged with the effort of our battle. The lynx yawned in answer.

You should not be here, Nagual, I sent.

The Cold Huntress is here.

Abaddon sensed my distraction and thrust low; I barely weaved aside, hammering the flat of my blade against his, deflecting it at the last moment.

She is, I admitted. *But Nefertari at least has the presence of mind to stay out of sight.*

Abaddon fought with the Talon held back and low the whole time, knowing it had no place in a spar, knowing also that coming too close to the weapon savaged my psychic sense with its bloodied resonance. As much as I had adapted to weather the pressure of its closeness over the years, if I narrowed my eyes I could still see the mist of death-echoes that surrounded its curving claws. That haze of psychic potency attracted countless unformed daemon-things; these too I could see if I focused. They prayed to the weapon. They whispered lovingly to it, an inhuman murmur of praise for all that it was capable of doing in changing the paths of the future. They sang their shrieking, howling songs in gratitude for all that it had done in writing the pathways of the past. In so many ways, as fascinating and disgusting as it was, the Talon was a taste of what would come when Abaddon claimed Drach'nyen.

Despite my distractions, I was winning. Having to keep the Talon back and low affected his balance, even though his Terminator war-plate enhanced his physicality far beyond mine. I had to hold Sacramentum in two hands, for it was the only way to meet the heavy blows powered by his bulky armour.

'Moriana,' he said, when our blades rasped apart, both swords raining sparks across the deck. 'You don't trust her.'

'I do not trust any seer,' I pointed out.

'No?' He backed away, his blade rising *en garde*. 'You trust Ashur-Kai.'

That was debatable. I certainly had no faith in his prophecies, for I had no faith in any prophecy, but I refused to be drawn into that discussion. I knew why he had detained me here, and it had nothing to do with Moriana.

'You should have killed Daravek,' he said in the face of my silence.

Ah, yes. Here it was. Punishment at last.

I had never deluded myself into hoping that the trivial task of journeying to Maeleum to examine telemetry fluctuation might serve as my only chastisement. Returning with evidence of the Black Templars' existence, and even bringing Moriana into our coven, was never going to earn forgiveness for my other failures.

I wondered, very briefly, if he was going to kill me. For a couple of heartbeats, when our blades whined and crashed, it seemed plausible. Would he do it, if Moriana had told him it was necessary to secure her nebulous future? I did not know.

And did I lean a little more strength into my blows when he reminded me that Daravek still lived? Perhaps. Perhaps I did. I said nothing, though. There was nothing to say. I would not deny my failure, nor make excuses for it.

'A target you cannot kill, Khayon.' He was defending with more ragged deflections, unable to match my speed. 'Is this fated to become a frequent occurrence? Do I need a new assassin? Should I send one of the others when next I need someone slain? Telemachon?'

My jaw ached with my clenched teeth. From far above I heard Nefertari's soft laugh. The next three blows that rained against Abaddon's blade sprayed flare sparks into both of our faces. Still I said nothing.

'You heard how Moriana speaks of Daravek,' Abaddon continued, grunting the words now, his own temper rising in mirror of mine. 'Whispers of destined threat and obstacles of fate.'

'Her words are meaningless.' I lashed back with an overhead cut, two-handed and descending. He took it flush on the blade; I heard the servos in his shoulder and elbow snarl at the pressure of holding me back.

Abaddon laughed as I disengaged, though he blocked the following blows as well, hurling me back each time with a toothy smile.

'I have wanted Daravek dead for decades, Iskandar. Yet still he lives. I have set my precious weapon against his throat five times, and yet still he draws breath.'

I am not without pride. No warrior is. I could accept my failure and bear the shame, but his mockery boiled my blood. I met the anger in his eyes with my own. Our blows were beginning to feel less like the strikes of a spar. They swung harder; they landed heavier. The Talon flashed at Abaddon's side, twitching. His voice was rising.

'Daravek unites dozens of warbands against us,' Abaddon pressed. 'He deadlocks our fleets. He laughs at us, pissing on what we're trying to build. And *still* he lives. Why is that?'

He was giving up ground, backing away slowly, parrying and deflecting without fighting back. I had him now. I could read the hesitancies in his movements that spoke of an inability to keep pace. Yet he laughed all the while, an angry and baiting laugh, meeting my eyes to share his bleak amusement at my failure. He was sincere. That was what ground my teeth together and stole the words from my tongue. This was no jest, no mockery for the sake of spite. He was sincere. Laughing at me, yet furious.

Moriana's promises of Daravek's ascension had added graver consequences to my inability to carry out Abaddon's orders.

The Talon crashed Sacramentum aside and Abaddon dropped his blade in the same smooth motion, pounding his free hand against my throat, wrapping around and lifting me with hydraulic growls of Terminator joints. My boots left the deck. I could not draw breath, and though a legionary can survive many minutes without oxygen, as I looked into Abaddon's wrath-rich eyes, I doubted it would be asphyxiation that killed me.

'Is it you that is broken?' The words were a beast's rumbling growl. Saliva bow-stringed between his teeth.

Master... Nagual sent from nearby. I did not move. To move would be to provoke Abaddon's rage, furthering its downward spiral. I knew these rages, and I knew they were earned more often than not.

Stay back.

But master...

Stay back, Nagual.

A breath of wind and a silken purr of alien technology heralded Nefertari's descent. Abaddon spoke to the shadows, though his eyes never left mine.

'Alien. Beast. If either of you take a single step closer, this turns from punishment to execution.'

The ceramite of his gauntlet closed tighter around my throat. My spine clicked and crackled. My jawbone pulsed with pain in time to my twin hearts.

'You are broken, Khayon.'

Abaddon dropped me. My boots thudded to the deck. 'Broken,' he continued, 'but not irrevocably.'

I drew a slow breath through my constricted throat,

watching him closely. My voice would not come. *Broken?* I asked, mind to mind.

'You no longer hate, Khayon. You have come to accept this exile inside the Eye. You no longer seethe with the need to revenge yourself on the Imperium for the wrongs done to us. You say you no longer dream of Wolves, and you shine with pride over it, as though it were a failing at last overcome.'

Abaddon shook his head, his golden eyes glittering with unspoken insights. 'Hate is valuable. It made you a killer. Hatred sustains us. Hatred is all we have. *Vindicta,* my brother. Vengeance. Our fuel. Our sustenance. Where is your passion to prosecute this war? Where is your need to see the Wolves of Fenris bleed for what they've done to you? For the life they stole from you? Where is your rage at the Emperor for censuring your Legion and forbidding the very gifts that set the Thousand Sons apart?'

I knew rage at Horus Lupercal, for deceiving the Wolves into destroying my home world. Rage at the Wolves themselves for their frothing, idiotic zeal and their ignorant beliefs. Rage at Magnus the Red, for offering us up on the altar of his martyrdom and failing to defend Tizca at our side.

But anger at the Emperor? One may as well hate the sun or the laws of physics. I said this to Abaddon, who shocked me by laughing.

'Look at the mastery you and your sorcerous brethren hold over the warp now. You are no longer Librarians questing blindly in the dark. You face the dangers, meeting them with open eyes. You are aware of the predators that swim in this infinite murk. Was the Emperor right to order you to remain ignorant?'

I could not answer that last question. In my hypocritical heart, I feared to give a response. The more I learned of the warp, the more the Emperor's mandate made sense. I could not pass the opportunity for power now, not when those around me showed no such restraint, but I could see why the Emperor had commanded us to do so.

The more familiar I became with the realm behind the veil, the more I mourned that the Thousand Sons, in our blind arrogance, had believed we knew everything worth knowing. We had stared at the sky and believed we knew everything of the stars. We had looked at the ocean's calm surface and believed there was nothing deeper beneath.

Abaddon saw my hesitation. He smiled without surprise.

'Do you see?' he asked me. 'Do you see what you've become? Moriana brings word of a weapon we might use, and rather than peer into the warp for ways to master it, you doubt that it can be wielded at all. Rather than devote yourself to slaughtering the one foe you failed to kill, you slink around the flagship – accusing, hesitating, holding back.'

He slammed a palm down on my shoulder, a brotherly grip, his golden eyes boring into mine. 'Rediscover your hate, Khayon. It began to fade when you hunted Daravek that first time, and it has depleted in increments ever since. I need you. My brother. My *blade*. Reforge yourself, for if we accept the Eye as our domain, we have already lost. It makes us nothing but broken weapons. This is a prison and a lair to lick our wounds. Not our home. Not our fate.'

I nodded, for agreement was the only reaction I could offer. I have torn souls open before, reading mind and memory, peeling back the layers of personality and flaying a man's essence to rifle through the heart of his being. Such torment left the victims of my interrogations nothing more than fractured husks. Abaddon's words had threatened to unmake me in the same way, so precise were his insights.

'It will be as you say, brother,' I said.

Abaddon lifted his hand from my armour. 'We stand on the edge of returning to the Imperium we built with our own sweat and sacrifice. Thagus Daravek will come for us before the end. I need him dead, Iskandar. No more excuses. I need him dead.'

I knew he asked the impossible of me, and may I be damned for lying to my brother, but I nodded my avowal. I agreed to do something I was sure I could not.

He turned and left me there, in that museum of futile wars. And with Moriana's destiny-soaked venom turned to honey in Abaddon's ears, we sailed for the edge of the Great Eye.

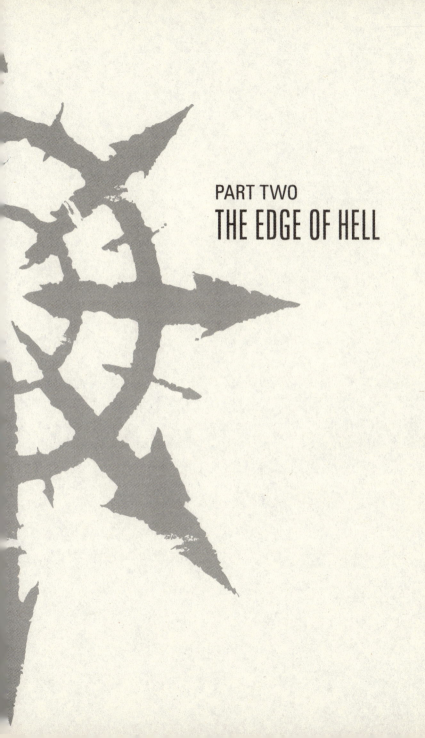

PART TWO
THE EDGE OF HELL

'...the ferrymen demanded we pay the price of freedom we paid as everyone must pay in coin of flesh of soul of blood of life we paid we gambled our future but it must be this way sacrifices must matter don't you see a sacrifice is only true if it drains the giver and nourishes the taker so we gave and the ferrymen took and we were lessened and they were enriched...'

> – from 'The Infinity Canticle', sequestered by the holy order of His Imperial Majesty's Inquisition as an *Ultima*-grade moral threat. Purported to be the unedited, raving confession of Sargon Eregesh, Lord-Prelate of the Black Legion.

VIII

OUTRUNNING THE STORM

The first ship to die was the *Inviolate*. It was a Terran-born destroyer, one of the oldest vessels in our fleet, and one of the most reliable. It had sailed the skies in the very earliest years of the Great Crusade, and though it was originally sworn to the VII Legion, the Sons of Horus had wrested it from its Imperial Fists masters during the Siege of Terra. Its current captain, the former Sons of Horus Reaver Chieftain Xerekan Kovis, was a calm and calculating officer with a gift for void battle. The *Inviolate* itself was a beautiful vessel, a spear-point cutter of a warship, swift and lethal.

It exploded after eleven minutes and nine seconds of red-lining instruments and warning klaxons, the stress upon its hull too much to bear. I watched it happen. I listened to the final calls of its command crew, laced with interference across the fleet-wide vox. The *Inviolate* buckled off course, falling out of alignment with the fleet, tumbling into the seething tides of fiery warp energy that thrashed and boiled around our armada. I saw it enveloped in those dissolving waves, its shields bursting as it plunged into them. I saw the ship's hull first crumple, crushed by the grip of impossible pressures, then come apart, pulled open as though it were nothing more than a child's toy.

I felt the *Inviolate*'s sorcerer-pilot's final thoughts: the split-second desperation of *Wait... Wait!...* that he unintentionally breathed into the burning night. I felt no fear from him; perhaps he believed he could still maintain control in that flash-fire second before he was bathed in the cascading energies of unreality. Whatever the truth, the mundanity of the sentiment was a breed of madness in its own right – the refusal of consciousness to realise its end has come. Rarely do we sound so human, but death, perhaps, is the great equaliser.

'The *Inviolate* has fallen,' Ultio called out across the bridge. Her voice betrayed her distraction as she faced forwards, floating in her immense life-support tank. Her crown of cognitive interface tendrils swayed in the fluid between the young woman and the hive of gestalt-brain engines fixed to the chamber's ceiling above her.

Her eyes were narrowed to slits, her teeth clenched, her outreaching hands curled into claws of effort. She wore an expression she had never worn in life, a rictus of such inhuman ferocity that it momentarily drew my eyes away from the oculus. Blood was beginning to stain the fluid close to her body, curling into the *aqua-vitriolo* in misty, sanguine threads from cuts appearing across her flesh. Around her, around all of us, the bridge was a red-stained place of fear-scent and thunder.

Abaddon clutched the handrail at the edge of his raised dais, his golden gaze locked to the storm kaleidoscoping outside the ship. The *Vengeful Spirit* juddered in its entirety;

we heard its central spinal stanchions growl, then whine, in the storm's grip. At the bridge's heart, the Anamnesis cried out in sympathetic pain.

The din of the vox rivalled the tempest tearing us apart. The voices of every captain in the fleet cried out in disordered unity, reporting their progress and roaring of stress fractures, of failing shields, of shipboard fires and uncountable deaths. I could hear space around us, the void itself, shrieking with the outpouring of souls dragged from dying bodies. Our fleet was populating the warp with the spirits of our slain.

We led the way. The *Vengeful Spirit* took the brunt of the tempest's tide, a wavebreaker vanguard that ploughed through the roughest thrashings of energy, shattering them to carve a route through for the smaller ships. New trails of blood inked the amniotic fluid from a fresh latticework of wounds across Ultio's body. She suffered as the ship suffered.

The *Promise of Absolution* was a jagged silhouette off our port bow, another of the forward battleships spearing ahead to take the worst of the boiling tides. One moment it was there, shaking and streaming fire from its battlemented hull; the next it was a lacerated hulk, killed too swiftly to even detonate. Torn-apart sections of the ship tumbled away into the warp's devouring essence. It was as if the entire ship had crumbled as part of an avalanche. We did not even hear any change in their final communications: one moment the captain was there, the next his voice was no longer present in the vox-web.

Delvarus was next to me, his boots magnetically locked to the deck, his gauntleted hands holding to the same crew rail as mine. He was Secondborn – the melange of daemonic entity and human soul – and as ever in his presence I felt the war taking place inside him, the eternal shifting turmoil between possessor and possessed. His eyes were blackened orbs in his dark flesh, curdled over with etheric cataracts, and though the warp had rendered him blind it had suffused his other senses with sensitivity beyond measure.

When the *Promise of Absolution* died, his face twitched as if in pain, though I knew it was far more likely hunger.

'Was that the *Absolution?*' His voice was a raised snarl. I could feel the need within him, the feverish desire to adopt what he and his brethren called 'the warshape', letting the daemon threaded through his flesh ascend to the fore in the hour of bloodshed. He fought the instinct, just as he fought the bite of the Butcher's Nails in his brain.

It was, I sent back, telepathy far more reliable than shouting amidst so many other voices. He twitched again, this time in true pain at his cranial implants reacting to the unwanted touch of my silent voice.

'There were almost two thousand warriors on that ship,' he said between clenched teeth. He didn't mention the tens of thousands of slaves, serfs, thralls and servitors, but even noting the loss of our brethren was a sentiment I had never expected from Delvarus, of all men. He said more, but the *Vengeful Spirit* kicked around us as it pounded through another devastating wave, casting the deck into flickering darkness for several seconds and intensifying the warning sirens.

Ultio screamed again, her voice razoring from the shouting mouths of a hundred gargoyles and fallen angels. The ship cried out with her, from its ram to its roaring engines, its superstructure groaning with torment.

As that dual cry rang through our minds, I looked up to

Ashur-Kai. He stood on his navigational platform above the bridge, eyes wide, long hair like a banner in the grip of a storm's wind. He was braced as we were all braced, though he saw none of us. His sight was tuned to the realm outside the ship, and his hands on the twin control columns sent impulses and commands to Ultio and to the *Vengeful Spirit* itself. I'd never seen Ashur-Kai and the Anamnesis move in such perfect synchronicity, their motions mirrored, each lean and tilt and adjustment coming in the very same second for both sorcerer and living machine-spirit.

Even their injuries were in symphony. The psy-stigmata that decorated Ultio's flesh showed across Ashur-Kai's face in the same constellations of ripping pain; three of those slashes torn open to the bone. Only when the ship crashed through the most forceful tides did they fall out of alignment, and Ashur-Kai's pale features would strain with the effort of finding that slipped harmony once more. The *Vengeful Spirit* was Ultio's ship; thanks to the Mechanicum's ingenuity, she was far more aware and attuned to her vessel than most machine-spirits could ever be, but it was Ashur-Kai, her void-guide, who saw the way through the storm.

If there was a way through this one.

I... do not believe there is. Evidently he had heard my careless thoughts.

The next ship to die was one of the nameless bulk cruisers that carried clans of beastmen warriors and warp-changed human slave soldiers. Its death lit the oculus as it veered wildly off course, rolling into the acidic tides either side of the turbulent channel we were carving, and a migraine crack of light flared sun-bright for half a heartbeat. A fraction of a moment later, it was gone. All that remained were the echoes of its captain's screams over the vox-web.

Three of Ultio's vox-gargoyles toppled from the gothic rafters and shattered into marble rubble across the deck. Another, one of the bronze sculptures with its features twisted in ecstatic agony, crashed onto one of the crew consoles with the sound of a great bell tolling, killing two humans and crippling a third.

I made my way to Abaddon, forced to move as a drunkard might across the shaking bridge and staggering over the corpses of the storm-slain. I gripped his shoulder guard, forcing him to face me. His face was his father's face, red-lit by the emergency illumination, flashing with the colours of madness that danced outside the dying ship.

We will not survive this, I sent directly into his mind. *The* Spirit *cannot endure this punishment.*

'We must break through,' he spat back through his filed teeth. 'We *will* break through.' And then, with the ever-surprising force of his own will, he spoke right into my mind. *I will not die in this prison, Iskandar. I will be free. We will all be free. We will bring our fury to the Golden Throne itself, and the husk enshrined there will weep with the homecoming of His abandoned angels.*

I met his eyes for what felt like an eternity, though I know it cannot have been more than a brief moment. Blood of the Pantheon, but he looked like his father then. The creature before me was Horus in body and blood. The only difference was the eyes. Horus had been hollowed-through by the powers he had sought and failed to control; Abaddon was drained by forever resisting them. The father had been but a host for the strength of others. The son was a bastion of his own will and endurance. I saw then, truly and for the very first time, just what value my lord could be to the creatures we call Gods.

What do you see, Iskandar?

I snapped back to the reality of our flagship burning, shattering around us.

What?

Outside the ship. Do you see their hands at work?

Abaddon knew none of my internal revelations. He wanted me to spread my senses beyond the warship's hull. Were we being held here? Was this hurricane the whim of the malevolent consciousnesses that acted through the galactic wound we called the Eye?

I cast my perceptions wide, breaking through the walls of the *Vengeful Spirit,* plunging into the firestorm of warp energy. I felt the cataclysm of forces at work, the shoving rage of our engines generating an equal pushback in the Eye's resistant tides. I saw our armada drifting apart, unable to hold cohesion in the chaos. I saw daemons, a billion daemons, a trillion daemons riding and leaping and melting out of the warp-matter to burst – laughing, howling, clawing – against our warships' hulls.

ISKANDAR.

I opened my eyes to my lord's face once more. Sparks sprayed elsewhere across the command deck. I could smell burning fur and sizzling blood. Beastmen cawed and croaked and brayed and bellowed and died. So many of them were dying.

'Stop the ship,' I said, and though there was no hope of hearing me over the thunder, Abaddon read my lips.

Is it them? he sent into my mind, fierce as a lance through the skull. I tensed and sought to back away from him, but he held me in place. The truth was that I did not know. Was this a move by the Gods in their Great Game? No one can know such things with certainty. But I know what I sensed outside the ship.

It is us, I sent back. *As we push, the storm pushes back. We push harder, it answers with thunder and acid and pain. Stop the ship. Stop the fleet.*

Abaddon released me and turned to the oculus once more. Fury, absolute in its intensity, blackened his features.

'The fleet...' Ultio began, and she needed to say no more. The oculus finished her thought, showing the shapes of our armada shrinking, falling behind, several more shaking beyond tolerance and beginning to shatter, others engulfed with wrapping shrouds of warp energy.

The *Vengeful Spirit* gave its most savage heave yet, throwing half of the command crew to the deck. Several crew stations detonated through their links to suffering pressure points elsewhere aboard the ship.

'The *Blood Knight*,' Ultio called out, and her voice became a messy merging of warship names as they fell out of formation in grotesque and swift disorder. 'The *White Sigil*, the *Hammer of Sarthas*, the *Halo of Blades*, the–'

Abaddon screamed. It was a wordless cry of raw emotion, the roar of a thwarted king without the power to protect his crumbling kingdom. Rage laced that cry, as one would surely expect, but there was also frustration – frustration that others could not provide what he needed of them, and vexation that his plans were being swept aside by the hands of pathetic, accursed Gods at this latest of hours.

'All stop!'

Every warrior and crew member not actively engaged in keeping the ship held together turned to him. Ashur-Kai was down on one knee now, teeth bared into an invisible gale, his skin lacerated with a thousand cuts that wept tiny trickles of blood.

'I... can get us through...' he wheezed across the vox. His

lungs sounded full of fluid, most likely blood. The warp was cutting him to pieces along with the ship.

'All stop!' Abaddon roared a second time.

'Lord... I can...'

Abaddon ignored him, his blazing gaze locked on the Anamnesis in her suspension tank. His voice was inaudible over the crashing, shaking bridge. All I saw was his mouth moving.

'Ultio. Signal the fleet. All stop, all stop.'

The protesting, failing ship was riven by new thunder as the engines banked and the retros bawled into life. The shaking, that heaving wrench of abused iron, slowly began to abate. I watched the oculus' compound-eye view of the ships in our armada as they slowed in our wake. The ravaging warp tides eased around them.

It took time to slow down, for our thrusters to bring everything into balance and for the warp's angry tides to finally settle. A warship is never silent, nor even truly quiet. Plasma reactors kilometres away send their living murmurs through every inch of metal. Crew speak, curse, breathe, shift. Power armour hums as it idles and snarls when its wearers move. The *Vengeful Spirit*'s command deck was louder than most, with the size of its crew and the Anamnesis' life-support tank with all its ticking, clicking ancillary cognition-machines.

The fleet clustered around us, drawing in close the way a pack of beasts approaches its alpha with their throats showing in submission. Abaddon watched them drifting into formation, saying nothing. I could sense the swift cycle of his thoughts but could discern none of their meaning.

'All stop,' Ultio called after what felt like an age. I looked across the bridge, at the wounded and the dead, at the smoky aftermath of our failure. We had failed. We were trapped.

Ashur-Kai descended from his platform, boots thudding on the gantry stairs, and knelt before Abaddon. He looked destroyed by his futile efforts, his eyes closed, blood scabbing across the host of psy-stigmata lacerations that covered his face and throat.

'I tried, Ezekyle.' Blood spattered to the deck by Abaddon's boots, spilled from Ashur-Kai's cut tongue. The warp had wounded him even there. 'I tried.'

There had been times before this – and there would be more to come – when Abaddon punished failure by execution. Sometimes, I must admit, these acts were delivered out of unrestrained anger, but more often as acts of calculated and precise mercilessness. To set examples. To establish boundaries. To spread fear, as all tyrants and warlords and kings have done, since time began and the first men and women ruled their brothers and sisters.

But he is not without forgiveness. He knows when a defeat was unavoidable. That distant day, as our armada sat becalmed in the seas of madness, he barely even looked down at Ashur-Kai before resting a hand on the other warrior's pauldron and lifting the sorcerer to his feet.

'You cannot fight fate, brother. But you did well to try.'

That choice of words rekindled life in the sorcerer's red eyes. Shame, yes, but life as well – something dangerously close to hope. 'Is that what you believe this was?' he asked Abaddon. 'Fate?'

It was Moriana, an insignificant wraith at Abaddon's side, who drew my eye. I felt my irritation rise with the way she stood in Abaddon's shadow, where she alone seemed unbroken. Defeat settled across the rest of us like a cloak;

Ashur-Kai and the Anamnesis were riven by warp-stigmata, and bodies of mutants lay across the bridge, yet she was the lone soul showing no unease at our continued imprisonment. She looked almost vindicated, as if this outcome had been a suspicion of hers since we brought her aboard all those weeks before, and here it finally stood confirmed.

'Greatness requires sacrifice.' She looked between those of us gathered there, one by one, until her gaze finally settled on Ashur-Kai. 'It always requires sacrifice. It is the way of all life. I tried to tell you this, Ezekyle.'

He shrugged her off, evidently not as in thrall to her words as we had feared. She drew breath to press her point.

'When the time comes, you cannot run from what must be done. Sacrifices must always be made.'

'Be silent,' I warned her. 'Look around you, prophetess. See the fraying tempers and defeated hearts of those nearby. Now is not the time to weave smug and mystical allusions to the preciousness of hindsight.'

Telemachon laughed softly behind his mask, though more in derision at my annoyance than agreement with it. Lheor gave Moriana a disgusted glance before jerking his chin towards Abaddon.

'So now what?' he asked.

The question hung in the air between us. No one had an answer.

In the long-ago Age of Sail, when vessels of wood and cloth rode the oceans of Terra at the mercy of weather and wind, there were fewer fates worse than being becalmed. Vessels without the breath of wind in their sails were doomed to drift in the ocean, too far from land for oars to be any salvation. That is the situation we found ourselves in. We were becalmed. To go forwards was to die, while to go back was to abandon all hope of a future. If we could not revenge ourselves upon the Imperium, why then did we band together in this new brotherhood? Why did we still draw breath?

Perhaps you think us stubborn. Perhaps you believe we should have turned away and sailed back from whence we came, back to those daemon-world fortresses and those savage blood-raids against our brethren. Perhaps it truly seems that simple to you. But then, it would. You have never been free. Freedom, once tasted, cannot be so easily forgotten. Life in the Eye was an existence of hellish, endless battle in the underworld. It has always been our prison and our crucible as much as our sanctuary.

Yet there we sat, motionless in the warp-touched void. There on the very edge of the Eye, we took stock of our losses. Seven warships lost with all hands. Five times that number damaged, some grievously. Thousands of legionaries gone, to say nothing of the mortal and mutant crews, or the priceless arsenals of wargear, gunships and battle tanks also fallen away into oblivion.

In that long-ago era, before we had conceived of the Crimson Path, before Abaddon wearied of Cadia and wiped it from existence like excrement from his boot, the only reliable route out of the Great Eye was the so-called Cadian Gate. There, reality cut a deep gouge into Eyespace and soothed the seething tides. Yet a route out of the Eye is useless if it cannot even be reached in the first place.

The worst aspect was that none of us had an answer to Lheor's question. None of us knew what we could do to free the fleet from this etheric stalemate.

The answer, when it came, was delivered in the form of destruction.

* * *

I sensed nothing of the first asteroid. It was too swift for our storm-compromised auspex scanners to track. We only became aware of it when the troop barge *Scarred Crown* blared warning cries across the fleet-wide vox-web, and by then it was already too late to do anything. The *Scarred Crown* was already dying, its diminished wreckage rolling and tumbling through space. The asteroid that had slain it had shattered in the impact – I watched a spread of huge rocks, each one streaming fire like a comet's tail, scattering into the misty void of Eyespace.

Ultio closed her eyes, pressing a hand to her temple. 'I...'

She got no further. Another asteroid speared through the fleet, this time killing the *Oath of Knives* with a heart strike, bursting the cruiser's void shields and driving through its core, triggering a terminal unleashing of plasma that instantly annihilated the entire superstructure.

Ultio turned in her blood-streaked fluid tank, hands tensing once more into claws. 'Translation signatures,' she called out. And then, with her eyes widening, 'Brace, brace.'

The engines fired, the ship's manoeuvring thrusters igniting along its starboard side. Every single soul aboard the *Vengeful Spirit* was thrown to the deck as the ship moved from all stop into a hard banking, rolling turn, the vessel protesting at the pressures put upon its hull.

The third asteroid still hit us. All power failed in the wake of that world-shaking crash; it took several seconds to reactivate, during which time we existed in a shaking, thrashing realm of absolute blackness.

When the illumination globes flared back to life, they cast their light over Ultio in her suspension chamber, psy-stigmatic bruises blackening the flesh of her back and shoulders. Blood trailed from her left eye, threading into the amniotic fluid.

'Relighting voids,' she mouthed as her gargoyles declared the words aloud. The ship stabilised, slowing in its roll. 'Relighting voids. Seeking. Seeking.'

On the oculus, views of Eyespace clicked through magnification filters as the Anamnesis followed the asteroids' trajectories back to their origins.

At first I thought we were witnessing our armada's shadow cast across the swirling mists of Eyespace. I realised my error when I saw the vessels moving, and more warships penetrating the haze following behind them.

'Shield failure,' Ultio called out. 'I am unable to rekindle the voids.'

Abaddon watched from his central dais, eyes gleaming with vicious captivation. 'Ultio, signal the fleet to form a defensive sphere. All warships are to protect the supply runners and troop barges. Run out the guns. All hands, prepare for battle.'

'Another projectile,' she warned.

'Destroy it.'

She tried, but she was wounded from the storm and too few of the *Vengeful Spirit*'s weapons were ready to fire. No matter how swiftly her gestalt mind operated, the calculations for void battle at such insane ranges required time and precision. We had the luxury of neither.

Torpedoes sluiced from their chambers, silently cutting the misty darkness of space. Several impacted on the surface of the inbound hunk of planetary rock but most went wide, running harmlessly onwards.

The frigate *Skies of Wrath* was already moving, rolling aside from the path of its oncoming doom. The asteroid hurtled past, illuminating the ship's voids as it came within sparking distance of the vessel's belly.

Around me, the command deck had broken into a miasma of activity. Crew shouted and raced between stations. Legionaries demanded answers. Machinery thrummed and clanked. But I was watching the oculus, ignoring the jostles I received from standing in the way.

I watched the last asteroid spinning away into space after missing the *Skies of Wrath*. They were more than mere dead rock. They echoed with familiar whispers, familiar cries, as though the asteroids were alive – or had once been.

The other fleet approached from the storm, sailing far calmer tides than those we had endured. Whatever forces had oppressed us offered no such resistance to these newcomers. They lingered at the very edge of our firing solutions, at a distance not only invisible to the naked eye but requiring intensive calculation to even lock weapons.

Only their weaponised meteors could reach us. More of them streamed through our spreading formations, but with our ships moving, there was no chance of striking at such a range with unguided projectiles. Only our own complacency and poor luck had allowed the deaths of the *Scarred Crown* and *Oath of Knives*.

One of the lead battleships ignited with a procession of successive lights along its backbone. Not damage, but a harnessing and release of energy. Another meteor burst forth from beneath the vessel's hull.

'They're using mass drivers,' I said.

Ilyaster, pale and parched as ever, stared at the oculus with his sunken gaze. Wearing our Legion's black only highlighted his emaciation and cadaverous pallor. He spared me a rheumy, unhealthy glance that still blazed with life.

'But why?' he asked.

I had no idea. 'They are not even aiming,' I replied.

The next asteroid speared past us, parting the misty matter of Eyespace. I felt it again, that murmur of familiar voices.

Ceraxia stalked closer to me, her bladed legs clank-clank-clanking on the deck. The dim light of battle stations cast her hooded features into absolute blackness. All I could see of her face was the faintest glint off the edge of one eye-lens.

'You sense something,' she accused me.

'Those asteroids. They sound like... They *feel* like...'

Like Maeleum. The same whispers I had heard on that dead world. The same choruses of ghosts.

'Blood of the Gods,' I swore, turning and ascending Abaddon's dais. He was watching another fusillade of vast rocks slash past us. 'Ezekyle. Those asteroids.'

'Their mass drivers won't hit us at this range. Not now we're ready for them.'

I waved his reassurance aside. 'Those aren't just void rocks. They've shattered the grave world. They're throwing Maeleum at us.'

Abaddon spat a curse. 'Thagus Daravek.'

I could only agree. Leaving our dominion behind had meant sailing far from the reach of our astropathic relays and telemetry beacons. The forces we had left to garrison our territory were pulled tight to the most critical regions, with skeleton fleets and warhosts around our primary fortresses, leaving the rest of our domain at the risk of invasion. We knew this was a risk. We accepted it as necessary.

And thus, we had no conception of what was transpiring in our absence. For all of our suspicions that Daravek might pursue us, we had no way of knowing what form that pursuit would take.

Now we did. Daravek had levelled Maeleum from orbit, and was hurling the planet's bones after us.

'As insults go,' Abaddon admitted through clenched teeth, 'I almost admire the bastard.' He called up to the Anamnesis in her containment chamber. 'Ultio, can we kill that fleet?'

She had already processed a multitude of estimates and probabilities. 'Yes,' she replied, watching the motionless armada that faced us. 'Casualties will be catastrophic on both sides but... Yes. We can kill them.'

Abaddon stared at the oculus, the same calculations firing behind his narrowed eyes. 'Daravek can't intend to fight here.' He spoke of the storm's instability around us, but also, I suspect, the fact that our fleets were so evenly matched. Forcing the issue here would be definitive, but practically suicidal.

'They have nothing that can match the *Spirit*,' Telemachon urged as he appeared at Abaddon's side. 'We should fight.'

'And if they cripple half of our fleet while we're beating them?' I countered. 'You ate that Templar's brain, the same as I did. You know what lies beyond the Eye's borders. We cannot afford to limp our way out of here with the real battle yet to come.'

The decision was stolen from us when the Anamnesis laughed, the sound resonating in tinny majesty from her damaged vox-gargoyles. She twisted in her blood-streaked fluid, her laughter bitter and dark. A moment later, voices rose from the crew consoles responsible for the vox-array.

'They are hailing us,' Ultio called out over one of the

human officers saying the same thing. 'Daravek wishes to meet on neutral ground.'

Abaddon added his laughter to the tempest of amusement already taking hold of the bridge. 'And what terms does he offer for this truce?'

The communications officer in his tattered finery replied, still holding one hand to his earpiece. 'You and him, Lord Abaddon. Each may bring ten warriors. You may choose the neutral ground upon which to meet.'

Ezekyle was still chuckling. 'Tell him I do not need ten warriors. Inform him that I will bring three.'

'Yes, Lord Abaddon.'

Abaddon turned amused eyes back to me. 'Is something amiss, Khayon?'

'Three warriors?' I asked. My disapproving tone spoke for me.

'I am Lord of the Black Legion,' he said, and it was the first time I ever heard him speak those words, naming us as our enemies named us. 'No one dictates terms to me. Let the coward bring his ten for protection. I will bring three, and we will smile throughout his tawdry truce.'

He bared his filed teeth in the ugliest of grins. 'And if the chance arises, Khayon, I want you to kill him.'

A GARDEN OF BONES

There were no worlds nearby to use as neutral ground. At least, none that we could reach from where we were becalmed in the heart of the storm. It was Nefertari who gifted us with an idea. She came to us, with Ashur-Kai at her side. They approached the rest of the Ezekarion as we stood around the stellar-cartography hololith presenting its unreliable imagery of the flux of nearby Eyespace.

Ashur-Kai spoke first, his voice softer since he had sustained the host of psychic stigmata wounds that had healed scabbily across his features. From his discomfited movements and the ripples of pain radiating from his thoughts, he was wounded within his armour, not just on his face. Injuries of psy-stigmata and war affliction are wounds to the soul as much as to the mind and body. They are notoriously agonising, enough to drive unaugmented humans far beyond reason. Worse still, I suspected that the lacerations to his flesh were mirrored on his muscles and internal organs. He was fortunate to still be alive.

'The alien,' he said with his typical distant politeness, 'has an idea.'

'Taial'shara,' she said. And she gestured at the hololith, to a patch of shifting Eyespace devoid of planet or moon or sun.

'Tulshery?' Lheor grunted. He had never deemed it necessary to learn any of the eldar tongues. 'There's nothing there.'

'Taial'shara,' Telemachon corrected him, murmuring with no small reverence.

Nefertari closed her eyes for a moment – an eldar gesture of agreement and trust – at Telemachon's perfect pronunciation. 'It was slain in the exodus begun with the birth of She Who Thirsts,' the eldar continued. 'You need somewhere to meet your foes? There lies Craftworld Taial'shara, its bones cold in the tainted night. Use its grave for your neutral ground.'

Abaddon spoke through a fanged smile. The idea seemed to appeal to him. 'Can we reach it, Ashur-Kai?'

'I believe so, lord.'

And so it was decided.

Abaddon was true to his word, taking only three warriors. Arguably the three most calculated to challenge Daravek's temper.

We arrived first, at Abaddon's choice. Around us rose the shattered arches and broken domes of wraithbone architecture, absent of the usual psychic thrumming that teased the senses in the presence of the alien material. As Nefertari had promised, Taial'shara was dead. Even daemons left it alone. Every shred of nourishment had been sucked clean from its husk, down to the plaintive whispers of its ghosts. All was cold. All was silent.

Have you ever walked through the deep-void palaces and spires of an eldar craftworld? They defy easy imagining. Each craftworld is an artificial city, born through alien ingenuity and pushed out to sail the dark heavens like a life raft. They are constructed of psychically resonant wraithbone and shielded against the touch of space. Domes are given over to habitation, others to inhuman hydroponics and agricultural cultivation, others to the eldar's many temples of war.

Every craftworld is home to a different eldar culture, each realm its own unique jewel in the night. Taial'shara, like so many others, did not escape the death of the species in time. As it fled the birth of the Youngest God, it was torn open and swept clean of life, trapped forever within the grip of the Great Eye.

After securing the landing area, we gathered together to wait in the shadow of our gunship. Its black hull showed the golden Eye of Horus set in the heart of the Eightfold Path; a reminder of our origins in rebellion, set now amidst the pathways of the future.

Abaddon came to me as I crouched by the edge of what had once been a reflecting pool, doubtless where the eldar of this botanical garden once meditated. I tossed a broken chunk of wraithbone into the dry, empty pond where only the ashes of plants remained. The hank of curved bone disturbed a smoky cloud of grey powder.

'Brother?' he asked me. His good mood was holding. If there is one thing Ezekyle has always loved, it is a challenge. He lives to test himself against worthy foes.

'All is well,' I assured him, rising to my feet. I cast my gaze across the shattered dome's landscape. If I let my senses drift and my eyes unfocus, I could see wraithly after-images of the alien jungle realm that had once thrived here. 'I was merely thinking.'

'Thinking of what?'

I gestured to the wraithbone ruins. 'This place. The serenity here. The silence. It tempts me.'

'I'll never understand your fascination with the eldar,' he said, thudding a hand against my back-mounted power pack in fraternal warmth.

'There is no mystery to it,' I said sincerely. 'They are a warning of what happens when the Pantheon controls a species, as opposed to a species showing caution in its dealings with the divine.'

Little did I know as I spoke those words just how familiar Taial'shara would become to me in time.

I was preaching to the choir, of course. His smile told me that.

Daravek and his cohort arrived in the fat-bellied mass of a Sykri-pattern Stormbird gunship, eclipsing our sleeker Thunderhawk. Death Guard symbols marked its scored hull, and its turrets tracked us in a display of tedious, unnecessary aggression. We remained still, and if unsurprised disappointment at needless posturing could be weaponised, I believe Abaddon's sigh would have slaughtered the Stormbird there and then, dragging it out of the air.

He alone seemed at ease. Ilyaster and Telemachon, as dispassionate as they could be, betrayed their tension in their stances. For my part, I could not look away from the descending gunship, feeling the dread gaze of its cannons, suspecting Daravek would simply end the truce by taking this chance to eradicate us. I could shield us with a barrier of telekinetic force, but a kine shield would avail us little if the craftworld crumbled around us.

The Stormbird's landing claws crunched onto the wraithbone platform. The gang-ramp slammed down, disgorging the eleven warriors we had been expecting.

They came in a clash of colours – every one of the Nine Legions was represented, even the Sons of Horus. I sensed Abaddon's amusement sour to annoyance at the sight of that warrior, though he let nothing show on his face. The bitterness was fleeting; it seemed little could dampen his mood of righteous confidence.

Daravek led them. Each was a warlord in his own right, but Thagus Daravek held their allegiance, either by willing oath or the servitude of thraldom. He strode forwards, boots sending cracks through the wraithbone floor.

The Gods hate us all – I have told you this – but they craved Thagus Daravek's attention. The warp murmured in the air around him, ripe with the spirits of disease and creatures of mutable fate, all of them chittering promises of golden futures and life eternal into their master's aura.

He furled his wings tight to his body. Those mutated pinions were surely too weak to lift him skywards in all his rot-crusted Terminator regalia. The metallic spines that thrust from his skin and bone alike were sheened with blood as thick and dark as unrefined promethium oil.

He stood opposite Abaddon, the two of them ten metres apart. On the ground between the warlords was a shattered pictograph of coloured glass, its original artistry long since destroyed, its meaning long since lost.

I confess, there was something kingly about Daravek that day. Abaddon looked as he always looked: a lord of war, a leader of men, a warchief. He was one of us, and first among equals. Daravek was something more, something that held itself above the warriors he led. In the Eye, where thoughts become reality, one could almost see the chains of submission from the legionaries' throats, bound to Daravek's clawed hands. I wondered what hold he had over their souls, whether it was a lord's mastery or something deeper.

'First Captain Abaddon of the Sons of Horus,' Daravek greeted my brother.

Abaddon replied with a warm, sincere laugh at his rival's choice of words. 'Thagus Daravek, Lord of Hosts. We meet at last.'

'It is a change,' Daravek allowed, 'to face you, rather than your useless assassin.'

'You would have faced me long before now if you would cease fleeing before my armies each time I come to kill you.'

Daravek made a show of his bleeding gums, which may or may not have been a smile. 'I see Khayon at your side now, making this our seventh meeting. Is that not so, Iskandar?'

'Sixth,' I corrected him.

He gurgled his amusement. 'No, assassin. It is the seventh. And the Masqued Prince is here as well? I'm honoured, Telemachon Lyras.'

Telemachon inclined his head in a respectful bow, but said nothing. Daravek turned to the last of our ambassadorial party.

'And, of course, I recognise my beloved brother Ilyaster.' He had been too canny to let anger discolour his voice so far, but poison seeped into his tone as he faced Ilyaster. 'How do you fare, traitor?'

The former Death Guard performed a shallower bow than Telemachon, the joints of his blackened war-plate snarling. 'I am well,' he said with a gaunt and vague smile. 'Thank you for asking. Forgive me, but I did not bring your ceremonial scythe, lord. It was melted down to make piss-pots for my slaves.'

To my shame, I had to force myself not to show any amusement, for I knew this to be true.

Daravek licked his decaying teeth. 'You did not deserve to wear the haloed skull, Ilyaster. I hope you wept as you tore the symbols of your true Legion from your armour.'

'From shame and shadow recast,' Ilyaster said, rekindling Abaddon's smile. 'In black and gold reborn.'

Daravek snorted. 'Let me introduce my warriors,' he said with undeniable condescension. He swept his hand across the gathered legionaries, but Abaddon interrupted him with a grinding scrape of the Talon's claws closing and opening.

'There's no need,' Abaddon replied, 'for I do not care what names your slaves bear. You wished to meet and speak, Daravek. We have met. Now speak.'

The Death Guard lord bristled, and one of his warriors stepped forwards, breaking their uneven ranks. He wore the mismatching green, black and red of the Sons of Horus' Reaver clans.

'I am no slave,' he spat at Abaddon. 'I wear my Legion's colours with pride, renegade.'

Abaddon's eyes never left Daravek. 'One of your dogs is whining, Thagus. I thought you had a better leash on their behaviour.'

Daravek ordered the warrior back into the ranks with a curt gesture. The Sons of Horus legionary reluctantly obeyed.

'Do you wish to observe the formalities before we negotiate?' Thagus asked. He spoke of the traditional duel between champions that many warbands enjoyed before a battle or before attempts at diplomacy. When warriors gather, there will always be such contests. Reputation is everything to us. In the Nine Legions, there is no more valuable currency than renown. When I sailed alone, I usually allowed Nefertari to do the honours. A great many mutants and warriors had fallen to her alien blades.

I had expected Abaddon to laugh at the idea, but he nodded once, his lip curling. 'By all means. Who will step forwards from the gathering of heroes that cower in your shadow?'

Daravek's champion stepped forwards at once. I knew him – Ulrech Ansontyn was one of the Lord of Hosts' more renowned warband leaders, and even before the rebellion against the Emperor, he was known as a gifted bladesman in the IV Legion. The light of the choked stars glinted from his filthy ceramite, as though proximity to Daravek had allowed the warlord's Gods-given blessings to spread. His visor was a slit of red, gleaming from within.

Ulrech drew a plain, durable power sword, the same metallic hue as his armour plating. He saluted Telemachon with a sweep of the blade, and his voice emerged through the portcullis faceplate of his crested Mark III helm.

'Long have I wished to face the Masqued Prince.'

The other warriors murmured amongst themselves. This promised to be a duel for the ages; even Ilyaster's yellowed eyes were lit with a fever that spoke of dark excitement.

Telemachon stepped forwards, as was expected of Abaddon's champion. No deadlier fighter existed within the Black Legion. He was already drawing his blades when Abaddon lifted the Talon, halting his advance.

'I have no need to waste my finest warrior's time,' he said with vicious reasonableness. 'Telemachon, stay back, please. Khayon?'

I believe I actually blinked in surprise. 'My brother?'

Abaddon aimed the Talon at the towering form of Ulrech Ansontyn. 'Kill him.'

I hesitated, and that triggered guttural laughter from the warriors opposing us. Telemachon murmured beneath his breath, some unknown sound of displeasure. He wanted this fight. I was inclined to let him take it, but my lord had spoken.

'As you wish,' I replied with far more confidence than I felt.

'No sorcery,' Daravek called out with a bladed grin. 'This is a matter for swords to settle.'

Abaddon gave a lazy gesture of agreement, and in doing so, I was sure he had killed me.

I stepped forwards, drawing Sacramentum, letting its silver length turn violet beneath the storm's tainted light. When I returned Ulrech's salute, he remained silent.

Daravek spoke as the two of us drew close. 'Ansontyn has killed thirty-one warriors in single combat. How many have you slain in these duels, assassin?'

'Three,' I replied. This caused fresh laughter from the ranks at Daravek's side.

Ulrech held his blade at the ready. The claws of unformed daemons caressed across his armour plating, where brass icons of skulled faces stared cold and eyeless. Spirits of pain ringed his own skull in a crown of bleak light. His voice was a peal of thunder.

'I dedicate your death to the God of Blood and Battle.'

I had thought he might say that.

He did not wait to see if I had a similar benediction; he attacked at once, his sword flaring to life and cutting the air with the waspish buzz of its power field. Sacramentum snapped to life with a much smoother purr, a testament to the artisanship of its creation.

Most champions, like Nefertari and Telemachon, are consummately talented in single combat. They are duellists as much as warriors – often more so – devoting their lives and souls to the pursuit of perfection in the art of fighting a single foe. I had expected the first exchanges of my duel with Ulrech to follow the same pattern: focusing on learning, not immediately seeking to kill. We would trade blows, study the positioning of one another's bodies, ascertain what schools of blade work we preferred and measure the flow and feel of the fight. This was how most duels began, where expertise and skill mattered far more than in the grinding crash of war. Though some duellists may not admit it, it also allows the muscles to warm, the blood to flow and the adrenal narcotics in our armour systems to flood through, buying time for a combatant to immerse himself in the fight.

Ulrech had other ideas. He considered himself far above me in terms of swordsmanship, or else believed he could kill me while his blood was still cold, for he advanced at once, laying into me with a succession of blows that I barely blocked with the flat of my priceless sword.

I gave ground with each parry. Several of Daravek's warriors shouted their approval to see me on the defensive already. They suspected a swift end to the fight.

The Thousand Sons were never renowned as the most martial of Legions, and it was often said we relied too heavily on our psychic gifts to win wars. There was perhaps some truth to this accusation, but we were individually no less skilful than our cousins among the other Legions, even before taking into account the years of blood and battle since Horus' rebellion. Where many warriors fought through instinct and rote, we added a scholarly approach to duelling, with mental techniques of focus in tune with the meditative kata found among the more philosophical martial arts. The principles of balance, of action and reaction, of how to lead an opponent into revealing the flaws of their technique and how to avoid their lures in kind – all of these aspects of battle were drilled into our consciousnesses in the years of our training on Tizca and the warfare that followed. Against our more savage or rigorously trained kindred, such personal discipline evened the odds.

So I was calm in the face of Ulrech's overwhelming force – at least outwardly. Such was the power and speed of his blows that I struggled to maintain my battle focus. I imagined Telemachon watching, disgusted with my performance. I imagined Abaddon's eyes on me, unblinking in their judgement. I was no longer unsure of his motives – certain, instead, that he had committed me to this fight in order to see me die. The rewards of my failures, reaped at last. And how apt that it would be before Daravek himself, and brought about by the Lord of Hosts' own champion.

Ulrech drew first blood. He took advantage of a poor deflection to risk a cut to my torso, carving a slashing ravine across my breastplate. The cheers from his brethren redoubled.

Focus, I warned myself.

Our blades met, locked close to the hilts. We were close enough for me to see the reflection of my black battleplate in the filthy silver of Ulrech's ceramite.

'Why do you stand with him?' I asked the Iron Warrior, seeking any hesitation in his movements. There was none. 'Why do you stand with Daravek?'

Ulrech held the lock for a moment until we both disengaged, stepping back as one. 'Abaddon is no less a tyrant,' was the swordsman's curt reply.

I did not argue that point. Our blades clashed in a series of swings and parries; I refused to give ground now, deflecting what I could and weaving aside from what I could not. We were only metres away from my brothers. There was nowhere left to go.

Ulrech was not as silent as I had suspected – he spoke as our blades' power fields repelled one another with snarls of abused energy.

'Why did you abandon your Legion?'

I confess, the question surprised me. 'To escape the shadows of our failed fathers,' I said. 'From shame and shadow recast. In black and gold reborn.'

'The battle cry of a false Legion,' Ulrech grunted.

'The battle cry of a new way. A new war.'

'You cannot outrun shame,' the terse warrior growled.

'Those who do not learn from the past,' I countered, 'are condemned to repeat it.'

We crossed blades again and again, neither of us managing to score second blood. I was getting the measure of his swordplay, which was at worst masterful and at best exquisite. Telemachon might have beaten him by now. It was all I could do to maintain the deadlock.

'I'm growing bored, Khayon,' Abaddon called to me. 'End it.'

Blood of the Gods, but I was trying. I feinted with a carving slash that became a throat thrust when Ulrech took the bait, only to have Sacramentum's blade hammered aside when the Iron Warrior instantly recovered.

'Maeleum,' Abaddon said to Daravek, across the duel. I

refused to let their words distract me. 'That was an inspired piece of spite.'

Daravek's immense wings rippled, wafting us with a breeze of charcoal-stinking air. 'Maeleum was the least of the insults I inflicted upon your domain, Ezekyle.'

Abaddon no longer sounded amused. 'Is that so.'

Daravek began to list his roll of the discord and dishonour his forces had inflicted upon us. For the weeks it had taken us to sail to the Eye's edge, months had passed for the Lord of Hosts' armada. They had rampaged through our territory, bringing ruin to our garrisons, raining destruction upon our fortresses.

Daravek related it all, battle by battle and fall by fall, in meticulous and lascivious detail. Ulrech and I punctuated the warlord's delighted screed with the thrum and crash of active power fields, our duel continuing throughout the recitation.

A legionary is a transhuman construct, but humanity still forms our cores. We are not created without flaws, and the individual motions of a battle or a duel are not always easy to recall, even to our eidetic memories. This is because of that most unstable of elements: emotion. Anger especially can cloud a warrior's otherwise clear recollection, staining memory red, bathing it in feverish heat.

With every word that left Daravek's mutated mouth, I found it harder to maintain my duellist's meditation. My focus began to slip. I started catching Ulrech's blows on instinct as much as by observance of his posture or prediction based on his muscle movements. Worse, I felt the insipid creep of unease needling its way through my mind – a physical sensation, cold down my spine. My meditative principles were the best chance I had at surviving this fight, and Abaddon, curse him, had invited Daravek to speak his venom at the worst possible moment.

On and on went the recitation of inflicted pain. Maeleum savaged by orbital bombardment, whole tectonic chunks of the world broken free and loaded into his fleet's mass drivers. We considered the grave world useless, but the symbolism in the act could not be ignored. And worse was yet to come.

Three of our warships now sailed with Daravek's armada, taken as plunder in battle, their defenders overwhelmed and their surviving crews enslaved to the whips of Daravek's overseers. The others were destroyed or lost in Eyespace, driven away from the regions they had sworn to protect.

Hostages had been taken from the warship *Song of Wrath*, the flagship of the modest fleet we had left to watch over our territory. Its commander, Ranegar Coval, was one of those captured.

I knew Coval well. A former Sons of Horus legionary and lieutenant to Fleetmaster Valicar, he was a stern and intuitive presence, adding his measured, aggressive wisdom to Valicar's cold, defensive calculations.

Daravek's men had peeled him from his armour with mining lasers, bound him with chains between two Land Raiders and torn him apart. While he still lived, torn in two, they had fed him to the daemon-hounds shackled to the command throne aboard Daravek's flagship.

Other fates for our warriors were no less dishonourable. Crippled and wounded, some were lowered into vats of industrial acid; others were slowly crushed beneath the slow-rolling treads of battle tanks while packs of Daravek's mutant slaves looked on and jeered.

The final insult came when Daravek gestured one of his

warriors forwards, almost to the edge of the duel. The World Eater dropped a stinking black cloak onto the wraithbone floor. At once I was struck by the reek of piss from the dark cloth, the stench old and rank and sour. The World Eater kicked the cloak to unroll it – I only heard it happen, as I could not spare the attention to look – but the reaction from my brothers told me the truth as easily as my eyes would have. Abaddon exhaled a feral breath. Ilyaster's armour joints growled as they tensed. Even Telemachon murmured a sibilant hiss, the closest he came to showing his displeasure.

The next time I disengaged from Ulrech I dared to steal a glance, and sure enough, I had guessed right. The cloth was not a cloak at all. The slitted Eye of Horus, set in the sunburst yellow of the Eightfold Path, stared open, stained, from the middle of the cloth.

The cloth had wrapped a handful of bones, still reddened with blood marks and stringy with ligaments, marked with the engravings of fangs where they had been gnawed.

The banner of the Black Legion. They had had taken one of our banners, used it as a funeral shroud for Ranegar Coval's daemon-chewed bones and then let their slave hordes soak it with streams of tainted piss.

Screaming marred the duel now. Throaty, wrathful roars that I didn't realise, until I ran out of breath, were rising from my throat. All serenity and meditative thought was lost, replaced by a red focus. I advanced on Ulrech, laying my entire weight into every blow. Sparks sprayed from protesting power fields. They shrieked together with the abuse of every clashing parry. I rained two-handed blows against him, faster than I could ever recall fighting, faster than I believe I have ever moved since.

He beat my guard several times, for I fought with almost no guard at all. Yet he failed to land any true wounds; every time his blade scored my battleplate, he was forced to pull back and defend himself again.

I knew I could not win. I did not care. Even when I had him on the defensive, he was a better, faster fighter than me. He gave ground, blocking and deflecting instead of risking any attack, but I could not break his guard down. I still did not care. Roaring, my senses choked by the waste-stink of our defiled banner and my brother's bloodstained bones, I attacked without thought of the wounds I would take.

I wanted blood. I wanted to steal life, as it had been stolen. I wanted revenge.

This is *vindicta*. This is what I speak of when I say it fuels the hearts of the Black Legion's warriors, when I say it beats with the blood in our veins. Revenge at any cost. Vengeance no matter what.

There was no revelation of truth suddenly burning in my mind, no flash of bleak clarity that dispersed the red fury. Later, Telemachon would offer his blademaster's perspective – that the only way I could win was to not care if I lost. All combatants still seek to protect themselves even in the bloodiest heat of battle. Even the World Eaters, when the Nails bite into their brains, will defend themselves on instinct and through the blessings of gladiatorial muscle memory.

That day, against Ulrech, I abandoned all efforts to survive. *Vindicta* flowed through my skull instead of rational thought.

I gave him my arm.

Willingly, as a sacrifice to slow his blade. It happened in a hundredth of the time it takes to retell. A backhanded blow to batter his sword aside. A flaring burst of a power field. A sonic boom that thunder-cracked my forearm.

I thrust forwards in the very same second. I will never forget the sick ease with which Sacramentum slid in – its hilt kissing the shattered ceramite of Ulrech's chest – nor the agonised flexion of his entire body as I twisted the blade where it was buried inside his primary heart. I pulled Sacramentum free with a sweeping yank, annihilating at least one of his three lungs on the way back out.

Blood sizzled, evaporating on my blade's edge. I was already moving, bringing Sacramentum down on Ulrech's sword arm, shattering his fist and the power generator in the blade's grip. On the backswing, I hammered my blade into his side, where it cut deep and stuck fast. He had staggered away, ruining a blow that would have severed him at the waist, but he was slowed by his internal injuries. I kept my grip on Sacramentum, stepped closer and dragged the blade free, my boot thudding into Ulrech's shattered breastplate for leverage.

I backed away from the Iron Warrior who, damn him, still refused to fall. One-handed, his organs doubtless aflame with pain and threatening to cease functioning, he still refused to yield. He watched, wheezing through his helm's grille, looking between me and his fallen, broken sword.

Fire ignited along my left arm. Pain suppressants squirted into my bloodstream, and I flinched at the sight of my arm ended at the elbow. The stump of ceramite spat a couple of sparks and dripped treacly blood as the wound already began to seal. I had never been mutilated before. I could not rectify what I was seeing with reality, not even when I saw my hand and forearm on the ground, the armour plating shattered.

I wanted to finish Ulrech. I wanted nothing more than to take his head and hold it high, crying out my triumph to the mad Gods that watched over us. I could feel the warp itself wanting the same fate, as unseen winds carried the whispers of daemons waiting to be born from the barbaric act.

But I lowered my blade. Against every instinct, I lowered Sacramentum and forced the words through my ragged breathing. In the earliest days, this was our way. Abaddon's offer had to be made. It was our Legion's law, whenever we faced an opponent worthy of hearing it.

'It is over,' I told Ulrech. He knew it as well as I did. 'But I would have you as a brother, Ulrech Ansontyn. From shame and shadow recast. In black and gold reborn.'

I felt Abaddon's eyes on me. I had expected my lord to be furious after Daravek's insulting recitations of his desecrations against us, but the opposite was true. Had his temper been a ruse? He was calm now, his aura tightly controlled, betraying only the faintest hint of amused pleasure.

What did I tell you, he sent to me silently, the words rich with pride. *You had to rediscover your hatred, just as I said.*

I was watching Ulrech. 'My offer is sincere,' I said to him.

And it was, though I admit that I wanted him to refuse. I wanted to kill him for everything he and the others of Daravek's armada had done, but I knew the words were right the moment I spoke them. I would never be able to forgive him, but I would trust his spite and rage at my side in the Long War.

His breath was a wheezing saw. It sounded like a chainsword choking on inferior fuel. Perhaps I had sundered two of his lungs and damaged the third, after all.

Ansontyn took a step towards me. And there he died.

His helmeted head rolled to the side. His headless body dropped to its knees and folded upon itself with that familiar, dull resonance of ceramite striking ceramite.

Behind the fallen corpse, Daravek swung his axe to the side, flicking blood from its blade. Some of those flecks landed on the black banner, which can only have been intentional.

'You petty creature,' I spat at Daravek.

'Khayon, it's over.' Abaddon beckoned me back to his side. I refused to heed him.

'You are next,' I promised Thagus Daravek. The numb throb of my amputated arm was an irritating distraction. I concentrated, forcing the flesh to reknit, beginning the process of regrowth that would take time even with psychic gifts. Yet I levelled my sword, pointing its tip at the warlord whom I had failed to kill so many times before. 'You are next.'

'They shame you, don't they?' he asked in calm reply. 'All of those failures.'

He could read my thoughts. Effortlessly. Never had I met any other sorcerer capable of piercing my mind without monumental effort, if at all.

'Khayon,' Abaddon called, louder this time, 'it's over.'

But I would not move.

'What is it you want from this moment?' Daravek asked me. 'What is it you imagine may happen? That with only one arm, you will best me blade to blade? That you will bring your mighty sorcery to bear against me and drag my soul from my body?'

I advanced on him, step by step. His warriors reached for their weapons, but I paid them no mind. As naked as I felt without Nagual and Nefertari hunting at my side, my blood sang with adrenal promise. I could kill him. I could kill Daravek now. I knew it.

He was grinning, a slit of blackened teeth in a peeled-back maw. 'Kneel,' he said to me.

And I knelt. My knees slammed against the wraithbone ground with an eerie chime. It was not the pose of a warrior pledging service, but that of a slave before his master. I sensed my brothers' shock, but it was nothing compared to my own.

Ezekyle, I tried to send in warning, but my silent voice was strangled, choked as surely as if the warlord's hands were at my throat. I tried to rise, only to find myself locked with muscle cramps, my lungs seizing, scarcely able to draw breath.

Daravek approached me, burning wings shedding feathers of ash, his rotting head haloed in ethereal majesty.

'Apologise for this unseemly display,' he said in a tone of infinite patience.

I will carve your heart from–

'Forgive me,' I said. My mouth had moved. The words had spilled forth.

'Forgive you for what?' A bubble of dark fluid swelled and popped at the edge of Daravek's mouth.

I tried to stand. Instead, my throat vomited forth more quiet, calm words of surrender. 'Forgive me for this unseemly display.'

'Well done.' He licked his teeth, making a show of tasting the oily saliva stringing between his fangs. 'I'd wondered, Khayon, if you were hiding the truth from your brethren, fearful they might kill you for it. But I see the ignorance in your eyes now, and I realise you are hiding nothing. You simply don't remember Drol Kheir.'

There was nothing I could do about the loathsome mockery in his tone. 'There is nothing to remember,' I replied, trying and failing to rise from my knees. 'It was a battle like any other.'

His grin shed a treacly spume of poisoned ooze, and he said the words that had irritated me for years, words I had heard a hundred times and more.

'Iskandar Khayon died at Drol Kheir.'

That stupid rumour. Nothing more than the kind of false word of mouth that so often travelled between warbands in the unreliable winds of our hellish haven.

Whatever control he held over me, it was loose enough then for me to speak. 'You are a fool,' I told him.

'I know you died, Khayon,' Daravek promised. 'I was the one to tear open your throat.'

The assault against my mind came without warning, too fragmented to be a memory but too vivid to be psychic implantation. Images and moments descended upon me, all out of any discernible order – and behind it, the strange touch of slow-dawning comprehension.

Running knee-deep in the polluted, hissing snow of Drol Kheir. Blood spray flecking across the white slush.

(blood my blood that is my blood)

Bodies half-buried in the snow, rimed with frost the moment they fell. Alchemical fog so thick it resembled morning mist. The screaming of warriors and mutants drowning in the toxic smog.

(do something sorcerer)

The kick of my bolter. The hammering of drop pods as Ashur-Kai's Rubricae joined mine, their arrival shaking the ground. The crash of my axe

(Saern the axe of Fenrisian forge-fires)

against a rusted, corroded crescent of a weapon: Daravek's axe.

(Iskandar Khayon we meet at last)

The rushing of air

(the crack of ceramite)

and a feeling of weightlessness, of suffocation, of eyes sucked dry, of fingers numbed with frostbite, of your own skull weighing an impossible burden, of

(you are mine, son of Magnus)

a pressure, like telekinesis but not physical, a pressure against the soul itself and not the body. The ground not just shaking, but rattling as the sun is eclipsed by the shadow of an iron god.

(Titans the god-machines walk)

The screaming whine of a war-horn, warning those beneath it. The ozone reek-taste of overcharged, suffering void shields. The rage-born howl of a wolf. The rending of steel beneath heavy fur and razor fangs.

(Gyre my wolf my lethal huntress torn from me destroyed by Horus Reborn)

The suction of blood. The loosening of bone. The mincing of meat.

(where is Nefertari why is she not here this was before she came to the Eye before she was my weapon)

And then, at the edge of the sensory siege, the pathetic mercy of release

(is this now)

(is this then)

The weakness and freedom of a puppet's strings cut. The crash of ceramite against wraithbone.

I looked up at Daravek now, here on Taial'shara, and exhaled a breath that tasted of old blood.

'You cannot kill me,' he said with sordid benevolence. 'You are mine, Khayon. I tore your throat open three centuries ago and ripped your soul from the wound.'

You lie, I knifed the words at him. *YOU LIE.* He deflected them with no effort at all.

'I have no need to lie, little slave. Reflect upon what you have learned this day. Reflect upon just whom you serve.'

I forced my gaze to the other legionaries at Daravek's side. Was it true? How many of them were soul-bound in the same way?

Daravek gestured with his axe. 'Now go back to your master, assassin.'

I gasped as I once more became the master of my own body. My muscles were in spasm, my nerves misfiring, but I rose to my feet through a red haze of pain, doing all I could to show I was not shaken by his effortless puppeteering of my body.

First I sheathed my blade over my shoulder. Then I ignited the defiled war banner with a psychic kindling, burning it to ash in the span of three heartbeats. And then I picked up Ulrech's iron grey helm, tipped it to drop the severed head onto the wraithbone ground and took the helmet with me – a trophy, to remember the moment.

Yet my hearts were pounding. Shame coursed through me, shame and defeat. My failures were cast into stark relief now, and I think until that moment Abaddon had doubted my reports of the failed assassinations. It took the evidence of his own eyes to convince him.

Now we knew why I had failed.

None of my brothers offered comment on my supplication as I returned to their ranks. Telemachon edged away from me, as if my enthrallment to Daravek were infectious.

Ilyaster applied armour cement to the stump of my arm after the most cursory examination; he was a practical creature, and losing limbs is hardly critical in terms of a legionary's injuries.

'Did you know?' I asked him. 'Did you know he killed me at Drol Kheir?' The words were madness in my mouth. 'Is it even true?'

I could see in Ilyaster's eyes that he knew nothing. After seeing me kneel he believed it was true, but no, he knew nothing for certain either way.

Telemachon had met Abaddon's eyes first, his silver face expressionless, but I sensed his slimy mirth at my weakness so brazenly revealed. He would doubtless speak with Abaddon alone – asking whether I could now be trusted, if I could ever have been trusted...

Abaddon was sealed to me. He showed nothing, betrayed nothing. I had at least expected anger, but even that seemed absent.

He called out to Daravek, 'Unless you have another champion that wishes to die, Daravek, it's time we spoke of this truce.'

'I think your pet has proved his point, as I have proved mine.' Daravek stepped forwards, mirroring Abaddon's movement. 'So let us begin.'

X

GHOSTS OF THE WARP

You know, as my gracious hosts, that my arm was restored between that day long ago and my captivity now. The changes wrought upon my flesh are visible as I stand here before you in this cell, shackled and blinded. My arm regrew – perhaps regenerated would be a fairer term – though it reformed in a far changed state than it had been before its loss.

It was my first mutation, and far from my last. Ahriman's Rubric banished mutation from the Thousand Sons, but only among those whom had little in the way of psychic talent, and only by destroying their physical forms. The rest of us are as prone to the warp's whims and our own sins as any other being dwelling inside the Eye. If you believe my former brother Ahzek is entirely unchanged beneath his Eye-touched armour, you are as dangerously naïve as he was when he unmade our Legion.

Ahriman believes he is perfectly unaltered. Did you know that? Yet I have seen the void that screams where his face used to be.

As we met with Daravek, I did my best to ignore the ache of loss and the maddening phantasm of pain in fingers I no longer possessed, silently reciting Prosperine focusing mantras.

'I can still feel my fingers,' I said under my breath at one point.

Ilyaster began to quietly detail the physiological reasons for this.

'Silence, fools,' Telemachon murmured, still focused on Abaddon and Daravek.

I understood why Abaddon had chosen to only bring three of us, and I daresay it made a statement to Daravek regarding how little he intimidated us, but we were heavily outnumbered thanks to my lord's posturing. I looked across the rank of warriors opposing us, recognising a couple of them from old battles. I had even served one of them, Ektral the Scaled, as a mercenary in the years before I wore the black. Whether these warriors comprised a new elite bodyguard for Daravek after Ilyaster and I had butchered his former kindred, or whether they were a gathering of lesser commanders meant to impress us, I could not be certain. All I knew was that we could not kill them all.

Had Moriana predicted the details of this meeting? Had she seen its outcome? As much as I wished to know, I did not dare to risk a telepathic pulse to Abaddon, lest Daravek hear our shared thoughts. It was galling enough knowing he had the ability to read mine.

The warp boiled in the night heavens above the broken dome. I heard its never-ending song louder here, as the essence of unreality whispered and sang to those who would be its champions. Abaddon and Daravek were nexuses for these half-seen, half-felt forces, though I could make out no real meaning in the voices calling to them. Not that 'voices' is even an accurate word, given the primal forces sinking gentle claws into both warriors' souls. Such nebulous sound was merely how my too-mortal consciousness conceived of the powers at play.

Watching the twisting sky put me in mind of Abaddon's confession after my return from Maeleum. When he had informed the Ezekarion of the pressures grasping at his spirit, that too had been a matter for intelligences not limited by mortality. Abaddon had little in the way of answers himself, merely citing a compulsion – a physical and spiritual need – to reach back into real space and seek the source of the warpsong he never stopped hearing.

'I see a sword forged in a sunset,' he had told us in a strained tone. 'I see a star dying, and its ash used to fuel the engines of a great throne of gold. I see the first murder, where brother kills brother, where the rage of the slayer and the agony of the slain becomes a tempest behind the veil.'

He had spoken like this for some time. I did not mock him for such poesies. I did not laugh at them; I dreaded them. Never had I witnessed him so close to breaking apart. Seeing Abaddon murmur of his haunted dreams in a prophecy-soaked whisper was one of the most unnerving sights I have ever seen. His golden eyes glazed over with cataracts of distracted madness, as though someone or something had reached into his brain to puppeteer his fanged mouth to speak on its behalf.

The warp promised him this unimaginable prize in a ceaseless song, and yet he had no way of knowing what this treasure truly was. Whatever it was, its presence was a clarion call throughout the empyrean's tides. It inhaled hope and exhaled promise.

'Is it a daemon?' Lheor had asked, as awed and uneasy as the rest of us. 'How can you trust such an offer?'

'I don't need to *trust* it,' Abaddon snapped back from his polluted reverie. 'I need only to master it.'

'It will be yours,' Moriana promised him. 'From the moment you claim it until you wear the Emperor's crown upon your brow, it will be your companion and your weapon.'

Few of us were convinced. Amurael spoke for us.

'For this,' he said, 'you would fight a war?'

'The war is sacrosanct,' Abaddon replied. 'And it is ours, not mine. We will return to the Imperium and bring fire to those deluded souls who fight beneath the False Emperor's banners. This is *vindicta*. This is why we wear the black. Whatever else waits outside the Eye, I will kill or claim as the need arises.'

We knew so little about Drach'nyen then. I think back to our ignorance in those nights with a sense of something akin to purity. For all the strength Abaddon's blade has granted to us down the centuries, and for all of the victories reaped with its screaming edge, it remains a cancer threatening to blacken my brother's heart. I believe none of its whispers. None at all.

Throughout the negotiations on Taial'shara, I layered my psychic resistances in the hope of defeating Daravek's casual rifling of my mind. All the while I watched for the ambush that seemed inevitable. Daravek had us where he wanted us. The idea he might not take this chance to kill Abaddon was laughable.

Worse was the thought that he could make me turn on my lord, and there was nothing I could do to stop it. Yet, if it was within his power, why had he not already willed it to happen?

There was no answer to this. At least, none that I could see.

His warriors' thoughts were calm and assured. They seemed certain of their dominance in the truce. They had come to make demands from what they perceived as a weaker foe, not to make an agreement with them.

The negotiations themselves were torturous, as they so often are between the Eye's warbands. Our relative strengths only added to the difficulty in reaching a resolution. Both sides had no wish to leave their fleets alone for too long, lest conflict break out according to some previously planned betrayal.

We could not destroy their fleet without taking horrendous casualties, diminishing any hope of bleeding the Imperium regardless of whether Sigismund's Black Templars waited for us or not. They could not face us without the risk of sustaining the same losses. The promise of mutually assured destruction had a way of calming even the fiercest hearts. Yet their demands rained upon us. Daravek wanted ships, warriors and materiel in exchange for holding off from an attack. Again and again he made his smirking insistences, assured that Abaddon would capitulate to preserve the bulk of our fleet.

'I will give you nothing,' Abaddon replied each time. When he wearied of Daravek's perseverance, he looked longingly at the Talon. Its autoloaders cycled in clanking response to his fading patience. 'Shall I tell you what I believe, Thagus?'

Thagus was taller than Abaddon – a rare sight given that Abaddon was cast in Horus' image. The Lord of Hosts, swollen by his supplication to the Powers, inclined his head in generous benediction, as if granting a favour to a particularly amusing servant. The three of us bristled at the insult, but Abaddon only smiled.

'Speak,' Daravek intoned.

'I believe you are likewise trapped in the storm.' Abaddon was holding his anger back, binding it tight, showing it only in the flashing gold of his soul-stained eyes. 'I believe the warp aided your pursuit of us, then cut you adrift in our wake, leaving you becalmed and with no idea why. I believe that the malignant essences we call Gods have brought us together here in the heart of this storm to play out a game of kings and pawns, just to decide where their favour should fall.'

'You have an admirable imagination, son of Horus.'

Abaddon refused to rise to the bait. 'I believe, most of all, that you are frightened of us.'

He scraped the Talon's claws together. Several of Daravek's warriors brought their hands inching closer to their bolters. We held motionless in response, lest mirroring their gesture provoke them into breaking the truce.

'You fear us,' Abaddon continued, 'because despite your raving speeches that we are betraying the Legions, and despite your petty crusades to destroy us, we not only survive, but thrive. We grow with every conflict. The icons of the failed Legions are sheared from ever more suits of armour, and the colours of shame are eclipsed in numbers no other warband can match. You fear that we are right, and that you are wrong. You fear us, more than any other reason, because you had to *chase us*. Because we were here first. Because we are the ones on the verge of breaking free, despite all your attempts in these last decades to hinder us. We have been working towards this fate, while you have done nothing but seek to stop us. We've fought for true unity, all brothers beneath the black banner, while you've fought against it in the guise of preserving the old, failed ways. We, Thagus, have acted. You have reacted.'

Abaddon's gaze had roamed across the other legionaries as he spoke, and now it returned to Daravek. 'And here we stand at our prison's edge. Even now you have no answers to give your men. Instead you force this meeting with us, praying you can glean insight into our plans and scavenge victory through threats. You'll lose this war, Thagus. You'll lose because you desire the Gods' favour and you fear it falling upon anyone else.'

Daravek opened his jaws. Black slime ran between the sewer grate of his teeth. 'You are not the only one to dream of the End of Empires,' he warned. 'You are not the only one that hears Drach'nyen's call.'

'No,' Abaddon admitted, 'but which one of us hears it louder? Who hears it clearer? The one seeking it, or the one chasing the seeker?' Abaddon turned away before Daravek could reply, speaking as he walked back to us. 'If you're so certain of your strength, Thagus Daravek, come test it against my Black Legion now. The *Vengeful Spirit* hungers.'

There should have been more. We all expected harsher words to follow and promises of recrimination. Such suspicions proved unfounded when in the very same moment, three of Daravek's warriors held fingers to their vox-beads, and Ashur-Kai's voice drifted through my mind.

Sekhandur.

Ashur-Kai, I sent back. *Do you remember Drol Kheir?*

Of course I do.

Did I face Daravek? Did he kill me?

Blood of the Pantheon, what foolishness is this?

Daravek implied that–

Don't be ludicrous, interrupted Ashur-Kai. *I must speak with Ezekyle, but his mind is walled too tight.*

What is amiss? Explain yourself.

Across from us, Daravek was speaking with his men, and a sudden disquiet radiated from their auras.

There are ships appearing before both fleets – unknown vessels of unknown allegiance, not sailing into the storm's heart, but simply manifesting before us.

Daravek's men are uneasy, I observed. *It is not one of their ploys.*

I have no idea what it might be. We have been boarded.

We... What?

In the same moment, Daravek aimed his axe at Abaddon. 'What treachery is this? You have broken the truce, Ezekyle.'

Abaddon rounded on his rival, eyes narrowed to platinum slits. 'We have broken nothing.'

We have been boarded. Ashur-Kai's silent sending was jagged with urgency. *A single legionary. It defies explanation. Every ship in the fleet is reporting the same phenomenon – a lone warrior manifesting upon their command decks. They are not moving, nor speaking. They merely stand there, watching us.*

I reached out to place a hand on Abaddon's shoulder and haul him back, only to see I had no hand with which to grip. It still lay on the wraithbone ground, metres away.

'Brother,' I said, 'we must return to the *Vengeful Spirit*. Ashur-Kai reports that we have been boarded, and–'

'You dare?' Daravek was calling out to us. 'You dare board our ships?'

Daravek's warships have been boarded, as well, I sent back to Ashur-Kai. *He suspects us of breaking the truce.*

I looked between the two opposed, confused groups of

warriors. One by one they turned to stare across the dusty garden with its eroded statuary, where a lone warrior walked from the eldar ruins.

He was dead. I thought that at once, as easily as if I had seen decaying flesh or smelt the rotting musk of decomposition. To my sixth sense, he was without a soul, a man disconnected from the mechanisms of life. And yet he walked closer, his armour the light grey of an overcast sky, tinged by the faintest pale green, his eye-lenses red-lit from within.

He was no daemon. Daemons have no souls, yet they are presences in the warp – they are the warp itself, and form writhing, drifting things before my psychic gaze. Yet he was no human. Humans have shining souls, and they are beacons in the warp's tumultuous night. Whatever this warrior was, he walked the line between mortal and immortal, fused with the warp yet not born from it, saturated by the immaterium yet not possessed by it.

He had a soul, I saw as he drew near, and it was still his own – a weak thing, a dim and shredded light.

There was a beauty in that, in the same way a lesser mind – reliant on the five mundane senses – might see beauty in a colour never before seen. Here before me was a kind of entity I had never believed possible, taking the form of a brother legionary.

What Legion or Chapter had sired him, I could not say. His armour was of a mark unknown to me then, not even matching the newer suits of Aquila-pattern battleplate I had seen aboard the Black Templars vessel.

We have encountered one of them ourselves, I sent to Ashur-Kai.

Daravek's warriors brandished their weapons at this newcomer. We did not.

'Name yourself,' Daravek demanded. I could see his knuckles tight on the haft of his axe.

The grey warrior turned his helmed head to each group in turn, showing no favour either way. The voice that emerged from his helmet grille was deep, though not unusually so for a legionary, and his words were preceded by a click of vox projection, just as any of our voices were.

'I am Saronos.'

Within his words I heard the telltale flow of respiration. He was dead to my sixth sense, yet alive to all others. My fascination deepened. Had he been one of us before undergoing these changes? Was he still one of us, but with mutations of the soul that set him apart?

The icon on his pauldron was not one I recognised, but it was nevertheless gravid with symbolism – two skulls set within an eight-spiked disc, one looking to the left, the other to the right. An inscription ringed the staring skulls, cast in dark silver and written in an unfamiliar dialect of High Gothic: *In Abysso Tollemus Animabus Damnatus.*

The exact translation evaded me, but I could make out its meaning: 'We bear the souls of the damned through the depths'.

'I am Thagus Daravek,' declared our rival. He strode forwards, confronting the newcomer.

'We are aware of what you name yourself,' said the grey warrior. 'You speak irrelevancies.'

'How did you reach us undetected?' asked Daravek. 'How have your men boarded our ships?'

Saronos kept his gaze steady. 'You speak irrelevancies.'

'Then what of your warband?' Daravek pressed. 'Where do your loyalties lie?'

'You speak irrelevancies.'

I do not know if Abaddon sensed something about the newcomer that I could not, or if he simply made the intuitive connection first, but he addressed the grey warrior, cutting past Daravek's useless questions.

'Will you guide us out of this storm?'

The grey warrior's armour joints purred as he looked between the two leaders. 'Yes, Ezekyle Abaddon, we will – if you meet our price.'

For a time, I watched through Ashur-Kai's eyes. I bore witness to his memories, seeing the spectral warships coalesce into being. They took shape on the oculus, at first ghostly and indistinct, becoming the same pale grey-green as Saronos' armour as they drifted nearer. Imperial ships, but built to patterns I did not recognise. They possessed enough familiar elements to suggest they had been brought into being by Standard Template Construct plans, but not by any that were in use during my years fighting for the Imperium. Like the Black Templars vessel, these warships were newer than those we sailed aboard.

The Anamnesis reached out through her amniotic fluid, her hands curling as though she were strangling the closest vessel. I felt every turret and forward cannon along the *Vengeful Spirit*'s hull grinding around to lock on to the far smaller ship.

That was when the grey warrior manifested before the several hundred primary bridge crew, coming into being the way Saronos had appeared before us. This warrior wore the same armour and showed the same symbol, though whereas Saronos conversed, this one remained perfectly silent. Warriors, beastmen and Ultio's mind-slaved cyborgs and robots all converged upon the figure where he stood by Abaddon's empty throne. He still made no move.

All of this I took from Ashur-Kai's mind. I took it and relayed it back to Abaddon.

'Tell Ashur-Kai to maintain a vigil,' he commanded, 'but make no hostile move.'

Ezekyle orders you to maintain a vigil, but make no hostile move.

As he wishes, came the reply. *The warrior with you – he speaks?*

He does. He speaks of prices to be paid, to guide us from the storm.

I felt a stab of irritation from Ashur-Kai, to be so far away from such a fascinating occurrence. It galled him. It galled him deeply.

Saronos named his Chapter, though each of us heard something different in curiously structured High Gothic. Ilyaster heard *Infernum Ductorii,* the 'underworld's guides', and Ezekyle heard *Umbra Larua,* the 'ghosts of the shadows'. When Saronos spoke the name, I heard him say *Kataegis Lemura,* the 'storm's spirits'.

Later, when we had heard others speak of the grey warriors, we would piece together a rough Low Gothic approximation of their name: the Warp Ghosts.

Saronos told us of his Chapter's purpose – that he and his kindred were ferrymen of a kind, guiding vessels through the warp. They would, for a price, guide one of our fleets through the storm and into the narrow channel of calm space that speared through the Great Eye and led to the Cadian System.

He swore in those ceaselessly calm tones that his brothers were born of no Legion, yet told us we spoke irrelevancies every time we asked how that was possible. He said the same when asked the year of his birth, or the patterns and classes of his small fleet's unknown vessels. Never did he display a loss of patience, nor appear to favour one warlord over the other.

'I do not trust these Ghosts of the Warp,' Telemachon murmured, giving the name he had heard Saronos speak.

None of us did, but what choice did we have?

Daravek, meanwhile, spat at the idea of negotiating with the grey warrior. 'What are your demands, spectre?'

'We demand nothing,' said Saronos.

'Then what is your price to free us from your storm?'

'It is not our storm. And the price for guidance out of these tides is for you to discern. You will be judged by what you sacrifice.'

Daravek spat at the idea. 'And if we kill you now? If we destroy your fleet?'

'Then we would die. You speak irrelevancies.'

'How can we trust your word in any of this?'

'Nothing I say will alter that choice. You speak irrelevancies, Thagus Daravek.'

'Very well.' The Death Guard warlord rested his axe on one shoulder, speaking with a confident grin that hid little of his fury. 'Here is my offer, ghost.'

'We are listening,' said the grey warrior.

'If you require ships for your fleet, I will give them to you. Ten. Twenty, if need be, from my war spoil. I will tear them from the Black Legion and lay them at your feet. If you desire slaves, I will grant you a million of them from the holds of Black Legion vessels. More, if that is not enough. Two million. Three. If you want access to my daemon forges or armament manufactories, it can be arranged. And once I claim what is mine by right, if you wish my favour in the future, then it will be yours without question.'

Blood of the Changer, the sheer magnitude of that offer. Most warbands would risk destroying one another over even one of those elements, let alone all of them. The right to use a powerful warband's forges and manufactories was the kind of opportunity many warlords never saw in the entirety of their lives. Daravek offered lifelong riches for any warband, and he did so with the arrogant generosity of a king laughing while scattering gold coins onto the street for peasants to fight over. Much of it was not his to offer – the ships and slaves he spoke of were still ours for now – but they could so easily become his if this deadlock escalated into war. Nothing he said was beyond the realm of possibility.

And most valuable of all was his favour. The regard and support of a warlord with Daravek's influence was enough to inspire any warband to acts of madness. Such patrons were rare indeed.

At my side, I heard Ilyaster exhale the same awed sigh at the wealth and opportunity being offered so royally. But Daravek was not yet done.

'And,' he added, through clenched black teeth, 'if it is souls you desire, then I offer you the souls of Ezekyle Abaddon and his miserable Ezekarion. Ask, and they are yours. I will harvest them with my own blade, one by one, when our fleets do battle.'

Saronos inclined his head, acknowledging Daravek's words before turning to Abaddon.

'We have heard the offer made by Thagus Daravek of the Legion Host. What do you offer, Ezekyle Abaddon of the Black Legion?'

My lord did not answer Saronos at once. He requested a moment to speak with his brothers, and turned to the three of us, his gaze raking over us in turn.

'I think back to Moriana's words,' he said softly. 'That "greatness requires sacrifice". That "one cannot run from what must be done". As much as I doubt her ultimate loyalty to us, and as much as I distrust her adamant beliefs, there is a cold truth to what she said. She saw this moment – not the souls gathered here, nor the offers that would be made – but she knew the time was coming when a great offer would need to be made. And now here we are, with her words echoing through my skull. The necessity of sacrifice.'

He gestured to me, indicating my arm. 'You showed it yourself, Khayon, this very night. Sacrificing your arm. Suffering a grievous loss to win an even greater victory. Without that loss, you would have died. How many myths and legends all grow from the same seeds? A multitude of tales preach that sacrifice is at the root of epochal progress. How many warriors throughout history have laid down their lives so that their nations would survive?'

For the first time in years he looked at peace, as if the decision he was making was a fight back against the pressures upon his soul. 'If you wish to beseech the God of War, you kill in his name and risk your own death. If a warrior wishes to join our newborn Legion, he is forced to balance individual glory and personal freedom with the cause we all share. He battles beneath my banner as well as his own. He carves the icons of his former life from his battleplate, and he stains his ceramite black. Sacrifices, all. Sacrifices made for greater gain.'

Abaddon hesitated, no longer looking at Telemachon or Ilyaster – only at me. 'A sacrifice is only meaningful if one surrenders something precious. You are a ritualist, Iskandar – a sorcerer, a philosopher. Is that not the truth of it?'

I thought of my father Magnus, and his ritual to send word to the Emperor. The many apprentices and cultists that lay dead on desecrated altars, even before we were rendered *Excommunicate Traitoris*. It had worked, though with devastating consequences.

I thought of Ahriman – my courageous, foolish, beloved, hated brother Ahriman – and the Rubric he wove that destroyed our Legion. He had sacrificed nothing of true worth. He believed in himself above all else, and he had been punished for his flawed attempt to cheat the Changer of the Ways.

I thought of the sacrifices I had made down the many years, as part of rituals, summonings, bindings… So many of them had involved blood and death, and the most powerful always demanded the most intimate of sacrifices. One did not deal with daemons without making sacrifices to them. The slaughter of a stranger holds almost no power, no emotional resonance. The butchering of a close brother, betraying his trust, is an act that sings out across the warp.

'By its nature,' I finally replied, 'a sacrifice must cost the giver. Otherwise, it is merely an offering. True sacrifices are fuelled by such depth of emotion that they echo into unreality. They are the offers that the warp hears, and the ones it most often answers.'

'They are the offers that *history* hears, brother.' Abaddon was smiling now, though there was no humour upon his visage.

He turned from us, walking towards Saronos. The grey warrior had not moved at all.

'What do you offer, Ezekyle Abaddon?'

Abaddon spoke his offer. It took far less time than Daravek's many promises, and was done before I could stop him.

I would have tried. I told myself that afterwards and I have maintained it through all the years and wars since. Had I known what he would offer, I would have tried to stop him. Instead he spoke, just a single sentence, and I had no time to do anything but stare in shock.

As soon as he had spoken, other warriors in the same grey-green as Saronos drifted from the shadows and from the air itself, striding forwards and taking form. Ten of them, twenty, fifty. They levelled their bolters at Daravek and his officers.

'Return to your vessels,' Saronos ordered Daravek's men. 'Your offer has been refused.'

Pus ran from Daravek's eyes in creamy mimicry of fury's tears. It took me a moment to realise they were maggots, hatching within his skull and spilling from his tear ducts.

'You have made a grievous mistake,' he warned Saronos and the grey warriors. Saronos' only reply was to draw his blade, a slow and stoic threat.

Wisely, they left without bloodshed. I doubted we had long before Daravek's armada attacked.

And we made ready to return to the *Vengeful Spirit*, for there we would offer up our sacrifice.

XI

SACRIFICE

Nagual and Nefertari awaited me on the bridge. The former came to me at once, trailing at my side, bearing his fangs and swearing to destroy whomever and whatever had wounded me.

He is already dead, Nagual. I killed him.

He offered, in his simple way, to find my opponent's soul in the warp and devour it for me, or bring it to me in his jaws that I might use it for my own purposes. I had no desire for either eventuality. Binding a soul is a monumental undertaking for a mortal. Few sorcerers manage it even once. Let Ansontyn burn. Let his soul journey on its way to oblivion.

Nefertari offered none of Nagual's open loyalty. She sat in a tiptoed crouch atop the backrest of Abaddon's command throne, her wings half-spread for balance. She leapt up when we entered and took wing, her arc carrying her over several consoles before she rested, perched on the railing of one of the upper balconies. Beastmen brayed and cawed up at her, all of whom she ignored. They despised her as an alien thing. The most attention she ever paid to them was when she hunted them as prey and flayed them as playthings. She paid them no notice now, however, because her laughter rang out across the bridge instead. She was laughing at me – more specifically, at my arm. There would be a lecture in my future about my blade skills.

Above all of us, Ashur-Kai's navigational platform was notable for its new presence: a grey warrior, cast in Saronos' image, standing in dreadful serenity and making no move at all. My former mentor remained up there, watching this intruder into his private realm. He greeted me with a psychic sending. I returned it, hiding my guilt for what was about to come.

What deal was struck? he sent to me.

I pulsed my memories of just what had happened. Ashur-Kai sifted through the scene in the wastelands of the craftworld, his own thoughts growing colder.

I do not know what Abaddon's offer entails, he admitted. *It could be anything at all.*

I said nothing. Unease serpentined its cold and greasy way through me.

Abaddon marched to the central dais. 'Ultio, report.'

The Anamnesis did not need to watch the oculus – her attention was spread throughout the ship's bones and gun-imagifiers – yet she stared at the oval screen with particular intensity.

'I sense presences aboard,' she said, sounding confused and distant.

'Report on the enemy fleet,' Abaddon clarified, eyes narrowing as he gazed upon the oculus himself. He sat in the command throne with an ungainly growling of Terminator armour joints. I shared a glance with Telemachon. Outside of negotiating with other warbands, our lord only ever occupied Horus' throne when gripped by irritation or fury. This seemed to be both.

'Ezekyle...' Ultio said, her confusion deepening, making her sound somehow younger. 'They... They are taking my crew.'

'I want you concentrating on Daravek's armada. Are they moving? What formations are they adopting? Focus, damn you.'

It was the first time I had seen her openly failing to heed his orders. 'I hear the same loss across the fleet in the voices of the armada's captains. These presences are leeching lives from our crews.'

Abaddon hammered his fist against the arm of his throne. '*Ultio*. I know what is happening. It's happening by my will. Now focus on what matters.'

Her eyelids flickered several times, evidence of immense cognitive processing taking place inside her gestalt mind. A moment later she swirled in her fluid, coming back to herself.

'Thagus Daravek's fleet is advancing,' she said.

Abaddon heaved a breath. 'Battle stations.'

'That will not be necessary,' Saronos said, from his place at the side of Abaddon's throne. 'We will guide you from here before they can engage you. But first, there is the matter of payment.'

We never learned the exact cost. There was no way we could, for no officer in the fleet truly knew the scale of the human communities dwelling within the bowels of their warships. Slaves bred other slaves, dregs bred other dregs, regiments of thrall-soldiers – the Lost and the Damned, you might say – merged and blended and split apart, all away from the eyes of their Black Legion masters. Some of our warbands enforced rigid discipline upon their human and mutant soldiers, while others threw them into war as a ragged tide and paid them no mind between battles. The same as any other vessel, the *Vengeful Spirit* was home to tens of thousands of unknown, unlisted humans eking out a living in the deeper decks.

In truth, we only descended into those levels for two reasons: to stir the rabble into a frenzy before deploying them as bolt fodder, or – far more rarely – harvesting their ranks for male children who would make viable candidates for ascension into our ranks. But we lacked the functioning resources to devote any real efforts to that process. There was no true recruitment, only stasis and slow depletion.

Our new allies, however, suffered no such limitation.

When Abaddon made his offer to Saronos, he had laid his ambition bare. He would escape the Eye, no matter the price.

How many children were taken from the benighted cities that spread throughout our warships' bellies? How many families living in those tribal clans and blighted depths cursed our allies for the theft of their young? These miserable questions have no answer. I suspect, however, that they took the children with the most promising souls first. The ones that would, in time, bloom with psychic strength. Not all, of course. But many. So very many.

And I suspect this not because of some misguided concern over their cruelty. No, I believe it is true purely because of what Abaddon offered them when he made his great gamble and threw his ambitions bare before us. His exact words were what mattered.

Saronos had watched my lord's approach. 'What do you offer, Ezekyle Abaddon?'

Abaddon had replied with only three words.

'Whatever you need.'

Saronos moved among us now, a grey figure amidst the ragged hordes of bridge crew. His red eye-lenses tracked left and right as his gaze lingered on the warriors present, drifting over the mutants and humans. He made his way across the command deck, all while our holds were being drained of potential recruits, the actions of the spectral Space Marines unopposed by anyone but the screaming parents of the stolen children. Their resistance was as useless as you can imagine. I am sure that unarmed hands scraped uselessly against grey ceramite, and that plaintive cries fell on deaf ears. The Warp Ghosts took what they had come for.

But that was not all they came for. Abaddon had promised a sacrifice, and offered them whatever they needed. This, they took.

'Ezekyle,' Ultio called down from her raised tank. 'The *Abyssal Shadow* reports that their void-seer is...'

She trailed off, looking up, lifting her gaze to the navigational balcony at the apex of the bridge's ornate architecture. Our gazes followed.

Three grey figures materialised out of the dark air, their dirty armour seeming to eat the sick half-light of the illumination globes as they advanced on Ashur-Kai.

I want to tell you that I had not expected this when Abaddon made his dreadful gamble. I want to say that I fought for my former mentor, that I opposed Abaddon's sacrificial offering and the bond between Ashur-Kai and I holds fast to this day. That would make for a pleasing beat in the song of this long saga: that despite losing so many brothers over the centuries, my oldest companion – the scholar that first taught me the rudiments of sorcery – remains by my side to the very last.

I want to tell you that I did not stand by, doing nothing but playing my part in his betrayal.

But I promised that every word on these pages would be true.

The truth is that I drew my sword. The truth is that I stepped forwards, my gaze raised, and called Ashur-Kai's name across the teeming bridge.

Boosters flared nearby. Telemachon and Zaidu struck the deck before me, rising from their swift landings and barring my way, blades in their hands. The Masqued Prince was silent, his facemask impassive and beautiful. Zaidu growled a wet, snarling laugh, a warning sound from the throat of a beast.

Yet it was Ashur-Kai that stopped me. Not Telemachon and Zaidu's needless posturing, nor even Abaddon's cold scowl at my reaction. It was Ashur-Kai, raising a hand to ward me away.

I should have guessed, he sent to me. *What else would the ferrymen of the damned need?* His silent voice was raw with icy, amused revelation. *This is their life. Their entire existence. They need more ferrymen.*

I felt him send a telepathic command to his Rubricae, commanding them to lower their weapons. They did so at once.

This is not brotherhood, I sent the words as a blade, knowing Abaddon would hear them.

Wrong again, boy, said Ashur-Kai, with the informal title

he had not used in centuries. *This is a sacrifice for a greater cause. It is the very essence of brotherhood.*

One of the grey warriors placed a hand on Ashur-Kai's shoulder. Another drew a curved dagger, its blade scratched with unreadable runes. He rested it under Ashur-Kai's white chin, its tip seemingly ready to plunge upwards through the jaw and into my first tutor's brain.

I could sense the Warp Ghosts speaking to him, but I heard nothing of their words and detected none of their meaning. Ashur-Kai closed his albino eyes and, barely perceptibly, he nodded.

If we fight them... I sent to him.

Then the fleet dies.

Amurael was at my side as well. Partly, I thought, to lend support against Telemachon and Zaidu, and partly to prevent me doing anything foolish that would antagonise the Shrieking Masquerade's commanders. He certainly bore no love for either of them beyond fraternal loyalty.

Nagual prowled to stand at my other side. I calmed him with a reluctant sending, telling him it was over.

I was wrong, however. Someone had yet to voice her say on the matter.

Ultio was still watching the theft of the sorcerer responsible for guiding her through the warp. In a move of near-flawless unity, every enthralled cyborg and war robot of the Syntagma across the bridge raised their weapons and aimed their shoulder cannons at the grey warriors in our midst.

'You are not taking him,' the Anamnesis stated. The lumoglobes flickered brighter, a sign of her rising temper. 'He belongs to the *Vengeful Spirit*. He is mine.'

Abaddon's eyes glittered. I could read the surprise there, subtle as it was. He had not expected this.

Moriana dared to raise her voice against the ship's heart, only for one of the Castellax robots to whirl on her in a grinding chorus of gear joints. Both of its industrial claws opened, like the threatening maws of iron dragons. Flame-projectors mounted on both forearms hissed, their pilot lights lit, ready to bathe her in twin gouts of alchemical fire.

'You will shut your mouth on my bridge,' Ultio told the prophetess. 'Save your poison for other ears.' Ultio did not deign to look at her; the Anamnesis kept her gaze fixed upon the navigational balcony. 'Grey Ones,' she called to Saronos' warriors. 'Behold your fleet.'

The entire ship shivered, coming alive, rolling in the storm's silence. We could feel the *Vengeful Spirit*'s gun decks rumbling as its city-killing cannons realigned, no longer locked on Daravek's distant fleet. Instead, they trained their lethal aim on the grey ships of our new allies.

'Ultio, enough of this,' Abaddon ordered her.

Was the ship's ancient machine-spirit at war with the new soul that claimed the vessel? I do not know. I know that Ultio hesitated – she was Abaddon's creature through and through now, despite her origins. When he spoke, she listened. When he commanded, she obeyed. But not this time.

'Release him,' she ordered the Warp Ghosts. 'Or I will reduce your weakling fleet to dust.'

This was the first time any of us had witnessed the potential reaches of Ultio's true autonomy. In time she would grow both more powerful and more unstable, as the hearts of our warships were prone to do through warp exposure. By the time we constructed our ultimate flagship, the *Krukal'Righ* – what the Imperium calls the Planet

Killer – she would be unrecognisable as the once-serene machine-spirit of the long-dead *Tlaloc*. Here and now, as she turned her ire upon the intruders threatening Ashur-Kai, she made her first independent stand.

'Eleven of my ships report the theft of their void-guides. I am willing to accept their loss as part of the Black Legion's offer. But you will release *my* sorcerer at once if you value the existence of that insignificant flotilla you call a fleet.'

Saronos turned to Ezekyle. 'Does the Black Legion choose to break the pact?'

Righteousness blazed in Ultio's eyes as she answered for our lord. 'Take another soul. Not him. Then the pact stands.'

I believe I sensed Abaddon's unease in that moment. With my lord, I could never be sure what was imagination or projection. He guarded himself too well, or he was guarded too well by the powers that increasingly hungered for his attention.

'The terms have already been agreed,' Saronos calmly intoned. They were almost his last words. Three of the Thallaxi cyborgs stalked towards him, ready to lance him through with ionised las-beams. Their lightning guns would cut him apart at close range.

I wondered whether in death Saronos would look any different from the rest of us. Whether, in fact, he had ever been human. He remained both alive and dead to my senses.

'Let him go,' Ultio repeated to the three Warp Ghosts still surrounding Ashur-Kai.

The Warp Ghosts raised their weapons. We raised ours. Everything was a half-moment from erupting into madness. I never learned if Abaddon was going to acquiesce to Ultio's will or not, for it was Ashur-Kai who spoke, his voice strained with the blade under his chin.

'Itzara,' he said quietly. He used her human name, who she had been before the surgical internment that had saved her life and changed her completely. 'The Gods orchestrated this drama, dear girl. Sometimes we must play our part in their traps, letting them sink their teeth into our souls, for the chance to fight another day.'

She stared up at him – resolute, unblinking, somehow both ardent and passionless, just as always. 'I will not allow this.'

Something passed between them, some telepathic exchange. It took only a moment, but there was no way to know the depths of that silent conversation. Telepathy allows you to convey a lifetime of meaning within the span of a single blink. I sensed the wordless flow of communication between them, and then Ultio's attention drifted, turning away, resting upon me.

'You are right, Ashur-Kai,' she said.

What did you tell her? I sent to Ashur-Kai. *What did you say?*

He met those words with silence. Meanwhile the ship's guns unlocked from tracking the Warp Ghosts vessels. The *Vengeful Spirit* rolled once more, bringing itself back to face Daravek's encroaching armada. Ultio turned with the ship, facing the oculus once more. Her refusal to speak anything more was a bitter shroud that she wore with pride.

Abaddon had watched all of this with a calm that boiled my blood. I shook Zaidu's clawed hand from my armour and looked to my lord.

I want you to remember this moment, my Imperial hosts, when I speak of Abaddon in the future. When I speak of the ways in which he excels militarily, or shows the gifts of truly charismatic leaders. I want you remember the pact he made with the Ghosts of the Warp, and the way he gestured with the Talon's scythe blades, indicating Ashur-Kai. My former mentor. One of the Black Legion's founders. One of Abaddon's own irreplaceable Ezekarion. The void-guide for the flagship of the fleet.

Remember this, as a display of the depths of Abaddon's ruthlessness. Some of you may see it as a virtue. Others as a failing. I cannot speak for you. But I want you to remember it, for it is part of who he is.

Ezekyle met Ashur-Kai's eyes, just for a moment. It was all that passed between them as a farewell.

'Take him.'

Early in my apprenticeship to Ashur-Kai, when I was a youth in one of the many Thousand Sons fleets, my mentor often pointed out my tendency to focus on the details to the exclusion of the wider picture. In the hours that followed his sacrifice, there are two aspects that cling to my memory with a clarity that would have vindicated Ashur-Kai's lecturing soul no end. My recollection of that flight should be meticulous in its detail. Instead, I find myself focusing on the aftermath of Ashur-Kai's vanishing.

The first thing to happen was immediate, yet noticed by almost no one else. Across the bridge, the nine Rubricae bound to Ashur-Kai's will were severed almost instantly from his control. I felt the psychic strands thinning, then give way with silent snaps. The nine warriors did not move. They remained as they were, their archaic and ornate boltguns held to their chests, inactive sentinels watching over the command deck and waiting for a sorcerer's commands. Now unbound, they were receptive to the authority of whomever would claim them.

We had other sorcerers among our ranks – some powerful, some lesser, and many capable of commanding Rubricae. I was reluctant to let the ashen dead that had belonged to my former mentor simply serve elsewhere, however. They had once been my own brothers, the warriors of the company I had captained.

It had been Ashur-Kai's personal preference to have his slaves artfully paint his automata guardians in the traditional Tizcan red of the Thousand Sons from before the rebellion. Their shoulder guards showed their true allegiance, however, cast in the black and gold of our new Legion. It was a striking image, and I had always wondered as to the spiritual significance behind the gesture. Far more commonly, our sorcerers left their Rubricae in the blue of the Thousand Sons, marking with them a single Black Legion pauldron, or they recast them entirely in the black and gold worn by all other warriors beneath our banner. I favoured the latter. In certain lights, you could see the warp-wrought blue of the Thousand Sons turbulent beneath the surface of the black, as though trying to stain its way back into being.

I turned to those crimson echoes of a long-lost past, reaching out to them with a psychic clutch I have become all too familiar with across the years.

I am Khayon, I told them.

Every one of them turned to me, some needing to look up from their places in the crew console pits, others looking down from the overhead gantries.

All is dust, they sent back, devoid of personality and life, hollow but for their lethality and obedience. Later, I would claim them, binding them to me. Later. Once I could bear to look at them for more than a few moments.

The second incident occurred when I was in my private sanctum, duelling with Nefertari, training to adapt to the cybernetic arm that Ceraxia's tech-priests had fitted. Days had passed, or perhaps weeks, in the timeless vagaries of Eyespace.

The arm had taken well, fusing to my flesh and offering the same strength as that I had grown used to all my life. Ceraxia had forged it herself, a fact that honoured me deeply, and from the elbow down my new arm was a contoured limb of burnished gold, shaped to match what I had lost. I had expected to be able to regenerate the original flesh through psychic manipulation, yet failed with each attempt. The flesh and bone refused to reform.

Ceraxia's artistry, then, was my only real choice. I regained the use of my arm, and slowly accustomed myself to the strangely dull sensations of its metal surface-sensors.

It was during one of our regular sparring bouts that Nefertari asked to look at the limb, amused at the engineering once I let her do so. She rarely touched me. We disgusted each other physically – she revolted me with her elongated, liquid alien otherness; I revolted her with my human crudeness and sloth, as well as with the corruption she so often pointed out was running through my veins.

But that day she gripped my wrist with a strength that had long since ceased to surprise me, her gauntleted fingers softly scraping against the adamantine-reinforced gold.

'It is changing,' she pointed out, looking at the shining metal. Her slanted eyes, inhuman and elfin, tended to blink too swiftly for even my enhanced vision to track. Only in moments of genuine surprise did I ever see a flicker of her eyelashes, in what passed for a languid blink among the eldar. '*You* are changing,' she added.

I pulled back from her, looking down at my forearm and palm. I closed and opened my fingers experimentally, hearing the quiet clicks and purring gears of the artificer's miracle I possessed as part of my body. Strange to think that those clicking cogs and servos were my joints now.

Nefertari was right. It *was* changing. Subtly but surely, where the flesh met the metal, the union was becoming an unnatural amalgamation of both. I looked closer at my fingers, where Ceraxia's perfectionism had driven her to render acid-etched engravings of my fingerprints, copied from my genetic records. They remained unchanged. On the other side, though, my metal knuckles were paling in a way I recognised from the transfigured, incomparably strong ivory that formed on the plating of some warriors' armour, binding them into their ceramite. Bone spurs were forming in the gold.

In time, my arm became what you see before you now, as I stand here chained to the wall. Witness the shining gold, etched with primitive cuneiform carvings that curse me for bringing my father Magnus to his knees. Witness the hand itself: how the gold still bears my fingerprints, yet the back of my hand bears that biomechanical slitted eye of gold-lidded, blood-filled glass. Witness the spurs of transmogrified ivory at my knuckles, hooked like vicious spines. I have killed with them, more than once.

But the process was only beginning then, and I could not have predicted its outcome.

It was as I regarded my arm that Tokugra, Ashur-Kai's crow, melted out of the shadows above me and fluttered to a rest on my shoulder. I had not seen the familiar since Ashur-Kai's capture, and had believed it simply perished without him, its form haemorrhaging back into the warp.

Boy. The greeting curdled directly within my brain, sounding like nothing any natural crow could ever produce.

You have not discorporated, Tokugra. Do you cling to existence long enough to provide a meal for Nagual?

My lynx gave a great yawn where he lay in feline repose. His tail swished once then stilled. The crow ruffled its feathers at this display, then began to preen itself. Every one of these acts were entirely unnecessary given the daemons' etheric states. Sometimes their symbolic lifelikeness amused me, and sometimes it irritated me, but it always managed to intrigue me. You could never be certain what traits a familiar would mimic from its host form. I have seen familiars take the form of books on mechanical legs that slam closed when threatened, and bio-clockwork knights that duel with vermin. Every sorcerer has his or her own tastes.

Boy, the crow sent again, more aggravated now. It was not bound to me, and found communicating with me either difficult or distasteful. I could feel its physical form becoming unstable with the strain of trying to force its thoughts into mine. What followed came in a toxic tangle of words, akin to a child's slumber rhyme.

One last echo of my master's pains, spoken before he was taken in chains. If the boy faces Daravek eye to eye. Tell him. Tell him. The boy will die.

Ashur-Kai's words. Or, rather, Ashur-Kai's warning, delivered through Tokugra's fanciful and fleeting mind. It was the most coherent communication I had ever received from Ashur-Kai's familiar, and I could sense how the effort cost the weakened creature much of its remaining strength. And there was more:

One hundred howls encaged. Beating heart of Daravek's

rage. Boy must listen. Boy must see. Do not know why. Howls are the key.

I reached for Tokugra with my senses, trying to keep its form stable, but the creature was not pacted to me, and I had no power over its corpus. I wanted more, needing to know far more of the context behind that warning, but the crow had done all it could. I suspected that even maintaining its form to reach me had required a journey of unknowable daemonic endurance. That was surely why it had taken so long after Ashur-Kai's disappearance.

I had no love for prophecy – not then, and not in the centuries since – but these were my former mentor's last words, sent at great cost. His final prophecy, telling me what I must do to stay alive when I faced Daravek. Will you consider me a hypocrite if I confess that those words took root within my mind? I did not know what to do with them – I did not understand them, but nor could I simply ignore them.

Thank you, Tokugra.

Boy, it sent back in acknowledgement. It took wing, melting back into the shadows overhead, swallowed by them. Unbound, it could not hold its form together for long, and it was gone, I was sure, back into the primal matter of the warp. I doubted I would ever see it again.

XII

TEMPLARS

Saronos had taken Ashur-Kai's place on the platform. Sometimes I came to the bridge to watch him stand where the White Seer had once stood, guiding the ship through the warp's unquiet tides. Ultio worked with him, her concentration absolute. What they lacked in the familiarity she had developed with her sacrificed void-guide, Saronos made up for with his unnatural mastery. He stood with both hands on the control pylons that Ashur-Kai had fashioned with his own craftsmanship, sending the adjustments in course and calculation through to the Anamnesis. She answered in symbiosis: leaning, tilting, swimming.

No journey through Eyespace is tranquil – the realm defeats all astronavigation attempts as often as it allows them – but the *Vengeful Spirit* no longer threatened to shake itself apart. Looking into the thrashing mess of energies outside the ship revealed that we sailed through channels of relative calm, as Saronos stared into the oculus and murmured soft, poetic chants in a tongue I had never heard before. Sometimes it seemed as if he was trying to soothe the ship's machine-spirit. Sometimes it sounded as if he were trying to add the coldly lulling words to a greater ritual taking place outside our perceptions. Whatever the truth, both occurrences were less troubling than the many hours he stood there in absolute silence, his head hanging slack. By what sense he looked out and discerned a path through the storm, I could not say.

Abaddon remained enthroned the entire time, staring into Eyespace with the same focus writ upon Ultio's features. Hunger radiated from him, a starvation that devoured him, reflected in the fevered glare of his golden eyes. He refused all conversation, only speaking to me once, with a single demand.

'Is Daravek following us?'

'How could he?' Lheor replied, at my side.

It was possible. I had to concede that. Perhaps even likely, if Daravek's sorcerers could find traces of our wake, or locate the same pathways Saronos and his Warp Ghosts were using. If they were pathways at all; Saronos was hardly forthcoming.

I was not the first one Abaddon asked. Ultio's sensors could not pierce this region of Eyespace, nor could any of us detect any signs of pursuit. The warp outside was a shroud, and we paid the price for its serenity by sailing blind to whatever might chase us.

All the while, I thought of Ashur-Kai's final warning. His last prophecy. If I faced Daravek, I would die. Did that mean a confrontation was inevitable? What if the Lord of Hosts pursued us?

Lheor was typically blunt on the matter when I shared it with him. He clacked his metal teeth together, feigning a bite at one of the unborn spirits of pain that drifted around his head in a red halo.

'You've already proved you can't kill him,' Lheor said of Daravek. 'So it hardly takes a seer to know who'd win the fight.'

Amurael, who often joined us in the sparring cages, concurred with Lheor, albeit less obnoxiously. 'You're looking at this the wrong way,' he added afterwards. 'Ashur-Kai wouldn't waste his last words relating something you already knew.'

I agreed. I had thought the same. 'He warned of me confronting Daravek eye to eye. It seems to be a warning to slay him without facing him.'

Amurael's fangs flashed in amusement. 'You've already tried that, Khayon. You wasted a year trying it.'

And well I knew it. 'Then I will try harder,' I said, hoping the words did not sound as hollow as they felt.

It was like this for some time, as we sailed onwards towards the Eye's edge. The Black Legion looked ahead to the promise of escape, but I found myself looking behind, thinking of duties undone, knowing there would be a reckoning before the last day dawned. I could not allow Daravek to live. Not after the mystifying power he had demonstrated over me. I would end him somehow. I would find a way.

'Abaddon would approve of you thinking like this,' Amurael pointed out. 'He'd consider it another encouraging sign of your *vindicta* returning.'

Lheor and Amurael were duelling as the three of us spoke. I was cleaning my weapons, maintaining them aloft with an insignificant whim of telekinesis. Three daggers, my ritual jamdhara blade, Sacramentum, my archeotech tri-mouthed laser pistol, my boltgun – all of them revolved slowly in the air before me, psychically stripped with a peeling, searing heat that flensed them of any corrosion.

'So the matter of my fury is something he discusses with you all? Does Abaddon speak of your failings as freely as he speaks of mine?'

That stopped their duel. Both of my brothers looked to me, and Lheor laughed with typically toothy malice.

'You realise that while you're away on your endless hunts, we have better things to do than discuss you? Some of us have wars to fight, Khayon. You can earn Abaddon's favour by cutting a few throats. The rest of us lead armies into battle.'

Lheor raised his blade again, beckoning to Amurael to continue the fight. 'Besides,' he added, 'I have no failings.'

The Warp Ghosts were true to their sepulchral words. They guided us through the storm, from the Eye's realm to the stark cold of real space.

How to describe that moment of freedom? The truth is that there was no exultation, nor even relief. The feeling was one of creeping awareness, an awakening that took firmer hold with every heartbeat. I had expected cheers and cries of defiant rage. Yet as the Eye's violet mists thinned, as we looked upon unpoisoned stars for the first time in a span of mangled chronology, the silence was deafening.

The shudders that forever ran through the ship's bones even in the Eye's calmest regions subsided, and the sudden quiet was practically a physical force, hammering against our senses. Some of the mutants and humans on the lower decks, mostly those who had been born within the Great Eye and never left its boundaries, for whom corporeal reality was an unimaginable concept, purportedly lost their minds. They had lived their lives with the sound and threat of claws raking against the hull. Without it... Well, reality was alien to them. I would not wish to speculate on the mechanics of their minds. All legionaries' brain patterns and cognitive functions are undeniably altered by our hellish sanctuary, but to have been born there and know no other existence? I tended to keep my senses away from their thoughts. Let that suffice.

Saronos lifted his hands from the navigational pylons. Ultio's breath was audible across the entire bridge, a relieved sigh from the mouths of her vox-gargoyles. Her ship had slipped free of those painful tides, returning to the natural void at last.

I no longer heard the whispering pleas and taunts of unformed daemons begging me to bring them into being. The chronometric runes at the edge of my retinal display began to tick in the right direction once more, marking time going forwards.

Ilyaster turned his skullish gaze to the oculus, which had become a painting of perfect stars. I did not know him well then, and his sunken features were slackened in an expression I struggled to recognise. At first I thought he might be weeping as he bore witness to our emancipation. With hindsight, I believe what I saw there was dread. We had been trapped in the underworld for so long, waging ceaseless war within our haven, that reality was now a realm of immense, insane emptiness.

Abaddon alone seemed unmoved by the transition. He listened to the crew stations sounding off their stuttering and overwhelmed status reports, then he received relayed word from the rest of the fleet as they drifted into real space in our wake. All of them made it through. Not a single vessel was lost. I had to check the records myself to ascertain that it was true, for I could scarcely believe such a thing was possible.

'Auspex,' Abaddon called to Ultio.

Even the Anamnesis was moved by breaking back into reality. Her eyes betrayed her disorientation, as she sought to process space that existed in a mere three dimensions once more, without the endless orchestra of madness tearing at her shields and the iron skin of her hull.

'I see nothing,' she declared. 'Ahead of us, the void is silent.'

'Keep your eyes open, my huntress. I doubt it will remain that way for long.'

Abaddon remained enthroned as Saronos approached him, and he bade the Warp Ghost rise when cursory obeisance was made.

'You have done all you promised,' Abaddon said.

'As was agreed,' Saronos replied.

'Though you leave several of my warships without void-guides.'

'As was also agreed. You speak irrelevancies, Ezekyle Abaddon.' My lord's lip curled at that in something approximating amusement.

Ilyaster approached, his black Terminator plate growling. 'What if we need your services again?'

Saronos turned his head to the newest of the Ezekarion. 'We have always served the Black Legion, when the Black Legion has met our price.'

I cannot have been the only one whose skin crawled with the temporal promise of the words. Abaddon's eyes narrowed to golden slits. 'You have *always* served us?'

A cawing cry sounded from the shadowed rafters, and a

daemonic crow spiralled down to land on the Warp Ghost's shoulder. It watched me with misted eyes, weak with the threat of discorporation, the smoke of its plumage thin to the point of transparency.

Tokugra?

It did not answer me. Saronos paid the daemon no heed either, even when it began scratching its claws on the mottled grey ceramite upon which it perched.

Saronos inclined his head respectfully to the warrior upon the throne. 'Goodbye, Ezekyle Abaddon.'

I found myself stepping forwards from the disorganised ranks, approaching the Warp Ghost, removing my helmet as I drew near.

'Hold,' I bid him. All eyes were upon me as I came almost within arm's reach of the grey warrior. 'Show me your face.'

The red eye-lenses burned with indifference. 'You speak irrelevancies.'

'Nothing I speak is irrelevant to me, or to my Legion. It is a simple enough request, Saronos.'

I had expected him to refuse. Instead, Saronos disengaged the seals at his collar, and the crow fluttered, shifting to his back-mounted power pack. There was a snap-hiss as Saronos' armour depressurised, and he pulled the helmet clear.

His skin was white, as was his long hair, the latter spilling free from its bindings as his helm came off. His eyes were red, and his face bore only minor alterations – the darkness of the veins beneath his sallow flesh was a map of the minor mutations in his bloodstream. He looked older than he had when I had last looked upon him, though he seemed no wearier, not even for the efforts of guiding the *Vengeful Spirit* and ferrying our souls back to reality.

Tokugra cawed, the sound ragged and weak. Murmurs began across the bridge. Ultio's gargoyles relayed her soft gasp. I glanced to Abaddon, only to see him watching with unsurprised acceptance.

I breathed Saronos' name, though not as it was now; I spoke his name as I had always known it.

'Ashur-Kai.'

His features did not flicker. They did not even twitch. 'You speak irrelevancies, Sekhandur.'

You know me, I sent to him. *You called me Sekhandur.*

'Do you remember us?' I asked him. He was already replacing his helm.

'You speak irrelevancies.'

'What happened to you, after you left us? For how many years have you been gone?'

His helm clicked into place with the crunching of pressure seals. His voice emerged through the vocaliser grille once more, as he told me, of course, that I spoke irrelevancies.

The bridge shivered with Ultio's sudden unease. 'I see another fleet in the dark,' she said. 'Approaching at attack speed.'

I had turned to her when she spoke. When I looked back to Ashur-Kai – to Saronos – he was gone.

On the hololithic display, the lone Warp Ghosts vessel that had accompanied our fleet, the *Tartaran Wraith,* was sailing back into the Eye's murky borders.

'Ashur-Kai...' I murmured.

ASHUR-KAI! I hurled his name into the warp, a plea to be answered and a command to be obeyed. There was nothing. Nothing at all.

Lheor thudded his palm against the back of my head. 'Forget them! Let them run. The war's about to start.'

Words escaped me. It was all I could do to nod.

We came about to face the new threat: the inbound fleet, its vanguard vessels still mathematically mystifying distances away. Deep-sight images relayed back ship after ship after ship... You must understand that when the Imperium speaks of Chapters, they have sacrificed the apocalyptic but disordered strength of a Legion for a surgical, precise special operations force. The Black Templars were a Chapter, but they were a Chapter on a scale the Imperium has not seen since the halcyon, blood-bitter days of the Heresy.

Abaddon laughed as image after image of sable-hulled warships stitched their way across the oculus. With the light of unhealthy mirth in his eyes, he spread his arms wide in a gesture of kingly acknowledgement.

'It seems we are not the only black Legion.'

When Ultio called out that we were being hailed, the command deck fell into hallowed silence. No one needed to ask which ship was sending the hail.

The image upon the oculus took several seconds to resolve, and between the distance at hand and the interference of nearby Eyespace, it remained flickering and grainy. The throne before us was fashioned of carved bronze and Terran marble, that blue-veined stone rarer than an honest man in the Nine Legions. Its high back and broad arms were flanked by stands of braziers and ascending candles, painting the white rock amber and casting flickering shadows across the dark warrior seated there.

Many legionaries and humans alike have mistaken Abaddon for his father, Horus. There was no way that this warrior could be mistaken for his primarch liege. His armour was black, as was ours. The ceramite layers were rimmed in gold, as were ours. It is said that our armour is black to obfuscate our past colours, and this is true, but I saw the very same mournful and hopeful defiance in the wargear of the warrior before me. The stain of failure clung to him as it clung to us, and rather than drape himself in funereal black out of a need for revenge, he had darkened his armour as a statement of atonement and redemption.

He reclined like an idle king, too stalwart to slouch, too alert to be resting, his hand on the hilt of a black sword. Every one of us knew that blade's legend. Many of us had lost brothers to its killing edge. Their blood had soaked into its black steel, running across the inscription marking its length. The oculus image was too flawed to read the words but I knew what they would say if the view resolved: *Imperator Rex*. The blade was forged to honour the Emperor, the king of kings, the Master of Mankind.

The warrior's hair was cropped close and whitened by time. A short beard framed the thin, scarred line of his mouth. Age had weathered his skin and frosted his hair, but his shoulders were unbowed, and no oculus distortion could hide the icy fury in his eyes. Vindication burned in that gaze. He had waited for us here, down the many decades, and he had been right to wait.

He was *us*, through a lens of loyal zeal, through a mirror of indignant righteousness. I would have known this even before I tasted his knight's brainflesh months before. I would have known it the second my eyes fell upon him, this ancient knight-king, enthroned on white stone and leaning upon a sword that had reaped an untellable number of lives during our doomed rebellion.

Abaddon was standing, staring, his glyphed teeth showing through parted lips. He was as awed as the rest of us. Knowing what was waiting once we broke free was one thing, but witnessing it with our own eyes was quite another. A smile dawned across his features, and his warp-lit eyes gleamed.

'Only you, Sigismund,' he said to the knight-king, 'would pursue a grudge to the very borders of hell. That's a hatred so pure, I can't help but admire it.'

The ancient knight rose, raising the blade in a warrior's salute, one I recognised from fighting alongside the Imperial Fists in brighter, better days. He kissed the hilt, then pressed his forehead to the cold blade.

'*I suffer not the unclean to live.*'

Abaddon's grin deepened. 'Blood of the Gods, it is good to see you again, Sigismund.'

'*I uphold the honour of the Emperor. I abhor and destroy the witch. I accept any challenge, no matter the odds.*'

Abaddon was laughing now. 'A true son of Rogal Dorn. Never show emotion when a chorus of oaths and vows will serve instead.'

But they were not vows. Not really. They were promises. He wrote those oaths for his Chapter to follow, but they were his words – not vows for his knights to emulate, but a promise to his foes.

Sigismund, once First Captain of the Imperial Fists, now High Marshal of the Black Templars, looked back at us from the bridge of the *Eternal Crusader*. And still he refused to address us. We were beneath him, undeserving of anything but his regal disdain.

In contrast, our bridge erupted with sound. Shouts and murderous cries were hurled towards the oculus, as the relief of escaping our prison and the surreal truth of being confronted by our former foes finally broke over us. It banished the stunned and useless silence that had gripped us upon emerging into the Cadian Gate, and we baptised the moment in an orchestra of bestial roars and jeers. It was a tide of sound from human throats, mutant maws and legionary helm vocalisers, a throat-tearing wave of derision and fury that made the stinking air of the bridge tremble. There was joy in that sound, and bitterness, and rage. It was an exorcism. A purging. It was *vindicta* given voice.

Sigismund looked at us as if we were nothing but howling barbarians. To him, perhaps we were. He still had not addressed us directly, and he did not change that now. He gave an order to his bridge crew and cast his cloak from his shoulders, freeing himself for the fight to come.

'*Attack.*'

Ultio's response was immediate. 'The *Eternal Crusader* is engaging.'

She didn't wait for orders. The *Vengeful Spirit* shuddered as it moved to match its sister ship. It had been centuries since they sailed the same skies. Now they would meet once more.

All-out void war is fought in spheres of engagement. The greatest fleets duel one another in a three-dimensional battlescape, with elements of each fleet occupying a spherical space of conflict. Within this sphere they keep their escorts, their fighters and their targets. In this manner, a series of individual battles forms the greater war, no different from the regimental shield walls of the Iron Era or the naval engagements of the Age of Sail.

How fine that sounds in principle. The reality is altogether messier. No battle plan survives contact with the enemy.

The spheres are ever-shifting loci, moving and realigning moment by moment with the unfolding battle. Keeping track of this untrackable miasma, where tens of thousands of lives are lost in every heartbeat and every attack must be made with streams of calculation, is a task for only our finest minds. A gifted void warrior is among a Legion's most precious resources. Abaddon, for all his skills, has never been a natural in the void. He has always thrived in the instinctual immediacy of a close fight. Valicar Hyne, named as the Black Legion's fleetmaster by Ezekyle, was one of our savants in this arena.

But none of our captains, Valicar included, could match the Anamnesis. Ultio was beholden to Abaddon and Valicar's orders, but they were beholden to her genius. She was the machine-spirit of the flagship – she was the ship itself – and yet she was even more. The Martian Mechanicum had originally constructed her to be the core of my first warship, the now-lost *Tlaloc,* encrusting her suspension tank with hundreds of mind-linked cogitators and harvested, vat-sustained slave-brains. They remade her into a gestalt entity, naming her the Anamnesis, yet it was only when she fused with the ancient and warlike machine-spirit of our Legion's flagship that she truly developed autonomy. As the heart of the *Vengeful Spirit*, she rediscovered mortal instinct and blended it with her cold and calculating mind.

Ezekyle was the one to name her Ultio, a wry reference to an Old Earth goddess of war and vengeance. And, I am sure it will not surprise you to learn, another word for *vindicta*.

With her enhanced senses bonded so closely with the *Vengeful Spirit,* Ultio had a perception of void war's oceanic possibilities that even the lords of the Legions could not easily match. She was one of the Mechanicum's very few successful prototypes in combining human awareness, gestalt consciousness and elevated intelligence within a machine-spirit, and this rarity made her as useful as any of Abaddon's warlords. Arguably, it made her more useful than any individual within the Ezekarion. More than once I had wondered if Abaddon's priority had been in acquiring my talents, or if securing my loyalty was merely a necessity towards gaining control of the Anamnesis. When I had asked him in the past, his reaction had been to break into laughter, which was no answer at all.

Abaddon was feverish from the moment he heard Sigismund give his order to attack. Despite our breaking free of the Eye, the Pantheon's singers and heralds cried ever louder for his attention. Strange to think that this was before he wore their mark and carried the daemon blade – in years to come, looking upon him as the Despoiler, the Lord of Chaos Ascendant, would be like staring into the heart of a sun.

Yet the Pantheon cried out for him, louder now that he was one step closer to the destiny they wished for him – a destiny he would both fulfil and deny for the rest of his life as the Gods' greatest chance of victory and the one man they could never trust or cage. Fire burned in his eyes as he stared at the *Eternal Crusader*.

The two fleets powered towards one another, far-sighted weapons firing on the faith of calculations long before a single ship was in visual range. The deck rumbled beneath our feet with the draconic efforts of the engines and the first volleys spat into the calm night. Individual battlegroups followed their assigned vectors, beginning to drift away to form their own engagement spheres. We had only just returned to real space, and already we defiled it with the scream of weapon batteries.

So began the first battle of the Long War.

Before the fleets joined, a period of suffocating serenity reigned. I was aware of the crew bracing around me, and of the clarion calls that sent warriors to their battle stations, pilots to their fighters and enslaved gunnery crews to their cannon decks. With the distance between the two armadas, for a time there was nothing to do but wait. I knew where Abaddon would want me to be when the time came, and so I remained on the bridge, awaiting his order.

My skull ached. It was more than a headache; it was a physical pressure upon the cranial bone that caged my brain. I could feel the blood vessels swelling behind my eyes.

Nefertari came to me, mellifluous in her alien motions. Her merest movements were all silk with no sensuality. Nagual was with her, almost overshadowing her in height and most definitely in bulk. My two trusted retainers, my two finest weapons, though circumstance had denied me their use in recent years. One, an alien maiden I no longer truly needed; the other, a simple-minded reflection of the wolf I had lost long ago.

Master, the lynx sent to me. I ignored him. I was watching the slow-growing specks that made up the enemy fleet. My remade fist closed and opened, a bionic bloom that betrayed my restlessness. My new machine knuckles purred.

'You are thinking of Ashur-Kai,' my eldar bloodward ventured. She was always so certain, her tone always so adamant, that it was strange to hear a query in her voice now.

'Yes and no,' I confessed. I *was* thinking of Ashur-Kai – of Saronos and the changes I had witnessed – but I was also dwelling on thoughts of Thagus Daravek. I felt us sliding inexorably closer to a final confrontation with the Lord of Hosts, and I no longer believed I could be of any help to Abaddon and my brothers.

Were they thinking the same? Would they see me as a liability and remove me? How strange it felt, to not be trusted by one's own kindred. I kept skimming their surface thoughts in search of any unease, but all of them were focused on the coming battle.

'Saronos,' said Nefertari, seemingly trying out the name's taste. 'Was the warrior in grey truly Ashur-Kai?'

'Yes. It was him all along. The dilations of time...' I began, only for Nefertari to silence me with a curt hiss between her teeth.

'So the White Seer lives, even after he was sacrificed. Why then do you seethe with such unbecoming melancholic unrest?'

'It is not Ashur-Kai that burdens me,' I admitted. 'Thagus Daravek said he killed me at Drol Kheir.'

Nefertari wore hydra gauntlets that day, devices of Commorran design that projected talon-like growths of living crystal, all to the wearer's whim. My bloodward used the violet crystal fingernail claws to tap out a slow, tinkling melody against the crew railing. It had the cadence of a lullaby, one warped and out of time.

Her grasp of the various Gothic tongues was masterful, but she struggled with her pronunciation. The eldar mouth and vocal cords were not suited to what Nefertari termed 'the animal bleating that you humans call language'.

'Drol Kheir,' she repeated the name. 'In our time together, allies and enemies alike have spoken of that place.' Her dark eyes watched the tense forms of the bridge crew as the warships closed the immense distance. The deck beneath us shivered with the distant roar of the *Vengeful Spirit*'s engines. 'Rumours of your demise are nothing new. Did you die there? Were his words true?'

'I do not know. It might explain the command he holds over my physical form.'

'It might also be the lie of a desperate monster seeking any advantage he can, as destiny slips through his fingers.'

'My memory of the place is shattered. Flawed.' Though that could be Daravek's manipulation as well. This was all so futile. My mind was working itself into knots.

I will kill him, Nagual assured me. I dismissed the beast's useless loyalty with a wave of my hand. Nagual had tried and failed in that ambition almost as often as I had.

'Why do so many of your brothers and cousins believe you died in that place?' Nefertari asked.

'Because I went into seclusion after Drol Kheir. I left the Thousand Sons conclaves still gathered at Sortiarius and sailed with Ashur-Kai, away from the rest of our Legion. We were unseen for decades.'

'Doing what, *voscartha*?' she asked, using the Commorran word for 'slave master'. I hesitated for a moment – she had never before betrayed any interest in my life before her presence within it. I felt the threat of a smile.

'We were seeking a route out of the Eye.'

She gave a knowing nod as the chronology slipped into place. It had been in that period that we initially came across Nefertari herself, adrift in a riven vessel of alien metal and living crystal. A lifepod of sorts, tumbling through the Eye's tides, with only one soul aboard.

She flexed her fingers and the violet crystal talons receded. 'In my experience,' Nefertari said in her thick, difficult accent, 'you *mon-keigh* make a great many claims when it comes to your own prowess, awarding yourselves title after title, your psyches awash with the hope that such posturing will intimidate your foes.'

'Undeniably true,' I admitted, 'though that is harsh criticism from a species that attaches poetic nonsense like "the Storm of Silence" and "the Cry of the Wind" to its demigods, no?'

'You are pronouncing the honorifics with a mumbling ineptitude that renders them meaningless,' Nefertari pointed out, 'and it is not remotely the same.'

If you say so, I thought.

'Indeed,' I said aloud.

'Perhaps he killed you and bound your spirit,' Nefertari mused. 'Perhaps he preys upon your fears. What difference does it make to you in the here and the now?'

'It makes every difference. If he has bound my soul to his will...' I trailed off, my discomfort growing. This was coming too close to matters I never wished Nefertari to know of – matters pertaining to her own existence. She cut onwards, ignorant to my reluctance.

'You are wrong. It makes no difference at all. If you see him, you must kill him. This is what must be done. It matters not what hold he possesses over you. It changes nothing.'

'My thanks,' I said, 'for this unwelcome and cold clarity.'

Distracted, I ran my bionic hand through Nagual's fur. The beast tensed, almost flinching back from me in alarm. Nefertari, far too inhuman to betray any real emotion, nevertheless let her glance flick to the motion. She recognised the gesture from the years with Gyre at my side.

I looked at the great *tigrus*-cat, meeting the flawed pearls of his eyes. I saw in his gaze how he feared me: he feared dissolution and banishment due to disappointing his master – as all thrall daemons do – but he feared *me,* as well. He feared my thoughts. He feared my temper.

I have not treated you well in our years together, have I, creature?

The huge lynx scored the deck with his talons.

You are strong, master, Nagual sent back with an acceptance born of instinct. He would serve me because I was strong, because I had shackled him to my will. He feared me but, for now, he would not defy me. I had expected this simplistic and somewhat hollow perspective, but Nagual surprised me with his next words.

And I am not Gyre. She alone tasted no torment from you.

I had never excruciated Gyre. She had never required torture or any other inflicted encouragement. Nor had I ever taken out my temper on her, for my long-serving wolf was a creature of cunning as well as lethality.

Nagual was all predation and destruction. Perhaps I had undervalued those aspects. It was something to think about when I had the luxury of time. *If* I rediscovered that luxury.

I touched my fingertips to my closed eyes, fighting through the miasmic headache still pushing at the insides of my skull. The indistinct haze of images from memories danced in a filter over my sight. The command deck around me was layered with the contours of places I had not been in decades. Brothers long dead stood at the edge of my vision. I could even hear their voices, not quite real, thinned in recollection, yet impossible to banish.

I was not the only one suffering. Most of the warriors remaining on the bridge radiated an aura of the same pain, and blood ran from the noses and ears of several mutants.

Tzah'q, one of the beastmen from the *Tlaloc,* snorted bloody filth from his nasal passages, sending it spattering onto the decking. He served as an overseer on the *Vengeful Spirit* just as he had on my old ship, and though he was ancient now – his fur whitened and his eyes milky – he needed no eyes to watch over the menials under his less than tender care. Horns of black glass jutted from his temples, and smaller spikes and spines of the same obsidian protruded from his chin and cheeks. He oversaw the menials and thralls, head jerking this way and that. Where furred, clawed hands had once gripped a lasrifle or a whip, now avian talons curled, wickedly sharp, held close to his chest. The Changer had blessed him – or cursed him, if you prefer – but I no longer healed the ravages of his age, for he no longer needed me to. The God of Fate had marked him well.

He huffed again, another short, breathy bark to clear his snout of the bleeding slime. The beastman sensed my scrutiny and bared his yellowing peg-teeth in a bitter rictus.

'Pain,' he grunted. An acknowledgement, not a complaint. 'Pain since we left the Eye.'

Tzah'q had been born in the Eye. He had never lived within the material universe. The weight of physics played upon all of us once more, but it was heaviest on those who were strangers to reality.

'It is time,' I replied.

'Time, Lord Khayon?'

'The pain you feel is time going forwards. You are feeling the weight of your bones and the running of your blood as your body ages around you. What you feel, Tzah'q, is the passage of time. That is why your mind aches.'

'Pain,' the beastman agreed. I did not care enough to read his mind to see whether he understood or not. It hardly mattered.

'Khayon,' Abaddon called to me. I left my thralls and ascended my lord's dais, ready to receive my orders at last.

When I say that he looked fevered, I am not doing justice to what burned in his gaze. You might call it a sick hunger or the purity of zeal, and both descriptions would be perfectly apt. What I saw in his eyes was a silent furore, a riot of restrained emotion. *If he were a beast,* I thought, *he would be salivating.*

Moriana was with him. She regarded me coolly. I ignored her.

'I can scarcely give it credence,' Abaddon said quietly. 'Free, at long last.'

'Free,' I agreed. 'But for how long?'

He gave a toothy smile, knowing of what I spoke. The Imperium would hear of this battle soon enough. We were a Legion, but our enemies would descend upon us with the strength of an empire.

'Long enough, my brother. Long enough. You know what I wish of you?'

'As always.' Closer to him, I could hear it now – the rippling song of the warp, spreading through his aura like blood misting through water. And within that shrieking harmony, words – words in a tongue that defied comprehension despite the many decades I had spent immersed in the warp's sacrilegious melodies. It was a song shaped for Abaddon alone, as the Pantheon crooned to him of fate and destiny. I wondered just what they were promising, and whether Moriana had whispered those same promises in my lord's ears.

One word permeated that siren howl, one word that was imprinting itself upon Abaddon's very bones and transcribing itself through his bloodstream. The only word I recognised.

'Drach'nyen,' I said aloud. 'I hear its song clearer out here.'
'As do I,' said Abaddon. Moriana stiffened at our words.
'Now is not the time for your suspicions, Iskandar.'

She rested her small, bare, human hand on the Talon of Horus. I was gratified by the caress of distrust in Abaddon's aura – no matter how he heeded her words, he was under no illusions. He seemed on the verge of saying more, but instead he shifted away from the slender prophetess and nodded to the oculus.

'Are you prepared for this, Khayon?'

Was that a second's doubt in his eyes? A momentary flicker of indecision?

I looked at the fleet bearing down upon us, and as vast as it was, it was no match for us in size. At the fleet's vanguard sailed the *Eternal Crusader,* and once more I saw the ancient knight in my mind's eye, so regal upon his throne.

'I do not think anyone can be prepared to fight Sigismund,' I replied.

'The Emperor's Champion,' Abaddon said quietly. This was the title that Lord Rogal Dorn had granted to his son at the Battle of Terra. And oh, how Sigismund had earned that title. 'You saw how old he is.'

'If you are trying to convince me that he will have lost his prowess, Ezekyle, you are walking a foolish road.'

'Perhaps so. He is the embodiment of all we are fighting against. He is ignorance incarnate, a puppet held up by strings of blind loyalty to the deceiving Emperor. But I can't hate him. Is that not insane, Khayon? There stands the avatar of all we seek to destroy – an Imperial legend – and yet I admire the man.'

'Admire the man,' I said. 'Destroy the legend.'

He grinned. 'Wise words.'

'Take me with you,' I added. 'I want to fight in the boarding assault.'

'Why?' Abaddon replied at once. His amusement faded

at my break with tradition. One of the Ezekarion had to remain aboard the flagship, to command Delvarus and to work with Ultio. It was the way of things. Without Ashur-Kai, I was the logical choice to remain, given my bond with the Anamnesis and my talents in guiding the Secondborn that served under Delvarus.

'Delvarus and the Riven can hold the *Vengeful Spirit* without me, and the ashen dead will answer to other sorcerers. I want to be part of the assault aboard the *Eternal Crusader*.'

'Why?' he asked again, as if he did not know. He merely wanted me to say it.

'To fight at your side. To have you prove, after Daravek's claims, that you still trust me.'

The Talon's claws clashed softly together. 'If I didn't trust you, you'd be dead.'

I reached for his mind to prevent the prophetess from hearing. *Is that true, brother? You do not trust Moriana, yet she still draws breath.*

He closed our psychic link with a pulse of dismissal. 'I need you here, Khayon.'

I heard the iron in his words. There would be no argument. I conceded with a nod, feeling every eye in the chamber turned to me, witnessing Abaddon's refusal. On one level I knew this was nothing but imagination born of bruised pride, yet still I felt those stares.

'Lheor will remain with you,' Abaddon decided. Ever the battle-king, he burned with vitality at the thought of boarding the *Eternal Crusader*. I could practically hear his racing pulse. 'And if you lose my ship, I may lose my temper.'

With those words, he left the bridge, trailed by Falkus and the black-clad Terminators of Abaddon's elite guard – once the Justaerin, now the Aphotic Blade.

I did not watch him leave. I focused my annoyance upon the oculus, where the two fleets sailed ever closer. The foe's spheres of engagement were falling into place as subfleets and battlegroups aligned in their individual formations. The deck shuddered as we veered ponderously aside from the first torpedo runs, the crew stations erupting in shouts and declarations of sensory data.

It was beginning now. Truly beginning.

'Sister,' Ultio called to the *Eternal Crusader,* the *Vengeful Spirit*'s sibling and the only Gloriana-class battleship in the enemy armada. On her face was an expression of consummate rapture. 'You missed.'

The bridge doors rumbled closed behind Abaddon and the Black Legion elite. The *Vengeful Spirit,* already juddering with the overburn of its engines, somehow sped up in unity with the Anamnesis' bloodlust.

XIII

VOID WAR

I have spoken of our fleet's might, but not its poverty. The many daemon-forges that would later answer Abaddon's calls were still in their infancy within the Empire of the Eye. Our Heresy-era technology was eternally degrading even back then, and we had little to use in place of our losses. Resources like ore-rich moons, shipboard foundries and Mechanicum manufactoria were as precious to us as fresh water: not only agonisingly rare, but also subject to their own sufferings. Legion warbands endlessly plundered such sites in the rabid hunt for shreds and scraps of advantage.

You have heard evidence of this carrion-feeding already. I have told you of Maeleum, of the raids and punishments it endured and of our undignified picking through its carcass. We were all vultures and carrion crows in those days. I believe we still are.

And if we were low on ammunition, if our armour plating was cracked, repaired and cracked again, the truth is that our fleets were in even worse shape. We had been beaten in the Heresy, we had been beaten into exile in the Scouring, and while the Imperium licked its wounds in the aftermath of our disappearance, we had spent that era waging war against one another.

For every vessel enhanced by mutation, another was cursed by it; for every cruiser sailing with admirable repairs or an undamaged hull, another was a shell of its former glory. Within Eyespace, our ships were subject to the erosion of the warp's touch, accelerating natural degradation, and reliable opportunities to dry-dock and repair a capital ship were staggeringly scarce. In the Eye, especially in that era, a functioning, stable shipyard was practically the stuff of dreams. They were always the highest priority for destruction if another warband wished to grind a rival into dust.

For a time, the newborn Black Legion had claimed and defended Niobia Halo – the shipyard and forge moon belonging to Ceraxia and Valicar. That custodianship had ended when Thagus Daravek led a warhost of Word Bearers and Death Guard to annihilate our docks and plunder the riches we had acquired. The installation was lost in the resulting battle. Afterwards, both Valicar and Ceraxia joined the Ezekarion as fleetmaster and armsmistress respectively.

Many of the vessels we sailed from the Eye into the waiting fire arcs of the Black Templars fleet bore the wounds of ages. The pressures of the storm that had barred our escape only added to the strains already placed on their hulls after centuries of civil war and sailing in the unquiet, poisoned tides of Eyespace. Imperial captains across the millennia often observe that the Traitor Legions and our thrall fleets are comprised of warships plundered from sectors surrounding the Eye. The Gothic Sector alone has supplied us with any number of ships across the many centuries. This is a sad necessity, as our Crusade- and Heresy-era vessels break down beyond sustainability, are lost to the warp's clutches or are simply destroyed in the ebb and flow of the Long War.

It is for these same reasons that you see our individual warriors equipped with ancient and unreliable patterns of weaponry, or reduced to using inefficient, outdated wargear. For all the strength that mutation and hatred bestow, erosion, decay and the eternal civil war between the Nine Legions takes more than its share.

We are mighty, but it is a tenuous might. Just as that day, when we outnumbered Sigismund's armada, our advantage was fragile. We did not have the luxury of carelessness. A great deal of our fleet's strength was concentrated in the killing power and endurance of the *Vengeful Spirit* and the other largest ships that once sailed at the vanguard of the Great Crusade. Most were changed significantly by their time in the Eye, and I knew their machine-spirit cores would be as disorientated by their return to real space as any truly living being.

I have no gift for void war. I have never been able to overcome the helplessness of being a witness to such grand destruction, with my fate entirely cradled by the vessel around me. Worst of all, void battle is not swift. Despite the fact thousands of men and women are dying with every passing second, the war itself plays out with unbearable traction.

I remained on the command deck as the battle began. The *Eternal Crusader* and the *Vengeful Spirit* powered towards one another, but they were not the first vessels to engage. That honour fell to the *Tyresian's Hex,* a light cruiser that sped ahead of its engagement sphere, immediately finding itself pockmarked with gas-venting wounds as an Imperial fighter wing clung to its skin like a haze of circling insects.

More of our vessels tore free of their formations, streaking ahead at the whims of bloodthirsty captains who were spurred on by the long-denied taste of vengeance. I shook my head at the sight, only for Lheorvine to snort at my disappointment. He was at my side upon the throne's elevated dais, watching the same images on the oculus. He sympathised with the warships falling out of formation to risk their own revenge.

'Undisciplined,' I said.

'Not everyone is a cold-blooded Tizcan,' he grunted back. His cranial implants were biting; one of his eyes kept twitching closed, and he had to suck saliva back through his metal teeth.

'We are soldiers,' I pointed out.

'*Soldiers.*' He made an insult of the word. 'Once we were crusaders, Khayon, and now we are warriors, but we were never "soldiers". Keep that foolishness to yourself.'

I swallowed my argument, following his train of thought. It was not the first time legionaries have disagreed over those semantics, and it would be far from the last. Some believed soldiering came down to discipline, or fighting for a state or a leader rather than for yourself. Some believed warriorhood was a matter of heart that elevated them above a soldier's station, while others considered it a state of barbarity that dragged them beneath it.

Some questions have no answers.

No matter how seriously we took warfare, no matter how adamantly we clung to our disciplined roots as a Space Marine Legion, many of our number were ultimately the raiders and marauders that time had made them. For better or worse, we would never have the ironclad discipline of a Throne-loyal Adeptus Astartes force. Even back then, we had lost much of the discipline we had once possessed as Legions of the Great Crusade.

'No argument?' Lheor grinned. 'Where is Khayon and what have you done with him?'

'I am in no mood for your jests.'

'Are you ever?'

'Please be quiet, Lheor.'

The ship shivered as the first lance strikes came close enough to caress it, and our void shields lit in reaction, brought into shimmering being. In her containment chamber-tank, Ultio pushed her hands forwards through the fluid. Her face was set in savage concentration.

As was mine. Ultio lived the battle as it unfolded, but I was limited to merely watching it, trying to follow its course through the inefficient vista of flickering hololithics and an oculus plagued by static.

The *Eternal Crusader* powered ever closer. The *Vengeful Spirit* felt tight around me, its every deck plate and hull wall taut with Ultio's excited fury. She wanted nothing more than to claw her sister ship to pieces with lance and broadside. From the viciousness writ upon her face, I thought she might even be tempted to ram the other vessel in her rage.

The ship gave a tremendous shudder beneath another barrage. The lights sputtered across the chamber.

'That was no lance strike,' I said.

'Look.' Lheor drew my attention back to the oculus. 'That's not good.'

Three vessels sailed in an elevated engagement sphere at a stand-off distance, too far from the wrath of our guns unless we broke off from the *Eternal Crusader*. Their delineation runes marked them as vessels unfamiliar to the *Vengeful Spirit*'s memory banks – Crusade-era Victory-class cruisers belonging to no Legion. I watched as the rearmost of the three daggerish vessels, thick with the flies of its lesser escorts, trembled in the void as it fired a city's worth of ship-wide stabilisers.

The impact struck us even before the ship's prow-mounted accelerator coils had flashed with their release. The *Vengeful Spirit* heaved around us, metal groaning under tension, bruises discolouring Ultio's dusky skin.

She gave a snarl that had no place emerging from a human throat.

Lheor grunted as the ship stabilised. 'Shieldbreakers,' he said.

'Sailing with minimal escorts,' I replied. 'That is bait if ever I saw it.'

'Sure enough, but it's one hell of an opportunity.' He wiped his mouth on the back of his hand. 'What's more important here? Killing Sigismund or claiming resources for the Long War?'

He had a point, and I was of a mind to encourage his rare tactfulness. I opened a vox-link to Abaddon, where he waited in his boarding claw. 'Ezekyle...'

'*We felt it,*' his voice crackled back, marred by interference. '*Nova cannon.*' He paused, doubtless reviewing the data from within his helm's tactical feeds, calculating how much damage they could inflict upon us before we reached the *Eternal Crusader*. If the imagery suffered battle interference up here on the bridge, it was likely little more than a spread of distortion across a helmet's retinal feed.

'*Proceed as planned,*' Abaddon decided, as we had all

known he would. '*Our escorts will catch up after we engage. We'll hold a quarter of their fleet alone if we have to.*'

'We can chase the cruisers down,' I argued. 'We can silence those long guns for good.' There was logic to this. Nova cannons require an immense sacrifice in time and effort to prepare, fire and reload, and were near worthless at close range. With Abaddon's order, we could tear through those three Victory cruisers like a mythical Terran lion ravaging through a helpless herd of extinct Terran elk. 'Should we not board them and claim them for ourselves? Think of the value of such prizes.'

'*Don't be tempted by lesser prey, sorcerer. It's a juicy ruse to lure the alpha predator away. They know if we go for their throat, we win almost at once, so they offer up tempting targets to test our resolve.*'

'The *Vengeful Spirit* is our greatest game piece on this board,' I replied to Abaddon. 'Let us win the war first, then you can face Sigismund.'

'*I will have his head,*' Abaddon snapped. His famous temper kindled at the threat of being denied close-quarters slaughter. I could practically sense him trying to wrest it back under control. '*Whatever they attempt is meaningless once we're aboard the* Crusader, *and nothing they can do will stop us boarding it. Ignore the ripe targets they lay in our path. Proceed as planned.*'

I tried one final time. 'We are here to raid, Ezekyle. We are here to gather our strength, not deplete it. We should take those ships for ourselves.'

Abaddon's reply was a static-laden dismissal. '*Valicar is fleetmaster. Let him take them or kill them as he sees fit. I want Sigismund, Khayon. I feel the hand of fate on my shoulder. This must be done.*'

There would be no arguing with him. Every syllable that left his fanged mouth seethed with *vindicta* – our greatest strength and our deepest flaw, embodied by Ezekyle, who has always been the best of us. I wondered how much of his eagerness was a desire for vengeance and glory, and how much was desperation to prove himself against the Legiones Astartes hero that had taken his place as first-favoured. Any warrior of the Nine Legions that says he fights without bitterness is lying.

There was more, and it was not tied into our gene-forged bodies or the preternatural depths of our bitterness. Abaddon was driven by a hunger far more mundane; warriors throughout history have always defined themselves by having the courage to face their enemies, and by the quality of the foes that fall before them. Of course Abaddon wanted Sigismund dead.

I spared a look at Moriana, who stood by Abaddon's empty throne. She could not overhear my conversation, for she lacked access to the vox, but she still smiled when she saw me take note of her.

I said nothing to Ezekyle. There was nothing to say. The link went dead, immediately punctuated by the rattling shake of the ship around us once more. Nova cannon projectiles, hurled by circular racks of gravitic impellers and accelerator spirals, detonated in plasmic cloudbursts the size of celestial bodies. The *Vengeful Spirit* tore through the detonation's savage aftermath, increasingly alone as our escorts fell ever further behind. Initially, we had been at risk of outpacing them with Ultio's aggressive charge, but now they were truly forced back: we could survive a sustained nova cannon barrage; they could not.

'We are about to be dangerously alone,' I said to no one but myself.

Moriana's smile was an unreadable crescent; it could have been sincere or vicious, I could not tell.

'Have faith, Iskandar,' she said. 'Trust in Ezekyle. Destiny rides at his side this day, and the Gods are bearing witness to his deeds. These are his first steps to becoming the vessel into which the Pantheon pours all of its promises.'

I sneered at the sentiment. 'I trust Ezekyle completely, prophetess. It is your Gods that I mistrust and despise. My lady, if you believe Abaddon will ever become their vessel, you have gravely misjudged the man you admire.'

'Time changes all things, Iskandar. Ezekyle is a soul of singular vision.'

'Your serene smugness makes my gorge rise,' I told her with exaggerated politeness, 'and I am telling you, Moriana, you did not see the expression he wore when he rammed the Talon through his reborn father's body. Abaddon is everything Horus is not. Your Gods may plague us. Some of us may even pray to them in times of dire need. But the son will never fall into the duped slavery that held his father in thrall. The sooner you see that, the sooner you will see why we follow him.'

She laughed aloud as the deck shivered around us. 'How confidently you speak of the future! Are you a seer now?'

'I am a man who knows his brother.' She paled at the force of my tone, perhaps suspecting she had pushed me too far.

Nefertari and Nagual drew near, the huntress playfully regarding her crystal claws, the great cat giving a low, burbling growl. I had not summoned them, yet they had read my mood perfectly.

'Remove this civilian from the bridge,' I ordered them.

For the very first time, Moriana looked hesitant as the daemon-cat and the winged alien regarded her with cold gazes.

'I am Ezekarion,' she said, and I could not help but laugh.

'That means Ezekyle is sworn to heed your counsel,' I replied. 'And it means I will not kill you, Moriana. It does not mean I want you on the command deck in the midst of a battle.'

'I'm staying here, Khayon. Your slaves won't harm me.'

'I say again, I am pledged not to kill you. I said nothing about not harming you. If I crushed your spine and plucked your eyes from your face, you could still mewl your prophecies to Abaddon.'

She swallowed, believing me and finally falling silent.

'Nagual, Nefertari, take her away. Guard her somewhere that any boarding parties will not be able to reach.'

Nefertari narrowed her slanted, alien eyes. 'It is time to leave, mon-keigh god-whisperer.' Nagual reinforced her words with a snarl.

Moriana backed away, dignified in defeat, though I could hear the rhythm of her quickened heartbeat as she retreated. When the three of them had left the bridge, Lheor approached me once more. I had the sudden and disquieting notion that he had retreated from Moriana's presence, hiding from her.

'She makes my teeth itch,' Lheor said quietly. His eyes were glassy and unfocused. 'I can't decide why.'

'I know why,' I ventured.

'You do?' Some of the caution bled from his gaze now she was gone.

'It is because she speaks like a primarch. Everything she says is wreathed in certainty and inevitability and dripping with righteous invincibility – the same deluded cries of our failed fathers. My patience for that kind of preaching ran out around the time we were fleeing from Terra with our tails between our legs.'

Lheor showed his metal teeth in a grin. Some were bronze in colour, some a dull silver. He replaced them periodically. I had never thought to ask what they were really made from.

'She *does* talk like a primarch,' he agreed. 'Though she drools less than Angron ever did, I'll give her that.'

Ultio thrashed in her suspension tank, her mouth silently wide, lips peeled back from her teeth. The choir of vox-gargoyles and drifting servo-skulls gave voice to her scream, loud enough to set the beastmen braying in worship.

In response to her feral shriek, the *Vengeful Spirit* heaved into a heavy roll, ramming its way through an ocean of streaming torpedoes. They were pinpricks against the Anamnesis' skin, the buzzing of worthless vermin.

Blood, she mouthed, and 'Blood,' her gargoyles hissed above us. 'Blood crystals in the bare void and twisted iron turned to melted slag and bursting bodies and decompression gasps and charred steel and rancid chemical fire and...'

On and on she spat the hissing curses, caught in a trance, staring at the *Eternal Crusader*. The beastmen shouted prayers and devotional braying to their entombed goddess, the heart and soul of the ship, loud enough to set the air shivering.

On the oculus, the black lance of our sister ship speared ever closer.

It is difficult to describe the *Vengeful Spirit* in battle without straying into theatricality, because a simple retelling of its deeds defies both reason and physics. You must bear witness to it fighting in order to believe what she is capable of.

Even before the Anamnesis was installed as the flagship's machine-spirit, reports from the Horus Heresy listed the vessel as performing manoeuvres of impossible agility and unleashing weapons of unknown, unnatural origin. These reports, while true, were just the beginning. The Eye changed the *Vengeful Spirit* in ways that went beyond the crenellations and bastions along its back and the dark goddess at its heart. Existence inside the Eye had bred insanity and lethality into its iron bones.

We tore past the *Eternal Crusader* that night, close enough that our void shields shrieked with contact discharge against theirs. Voices immediately overlapped as they shouted status updates. Shield strength reports were bellowed across the chamber. Three of the beastmen crew roared that the boarding pods had been fired from their housings. A fighter escort wing had already spat free from their launch bays, tasked with shooting down any missiles tracking our boarding claws; the pilots' chatter spilled across the vox as they flew and fought and died. Weaponmasters and gunnery overseers bawled orders into their consoles as the oculus filled with the *Eternal Crusader*'s shield-lit spinal castles.

Voices, voices, voices. Sirens, fire, thunder. Shrieks, detonations, death.

It sounded like Prospero. It sounded like Prospero burning under the Wolf King's rage.

And then we were past them. We dived through a loose phalanx of the *Eternal Crusader*'s escorts, our guns silent, every cannon and turret across the ship holding its breath. Projectiles still rained and burst against our shields, but we lanced onwards without firing back.

Ultio was the reason why. She silenced the thousands of cannons slaved to her will, and her worshipful crew obeyed. She rolled in her suspension tank, arching her back, every muscle in her body taut, sinews standing out on her flesh with almost emaciated ferocity. Her jaw was clenched hard enough to risk shattering her teeth. Her eyes, the same dark shade as my own, were rolled to show bare whites.

The ship heaved around us, gravity generators straining to keep pace with the speed of our turn. Weighted air slammed many of us from our feet; I remained standing by locking my boots to the deck.

On the oculus, the *Eternal Crusader* was beginning to lean into a hard turn, one that would still take a minute or more to complete. The *Vengeful Spirit,* without slowing an iota, pulled up, inverting its pitch at full speed, rolling to face the way it had come. At the moment we aligned with the *Eternal Crusader* dead ahead, the engines roared even hotter.

Physics disallows such a manoeuvre at such speed, but it took place in the span of my twin hearts beating no more than ten times.

The *Eternal Crusader* was still in the first motions of its turn. The Anamnesis raked at its image with her clawed hands, and lance fire streamed silver-white from the *Vengeful Spirit*'s prow. Torpedoes flew behind those glittering beams. A city-killing's worth of incendiary rage caught the *Eternal Crusader* unprepared, spreading migraine prism-light across its suffering void shields, then bursting them to rain fire upon its unprotected hull.

'The *Crusader*'s shields are down and Lord Abaddon is aboard her,' Ultio voxed to the fleet. 'Cripple her, but remember – she is mine to kill once this is over.'

The Anamnesis leaned the *Vengeful Spirit* into a more conventional roll, coming about to face the closest Black Templars ships. There was a deathly light in her eyes – she wore the expression of a child learning it can inflict pain on helpless insects, burning them with sunlight through a focusing lens and pulling off their legs and wings.

And that is when the true fight began.

The *Eagle of Old Earth* was a destroyer, aligning itself into an attack run before we had fully come about. Its weapon batteries banged into the void, spreading impacts across our shields – and there it should have ceased, using its speed and manoeuvrability to escape. Instead it lingered for a second volley, its captain likely buying time for the *Eternal Crusader* to finish its own course changes. But Ultio was done with her sister ship; that was Abaddon's prey now. The Anamnesis had a fleet to kill.

The *Eagle of Old Earth*'s shields lasted all of seven seconds beneath our broadsides as we cut past. The cityscape of Hecutor macrocannons along our port side screamed their sunfire against the *Eagle of Old Earth*'s naked hull, annihilating the smaller ship in a supernova of bursting plasma. Ultio did not even react. She was already focused on the vessels ahead, above, below – the Black Templars had our flagship isolated and were closing in for the kill. The ship shook endlessly around us, gravity fading or pressing down upon us with punishing force as a consequence of Ultio's movements.

Lheor, his features twitching with the bite of his cranial implants, worked from a handheld hololith projector, studying a flickering layout of the flagship. Red runic markers denoted the estimated position of Black Templars boarding teams. I tuned out his words as he conveyed information and orders across the vox, keeping Delvarus and his Riven squad leaders appraised of the intruders' locations.

'Fewer than I'd have expected,' he said to me.

We both knew why. The bulk of their strength was still aboard the *Eternal Crusader,* luring Abaddon and our inner circle into their territory.

'More than enough to keep Delvarus entertained,' I replied with a calm that I did not entirely feel. *And to slaughter several hundred mortal crew,* I thought, though I kept the words from Lheor's mind, not wishing to inflame the pain engine in his brain and distract him from his task.

He spoke into the squad-relay vox for another few seconds, then regarded me with twitching eyes. 'This is woeful and bloodless, brother. We should be down there fighting with Delvarus.'

'Or aboard the *Crusader.*'

'Or there,' he agreed.

I tuned into Delvarus' vox-feeds, only to be met with raucous screaming, howling, jagged laughter and leonine roars. Bolters crashed in the background. Wherever Delvarus was, he was reaping his share of lives.

The Riven was Delvarus' warband, a host of Secondborn I had helped create over time, binding daemons within mortally wounded warriors and, whenever the chance arose, prisoners we took in battle. In later years, Imperial forces have encountered Black Legion squads wearing the daemonically tainted armour of loyalist Chapters, as I – and my apprentices – have bound Neverborn into our captives. Before my journey to Terra and my surrender to the Inquisition's care, I kept a coterie of such bodyguards myself: Blood Angels, Ultramarines, Imperial Fists and several of their Successors, their souls shattered and subsumed by the presence of the daemons riding their husks. It makes for a delicious insult on the battlefield. In those early days, however, Delvarus' warband were largely comprised of sacrificial volunteers from the Sons of Horus and the World Eaters, as well as prisoners from the other Legions.

'The Riven are enjoying themselves,' Lheor muttered. He was rocking slightly now, unable to keep still, suffering from an erratic, adrenal energy he could do nothing to discharge. I would have told him to join the fighting, but he would have refused me. He was a warleader, an officer and a lord in the Legion, and his place was coordinating his brethren. He would do his duty no matter how much he craved to shed blood in its place.

Ultio sailed us through an ocean of enemy firing solutions, treating the ship around her like a steed to be reined to her will and coaxed to give evermore speed. She acknowledged every one of our foes in a descending list of priorities, one that shifted moment by moment based on threat calculations of armament, support and positioning. Her attention was absolute – she chased her prey one after the other with meticulous precision, inflicting enough damage to sunder shields and cripple or kill before immediately refocusing on another target.

The heavy cruiser *Adamantine* sought to bar our path and block us within a crossfire of several vessels. The *Vengeful Spirit* banked into a roll like a bullet leaving a rifle, our port and starboard broadsides fireworking into the conflicted night, discharging at the vessels around us as we twisted and dived towards the *Adamantine*.

Our prow batteries were lances and grativon pulsar arrays. The former ruptured the *Adamantine*'s shields in a disintegration of shredding light, before the latter crushed the warship's forward decks in a mangling compression of molecules. Its bridge was among those decks that collapsed beneath this manipulation of its mass, and Ultio torpedoed the still-sailing wreckage to send it spinning aside.

It was not quite enough. Ultio finished the execution up close – the *Vengeful Spirit* rammed the headless cruiser aside, savaging it with a second graviton volley that collapsed another immense section of its superstructure. Within a heartbeat she was rolling us again, chasing another foe.

I could take it no more, this realm of thunder and shaking walls. I closed my eyes and reached out, seeking a battle I could contribute to.

I found Amurael almost at once. I rode within my brother's mind as his assault team made its way through the *Eternal Crusader*. I could not be with them in the flesh, so I journeyed with them in spirit.

As I sank into Amurael's senses, an unwelcome familiarity gripped me. I had been aboard the *Eternal Crusader* twice before, both times as an ambassador to the Imperial Fists in shared theatres of war. How strange it felt to enter those halls not with curiosity and respect, making overtures to another Legion in the Great Crusade, but with blades in our hands and hate in our hearts.

I clung to Amurael's thoughts. He felt me there and did not resist, though I would not exactly call it a welcome, either.

Through his senses, I experienced the battle. The air clattered with the metallic coughing of boltguns and the shrieking beams of the few volkite weapons we possessed that still functioned. Each breath I drew was spiced with the fyceline stink of shell propellant or the scorched ozone of steaming metal. Amurael's warriors comprised a ravening horde – squad by squad they massacred their way through the *Eternal Crusader,* butchering even unarmed mortal crew, wasting precious ammunition as if we possessed an abundance of such riches. All caution was cast aside. Our men could not be reined in now, even if we had wanted to do so.

The Black Templars met rage with wrath, charging down corridors to crash against the advancing, disorderly tides that had invaded their domain. Again and again, we were locked against shield walls of ceramite plate, where vision thinned to the motions of flashing blades and rattling chains.

We bled. We sheeted with sweat. We swore. Fists and pistol grips pounded against helmets. Chainblades carved their whining way through armour joints or sprayed useless sparks against reinforced plate. Amurael needed room to swing his sword – in close quarters, a warrior needs a shorter, thrusting blade, not a duellist's longsword – and many were the times Amurael's blade was fouled by a poor angle or snarled in a Templar's body, struggling to withdraw after a killing blow. The warriors we faced ground against us in an unceasing horde, sounding out battle cries and oaths to the Emperor, roaring into our faces. Those behind us, our own brothers, howled in frustration, unable to reach through the tight ranks to kill the foes they had waited centuries to face again.

Blood misted the air. Tabards and robes ignited under flamer gouts and spraying sparks. Every heartbeat was punctuated by another crumpling crack of a bolt shell detonating inside a body. We killed blindly in that press of arcing weapons and flashing limbs.

The tide would turn in one tunnel, only for another squad of black knights to meet us at the next junction or around the next corner.

I remained peripherally aware of the *Vengeful Spirit* around me, shivering and shaking as the other battle raged. I could make out Lheor's murmurs as he relayed orders to the Riven and his own squads from the War God's Maw.

Riding Amurael's mind was exchanging one sense of helplessness for another, but at least aboard the *Eternal Crusader* I was with my brethren and could be of some use to them.

Amurael called his racing, bleeding squad to halt. Several of them actually obeyed.

What is it? I sent to him, speaking within the mist of his senses. His thoughts were a furious stream of consciousness in the near darkness of the *Eternal Crusader*'s repetitive corridors.

Scanner. Need my auspex. The fighting is unreal. Gods, these bastards can fight! We're falling behind Abaddon.

You are not behind. You are ahead of almost every other assault force. Only Telemachon and the Shrieking Masquerade are ahead of you.

How do you know? he asked. *Where is Abaddon?*

He is embattled in the secondary starboard colonnades, I replied. *His boarding pods took suppressive fire on approach, so he is fighting undermanned. And I know because I know where all of you are. I can hear the songs of your thoughts even over this distance.*

Where is Telemachon? I have to link up with him, and he's refusing to answer the vox.

I resisted the urge to laugh, which was no easy feat. *Telemachon seeks the glory of slaying Sigismund alone. He will not come back for you, Amurael – he is thinking of nothing but casting the Black Knight's severed head at Abaddon's feet as a gift for our lord. Move west and regroup with any of your sergeants still able to follow orders. There is a concourse not far from here that leads to the spinal tributaries.*

Amurael spat acid onto the deck. *Thank you, brother. You should be here, Khayon. I could use you at my side.*

I wanted nothing more than to be there, instead of bloodlessly watching from afar as our Legion won its first victory against the Imperium.

Abaddon cannot trust me. Not after Daravek.

Perhaps, he agreed, too easily for my tastes.

Amurael moved again. I slipped free of his thoughts and opened my eyes. Ultio was screaming. It took me a moment to realise it was a cry not of rage, but of pain.

Blood stringed through the fluid of her suspension tank. The cables that crowned her, binding her skull to the logic engines at the top of her life-tomb, were tangled and leaking coppery oil. Psy-stigmata showed in an ugly patchwork across her skin – some of it taking the form of cuts and rents, others showing as bruises.

As weariness descended upon her, or as pain crept across her thoughts, her control over the vessel slipped. This was nothing I had not seen many times before: the Anamnesis forced to speak orders to the command deck crew instead of relying entirely on her control as the ship's machine-spirit. She was doing so now, maintaining a barrage of clear, concise orders.

'...eighty degrees portside yaw, accelerating at once. Fighters and bombers to flock to the *Falkata* as we come about. Formulate attack runs against its defensive broadsides. Shields failing in thirty to ten seconds. Begin the siphon of plasmic conduction to relight the shields. Starboard fore-gunner decks, be ready to fire in twelve seconds. Target the *Ophidian Gulf* as it passes through our firing solution – shatter its shields and vox the *Ecstasy of Fire* with orders to chase it down. Prepare the ultima torpedo array for vortex lock upon the *Prideclad* when we shift to the fourth subquadrant. Shields failing in twenty-five to five seconds. Brace for inevitable bombardment as the shields fall... There. The *Arcus* and the *Sword of Sigismund* are bringing lances to bear – brace for impact, brace, brace...'

When the shields fell, they fell with a seismic sound wave that jarred the *Vengeful Spirit* to its industrial bones. The shuddering intensified as weapons struck the naked hull with impunity, yet Ultio – bleeding and bruised – was immersed in the killing fields before her. The ship banked and rolled with her will, or moved at her command when her will was no longer sufficient. Impacts rained against us. Our weapons spat back. Beastmen roared around me.

Lheor abandoned his console and shouted for his arming slaves. Saliva had formed a sheen on his chin, and by the light of his bloodshot eyes, it would not be long before he lost himself to the Nails.

'Boarders from the *Blade of the Seventh Son*. They've gained the primus tributaries.' That was dangerously close to the bridge, and though the Riven were scattered across the ship, it was the War God's Maw that held the sectors around the command deck. Lheor was going to join his warriors.

Three heavily augmented beastmen, from Lheor's ruddy-furred Khorngor clans, brought his heavy bolter and ammunition feeds. Another carried his chainaxe, and yet another bore his helmet. Lheor tore the weapons from their clawed hands and leaned forwards for the last of the beastmen to affix his crested helm in place.

'May the God of War be with you,' I said, not without an

edge of sarcasm. His eye-lenses glowed as his helmet seals locked, and he hefted the brutal cannon he favoured no matter the battlefield.

'What did you just say?'

'Nothing,' I smiled. 'Good hunting, brother.'

'Don't lose the battle while I'm gone,' he said, as if I had anything to do with Ultio's talents in the art of war. I could give her orders, but she needed none. This was her arena, not mine.

Lheor summoned the handful of his warriors present on the bridge and led them into the corridors that formed the *Vengeful Spirit*'s veins. I briefly listened to the clicking vox chatter as he rallied several of his squads on the way. It synergised, in a way, with Ultio's stream of orders and the shivering thunder impacting upon the hull: a perfect storm of sound.

I turned back to the oculus as the cruiser *Arcus,* once of the Imperial Fists warfleet and now of the Black Templars armada, detonated in our wake.

At the heart of the braying beastman herds and a world of dark steel shaking around me, I seated myself on Abaddon's throne, eyes half-lidded with the onset of a meditative trance as I watched the Black Legion's fate playing out before me.

Time passed.

Lives ended.

Warships died.

I watched fire tear through pressurised sanctuaries and cease to exist once it kissed the void. I watched the blazes slough the flesh from bones, before breaking those bones down to ash. I watched torpedoes streak and swerve and drill and detonate. I watched lance beams carve through consecrated armour that had endured the tides of hell itself. I watched ships full of my brothers crumble in ruin, populations of the mutated and the mad sucked in corpse-falls from sundered hulls. I watched vessels that had anchored proudly in the skies above Terra now dying in droves, as Sigismund's sons were reduced from an armada to a fleet, and from a fleet to scattered formations.

I watched it all. It was art.

I listened to my brothers shrieking and killing and dying. I listened to my cousins, those still loyal to the Throne, roaring and bleeding out and spending their final breaths on foul oaths that cursed us and mocked us for our treachery. I listened to Ultio's endless orders, not only to the crew but to her Syntagma war robots and cyborgs, directing them to stand with the Riven and the War God's Maw. I listened to the grind of straining metal and the thunder of guns that could – and had – killed cities. I listened to the sirens and the screams and the mechanical pulses of my armour's biosign systems.

I listened to it all. It was music.

I sensed the spillage of souls into the warp. I sensed the outburst of panicked, confused, blood-maddened, death-drunk spirits of the violently slain, tumbling into the realm behind reality. I sensed the wet laughter of gorging daemons. I sensed the ebb and flow of the empyrean's winds, blowing harder behind the veil, fuelled by the glut of freed souls. I sensed death after death after death – those who did not know they were dead; those that fought uselessly as they fell into the waiting, gaping maws; those that cried wordless defiance as they were torn apart by daemonic claws. I sensed the daemons that would be born in the aftermath of this battle. I sensed how they loved us for this slaughter, and how they hated us for its mortal limits – for no matter the slaughter we perpetrated, it was never enough, never enough.

I sensed it all. It was beautiful. Hatefully beautiful.

And, last of all, I felt when Abaddon reached Sigismund.

I felt the moment's curious formality, and felt the searing emotions in my lord's twinned hearts. I felt the vindication of glory to be earned. I felt the thwarted fury of a man forced towards a fate he did not, yet, adore.

I closed my eyes, leaving the rolling, burning, fighting *Vengeful Spirit* behind.

When I opened them, Sigismund sat enthroned before me.

'So,' he said, 'you have returned.'

XIV

HAMMER AND ANVIL

He burned with life. It seared through his veins. The righteousness of his cause haloed him, bathing him in the corona of a faith that was wholly unreligious, but faith nevertheless. I stared up at him beyond the ranks of his huscarls, those warriors who we would learn in later wars were called Sword Brethren, and I realised then just how it was that Sigismund still lived even after all this time. He had survived for a thousand years because he refused to die. He hated us too much to sleep in his grave with his duty undone.

Sigismund watched us through the chamber's surreal calm. Blood marked his armour and tabard, medals of honour earned from the Black Legion bodies spread across the hall of white marble and black iron. He had not been idle in defence of his ship. It seemed he had chosen this chamber of reverence as a place to make his final stand.

'So, you have returned.' He spoke to all of us, his voice ancient but uncracked. 'I never doubted you would.'

His Sword Brethren were battered, bloody and exhausted. Our warriors facing him were no different. Several were still breathless and bleeding, their wounds scabbing over even now with the effects of their gene-wrought organs.

Abaddon was filthy with gore. The souls of those he had slaughtered to reach this chamber circled him, unseen and silent, a halo of smoky misery trailing away into nothingness as the warp pulled them into the oblivion of its maw.

Sigismund rose. He held the sword of his office, what the Imperium knows as the Sword of the High Marshals. The Black Sword, his favoured weapon for so many centuries, was sheathed at his hip. The straightness of his back and the power within his posture surprised me, though the dozens of my dead brothers spread across the deck should have dissuaded me of any illusions that Sigismund would be enfeebled by age. He had carved his way through several of the Shrieking Masquerade, although, looking through Amurael's eyes, I did not see Telemachon or Zaidu among the slain.

Abaddon stepped forwards to meet him and gestured at us to lower our weapons. Sigismund did the same to his men. Both commanders were immediately obeyed, and the insane serenity stretched on while the *Eternal Crusader* shuddered and burned around us. The oculus, I noted, was tuned to watch the *Vengeful Spirit*. Our flagship rolled in the void, streaming fire and ice and air from her wounds, her cannons screaming silently into the darkness. She was duelling several smaller vessels, twisting to them each in turn, cutting them apart methodically with lance volleys that streamed through space, bright as the arcing flares of Terra's sun.

There was a shiver of disorientation as I witnessed the

burning ship where my body sat in Abaddon's throne, so distant from where I watched behind Amurael's eyes. That sense of dislocation did not last long. Adapting to such sensory perceptions was an elementary aspect in the principles of Tizcan meditation; I was taught the techniques before my eighth birthday.

Abaddon addressed the approaching knight. 'I see time has blackened your armour, as it has ours.'

Sigismund stopped within blade reach, but neither of them lifted their weapons. 'I looked for you,' he said to my lord, 'as Terra burned in the fires of your father's heresy. I hunted for you, day and night. Always lesser men blocked my way. Always they died so that you might live. But I have never stopped searching for you, Ezekyle. Not through all these long years.'

Abaddon's rage, ever his greatest weapon and most crucial flaw, had deserted him. I watched him through Amurael's eyes, and he looked ravaged.

'Don't make me do this,' Abaddon said. 'Don't make me kill you.'

He even cast his sword down with a crash of iron, such was his passion. 'You cannot have lived all of these centuries and seen nothing of the truth, Sigismund. The Imperium is *ours*. *We* fought for it. *We* built it with blood and sweat and wrath. *We* forged it with the worlds *we* took. The empire is built upon foundations of our brothers' bones.'

The old knight stared impassively. 'You lost the right to speak for the Imperium when you brought it to its knees. If you loved it as ardently as you claim, Ezekyle, you would not have pushed it to the brink of ruin.'

My lord overshadowed Sigismund, standing far taller in his Terminator plate. He gestured to the warriors around the room, taking them in with a single sweep of the Talon; they were all in black, though fighting on different sides.

'We are the Emperor's angels.' It horrified me to hear the dark kindness in Abaddon's tone. When he needed his wrath more than ever, he was trying to reason with the one Space Marine that could never be reasoned with. 'We didn't rebel out of petty spite, Sigismund. We rebelled because our lord and master played us false. We were useful tools to bring the galaxy to heel, but He would have cleansed us from the Imperium the way He purged the Thunder Legion before us, wiping us all from history like excrement from His golden boots.'

Sigismund was a statue, his face carved from coloured marble. 'I am sure some of you are convinced you fell from grace for those pure, virtuous ideals. You have had many centuries within your prison to repeat those claims to yourself. But they change nothing.'

I have seen Abaddon quell crowds and strike fear into entire populations with the ferocity of his invective, and I have seen him win over some of our most hostile enemies with the fire of his charisma – but in that moment, as he stood before Sigismund and came face to face with the avatar of the empire we had burned and been forced to abandon, I believe he suffered a rare, rare moment of conflict within.

Sigismund was a man to whom duty and law were inseparable from living and breathing. He cared nothing for our righteousness. He did not call us arrogant. He did not even say we were wrong, because he cared nothing for the whys and wherefores of what we had done.

We were traitors. We had betrayed our oaths. We had risen against the Emperor. That was enough.

He could not, or would not, see that we had risen against the Emperor for the sake of the Imperium. And yet, I confess that seeing him standing there, regal and ancient in his absolute certainty, I felt the same doubt that I sensed in Abaddon.

Distinct and cold, this feeling lasted only a moment in time, nothing more. Perhaps its brevity was because I did not turn from the Emperor for the sake of the Imperium or for the sake of any ranted truth. I, and my Legion, rebelled to survive. We were betrayed, and so we damned ourselves just to keep breathing. There were as many reasons to rebel as there were rebels.

Sigismund remained motionless and said, with infinite patience, 'You keep speaking, Ezekyle. Do I look as though I am listening?'

I saw the shift in Abaddon's features as he discarded any hope of Sigismund understanding our cause. I saw wryness there as well, chastening himself that he had dared to hope Sigismund would be able to understand why we had turned from the Throne.

'No pity, no remorse, no fear,' Abaddon said with a smile. 'Blessed is the mind too small for doubt.'

He did not wait for a reply. He held out his hand for his sword. Zaidu moved forwards, picking it up and placing it in Abaddon's hand before backing away.

Sigismund mirrored the gesture in reverse, handing the Sword of the High Marshals to one of his huscarls, who moved away with the relic held in reverence. Sigismund drew the Black Sword in its place, raising it to salute Abaddon with the same cold formality he had displayed unceasingly thus far.

Abaddon raised his blade, and Amurael flinched, not of his

own accord but through the exertion of my will. Instinct ran through me with quicksilver breath. So fierce was my ache to witness the fight that I had to restrain myself from taking hold of my brother's body and stepping forwards in his place.

Sigismund had the advantage of reach with his long blade; Abaddon held the advantage of strength in his Terminator plate. My lord would fight with weighty disadvantage of the Talon upon his balancing hand, but it gave him a devastating weapon if the duel allowed him a chance to use it. Sigismund would be faster in his ornate power armour, but there was no way of knowing how much age had slowed him.

And still the gathered warriors on both sides stood in awed silence across the devastated chamber. It seemed human thralls were not permitted here – none lay dead on the mosaic floor, at least – leading me to believe it was some kind of knightly sanctum for the Black Templars' rituals. Nine of Sigismund's Sword Brethren stood opposite almost forty of our own warriors; I could not make out exact numbers without forcing Amurael to turn his head.

Abaddon and Sigismund's blades met for the first time, a skidding clash that sprayed sparks across both warriors. I thought it might have been a signal for both sides to charge, for us to butcher Sigismund's elite while our lords battled, yet there was no such uproar.

I felt the acidic squirt of adrenal narcotics pumping through Amurael's bloodstream, injected by his armour in response to his battle hunger. He flinched and winced with the crashing blows of the warlords' blades, and he was not the only one to follow the fight with such ferocious focus, doubtless imagining he wielded a sword in Abaddon's place.

Their crashing blades brought a storm's light to that place of austere darkness. Lightning sheeted across the cracked marble walls and illuminated the stained-glass windows, bathing the cold statue faces of Black Templars heroes in flashes of even colder illumination. Those stone worthies looked on, only marginally more stoic than the watching warriors of both black-clad hosts.

In the years after this duel, those of us fortunate enough to witness it have spoken in terms both trite and profound of how it played out. One of Zaidu's preferred claims is that Abaddon led Sigismund the entire time, that our lord laughed all the while as he toyed with the ancient Black Templar before delivering the death blow. This is the tale related by the Shrieking Masquerade's various warbands, and one that Telemachon has never contradicted.

Amurael once described it in terms I preferred, saying that Sigismund was ice and precision, while Abaddon was passion and fire. That bore the ring of truth from what I saw through Amurael's own eyes.

Sigismund knew he would die. Even if he defeated Abaddon, he and his warriors were outnumbered four to one. His ship still rolled in the void, still burned within as our boarding parties swept through its veins like venom in its bloodstream, but if the battle for the *Eternal Crusader* was still in doubt, there was no such mystery surrounding the endgame within this chamber. Even if fate or a miracle of faith spared Sigismund, the rage of forty bolters and blades would not.

And Sigismund's age did show. It slowed him, the finest duellist ever to wear ceramite, to a pace that was no faster than Abaddon in his hulking Terminator plate. He lacked Ezekyle's enhanced strength in that great suit of armour, and age and weariness robbed him even further. He was already decorated in the blood of my slain brothers; this was far from his first battle of the day. Were his old hearts straining? Would they fail him now, and burst in his proud chest? Is that how the greatest of Space Marine legends was fated to end?

I found the signs of Sigismund's age unconscionably tragic – a fact Ezekyle later mocked me for, calling it a symptom of my 'maudlin Tizcan nature'. He remarked that I should have paid more heed to the fact that the Black Knight, at a thousand natural years of age, could still have stood toe to toe and matched blade to blade with practically any warrior in the Nine Legions. Age had slowed Sigismund, but all it had done was slow him to a level with the rest of us.

I did pay heed, of course. The outcome of the duel was never in question, but that did not mean I was blind to Sigismund's consummate skill. I had never seen him fight before. I doubted anyone but the Nine Legions' highest elite could face him and live even now, and at his best he would have rivalled any being that drew breath.

(Iskandar.)

Sigismund's artistry with a sword is best summed up by the way he moved. Duellists will parry and deflect to keep themselves alive if they have the skill to do so, and if they lack that skill – or simply rely on strength to win battles – then they will lay into a fight with a longer, two-handed blade, trusting in its weight and power to overcome an enemy's defences. Sigismund did neither of these. I never saw him simply parry a blow, for every move he made blended defence into attack. He somehow deflected Abaddon's strikes as an after-effect of making his own attacks.

Even Telemachon, who is possibly the most gifted bladesman I have ever seen, will parry his opponent's blows. He does it with an effortlessness that borders on inattention, something practically beneath him that he performs on instinct, but he still does it. Sigismund attacked, attacked, attacked, and he somehow deflected every blow while doing so. Aggression boiled beneath his every motion.

(Iskandar.)

Yet Sigismund was wearing down minute by minute. Air sawed through the grate of his clenched teeth. Abaddon roared and spat and laid into him with great sweeping blows from both blade and Talon, never tiring, never slowing. Sigismund, in contrast, grew evermore conservative with his movements. He–

(Iskandar.)

–was tiring beneath the pressure of Abaddon's rage, the spraying sparks of abused power fields now showed his stern features set in a rictus of effort. In so many battles, whether they are between two souls or two armies, a moment arises when the balance will shift inexorably one way over the other: when one shield wall begins to buckle; when one territory begins to fall; when one warship's shields fail or its engines give out; when one fighter makes a cursory error or begins to weaken.

I saw it happen in that duel. I saw Sigismund take a step back, just a single step, but his first of the battle so far. Abaddon's lightning-lit features turned cruel and confident with bitter mirth, and–

Iskandar!

I opened my eyes. It took me several seconds to detach my senses from Amurael's, so strong was the temptation to dive back into his mind and watch the duel between the two warlords.

'Iskandar!' Ultio called again. She was embattled, calculating attack vectors, flinching with the psy-stigmatic pain of impacts against the *Vengeful Spirit*'s bare hull. Blood trailed from her nose and ears, leaking into the amniotic fluid. The bruises that had decorated her flesh at the battle's beginning had ripened and split open, layering her skin in fresh gashes. Her left arm looked broken at the wrist and she cradled it close to her chest. One of her eyes was swollen closed. Worst of all, parts of her body had been reduced to raw muscle, leaving her partly flayed. The war was carving her apart. If her wounds were a representation of the *Vengeful Spirit*'s damage, Abaddon would be returning to a half-slain flagship.

A brother's urge overcame me: the need to pull her from the battle, to protect her. Its intensity stunned me, for... But we were long past such foolishness. She had been the machine-spirit of Legion warships for far longer than she had been my mortal sister, and the Anamnesis had always claimed to recall nothing of her human genesis.

The entire bridge was stained red with emergency lighting and flooded with shouting crew, yet I heard her gargoyles' synthetic murmur.

'Something is wrong,' they chorused. 'Can you not feel it?'

The oculus showed warships sailing, burning, breaking apart... I saw nothing wrong, nothing grave that required my attention so suddenly. I turned from the screen to the hololithic mess that tried to track and display every ship committed to the battle across every engagement sphere. It offered no answer either, save that we were winning. Slowly, surely, we were winning. For the sake of the Imperium and the warning they would need to carry, the Black Templars would surely fall back soon. Their blockade was already torn asunder with spatial holes we could break through, but our captains were caught between feasting on their loyal brethren and not wishing to risk turning their backs on them.

I calmed my breathing, letting the adrenaline of Abaddon's duel bleed away. I *did* feel something. A presence. A disturbance. If you have walked through the wilderness and heard the distant roars or howls of native predators carried on the wind, if your skin has prickled in a too-human reaction of instinctive awareness, then you know the feeling of which I speak.

I leaned forwards in Abaddon's throne. 'Ultio, bring your auspex arcs around and sweep subquadrants fifty-five to fifty-nine.'

'That is behind us.'

'I am well aware of that.'

'Piercing alignment,' she replied, her attention still divided. 'Resolving. Resolving. Resol– I see dead space in the named quadrants. Nothing but the void.'

'Tight-beam focus on subquadrant fifty-six,' I ordered. That was far behind us. Directly behind us. It was the way we had come, the very subquadrant in which we had emerged from the Eye's storm. Several of our bulk landers and troop ships remained there, held back from the shooting war. They were specks on the oculus, several minutes' sailing away even at full speed.

Ultio spat her wordless anger at another vessel nearby, raking it with her starboard guns and rolling the *Vengeful Spirit* slowly away. I saw the momentary flicker of distraction on her features as her crew cast the auspex scan in a tight beam array to the coordinates I requested. She could no longer manage the ship's systems alone, engaged as she was.

One of the Tzaangor beastmen crowed at me in her raucous tongue. I had already read the meaning from her mind before she finished croaking in what passed for her kind's language.

From the storm, she said. *They come from the storm.*

I cursed the Shifting God in that moment, which is as close as I had ever come to uttering a prayer to Tzeentch.

As I watched the specks multiply on the oculus, streaming in from the storm's edge, I mouthed one word, tasting its foulness on the back of my teeth.

'Daravek.'

He had followed us. I did not know how, let alone how he had made such decent speed and whether his fleet had suffered in the effort, but he was here, and he was behind us, and our fleet was already utterly engaged in breaking the Black Templars' blockade.

If Daravek attacked now, he could – he *would* – finish us. We would never recover from this evisceration between the descending hammer and the unbroken anvil, and once we were devastated, he would finish the remaining Black Templars and sail undeterred into Imperial space, stealing our glory.

If he killed us here, then to capstone our legacy of failure, all we would have achieved was to pave the way for him.

'Ultio,' I called out, 'we–'

The ship heaved around us, a jarring slam that struck with enough force to kill power to countless critical systems. The lights died. Gravity died with them, then returned tenfold at the wrong angle, no longer keeping us on the deck but throwing us backwards. Bodies hurtled through the dark air, colliding with one another in bone-shattering impacts and pulping against the bridge's walls and ceiling.

In the darkness, Ultio screamed. I do not mean she bellowed in fury or that she cried out. She screamed. It was torment made manifest, a sound that even the lifeless gargoyles conveying her vocalisations could not rob of its pain.

I did not know what hit us. Damage reports clattered from unattended consoles. I was sure the ship was dead in space, only disabused of that belief when I felt the thrum of deep, full thrust resonating through me.

We had not been rammed. We had not been struck by a nova cannon. Ultio had accelerated, full burn, without fail-safes or brace warnings, channelling the *Vengeful Spirit*'s entire reactor sector's output into the engines.

I twisted in the dark, clawing my way through a gravity forty times in excess of Terra's, hearing the creaking of bones among the pressure-crushed crew. The soft tissue of my eyes was distorting, clutched tight in an invisible grip; I could feel the harp-thread snaps in my eyeballs, each one a dagger pinprick of blood vessels breaking. The stench of blood surrounded me from others nearby, some crying out as they bled, others lost to unconsciousness, the reek of their suffering forming a miasma that coated my skin. Similar scenes of destruction were playing out across the ship.

Cease! I sent to Ultio. *You are killing your crew!*

I felt her reach back to touch me, mind to mind. She so rarely did that; the Anamnesis' psychic component was essential to her function, especially in commanding her Syntagma cyborgs and war robots, but she always shunned allowing me to get too close to her thoughts. What spilled across the connection now was an acidic flood of boiling, overlapping panic.

Ezekyle is wounded I must reach him we must I must he is our lord he cannot die we have to reach the Eternal Crusader *we have to–*

But she was wrong. She had to be wrong. Abaddon could not be wounded. And I would prove her wrong as soon as I saved the ship's crew from a crushing death in the pitch darkness. My suit's sensors registered the gravitational force still rising, now powerful enough to rupture organs. In her frantic grief, she would slay us all.

Slow. The. Ship.

But Ezekyle is hurt he

YOU ARE KILLING US, ITZARA. YOU WILL KILL EVERY SOUL ABOARD THE SHIP.

I... I...

She buckled. The ship fired retro thrusters and banked its reactors, and the gravitational forces eased, breath by breath. The emergency lighting reactivated, showing me a realm of crimson silhouettes and scarlet shadows in an artistic recreation of a charnel house.

'I am not Itzara,' she whispered through her gargoyles. 'I am Ultio, the Anamnesis.'

I let that go unanswered as I took stock. Bodies that I had feared were corpses began to move. Crew casualties would likely be significant, but the *Vengeful Spirit* held the population of a small city. I had brought Ultio back from the edge before she could do too much damage.

Or so I hoped.

The image on the oculus reformed from static nothingness to a cluster of warships we had left behind, now left to give slow chase. I hauled myself back to Abaddon's throne and keyed in a code to realign the oculus once more. It flickered to the chosen coordinates, showing an armada of

Nine Legions vessels pouring from the edge of the storm. I recognised not only individual patterns of craft but individual ships themselves – vessels I had sailed beside or fought against during my years within the Empire of the Eye.

There was no doubt now: the Lord of Hosts had followed us.

'Ezekyle,' Ultio said aloud, her tone lost, distracted.

Be silent, I sent to her, the command ironclad. If her fears were true, the crew – the Legion itself – must not be informed. Not yet. Not until the Ezekarion had weighed its options.

On the oculus, our fat-hulled troop transports were wallowing away sedately from their pursuers, while the picket of escorts we left to protect them were doing what little they could to cover the retreat.

Already Daravek's vanguard ships were overtaking them, cutting them apart with lance strikes and torpedo barrages. Behind this slaughter came the cruisers and battleships of the Nine Legions, their crews no doubt euphoric and disorientated in equal measure at their freedom. It would not take them long to realise that fortune or the will of the Pantheon had brought them back to reality with the perfect chance to silence us forever.

Tzah'q limped over to me, spitting blood. In the chaos of Ultio's fear, the bridge overseer had lost his weapons.

'Must fight, master. Must fight Lord of Hosts. No choice. Must fight.'

More ships broke through into real space, with yet more bladed shadows taking shape behind them. Time was anything but an ally. I could practically hear the Gods howling with laughter at this latest test.

'Master?' the beastman repeated, whining for an answer.

I silenced him with a gesture and reached out with my senses.

Ezekyle.

Nothing. Nothing at all.

Amurael?

Khayon! Throne of Terra, we—

No. Listen to me, Amurael. Thagus Daravek's armada has torn its way into reality behind us. Our rearguard is already burning. We are caught between the Templars and the Legion Host and cannot fight both. I cannot reach Ezekyle. Where is he?

Our psychic link wavered. I sensed more than heard boltgun fire, and felt the kick of Amurael's bolter in his fists.

Amurael?

We are embattled. Gods' piss, Khayon, when Sigismund fell, it drove these bastards into blood madness, but we are close. Another few hours, brother, and this ship is ours.

Sigismund is dead? Abaddon killed him? I sensed the clatter of more bolt-fire, and the heft of a heavy power sword in Amurael's hand. *Amurael, I need answers. The fleet is dying. There is no time for this.*

Ezekyle is with Falkus and Ilyaster. The Aphotic Blade *is evacuating him.*

Once more, dread made its icy way through my veins. *Abaddon is wounded?*

His answer was the breathy, exhausted ache of battle heat. I could sense him slipping from me.

Amurael, you have to abandon the Crusader. *We have to regroup. If we remain divided like this, Daravek will tear us apart.*

Red heat and flashing pain bleached our telepathic link. Amurael had been struck by a bolt-round himself.

Hnh. Khay–

He was gone, either dead or too wounded to maintain the necessary concentration. I could not reach Falkus or Ilyas, no matter how I tried – not with my powers, nor with the mundane connection of the vox. I was entirely in the dark.

Telemachon, I tried, plunging into the buzzing, venomous nest that passed for his mind. His psyche opened like a blossoming flower in welcome, closing with savage glee around me.

Lekzahndru, he purred. I could sense him fighting, weaving his sword dance through his foes. He was exultant, laughing as he fought.

You have to abandon the assault and lead the others off the Eternal Crusader. *Daravek has broken free behind us.*

His exultation turned to poison. I felt him suddenly seeking to repel me, to throw me out of his thoughts. *Coward! We can take the* Crusader! *We are mere hours from victory. Ezekyle would never allow this retreat, Khayon.*

What has happened? What happened to Ezekyle?

He is with Falkus and Ilyaster now, but if he lives, I will tell him of your treachery.

If he lives? Telemachon, for the sake of all that is sacred, what happened?

He did not tell me at once. He invited me to see for myself, opening the viperous pit of his memories to allow me insight within. The perversions of Telemachon's brain patterns were beyond my taste and tolerance, and although he lacked psychic strength, he possessed a supreme sense of will. His beckoning stank of a trap.

Tell me, I ordered him, and for a wonder he replied.

They fought. Abaddon won, but was wounded. That is all that matters, isn't it?

There was no time to deal with his pettiness; he had already wasted precious seconds better spent elsewhere.

Get Abaddon off the ship, and ensure none but the Aphotic Blade sees that he is wounded.

I felt him bristle at the orders. *Who are you to command me?*

You wish to argue this now, of all times? Get all of our warriors back to their boarding pods. I sent the words, knifelike and raw, into the meat of his mind, caring nothing that it hurt him, caring even less that he took a dark and drooling pleasure from the pain. *Abandon the assault on the* Eternal Crusader, *or I will leave you there to rot as the Templars' captive plaything.*

We can take the Crusader, *you filthy coward. The Legion has never conquered such a prize, and it is within my reach! You think you can deny me this glory? Is this your pathetic vengeance for failing our lord? You wish to drag me down into failure with you?*

I was already disentangling my thoughts from his, ready to cut him free. He sensed the thinning of our contact, and roared at me with the kind of frothing, feral desperation I would have expected from Lheor in one his rage-seizures.

I brushed his anger aside with ease. He had no telepathic talent himself.

You have your orders, 'Masqued Prince'. Obey them or be left behind.

I opened my eyes once more, back to a world of strained red lights and beastmen crews bleeding and braying and cawing. Tzah'q still looked at me, his beady animal eyes pleading for a command.

Before I could speak, the oculus resolved into the familiar face of Thagus Daravek, saliva stringing from his chin and jowls, a smile of ruthless self-satisfaction upon his disease-fattened features.

'*Iskandar.*' He turned my name into a sound of hateful luxury that lasted unpleasantly long on his tongue. '*Where is Ezekyle, assassin? I have come to offer him one final chance to grovel and acknowledge me as the Lord of the Nine Legions.*'

Lheor would have made a cutting remark. Telemachon would have used his wit. But for better or worse, I am not my brothers.

'I am going to kill you,' I said.

'*Those are words I've heard you speak before, Khayon. Let me guess what your next words will be, hmm? You are about to demand to know how I managed to follow you.*'

'Not quite,' I replied, and cut the communication link to spare myself his oozing smirk. 'Tzah'q,' I said, turning to the waiting overseer, 'ready the crew to fight.'

As he grunted and left, I looked up at Ultio. Her eyes were glazed as she saw through her auspex scanners and the trajectory calculations of her guns. I hoped it was that alone, and not the shock at her sensing Abaddon's injury. Her psychic bond with the Legion's lord had served them both well so far, but if Abaddon did not recover from his wounds...

No. The truth was that it did not matter. If Abaddon did not survive, there would be no Black Legion. We would devolve into feuding warlords fighting over the Legion's bones before his corpse was even cold.

Ultio shifted in her blood-darkened suspension fluid, looking down at me, perhaps alert to the turmoil inside my skull. Fear tainted her features with lines of tension she had never worn before. She did not know where to sail, nor whom to fight.

'Our Legion is dying,' she mouthed, and her gargoyles spoke the words with a gentleness I had not thought possible.

'Yes,' I agreed, 'it is. But we can save it, sister.'

Your sister is dead. I am the Anamnesis, she thought, but bit back from speaking it aloud. She had never hesitated with those words. For the first time since ascending to command of the *Vengeful Spirit*, she was sure of absolutely nothing.

'What do we do?' Ultio asked me, informally mirroring the question being asked a hundred times across the fleet-wide vox by a hundred warlords, captains and officers. 'Which fleet do we fight?'

I watched the oculus, where three fleets were tearing each other apart in the void. Every advantage we held, every advantage we had worked for all these decades, was haemorrhaging away like air from a ruptured hull. I could not reach Abaddon for answers – and what answers were there, even if he had been by my side? We could stand and die against one foe, or turn and die against another. We could not even flee in cohesion: Daravek had denied us our only avenue of retreat, and the Black Templars' remaining blockade prevented us pushing forth into the Imperium.

The choice I faced was no choice at all.

'The only way to survive this battle,' I said softly, 'is not to fight it.'

Ultio stared down at me, aghast. 'We cannot disengage. We will be butchered by both sides.'

I refused to let her horror, or the promise of Abaddon's fury, dissuade me. 'I am not speaking of disengaging in an orderly retreat,' I told her. 'Hail Valicar aboard the *Thane*.'

She did so. I retook Abaddon's throne – the very throne

that Horus had once sat upon when he waged war against the Emperor – and spoke to the Legion fleetmaster.

'Valicar, it is time to get the hell out of here.'

Valicar's voice crackled across a private command channel. His Olympian-slum accent was almost a drawl, punctuated by the booming of the battleship *Thane*'s weapons batteries. '*Easier said than done. Even a retreat will kill us.*'

'Not if we sacrifice several vessels to stay behind.'

He barked a bitter laugh. '*Good luck finding volunteers.*'

I told him what I wanted, and what was going to happen. He knew it was an order, and though he held rank above mine in matters of void war, he offered no argument. As proud as he is, and as much as the truth bit into his pride, Valicar has always been a practical soul.

'*Give the order,*' he acquiesced, '*and may the Gods be with you, Khayon.*'

'I rather hope they are not,' I replied before cutting the link. 'Ultio, give me fleet-wide vox.'

The connection clicked and held. 'Fleet-wide vox,' she confirmed.

'This is Lord Iskandar Khayon, commanding the *Vengeful Spirit*. I speak with the will of Lord Abaddon and bring the judgement of the Ezekarion. All warships, do not – I repeat, *do not* – engage Thagus Daravek. All engagement spheres will work in isolation to peel their embattled formations away from the Black Templars. Do not hunt for trophies or prize vessels. Do not seek to destroy any Templars warships. Do not linger in orderly disengagements and drift into other engagement spheres to lend aid to other vessels. There is no time. You will be overrun. Recover your boarders, abandon any attacks and break off from the battle. Scatter the fleet. I repeat – scatter the fleet.'

The *Vengeful Spirit* came alive around me, powering up for what would come next. Amidst the acknowledgements, an unexpected reply crackled back.

'*Magician,*' Lheor voxed, his voice rough and weary, '*who volunteered to stay behind and cover the retreat?*'

'I believe you can guess the answer to that, Firefist.'

'*Of course.*' He sighed. '*And don't call me Firefist.*'

'Then do not call me "magician". That is a word for children and charlatans.'

He hesitated then, though not because I had corrected him. I could almost hear his thoughts working through the barriers of the biting Nails. '*We're not staying out of any sudden nobility, are we? We're staying because you want Daravek's head.*'

'Two correct guesses in the same hour,' I replied, watching Daravek's armada swinging into view as the *Vengeful Spirit* came about. 'This is a day of rare genius for you, my brother. Next you will tell me you have learned how to read.'

XV

LORD OF HOSTS

Some hatreds cannot be overcome. The Nine Legions, subject to the whims of the Gods that stir fate around us, have always been their own worst enemies. When Abaddon's name is spoken in awe, much of that hateful and jealous reverence is because he does what no other warlord can do: he unites the Nine Legions, even if only briefly, and leads them to war. Horus had half of the Imperium loyally on his side: organised, unified, strong. Abaddon has to piece together the armies of the damned from the depths of hell, where they have spent eternity drowning in their own madness and despising each other as enemies.

Our chance to enter the Imperium as a potent and unified fighting force was broken, our ambitions cast away by the reality of Daravek's treachery.

To say we ran from Daravek and the Black Templars is to undersell the scale of flight that took place. We did not retreat. We fled. The fleet scattered in every direction, *vindicta* cast aside in the name of survival. Perhaps not one of our proudest moments, but certainly among the most tactically sound. There were no good choices. We chose the least of all evils.

I will not deny that there was something of a cockroach's cowardice in what we did, scurrying away from the light of powerful enemies. But there was also laughter. We were abandoning the remaining Black Templars ships to face a fresh fleet, and we were leaving Daravek's Legion Host like sand slipping through their fingers. They had wanted to confront us and crush us, and instead the Black Legion turned and sailed in a hundred directions at once. Within minutes there was no cohesive fleet to even attack.

It was not what we had wanted when we envisioned our escape from the Eye. It shattered all hope of waging a cohesive war, for this verminous scattering left us disparate and weak, each ship isolated within the Imperium. We were leaving enemies behind us, facing enemies ahead of us and were beginning our war on the weakest possible footing. But we would be alive. Necessity – ever a merciless mistress – forced our hand.

A formation led by Vortigern's ancient vessel, the battleship *With Blade Drawn,* broke the widest hole in the Black Templars' blockade, through which several vessels managed to run to freedom. The stubborn Calibanite attempted to come back until I dissuaded him with a direct command. He was the first member of the Ezekarion to break free, and it was vital that he did what he could to reunite the fleet far from here if the rest of us fell.

Ships broke off in the middle of attack runs, veering and rolling aside, awakening their warp engines with no regard for minimum safe cascade distance. I watched the *With Blade Drawn* recede on one of the insect-eye facets of the oculus, and I did not breathe easier even when it ripped a whirlpool of reality open to dive into the warp. This close to the Eye, the warp was desperately unstable. All our warping ships were really doing was forgoing certain death for a likely one.

Ultio spoke of every escaping ship in a litany of focused, tight-voiced triumph. Life sparked in her eyes with each name.

'*With Blade Drawn* is away,' she said. '*Talonis Praxia* is away. *Excoriator* is away. *Zeta* and *Sigma* are away.'

I was watching the *Zeta* myself when it dove into its warp rift, and saw how the tendrils of lashing lightning from the wound in reality clutched at the ship and practically sucked it into the waiting maw. A Black Templars vessel was within the range of its warp cascade, and the ship turned in burning, spiralling rolls, dragged into the rift behind the *Zeta* without the preparation of navigational arrays or its Geller field activated. I sensed the outpouring of panic, and the brief, harrowing agonies endured by the destroyer's twenty thousand crew as unreality flooded their decks, dissolving them and eating them alive.

Several vessels were destroyed by their own warp cascades, and I still shiver to think of the many warriors lost that day. Their ships detonated on the lips of their warp tears or were cut down by Black Templars' fire on the cusp of escape. I saw the *Anchorite* lancing into the warp only for its engines to ignite as it entered, iron flying into the void and trailing fire in its death throes thanks to a Black Templars missile frigate. Nor was it the only vessel to suffer such a fate.

So I will not say we escaped unscathed, but the bulk of our fleet did manage to tear itself free.

The *Thane* sailed hard, weapons bellowing, drawing alongside the badly damaged *Eternal Crusader*. Ultio's attention wavered then, and I suspect every psychically gifted soul in the fleet felt her hunger to turn back, to finish the *Eternal Crusader* herself, to recover our boarding parties and execute Sigismund's flagship in a firestorm of *vindicta*.

For all of the *Thane*'s size and strength, even a wounded Gloriana battleship outclasses any rival. The limping, torn-open *Eternal Crusader* turned its guns upon Valicar's warship and ravaged it with barrage after barrage, taking precious little damage in return. Fighters spewed from the *Thane*'s bays, and bombers swarmed in a slower tide behind them. All of Valicar's focus rested not upon killing the *Eternal Crusader*, but on keeping it engaged. He had to prevent it from chasing down our fleeing ships, as well as covering the withdrawal of our boarding parties and defending their returning pods.

I watched the *Thane* burn, its shields down, its hull pockmarked with explosions, and I wondered if I had sent Valicar to his death. If I had then Ezekyle, Telemachon and the several thousand warriors we had deployed aboard the city-sized *Eternal Crusader* would die next. Even if they managed to take the ship within hours as Telemachon insisted, they would possess a crippled flagship, her crew in open rebellion, and would be overrun by dozens of Daravek's vessels before they could ever claim their prize.

They had to withdraw. Valicar would impress that upon them, I was certain.

As our fleet scattered, the *Vengeful Spirit* speared on. The Black Templars, faced with another fleet that vastly eclipsed their diminished strength, began to fall back themselves.

They retreated in far saner coordination, racing for the system's Mandeville point to enter the warp at a safe distance, avoiding the threat of warp cascades. It ached to watch them withdraw, knowing they would sail across the Imperium and spread warning of our return. Any element of surprise we might have grasped had been cruelly stolen from our clutches.

Daravek would pay for that.

The Lord of Hosts was bold, and the flagship of his Kryptarus warband – the Death Guard battleship *Domina* – sailed at the vanguard of his fleet. It pulled away from the troop ships it had been firing upon and aligned with us, ready to pitch its might against the wounded *Vengeful Spirit*.

They would board us, of that there was no doubt. The *Vengeful Spirit* was a treasure no warlord could resist.

Our arrival forced several of Daravek's ships to break off from their slaughtering runs, and Ultio's laughter rang out across the bridge as she tracked them in a spread of hololithic runes. I followed the unfolding data stream, seeing at once what had spurred her amusement.

'His fleet,' she said aloud. 'It is disintegrating.'

She was wounded and distracted so I could forgive her hyperbole, but she was not entirely incorrect. The Legion Host was veering apart, craft by craft, warband by warband. Their captains had returned to the material realm and had concerns far beyond Daravek's grudge with Ezekyle. They were tasting freedom as keenly as we had, and now took fate into their own hands, deserting him.

'Do not fire on any warships abandoning the Legion Host,' I ordered. 'Focus all fire on defending our troop transports. Come in close enough to entice boarders, Ultio. We want them to feel welcome.'

'Compliance,' she agreed.

'And remain engaged only until Valicar reports recovery of the boarding teams. As soon as the *Thane* voxes success, disengage at once.'

'It will be done,' she promised.

As I watched Daravek's flagship power closer, Abaddon's words returned to me unbidden, from the night we had sparred and he had delivered his judgement of my failings in *vindicta*: 'We stand on the edge of returning to the Imperium we built with our own sweat and sacrifice. Thagus Daravek will come for us before the end. I need him dead, Iskandar. No more excuses. I need him dead.'

Ezekyle, damn him, had been right yet again. This was why he left me aboard the *Vengeful Spirit*. Not out of distrust at all. Quite the opposite.

My pulse quickened.

'Boarding pods incoming from the *Domina*,' one of the human crew called. I was smiling now, unable to stop myself.

Nagual, come to me.

Master? The beast rose from my shadow, melting out of the blackness, padding onto the deck behind me. I sent him a ripple of approval at answering my summons so swiftly.

I drew Sacramentum and observed my reflection in the silver blade. I was still smiling. Grinning, in truth – the face that looked back at me was all teeth and narrowed eyes, like Lheor when he fought for the War God's favour.

One way or another, Nagual, it is time to finish this.

Though I have watched my home world burn around me, and have committed massacres and commanded genocides, I still balk to remember that day's battle in its entirety.

Every action echoes within the warp, and the fighting was savage enough that the daemonic choirs shrieked behind the veil with a multitude of monsters waiting to be born.

For almost every soul aboard a warship, void war is a diminishment of the senses, with the world around you reduced to the tremors of the deck beneath your feet, the thunder of guns against the hull and the tight, hot cacophony of fighting in confined corridors. Inside a warship, you are fighting through an expanse of territory the size and complexity of a city, and existence shrinks to the ceaseless work of fighting tunnel by tunnel, sealing boarding breaches or holding them open, answering relocation orders, following the layout hololiths, dragging bodies aside to clear the way or using them as barricades – all without knowing if the ship around you is already dead. Has the bridge been taken? Is the external war going well, or are you already doomed? How much of the ship is already overrun by boarding parties?

There is no order, no overview. It is trench warfare, moment-to-moment tunnel fighting and guerrilla insurgency all at once. Sanity returns only in the brief cessations when you steal enough time to calculate where you are needed next, or needed most.

I was with the War God's Maw, the raiders and barbarians that fought beneath Lheor's banner. Their black armour was encrusted with the brass emblem of their divine patron, along with Cthonian runes and Nagrakali hieroglyphs promising blood and souls and skulls in the War God's honour. The Eye of Horus upon the Eightfold Path showed in dirty gold upon their battleplate.

I fought with Nagual and Lheor at my side, killing to the metallic crashing of a heavy bolter and the guttural roars of a tiger-like beast that had been extinct for centuries. We advanced without thought of tactics, wading into the disorder, willingly becoming part of the wretched fever that possessed the ship's deepest decks.

The hallways of a Black Legion warship are realms inhabited by innumerable horrors. Mutation is rife within the bowels of our vessels, proceeding unchecked and largely unknown, sometimes for entire generations. Clans of debased mutants and beastmen may dwell down there, but the deepest decks are often too hostile for any true mortal life. Squads and warbands are assigned on purging expeditions, and not all of them return. Those that do speak of entire bio-daemonic ecologies thriving in the lowest decks, where the air turns to poison and the walls are rippling caverns of undulating flesh, crystallised blood and exo-flora shaped from human bone.

We fought Daravek's boarding parties through these halls, and we fought the halls themselves. Warriors that fell wounded were devoured by the ship, or by the daemon-things that lived within the ship's malleable bones. Revenants centuries removed from any sort of genetic purity leered out from the walls and vomited steaming black bile onto legionaries fighting on both sides. Colonies of blind and lost things that could not possibly conceive of sunlight rose against us, and we cleaved through these desiccated husks for the simple sin of daring to bar our way. Partially articulated corpses with amputated limbs shrieked and clawed at our boots.

In one chamber, we fought blade to blade beneath a roof comprised entirely of ivory. Only when stray bolt shells cracked the material above and sent shards clattering down upon our armour did I realise that, somehow, the dome above us was made of human teeth.

Most of the time I could scarcely hear Nagual's roars or the gunfire of our advancing horde. The half-alive monstrosities that made their lairs in the choking dark pressed their lizard-brain thoughts against mine, filling my senses with stupid hungers and sick desperation. I was sweating with the effort of keeping their primitive urges from tainting my focus.

Ultio was with us in the form of her Syntagma cyborgs and war robots. They marched in ragged step, painting the air with gore with each sweep of their industrial claws and ionising the reeking air with spears of lightning from their arm cannons. Flesh that was not truly flesh burned with a stench that defied natural law, its intestinal resonance clinging to our armour, infiltrating our oxygen supplies, sinking into our pores.

I killed World Eaters that day. I killed Death Guard and Sons of Horus. I killed a warrior of the Alpha Legion, throttling him until his consciousness began to slip and then breaking his head open against the deck. I killed Night Lords and Emperor's Children and Iron Warriors and yes, even Thousand Sons. I put my blade through the open mouth of a charging legionary in spiked plate, and I hacked another into limbless wreckage. I pulled the front of a warrior's skull free with my bare hands. The sound he made as his head was torn apart was something less than human.

I killed some of them with leaping arcs of incinerating warp lightning. I killed others by igniting the air around them with fell flame, birthing daemons inside the incubating chambers of their hearts or aging them by forcing their bodies to decay where they stood. The veil was thin amidst the destruction, and skittering, stalking, blade-bearing daemons were brought into being amidst both sides, needing no summoning, granted genesis purely by the saturation of slaughter.

Daravek's men killed us in return, depleting the Black Legion's ranks in the very heart of our own flagship. The butcher's bill for that boarding action ran into the tens of thousands as the intruders devastated their way through the crew.

Of our warriors, the Riven suffered most, brought to the brink of annihilation. At times we were forced to vault their swollen bodies, the daemons within them as dead as the Space Marines they had possessed. We hauled our way through dozens of corpses frozen in the warshape, where daemon and man melded into a lethal amalgamation of killing prowess. At times, both attackers and defenders used the Riven's bodies as barricades. Necessity, a goddess as cruel as any of the Pantheon, was surely laughing that day.

Later, I would care. Later, I would reflect on the lives reaped. At the time, such thoughts were beyond me. I ran through the halls, my black battleplate awash with blood, yelling with Lheor and his men in undignified zeal.

'Daravek!' I shouted aloud, my voice echoing through the mutated corridors.

Daravek! I sent in brutal, blunt psychic pulses, again and again.

Nagual roared with every sending, his rage matching mine. I saw the ship through his senses as an ever-shifting haze lit by the flickering soulfires of living beings. I rammed Sacramentum down into the twitching bodies of the legionaries he tore apart and left on the deck, while he fell upon those I left wounded, eviscerating them with fang and claw. Never had we hunted in such harmony.

I came upon Thagus Daravek in the middle of a firefight,

as he sought to battle his way to the bridge. He was screaming Ezekyle's name in a frothing incantation, demanding that Abaddon show himself, whining that he was forced to massacre his way through the Black Legion's dregs because its overlord was a coward.

It did not occur to him that Abaddon would be aboard the *Eternal Crusader,* let alone that my lord might already be dead, slain by a hand far more righteous than Daravek's own.

The corridor was unremarkable, the same as any one of a thousand other thoroughfares inside the ship. The floor was strewn with an uneven ocean of wreckage from destroyed Syntagma automatons. Bodies in black armour added shadows to the scorched metal and sprays of sparks.

One of the wounded Syntagma Thallax turned its domed face up to me from where it lay on the floor. A bloody, wire-veined skull within the broken face-dome stared out through the mechanical implants that served in place of eyeballs.

'*Thane,*' it said in a distorted squeal of abused vocalisation. '*Thane.* Reports. Boarding. Parties. Recovered.'

'My thanks, Ultio,' I replied. 'Now get us out of here.' And then, looking across the battling warriors, I shouted, 'Daravek!' and ran into the fray.

I did not see Delvarus die. He was already a twisted shape at Daravek's feet: winged, crowned with horns, bearing weapons that had fused to his skin as he wore the war-shape. The mangled, mutated snarl of his helmet's faceplate was slack in death. The axe blow that slew him had opened his torso from throat to groin, spilling a feast of wretched guts upon the floor in a heap that still quivered with remnants of daemonic life.

He had not been Ezekarion, but he had been a ranking Legion officer, both capable and loyal. In redeeming myself, I would also avenge him and his fallen brethren. It was with that thought in mind that I stepped into the iron-raining, explosive storm of bolt shells, a kine shield projected before me, altering all incoming energy into sound and light. It was like pushing a sun-flare before me; even I had to turn my gaze from it until my genhanced eyes adjusted.

'Assassin!' I heard Daravek call. 'Where is your master, dog?'

He stamped on Delvarus' remains, grinding the Secondborn's helmed head into the deck, triggering a spillage of cranial blood and pulped brain matter. 'Where is Abaddon?'

He does not know, I realised. And in that moment, confronted with Daravek's ignorance, I felt the certainty of revelation. Ashur-Kai's final words lashed through my mind – Tokugra's crude, stupid poetry, conveying my former master's final prophecy.

My answer was to charge, blade in hand. No more threats, no more words. I had learned my lessons where Daravek was concerned. He laughed and met my charge with his own.

There was no knightly duel for us, no austere surroundings or awestruck witnesses. We ran at each other, shooting, cursing, sprinting – a scene no different from every other warrior around us.

Axe met sword in the snarl of conflicting power fields. I chanted as I fought, repeating a Tizcan mantra of focus, channelling my will into my flesh to move swifter, strike harder. The effect was narcotic, and the lactic burn of overworked muscles was a small sacrifice for the chance to see Daravek's spined features go taut at needing to brace against my sudden strength.

We were face to face, blade-locked and straining. A bolt shell impacted at the side of my knee, threatening to unbalance me. Three shells cracked and burst against Daravek's warped Cataphractii shoulders. He only heaved with renewed force.

I spat full into his face, immediately rewarded with the hiss of dissolving flesh as the acid of my saliva started eating into his cheek. I had wanted to hit his eyes but he twitched aside at the last moment.

'Give up, Khayon,' he whispered with sickening relish. His cheek and the edge of his mouth was dissolving inches away from me, yet instead of showing pain he unfurled a tongue almost half a metre long and lashed it across my face. He chuckled as I turned my head, holding my breath against the stink of his infected teeth.

'Give up,' he said again, the words laden with command.

I was ready for it. I *thought* I was braced for it, yet my arms weakened in the wake of his words. My grip strained. My arms trembled. The battle around us no longer existed. Resisting his will was all I could do. My senses could tolerate nothing else.

He was pushing me back. My boots skidded on the deck with twin, grinding squeals. I spat again, only for him to weave aside once more. He came back grinning, assured of victory.

'Give me your sword, Khayon,' he breathed into my face.

I could not speak. I could not summon the energy for anything but resisting his overbearing strength. Instead I reached for his thoughts, my silent voice stitching through his mind in a jagged stabbing.

NO.

As the single word lanced into his consciousness, I closed

the clutch of my reaching thoughts around his brain. I snared his mind, cradling it, threatening to crush it, tendrilling my senses deep within his skull.

Doubt flickered across Daravek's transfigured visage. His hesitation lasted less than a fraction of a breath, but it was enough for me to set my balance against him once more.

I know how you followed us, Daravek. You followed me. Not fate. Not destiny. Not Abaddon. You followed me. I suspected it the moment you broke from the storm. Ashur-Kai dreamed of it long ago, without understanding the truth. I knew it for certain when I saw you bellowing Abaddon's name, unable to sense him. And there is only one way you can possess this much control over me.

We are Space Marines. We know no fear. But what flashed in Daravek's crusted eyes was as close to fear as we can come, and by the blood of the Pantheon, it was a beautiful sight.

'Khayon,' he grunted. I shook my head, refusing to hear.

You have something that once belonged to me.

It was all the warning he had. I tore it from him, that aspect of myself that he had stolen through his own sorcery. That shard of my soul that had allowed him to pretend he had conquered and killed me at Drol Kheir; that piece of my heart that let him remake my memories; that element of my psyche that allowed him to manipulate me and defy my every attempt to kill him. I ripped it from his blood and brain, forcing us apart in a telekinetic burst, my hands curled into claws as if tearing the truth from his body were a physical act as much as a psychic one.

It did not come willingly, and it did not come gracefully.

The essence streamed from Daravek's flesh in ribbons of misty blood, coalescing, taking form. I backed away, blade in hand, knowing the shape it would take, telling myself I was ready for it. If I could kill it, Daravek's hold over me would be nothing but a shameful memory.

The essence shifted, whirled and formed. The creature that stood before us, defending its new master, glared with white eyes cracked by lightning-bolt blood vessels, baring its obsidian teeth in bestial challenge.

Nagual roared back. He matched the beast's size and bulk, his fur formed of the same smoky corpus, his claws and jaws the same unbreakable black glass. My Prosperine sabre-toothed tiger roared, louder than any sound I had heard before, louder than any sound I have heard since. A daemon's rage and hate poured into a single word. A name.

GYRE.

The wolf – once *my* wolf – turned to face this new foe. They leapt as one, both huge daemon-beasts crashing through the ranks of fighting warriors, a flailing tempest of flashing talons and biting fangs.

I was already running. Sacramentum sang in the fyceline-stinking air. Daravek parried, his axe raised to deflect – but Sacramentum, the blade forged from the scavenged sword of the primarch Sanguinius, cleaved through the lesser weapon's haft and kept falling. It fell through Daravek's hand, splitting it in twain; through his armoured wrist, severing the arm at the elbow; and biting deep into the Lord of Hosts' collar, sinking in a crunching snap all the way into his chest.

'Drach'nyen...' said Thagus Daravek, meeting my eyes in disbelief.

I wrenched the sword up, out and free. The Lord of Hosts' head rolled away, tumbling beneath the shifting feet of the battling warriors nearby. His rotten wings fell like decayed sails, slapping wetly onto the deck.

Nagual, I sent. *My lynx.*

Gyre was howling. Nagual was snarling. The former sound was the kicked-dog whining of a wounded canine. The latter was the wet snarl of a great feline hunter making its kill.

Felines, when fighting for their lives, will bite at their foe's throats – and if such instinct fails, if they are pinned onto their backs beneath another predator, they will kick with their hind legs to rip open their prey's belly and disembowel their foe. Nagual was doing both. Gyre, this tainted, changed incarnation of the wolf that had served me loyally for so long, was above the lynx. She should have been snapping her jaws down at Nagual's face, but the *tigrus*-cat had his sabre-fangs deep in the wolf's throat, while his huge clawed paws tore at the canine's flanks. Kick after shredding kick tore daemonic ooze from Gyre's belly, spraying corpus slime with every slashing rake.

With a roar that would have done a true Prosperine lynx proud, Nagual rolled and hurled the wolf aside. Gyre's shredded bulk crashed to the deck before me, and I advanced upon her, clutching Sacramentum tighter.

Nagual pinned her, jaws clamped around her throat again, keeping her borne to the ground. He radiated a proud rage, and I pulsed back wordless, relieved gratitude. He had served me well this day.

Gyre looked up at me. She knew me – I saw it in her eyes – but she was no longer my daemon. The tutelary that had guided my studies on Prospero was gone, as was the daemonic familiar that had saved my life and possessed a Fenrisian wolf, becoming my huntress for so many years until Horus Reborn destroyed her.

Now I knew why I could never resummon her. Now I knew why all my nights psychically reaching into the warp and sacrificing human lives in the attempt to recall her to my side had failed time and again. Daravek had claimed her for himself. My first and most precious daemon, to whom I had bound myself far too closely years before. She had become a pawn, as had I, in Daravek's long game to destroy Abaddon.

The wolf that had saved my life so many times snarled and frothed and writhed as it stared hatefully up at me.

I lifted Sacramentum. Though my sword would rise and fall many more times in the cleansing of the boarding parties threatening the *Vengeful Spirit,* as we purged the remnants of Daravek's failed ambition, no other blow pained me like that one.

Stay dead this time, I told her. *Let me remember you as you were, not as you have become.*

She barked bloody froth. The sword fell. And the last evidence of Thagus Daravek's plan to become Warmaster of Chaos was banished with the dissolving body of a daemon-wolf.

XVI

SILENCE

Days after the battle, the silence was still deafening. Yet there was safety in that silence, the very antithesis of the Eye and the battle we had fought to break out of it.

We hid deep in the true void, the *Vengeful Spirit* and the *Thane* drifting together in the space between the stars, surrounded by a significantly diminished flotilla of escorts, light cruisers and captured Black Templars frigates. Soon we would need to reunify our scattered fleet, but for now we drifted in hidden serenity at one of the prearranged muster points, preparing for the coming war.

I stood with Nagual, distractedly running my hands through the daemon's fur. I listened as my lord spoke of the future.

'This is an opportunity like no other,' Abaddon said to me. His voice crackled from the speaker vanes at the sides of his medicae tank. He floated in suspension fluid similar in both shade and bloodstained taint to the amniotic fluid within Ultio's life-support cradle.

The three of us were alone – this deck's apothecarion was empty upon pain of death; a squad of the Aphotic Blade stood guard outside – and only the Ezekarion were permitted to enter. Of the Ezekarion, only Amurael and Ilyaster were permitted within to tend to our lord's wounds.

A rebreather mask bound to his face supplied oxygen and conveyed his words. He was stripped of his armour plating, his pale bulk in the murky fluid somehow reminiscent of a necromantic experiment. The scar began at his cheek, then thickened as it descended to his collarbone, ending at the ruination of his chest. Sigismund had struck true, destroying several of my lord's internal organs, necessitating their cloned regrowth.

I had offered to heal him with my biomantic manipulation. 'I can encourage the flesh to regrow,' I pointed out. It was unreliable, but no more so than cloning.

He had refused. It was, he stated, a matter of trust. By relying on Ilyaster's cloning ministrations, he proved the depths of his trust in Ilyaster.

'Cloned organs are vulnerable to cancerous growths,' I pointed out, to no avail. Cancer was, after all, nothing more complex than natural cell replication gone awry, and adding artifice to the process only heightened the risks. But Abaddon's mind was made up.

As he floated in the tank, naked of armour and dressed only in a plethora of old scars, that age-old suspicion resurfaced amidst my thoughts. He had always been huge for one of our kind, and had always possessed his primarch's features, in the way many of the former Sons of Horus tended to do. It was common knowledge even during the Great Crusade that no Space Marine took after their primarch as obviously as Ezekyle Abaddon took after the Warmaster.

But seeing him stripped of battleplate and pretension alike, the similarity between dead father and living son was nothing short of revelatory. I finally gave voice to a question many had considered, yet none had dared ask.

'Are you Horus?'

His golden eyes glinted with amusement. He dragged in a slow breath through his rebreather.

'I am Ezekyle Abaddon,' he said through the medicae tank's speakers.

'That is not what I meant.' I shook my head and gestured to him: this immense figure in the suspension tank, with slabs of muscle over muscle and a demigod-like stature that had led to this legend being whispered throughout the Nine Legions, a legend that would one day be whispered across the galaxy. 'Are you Horus? Are you his clone? His... son?'

He laughed, the sound wet and tinny over the speakers. 'What do you believe, Khayon? Do you think I am?'

I saw no reason to lie. 'Yes.'

This delighted him. I was not sure why.

'And if I were, brother – if I were merely Horus remade, recrafted, with a twist in my gene-code here and an alteration there, would it change anything?'

I had to think about that. I looked into his eyes but saw no answers there, only amusement.

'Perhaps. Perhaps you have always been a genetic twin of your primarch. Or perhaps Ezekyle Abaddon was slain in his pilgrimage across the Eye, and you are one of Fabius' creations in his place. How am I to know?'

This, too, delighted him.

'So yet again we come back to trust, my brother.'

'So it seems.'

'Let me ask you this, Khayon. What does it matter? Clones,

sons, fathers... Let the herd whisper whatever truths they choose. Our eyes are set on worthier goals. We look to the future, not the past.'

I acceded with a nod, knowing that there was no answer to be had here. Knowing, ultimately, that he was right. It did not matter.

At least, not if he was on our side.

'You spoke of an opportunity,' I prompted.

'You did the right thing,' he countered. I flinched, taken by surprise. 'You were right to scatter the fleet, brother.'

'I know. But it is gratifying nevertheless to hear you agree with my actions.'

'And you slaughtered Thagus Daravek. Did I not tell you that you could?' He shifted in the suspension fluid, his eyes wild and bright. 'And was it not, as ever, a matter of *vindicta*?'

'It was,' I conceded.

'Between our freedom and Daravek's death,' he began, and his gaze turned fierce, shining with ambition, 'opportunity dawns like never before. The Templars will return, and they won't be alone. They'll bring the wrath of the Imperium at their backs. And what will they find?'

'Is this question rhetorical?'

'Humour me, my assassin, humour me.'

'They will find worlds aflame. Outposts destroyed. Fleetyards raided. Shipping lanes plundered.'

'All true. But they will find raiders and reavers performing those acts. Scattered warbands and isolated warlords. Not an army. Not the Nine Legions.'

I saw where he was leading, now. 'And with Daravek dead...'

'There has never been a finer time to unify the Legions

in the hatred we share. Once we have unified the Black Fleet, we will bring the warbands of the other Legions to heel through temporary alliances and offers of mutual warfare. Some will betray us. Some will reject us. But we need unity now, Khayon. Let us rise above petty piracy and wage open war once more.'

It sounded grand, and it was the perfect truth. But it was not the truth entire.

A silken thread, too fine for an unaugmented human eye to make out, lay on the deck. It was approximately a metre long, the shade of a dead tree under an overcast sky.

A hair. A hair to match the faint scent of Abaddon's previous visitor.

I wondered how long ago Moriana had been here. I did not need to wonder what she had said.

'Open war in the segmentum,' I dared to say, 'will also serve your other purpose.' It was not a question, nor did he insult me by feigning ignorance.

'Drach'nyen calls, Khayon. That weapon will be mine.'

Nefertari had protected Moriana throughout the boarding actions. I would, in time, come to regret giving her that order, and regret how well she had obeyed it.

But I did not yet know what a curse the blade would become, nor the madnesses that its black spirit would whisper into all of our minds. Even if I had known then, would I have argued? Abaddon would never have listened. Ambition is ever his closest brother, closer even than the Ezekarion.

'Tell me something,' I said, 'before I leave.'

'Speak.'

'Sigismund. How did he wound you?'

Abaddon fell silent, the vicious vitality of ambition bleeding away. The black rebreather covered much of his face and the murk occluded some of his expression, but I believe for the very first time I saw something like shame flicker across my lord's face.

How curious.

'He wouldn't die,' Abaddon said at last, thoughtful and low. 'He just wouldn't die.'

I did not need to skim his mind for insight. Just from his tone, I knew what had happened. 'He baited you. You were lost to rage.'

I saw the muscles of Abaddon's jaw and throat clench as he ground his teeth. 'It was over before I knew he had struck me. I couldn't breathe. I felt no pain, but I couldn't breathe. The Black Sword was buried to the hilt, like the old man had sheathed it inside my chest.'

Ezekyle's voice was soft across the speakers, cushioned by the bitterness and fascination of reflection. His words were almost staccato whispers, each one a drop of acid on bare flesh. 'The only way to kill me was to welcome his own death, and he did it the moment the chance arose. We were face to face like that, with his blade through my body. My armour sparked. It failed. I lashed back. His blood soaked the Talon. He fell.'

I remained quiet, letting Abaddon's tale unspool. His eyes were looking through me, not seeing what was, but what had been.

'He wasn't dead, Khayon. He was on the floor, sprawled like a corpse, disembowelled and torn in two, but he still lived. I was on my knees, forcing my dead lungs to keep breathing, kneeling over him like an Apothecary. The Black Sword was still through me. Our eyes met. He spoke.'

I did not ask Abaddon to tell me. I reached into his thoughts then, tentatively at first in case he rebuffed my presence.

Then I closed my eyes, and I saw.

The Black Knight, fallen and ripped apart. His Sword Brethren gone or dead, I did not know which. Red staining Sigismund's tabard; red decorating the deck beneath and around him; red in Abaddon's eyes, misting his sight.

Blood. So much blood.

Here at the last, he looked every one of his years, with time's lines cracking his face. He looked upwards at the chamber's ornate ceiling, his eyes lifted as if in reverence to the Master of Mankind upon His throne of gold.

Sigismund's hand trembled, still twitching, seeking his fallen sword.

'No,' Abaddon murmured with brotherly gentleness, through the running of his blood and the heaving of his chest. 'No. It's over. Sleep now, in the failure you have earned.'

The knight's fingertips scraped the hilt of his blade. So very close, yet he lacked the strength to move even that far. His face was the bloodless blue of the newly dead, yet still he breathed.

'Sigismund,' Abaddon said, through lips darkened by his own lifeblood, 'this claw has killed two primarchs. It wounded the Emperor unto death. I would have spared it the taste of your life, as well. If you could only see what I have seen.'

As I stared through Abaddon's eyes, I confess I expected the triteness of some knightly oath, or a final murmur in the Emperor's name. Instead, the ruined thing that had been First Captain of the Imperial Fists and High Marshal of the Black Templars spoke through a mouthful of blood, committing the last of his life to biting off each word, ensuring he spoke each one in shivering, sanguine clarity.

'You will die as your weakling father died. Soulless. Honourless. Weeping. Ashamed.'

Sigismund's last word was also his last breath. It sighed out of his mouth, taking his soul with it.

In the apothecarion I opened my eyes, and found I had nothing to say. Words eluded me in the wake of Sigismund's final curse.

'Falkus brought Sigismund's body from the *Crusader*,' Abaddon told me. 'He carried it himself.'

Still I said nothing. Whether he desired it as a trophy – to join Thagus Daravek as an articulated skeleton crucified above the oculus – or whether he wanted to desecrate Sigismund's corpse to some divine end, I could not guess.

Abaddon looked incomparably weary once more, and I took the quiet as my cue to leave. He did not object.

'There is something I must do,' I said by way of farewell. 'One last thread to cut.'

He did not answer, nor did he watch as I left. He was seeing Sigismund again, dwelling on replies he could never speak to a brother he had once admired and who had died despising him.

I sensed no sorrow from him as I left. I sensed nothing at all. And that hollowness, that emptiness, was somehow worse.

Sargon had gathered a small conclave of warriors within his suite of chambers, and they stood in the candlelit space of his prayer chamber, speaking amongst themselves, awaiting the former Word Bearers Chaplain to begin proceedings. I had asked Sargon to gather them, and to take their sworn oaths in the privacy of his sanctum. If I sent the summons myself, it would have woken their suspicions in ways I wished to avoid.

Eleven in total. Eleven surviving warriors that had witnessed the battle between Abaddon and Sigismund. It should have been twelve, but Zaidu was not there – Telemachon had done as he always did, and ensured his favoured lackeys answered to no one but himself.

I chose not to let it concern me. I had business enough with these eleven souls. Two of them were warriors of the Shrieking Masquerade; the rest were from Amurael's warband, the Flesh Harvest, warriors he had trusted with his life on countless occasions.

Sargon bade them remake their oaths of silence – oaths they had already sworn to Telemachon and Amurael aboard the *Thane*, murmuring vows never to speak of what they had seen. No one outside those present for the duel itself could be allowed to know that Abaddon had come so close to falling in battle against Sigismund. Such unwelcome truths had no place in the legend we were carving.

They all reaffirmed without objection, honoured by the ceremony. Each of them knew that deceit meant death, and that keeping their word meant the Ezekarion would look upon them with favour. This could be a grand opportunity. Leadership of squads, even lieutenants' roles in a warband, were not out of the question. Fate had given them leverage and brought them close to the Ezekarion. They had no desire to squander this opportunity by proving themselves unworthy of it.

These were the thoughts I felt from afar: the ambition, the temptation, the hunger. None of them had broken their oaths. They cherished the chance to be loyal.

Sargon consecrated them, one by one, with blood blessings of the Eightfold Path gently drawn upon their foreheads with a gore-wet thumb. He dipped his fingertips into a bowl of slave viscera and whispered that the Pantheon would look kindly upon each of them for keeping their lord's secret.

When Sargon was done, he tipped the bowl to his lips and drank the remaining gore. With care and patience, he placed the empty receptacle down and gestured for the warriors to leave, thanking them once more. They filed through his training room and across the bare metal deck, not yet beginning to speak amongst themselves. Their auras were alight with pride, with the sense of being inducted into secrets that were denied to their brethren.

The bulkheads at the north and south of Sargon's armoury sealed on grinding tracks, ending with cacophonic bangs of metal on metal. As both doors crashed closed, I stepped from the shadows before the eleven warriors.

I did not say anything. The charade was over.

Even if I had wanted to speak, there was no time. Several of them realised what was happening at once. The two Raptors of the Shrieking Masquerade cried their piercing, weaponised hunt calls, reaching for chainblades and gunning them to life. In the same moment, four of the others went for their bolters and opened fire. The shrieks drifted past me, ignored. The bolts slammed and burst against a kine shield I raised with a gesture of my bionic hand.

I did not tell them to surrender and give in to the inevitable. I could have promised them it would be swifter and without pain if they accepted their fate, but I did not wish to lie to them. It was going to hurt whether they submitted or not.

'Hold fire, hold fire!' one of them, a squad leader, roared. He battered the others' guns down. 'Lord Khayon,' he said, and looked at me with the faith of a true believer. 'Lord Khayon, you don't need to do this. We swore an oath. We would never speak of what we saw.'

I admired his level-headedness. I did not admire his naïvety.

Nagual leapt from the darkness, the *tigrus*-cat's size and weight bearing the sergeant to the deck and eclipsing him in moving, clawed shadow. Ceramite warped. Blood arced and stank in the air. The remaining ten warriors moved without unity, shouting and firing and charging and seeking to flee.

I hurled them away in every direction, pinning them to the walls with an outburst of telekinetic force, slamming them back against the iron in mimicry of high-gravity acceleration. Each attempt to wrench an arm or leg free of their pressurised bindings ended with the limb thudding back into place with magnetic force.

Enough.

The beast stopped its noisy feasting at once. The sergeant was still alive. He lacked a functioning throat, a chest and one arm, but he was still alive. The remains of organs pulsed slickly, slowing, in the broken shell of his chest.

'Lord...' he managed to murmur through black, stinking blood. The man's endurance was nothing short of amazing. 'Don't... give us... to your eldar.'

I smiled at the man's dying request. I could, at least, grant his last wish.

'You are not traitors,' I replied. 'You will not suffer a traitor's fate. Goodbye, Sergeant Havelock.'

'Lord–'

Sometimes I still wonder what he was going to say. His attempts to speak were cut off by the blackening and swelling of his flesh, by the splitting and shattering of his armour plating, by the unformed words melting into a throaty scream of mutating vocal cords.

Feathery wings burst, tattered and bony, from his back. The elongated avian beak that stretched and cracked from his face was stringy with bloody saliva.

Come, Nagual.

Master, the daemon acknowledged, following me at once.

I left the chambers with Sargon and my familiar at my side. Once the bulkheads were sealed again, I relaxed my psychic grip on the ten warriors pressed to the walls. The way they clawed at the hull and the sealed doors was almost musical, the muffled sounds of their captivity.

Bolters barked, sounding like distant thunder. Bodies crashed against metal. Legionaries shouted and then fell silent.

Something vast cawed loud enough to shake the corridor outside the chamber, but I had been careful in my preparations. The creature – a ragged, black and raven-like example of its daemonic choir – would be weakened at once by the sigils of draining imprinted upon the walls. Its life span in the corporeal realm was measured in a matter of heartbeats after its executioner's duty was done. Already its enraged laughter began to fade as its physical form dissolved.

I looked to Sargon. 'I apologise for the mess you will find in there.'

He blinked slowly, uncaring. I doubted he would even allow his slaves to cleanse the chamber. He had no aversion to such decorations in his sanctum. I left him there, left him listening to the Lord of Change dying in banishment, and returned to my other duties. With the Black Legion scattered and weakened, we had to ensure its first crusade was not destined to be its last.

Soon we would bathe Segmentum Obscurus in fire.

'...that is his blade I know that sword it is Sacramentum you lie you lie Khayon would never allow himself to be captured you lie you lie you breathe lies YOU LIE my brother would flense your souls wither them peel them from your bodies Khayon is not here you could never capture him he cannot be here he would come for me he would carve your souls from your bones he would save me Khayon KHAYON KHAYON KHAYON KHAYON PLEASE KHAYON...'

> – from 'The Infinity Canticle', sequestered by the holy order of His Imperial Majesty's Inquisition as an *Ultima*-grade moral threat. Purported to be the unedited, raving confession of Sargon Eregesh, Lord-Prelate of the Black Legion.

TERRA

We were free. Free of our prison, sailing at the vanguard of a colossal invasion of Imperial space.

Our escape plunged the entirety of the Segmentum Obscurus into war. The conflict that raged for decades – that which you call the First Black Crusade – would eat at our resources as much as it replenished them, stealing as many gains from us as it granted.

You know of the purges and sterilisations and recolonisations that followed the war, seeking to sear our existence from the minds of the Imperial faithful. We have forever been the Imperium's dirty little secret, a truth never more pronounced than when the Adeptus Terra moves upon its own citizens, forcing them to forget we ever existed.

And there is so much yet to tell of the First Black Crusade, with its years of protracted war against the increasing tides of Imperial resistance.

There are those among the Legions that regard the devastating conflict as an unmitigated victory, and there are those that see nothing but harrowing loss in the defeats they sustained.

The truth, as ever, is in the grey that exists between the black and the white. We did not call it a crusade. To us, it was the opening campaign of the Long War, and even that suggests a level of organisation that could scarcely exist. There was no overall conflict to judge. It broke down into a hundred wars between individual fleets and warbands rampaging their way through the segmentum. Warlords from the Nine Legions sought their own glory; champions shed blood and raided slaves and offered sacrifices in the myriad names of the Pantheon they either willingly served or courted for favour.

Cadia was no fortress world in that era, and lacked the defences it boasted in the millennia since, but the Imperium rose against us with inevitability if not alacrity, and we were forced into a protracted war that devastated both sides. The Black Templars and the Imperial Fists led the war – the vengeance they inflicted upon us wove scars across flesh, armour and pride that some of us bear to this day, nine thousand years later.

Soon I will speak of Uralan. Soon I will relate all that transpired in the Tower of Silence, where Abaddon claimed the daemon blade Drach'nyen, that weapon of lies and broken promises. We had to fight for years to reach Uralan, and then we had fight our way through the many madnesses that infested the spire itself.

It is but one story in the Black Crusade that unfolded.

But if we must pause our interrogation here, then allow me to speak of one final matter. It will grant you a greater understanding of my Legion – its noble savagery and its dark codes of honour – and perhaps offer insight into the prisoner you see bound before you now. This was something we shared with all humanity, but I suspect even your Inquisitorial masters may not know it ever happened.

Let me tell you, Siroca, of how we truly declared the Long War.

It was not with the anger of the *Vengeful Spirit*'s guns, nor with the garbled, shrieking vox-transmissions of burning ships and falling outposts. No, I speak of the formal declaration, unknown even among the Nine Legions but for the Ezekarion that gathered at Abaddon's side.

You see, even in our vaunted malignancy, we still observed the formalities. War must be declared.

Sigismund was chosen for this responsibility. It felt right that he should carry our words back to the Imperium, back to the Throneworld itself, and it was a solemn conclave that gathered around his corpse.

One of the Black Templars ships served as Sigismund's mausoleum. I was one of the four warriors that had carried him there, a pallbearer for our first Imperial foe. We had laid him upon one of the command tables in readiness.

Abaddon handed me Sigismund's blade – not the Sword of the High Marshals, for that was gone in the hands of the surviving Black Templars, but Sigismund's favoured blade, the Black Sword that had ripped through Abaddon's own armour. My lord bade me carve our declaration along the length of the blade, and I did so with the point of my ritual jamdhara dagger and the acetylene kiss of psychic fire.

Once it was done, we lay the cooling blade upon Sigismund's corpse and closed his hands around its hilt. No effort was made to hide the wound that had slain him, nor to mask the mangled ceramite and bloodstained mess of his tabard. The knight-king's chin was bathed with bloodfall as well – Abaddon wiped the worst of it from the old warrior's bearded features with a care that would astonish any Imperial witness.

Abaddon touched the slash across his own face, a mark left by Sigismund's blade, a mark that Abaddon would carry with him down the many centuries to come. He keeps that scar to this day, a reminder of one of the worthiest foes we ever fought and the moment the Great Crusade truly came to an end.

The ship we chose was the light destroyer *Valorous Vow*, a name I found almost saccharine, but one I had to confess was at least apt. We crewed it with servitors and sacrificial slaves, and ensured its databanks were spooled with all available data of the First Battle of Cadia, from our emergence from the Eye to the breaking of the Black Templars, even down to helm-feed imagery of Abaddon's wounding and Sigismund's death. We held nothing back, pouring in all of the objective, wordless data and hololithic recordings for the *Valorous Vow* to carry back to Terra.

From the bridge of the *Vengeful Spirit* we watched the small, swift vessel turn away from the fleet and tear a hole in reality, before plunging into the warp on its long journey home. The distress beacons we had lit aboard her suddenly fell silent, as did the repeating loop of its active transponder. It would declare its name, and its burden, until its destruction. As we watched it vanish, sucked into the miasmic puncture in the universe, we hoped it would make it to its destination.

We would learn many, many years later that the *Valorous Vow* did indeed reach Terra. The message we sent was delivered to the High Lords themselves, though there is no telling how many heard it beforehand, and what they made of the *Valorous Vow*'s appearance.

In my own imaginings, I like to picture the High Lords' lackeys boarding the ship in Terra's vessel-choked orbit, and moving chamber by chamber, corridor by corridor, every step closer towards revelation. Surely they killed the servitors and thralls we left aboard as crew. So be it. I shed no tears over their fate.

But what did those first Imperial souls think, when they looked over the carcasses strewn across the command deck, as their weapon barrels cooled and their chainswords idled? What passed through their minds as they approached Sigismund's funereal form, rotting in his armour, yet honoured by those that had slain him?

And what did the High Lords themselves make of our declaration? Did one of them cradle the first Black Sword in her hands? Did one of them touch my inscription with his bare fingers? Did they return Sigismund to his bloodied Chapter, or does he lie on Terra, entombed on the same world as the Emperor he so ardently served? Did they stare in disbelief at the data recorded in the *Valorous Vow*'s archives?

And if they gave credence to the footage and the hololithic spools, did they feel any sorrow or regret at not trusting Sigismund in life, when they had believed us dead and gone, leaving him as the only sentinel out there beneath the Eye's light?

The message Abaddon commanded me to sear into the Black Sword's steel was not long. You might think it would be a boast, the petty glorification of one warlord over another, or a spiteful threat in the wake of our freedom.

It was no such thing. The message was a mere three words. I burned them into the Black Sword with an artisan's care, feeling the weight of history upon my shoulders as I worked.

And in my mind's eye, I can see the High Lords of that dim and almost-forgotten age – their naked eyes narrowing, their bionic replacement lenses rotating and half-sealing, as they too felt the pressure of history shroud them at the sight of the three words I had carved.

You know what those words were, do you not, Inquisitor Siroca? Is that a smile I hear in the faint wetness of your moving mouth? Why, I believe it is.

With those three words we declared the Long War. Words that would, in time, rise from our throats as the battle cry of the Black Legion. Words that encapsulated all that we had been, and all that we had become.

We are returned.

ABOUT THE AUTHOR

Aaron Dembski-Bowden is the author of the Horus Heresy novels *The Master of Mankind*, *Betrayer* and *The First Heretic*, as well as the novella *Aurelian* and the audio drama *Butcher's Nails*, for the same series. He has also written the popular Night Lords series, the Space Marine Battles book *Helsreach*, the novels *The Talon of Horus* and *Black Legion*, the Grey Knights novel *The Emperor's Gift* and numerous short stories. He lives and works in Northern Ireland.

YOUR NEXT READ

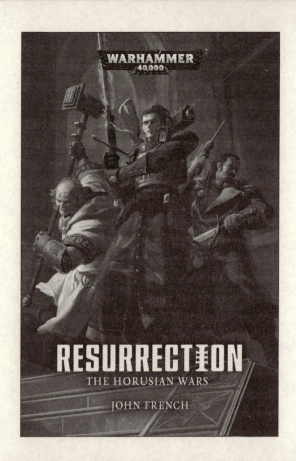

THE HORUSIAN WARS: RESURRECTION
by John French

Summoned to an inquisitorial conclave, Inquisitor Covenant believes he has uncovered an agent of Chaos and prepares to denounce the heretic Talicto before his fellows…

Find this title, and many others, on **blacklibrary.com**

YOUR NEXT READ

CASTELLAN
by David Annandale

When Castellan Crowe and his force are lost in the Cicatrix Maledictum, the Imperium they return to is different... and much deadlier.

Find this title, and many others, on **blacklibrary.com**

JOIN THE FIGHT AGAINST CHAOS WITH THESE COMIC COLLECTIONS

WARHAMMER 40,000
VOL 1 / WILL OF IRON

GEORGE MANN
TAZIO BETTIN
ERICA ANGLIOLINI

WARHAMMER 40,000
VOL 2 / REVELATIONS

GEORGE MANN
TAZIO BETTIN
ERICA ANGLIOLINI

WARHAMMER 40,000
VOL 3 / FALLEN

GEORGE MANN
TAZIO BETTIN
ERICA ANGLIOLINI

WARHAMMER 40,000
DEATHWATCH

AARON DEMBSKI-BOWDEN
WAGNER REIS

BLOOD BOWL
MORE GUTS, MORE GLORY!

NICK KYME
JACK JADSON
FABRICIO GUERRA

DAWN OF WAR III
THE HUNT FOR GABRIEL ANGELOS

RYAN O'SULLIVAN
DANIEL INDRO

AVAILABLE IN PRINT AND DIGITALLY AT
TITAN-COMICS.COM

© Games Workshop Limited. All Rights Reserved.

GAMES WORKSHOP